MARIE FRANÇOISE HUC

Love and Danger in the Time of North America's Wars

IAN BRUCE ROBERTSON

ALSO BY THE AUTHOR

While Bullets Fly

A soldier is badly wounded in a mobile, fast-moving theatre of war. Without urgent surgery he will die. There are no helicopters to move him out to a hospital.

This was the problem faced by the military medical authorities in the Second World War. Their solution: take the medical services to the wounded! They set up mobile ambulance units, field dressing stations and blood transfusion units, all based on trucks so that they could move swiftly to keep up with the troops.

They also set up field surgical units that were mobile operating rooms based on three trucks and managed by the surgeons themselves. They operated in everything from tents to wine cellars, abandoned schoolhouses and hospitals to monasteries and cathedrals. Working often in conditions that would be condemned in modern hospitals, they did whatever it took to save lives.

This is the story of one such unit, the 2nd *Canadian Field Surgical Unit under the command of the young surgeon Rocke Robertson.*

The Honourable Aleck

...is the true story of the life and times of Alexander Rocke Robertson and Margaret Bruce Eberts, Aleck's cousin and beloved wife 'Maggie'. They were

born and raised in Chatham, Upper Canada, and came to British Columbia in the 1860's.

Well-known and highly respected in BC's courtrooms, Aleck was also Mayor of Victoria, a member of BC's first provincial Cabinet, and BC's first Canadian-born Supreme Court Judge, all before his untimely death at the age of 40.

The combining of the colonies of Vancouver Island and British Columbia, and then confederation with Canada, give a dramatic backdrop to the story. Aleck's passionate correspondence with Maggie throughout their lives, and their warm and loving family life with their many sons in early Victoria, show the human side of those turbulent times in early BC.

FriesenPress
Suite 300 - 990 Fort St
Victoria, BC, Canada, V8V 3K2
www.friesenpress.com

First Edition — 2016

Thanks for the map in Appendix 1 to The Incredible War of 1812, A Military History, by J. Mackay Hitsman, updated by Donald J. Graves, published in 1999 by Robin Brass Studio Inc.

ISBN
978-1-4602-8423-0 (Hardcover)
978-1-4602-8424-7 (Paperback)
978-1-4602-8425-4 (eBook)

1. Fiction, Historical

Distributed to the trade by The Ingram Book Company

FOREWORD

I have been fortunate that my family – my parents and other ancestors – have made a habit of writing things down. Diaries, notes, letters, even books – if there was something worth telling about and remembering they wrote it down. This has given me a windfall of ideas and facts to write about. I stress that I have drawn on this material not because I wish to tell family stories, but because they are great stories themselves.

My first book, *While Bullets Fly,* drew on my father's voluminous letters sent home to his family while he was in England during the Second World War, his official diaries when in action in Sicily and Italy, and numerous short pieces written upon his return.

For *The Honourable Aleck* I had the enormous collection of letters and other documents produced by Alexander Rocke Robertson (1841-1881) and his wife Maggie and their families and friends. I also had a wonderful book on the history of the Eberts family, published in 1944 by Edmond Urquhart Melchior Eberts.

In both cases I had so much accurate information from these sources, as well as many other library and internet sources, that I was able to write the books in the creative non-fiction genre.

This time, with *Marie Françoise Huc,* I have some solid family history thanks mainly to Mr. Eberts, but not enough to write a non-fiction work. So this book is an historical novel based on the life and times of Marie

Françoise Huc. She was my great.great.great.great grandmother and yes, she really did live the amazing life I have described.

Aside from the Eberts book, I have drawn on numerous historical references in the internet, books on early Quebec and Montreal, and the very useful *The Incredible War of 1812* by J. MacKay Hitsman, updated by Donald E. Graves. For the history of Detroit I have used the first two volumes of *The City of Detroit, Michigan, 1701-1922,* the massive work produced in 1922 by Clarence Monroe Burton, William Stocking and Gordon K. Miller.

Many of the names in the book are real, but there is a liberal sprinkling of names for characters I have had to invent. The real people are identified in Appendix 2. Although the book is entirely in English, the Eberts family would have spoken French during their time in Quebec, and generally in their home in Detroit.

I am, once again, indebted to my wife Bonnie for her wonderful patience and assistance. Her ideas and comments throughout the writing of the book have been invaluable. I am grateful to my brother Stuart for his helpful advice on all aspects of our family history. And finally, thank you Glenys Galloway for your thoughtful editing.

Ian B. Robertson

INTRODUCTION

After the British took Quebec in 1759, their control over the French-speaking population strengthened steadily, and was confirmed in detail when the British Parliament passed the Quebec Act in 1774. The vast area had a strong overlay of British law, military control and commercial activity, but continued with its distinct French character, administration and religion.

The revolution in the American colonies to the south began in 1775. The leaders of the revolution thought it a good idea to include Quebec in the new country they were establishing, and invited French Canadian leaders to join their deliberations. Receiving no answer, they decided to take over the lands to the north by force.

In 1776 American troops and militia invaded Quebec, took Montreal and laid siege to Quebec City. But with the arrival of reinforcements from England the invasion was defeated, and the Americans were forced to retreat up the Richelieu River system, across Lake Champlain to Fort Ticonderoga. In July 1777 British forces out of Quebec took Ticonderoga and continued south with the intention of excising the New England states from the rest, returning them to the British fold. It was an ill-fated adventure. They were defeated in subsequent battles, climaxing in their disastrous defeat at Saratoga.

The American Revolution continued, but the Americans gave up, for the moment, their claims to the British controlled lands to the north. In 1783 the Treaty of Paris ended the war between Great Britain and the United States of America, and established the boundary between the United States and British North America. But then in the 1790s tension started to build as the Americans cast their eyes once again on the prize to the north. The tension reached its climax in the war of 1812-14.

Marie Françoise Huc lived through these troubled times. Her life was at first peaceful and sheltered. Then it became lively, loving and happy, until a terrible turn of events changed her life forever. She knew hardship and war, and the loss of children. War was a constant in her life.

She had love, but it was a hard life.

Contents

I

THE MARKET – 1778

Marie felt the eyes of men on her, soldiers and civilians alike, young and old, as she and her father strode through the market to their appointed booth. She knew that she was pretty and could expect some attention, but she couldn't help blushing at those stares that implied a familiarity that did not in fact exist. It was good that Papa was there. He kept a close watch on her; nobody would dare challenge old Sergeant Gregoire Huc.

Autumn was always Marie's favorite time of year. The cloying heat of summer was gone, leaving warm sunshine and fragrant breezes scented, but just, with the first hint of more serious weather ahead. This was the joyful time of the harvest markets in Montreal, of thanksgiving for the bounty of the harvest and (hopefully) celebration of another year of peace.

The autumn of 1778 was the first time that Marie had been called upon to help her father in the markets. Gregoire was a cutler by trade, and used the markets to expand his range of customers to newcomers, and to farmers who came so rarely to town. Marie found it exciting with all manner of food, implements and other goods spread out on the tables and along the streets, presided over by farmers and tradesmen eager to sell. The stalls where food and ale were sold were particularly lively, growing ever more so as the days progressed into evenings of celebration.

Gregoire had come to Quebec back in 1757 as a Sergeant in the French army. He had been wounded in the leg in the Battle of Quebec and the wound, clumsily healed, still caused him some pain. After the fall of Quebec in 1759, and then Montreal in 1760, he had decided to stay on in Montreal and ply his trade. He had received a reasonable education back in France, and understood full well the implications of those defeats. He knew that he had to live with the English masters, so he accepted it and got on with his life, hoping to include British people in his still unsatisfactory list of customers.

He was a strong, clever man, blessed with a great, shaggy head of hair now showing strands of grey, and a well-trimmed beard. He had a good head and steady hand for his products, although he was not totally comfortable with the intricacies of business. Thus he had been able to make a reasonable living, but never quite to the level at which he could feel secure.

His proudest success had been courting and marrying Judith Marie Charbonneau, daughter of a respected Quebec family. Judith's quick wit and happy laugh appealed directly to the heart of the soldier right from the first time that they had met in his shop. The Charbonneau family was reasonably well off, albeit not wealthy, and they had great plans for their attractive daughter. A marriage of prominence would help the fortunes of the family.

Unfortunately, the new British administration that now controlled Quebec had confused the issue somewhat, as the most important people were now British and Protestant, and the Charbonneaus did not wish to see their daughter fall into such hands. Thus in the end they had accepted the proposal of young Huc for Judith's hand. He was not senior in military rank, but he was well respected as a decorated and wounded veteran, and in any event Judith had been attracted to him, and had made her choice known in no uncertain terms.

The dowry offered by the family had included a comfortable house in Boucherville, a small community on the south shore of the St. Lawrence River, opposite Montreal Island. Gregoire and Judith had moved in and become a lively part of the local community. Gregoire's problem, his challenge, was to earn enough money through his trade to run the house and feed the occupants.

The couple had set about immediately to have children, and their first-born had been Marie Françoise, born in April 1765. They had hoped to produce a boy as first-born, but little Marie stole their hearts immediately, and they were content in the knowledge that a boy would come along in due course. Unfortunately, Judith had several miscarriages, and was unable to bring another child, whether boy or girl, to term.

Thus Marie Françoise Huc grew up as a protected only-child. By the fall of 1778 she was a beautiful young woman, bursting with happiness and promise. She was of medium height and, although only thirteen years old, had a well-proportioned body and the face of an angel. Knowing as he did the ways of soldiers, of whom there were many in the community and in Montreal, Gregoire kept a careful watch on his daughter. Her parents wanted only the best possible match for her, a match that would bring her happiness, and perhaps offer them some distinction and even some financial security. They assumed, as did their community, that she would marry a Catholic.

Gregoire did not want his daughter to be seen to be involved directly in trade, as that would be damaging to her prospects. But by simply being there in the market, near his booth, she would naturally attract men to come closer to view her father's wares. She would smile at them, and perhaps offer a polite greeting if the potential customer was of an appropriate type, and they would feel welcomed and might make a purchase. She was dressed nicely for the part with a simple flowered dress, sun bonnet and frilled parasol.

In the early afternoon a young, well turned-out gentleman approached the booth. He was clearly 'the appropriate type', so Marie prepared her best smile for him, and he glanced at her and smiled before going up to the booth and greeting her father like an old friend.

"Ah, Sergeant Huc, how nice it is to see you on this fine day. I trust you are well?"

Marie saw her father smile broadly as they shook hands. "I am, Dr. Eberts. Thank you. And you, Sir, I hope that this cool weather pleases you?"

"That it does Sergeant. It's good to have that damp heat behind us, and no snow as yet to slow us down! But I say, what a fine array of implements you have here today. These serving spoons are particularly well formed."

"Thank you Sir. But here, please may I introduce my daughter Marie. Marie, come and meet Dr. Herman Eberts."

Marie had heard of Doctor Eberts. Her father had spoken of him on several occasions, always with great respect. She offered her hand to the doctor in the manner taught by her mother for important introductions. He accepted it gracefully and firmly, and bent over it as he looked into her eyes and said "Mademoiselle Huc, it is a pleasure to meet you. Tell me, are you enjoying the market?"

"I am Sir, thank you." She noticed the slight Germanic accent in his French. She also noticed that his eyes were an interesting dark blue, part of an attractive, strong face. In fact, as she had already noticed when he first arrived, he was very handsome, with a sophistication that could have come only from a European upbringing. He was tall and strongly built, dressed casually for the market but with a quality that showed his rank in the community.

Dr. Eberts looked to be a man who combined intelligence with an enjoyment of people, and of life itself. Marie saw all of this in that one glance over her hand, and then she sensed something more as he released her hand, perhaps somewhat reluctantly, but continued to speak to her. She felt that he was not dwelling on their conversation simply to be polite. No, this older man – he must be at least twenty-five – seemed to want to talk with her, to hover over their first meeting.

But it could not last long in this noisy setting. Finished with a browsing customer, Gregoire turned back to them. "Come Doctor, if you linger any longer I shall have to insist that you sample my wares!"

Herman winked at Marie, and then turned to Gregoire's table and reached for one of the serving spoons that he had admired earlier. "Of course, Sergeant Huc, I must do my duty!" They both laughed, and then Herman said that he would like to purchase the spoon.

"Excellent choice, Doctor! Now then, I would like you to take it as a gift from Madame Huc and myself. We are most grateful to you for your assistance with my wound."

The doctor responded in equal grace and good humour. "You are very kind, Sergeant, but I must refuse your offer. Sergeants are always the most businesslike of our brave soldiers, and I must insist that you pursue your business in this case as well. It is only right. So please, name your price for this delightful spoon."

Looking relieved, for he needed the money, Gregoire named his lowest possible price and the deal was done.

"I thank you, Sergeant. Now then, I will be making my rounds in Boucherville later next month. The timing would be ideal to take another look at that leg of yours. May I call on you then?"

"Of course, Doctor. I will look forward to seeing you then, and Madame Huc will, I am sure, be prepared to offer you some refreshment."

And so they parted on the happiest of terms, Herman paying his respects to Marie as he moved away from the booth. When there was a pause in their business, Marie asked Gregoire about the doctor.

"I know you have mentioned him before Papa, but I didn't realize that he was so, well, stylish. So forceful."

"So handsome do you mean, my dear? Oh yes, he's a fine gentleman, to be sure." Marie blushed, to Gregoire's delight.

Gregoire explained that Dr. Eberts was from a family connected to royalty in Austria. He had come to Quebec two years ago when his Hessian regiment was engaged by the British to help them deal with the American invasion here in Quebec, and the revolutionary war in the south.

"And has he been in the fighting, Papa?" Marie asked.

"Yes. I am told that his regiment was involved in some actions that first year, and then spent the winter here in Montreal. Last year they marched south, but he parted company with them and left the army."

Marie frowned. "Oh dear! Did he desert his comrades?"

"Oh no, my love, he was given an honourable discharge, so he was leaving the army as a gentleman, and the army thanked him for his service. Then he was free to come back to Montreal to set up his medical practice. And he's been well received here, I can assure you, and not just because he's well turned out. He's an excellent doctor, much better than most of the charlatans who call themselves 'doctors' in this place. So the British are pleased that he is here. He takes care of their people, and I hear that he's a welcome guest at their garrison. They have also been most generous in making him accessible to soldiers like me. I could not afford his services otherwise."

"But Papa" said Marie, "I thought that most of our community did not like the Hessians."

Gregoire frowned. "True, some people call them 'mercenaries', and wonder why the British needed to engage them in the wars over here. And he is a Lutheran, so not popular with our church people. But of course, there are always exceptions, and he seems to be a particularly nice sort of fellow. And really, you know, we should not be critical of the Hessians. They came here to do a job, to help us get rid of the Americans, and they did a good job. Indeed, I'm told that many of them intend to stay here and settle down."

2

THE DOCTOR COMES CALLING

Marie lived a happy life at the family home in Boucherville. The town was small, dominated by the impressive Catholic Church *Sainte-Famille,* the pride of the community. Her parents could not afford servants beyond a part-time cleaning and laundry lady, so Marie worked with her mother, cleaning, cooking and carrying out the numerous small tasks that made up the work day in their house. This left her little time for reading and study, but she did what she could in the time available, poring over the books in her father's study, and taking what she could out of the lessons at the local church school. She attended church faithfully with her parents, and was captivated by it. She adored music, and was accomplished at the pianoforte. Her studies gave her some visions of life beyond this small community, and she sometimes daydreamed about a life of adventure, perhaps in an exciting, far-off place. But there was little prospect of that, and in any event she was happy and contented, well loved by her parents and with a lively group of friends.

She knew from her reading and the whispers of her friends that there was a magic ingredient in the relationships between boys and girls, men and women. She understood that it involved attraction, and certain physical activities that sounded peculiar and made her blush, just with the thought. The way that the boys looked at her at church and school gave her a hint, and she found it all interesting and perhaps even stimulating.

Exciting? No, not that, and she certainly had no intention of rushing into any sort of improper situation. Marriages of women at very young ages were well known in this area but still, at thirteen she was interested only in looking and thinking. In any event, no matter what her intentions, her parents would make sure that any relationships with men would be carefully controlled.

At dinner in late November Marie's father told the family that he had received a note from Dr. Eberts asking if he might call on Sgt. Huc the following Thursday to inspect the progress of healing of his leg wound. Gregoire said that he had of course accepted, even though this would mean closing his shop early.

To her surprise Marie found that she looked forward to seeing the doctor again. He was such a nice man, and so good looking! She pictured him as he had been at the market, and felt a warmth creep over her as she recalled him kissing her hand and then looking over it, into her eyes. But that was silly. He was an important and busy man, she a young and unimportant girl. Ah well. Her mother's instructions to her for treatment of the guest were familiar ones: after the examination the parents would settle with the doctor in the parlour. Marie should prepare and bring in the tea and cakes when called for, greet him politely, and then stay or go as prompted by her parents.

The doctor arrived the next Thursday at precisely 3pm, blowing on his hands to warm them in the frigid air that was now blanketing the area. His buggy made tracks in the light snow on the pathway up to their front door. Gregoire took the conveyance into the small barn beside the house, secured the horse, and then invited the doctor into the house. Judith and Marie met them in the entrance hall, dressed nicely for the occasion and smiling with welcome. Gregoire introduced Judith to the doctor, who kissed her hand graciously as she welcomed him to their home. Gregoire then turned to Marie.

"And this is our daughter Marie. You will perhaps recall meeting her in the market this fall?"

"I certainly do, Sergeant. Mademoiselle Huc, it is a pleasure to see you again." His smile was warm and, as with Judith, he took Marie's hand and kissed it formally.

Introductions made, Gregoire led Herman to a side room for his examination. The women went to the kitchen to prepare the tea and cakes, and then Judith left Marie there and placed herself in a welcoming position in the parlour. Ten minutes later the men emerged from the examination, and they were all seated. After some lively conversation about the snow and the unusual cold, Judith called into the kitchen for Marie to bring the tea.

Marie settled the tray on the low table in front of her mother. "Thank you Marie" said Judith. In the friendly atmosphere that prevailed, she decided that it would be good to have Marie stay on, to learn from the conversation. "But my dear, there are only three cups here. You have forgotten yourself! Oh, do fetch a cup and join us!"

Marie returned from the kitchen as Judith was pouring the first cup, and she passed the tea and cakes with a practiced hand. The conversation flowed easily, touching on the outrageous politics in Montreal and Quebec, the cold and snow, and prices of various food products. The men would clearly have liked to discuss the war in the American colonies to the south, but good manners forbade such talk in the presence of ladies. In a pause in the conversation Herman turned to Marie and asked her about her studies. "Your father has told me that you enjoy reading, and are an excellent musician. Tell me Mademoiselle, what are the subjects of most interest to you?"

Marie was thrilled that such a fine man would ask her such a question. And she did not take it as simply politeness – a refined man showing formal respect to a young woman. She sensed that he was actually interested in her, awaiting her reply with a friendly smile.

"Well Sir, I enjoy my religious studies, and of course my music. But I'm also finding great interest in the study of French literature, and also in the subject of geography, although there is not much of that. I do not study the war in the south, nor do I wish to think of it, for it is a cruel thing. It's sad that there is so much hatred and anger in the world."

She came to a sudden stop, blushing at her impertinence delivering such a lecture to her elders. But the doctor nodded and smiled.

"Well spoken, Mademoiselle! I quite agree. Mind you, were it not for such wars I would still be living in Europe, and would never have met you and your charming family. So perhaps war has its good points too, with your reservations, of course."

Judith sighed with relief, and guided the conversation into safer waters. But she did notice as she did so that the doctor had great trouble taking his eyes off Marie, issuing warm smiles in her direction whenever she turned to him. Ah well, so it is with beautiful young women! Men are such fools – even fine gentlemen like the doctor! They can never resist a pretty smile or a well-formed bosom, even for a moment. She had enjoyed such attentions in her day. Her daughter deserved the same. If only the right man would come along...

The Christmas season in Montreal and the surrounding towns was celebrated in sharp cold and beautiful snowfalls. This contributed to the festive air, for the cold made for rosy cheeks and great consumption of mulled wine.

Marie and her parents saw Herman twice during the season – once in the market where they were both searching for vegetables, and once at a festive carnival arranged by the merchants of Montreal. On both occasions the doctor greeted the parents first, with great warmth and good humour, before turning to Marie. She felt a tingling in her heart as he pressed her hand and asked how she was, and what she was doing to celebrate the season. The parents looked on with pleasure, as it was good to have this distinguished medical man as a family friend. They were not aware of what was really happening in those innocent conversations.

Herman was, in fact, already in love with their daughter. He had met her just those two times, but it had been love at first sight, with confirmation at second sight. At these meetings at Christmas time, in spite of his rigid upbringing, professional discipline and worldly experience, he could scarcely contain himself from grinning like a fool at the very sight of the girl. Marie, for her part, sensed that something special was happening, and found it exciting – whatever 'it' was!

In early March of 1779 Marie's mother told her that the doctor had sent a note asking to call upon them to discuss a matter of great importance. Mme. Huc had no idea what that matter might be, but alerted her daughter to be prepared to serve tea.

As previously, Gregoire greeted Herman at the front door, stabled his horse and brought him into the house. Herman told him on the way in that he wished to speak to the parents in confidence, so after Marie had brought in the tea, Gregoire thanked her and asked her to withdraw. Judith served the tea amidst disjointed comments on the weather, and then the Hucs settled back and waited for Herman to state his business.

"Sergeant Huc, Madame, I am here to seek your permission to pay court to your daughter Marie." Ignoring the startled looks on their faces, he pressed on. "I realize that this request may come as a surprise to you, especially as I am several years her senior, and have known her for such a short time. I have, however, found her to be most attractive and intelligent, and I have developed feelings towards her that are so strong that I am impelled to make this impulsive request of you. I realize, of course, that my feelings for her may not be reciprocated, at least to the same extent, and you may yourselves have reservations about me, especially as I am not of the Catholic faith. Whatever the situation, I would be pleased and honoured to visit her here and, over time spent with her and yourselves ascertain if there exists a basis for a long-term relationship."

He stopped and gazed at his feet and then out the window, giving the Hucs time to think and to glance at each other and exchange their silent thoughts. The Hucs were surprised at first, but their thoughts turned quickly to the question itself. The Catholic thing was an issue that would have to be dealt with, but the age differential was acceptable, and Dr. Eberts would certainly be a prestigious connection for the family. But what if Marie was not in favour of this request?

That would be discovered over time. Right now there did not seem to be any reason to be anything but forthcoming, albeit in a cautious way. Gregoire rose to his feet, followed immediately by Judith and Herman.

"Dr. Eberts, we are honoured by your request. I know you will understand that we wish to consult with our daughter and give the matter due consideration before responding, but I assure you that we will be in touch with you shortly."

Herman thanked them for their time and their consideration, and departed without fanfare.

When Gregoire came back into the house after waving good-bye to the doctor, he found his wife and daughter in excited conversation in the parlour. Blushing furiously and with her hands clapped over her mouth, Marie had just said "Oh Maman!" as he entered. He sat down opposite them and smiled at her, and the three of them sat in total silence for a moment before bursting into lively chatter.

The parents were excited, their minds racing. They both knew instinctively that within this conservative community there would be problems with an older man, a foreigner and not a Catholic, marrying into their family. But on the other hand, this could prove to be a brilliant match, and not just for Marie.

Marie's mind was not racing. Rather, she was calm, having collected herself quickly after that first rush of surprise that she had expressed so eloquently to her mother. She had known that there was something special about the doctor, and so it was! She had known that she was ready to start learning more about life and love, and now it would happen! She had a feeling of being in the small room that had been her life so far, but now there was a door opening, and a whole new world beckoning to her to come through.

3

COURTING – 1779

The heartening signs of early spring were the backdrop to Herman's first call on the Hucs with the new understanding in force. It started with the usual tea in the parlour, brought in by Marie and served by Judith. The Hucs were shy and found it difficult to start conversation, but Herman was happy to be there, enchanted with the company, and showed it with lively talk that soon had them relaxing and even laughing at times.

Then, as if in response to a secret signal, Judith rose and asked Gregoire if he would like to help her "put the things away". Gregoire was at first confused by this strange invitation, but suddenly came to his senses, rose to his feet, picked up a plate and followed his wife from the room. Herman and Marie rose from their seats in respect, and then sat down again to begin their courtship.

It began with Herman smiling at Marie, and Marie gazing red-of-face at the floor. But that did not last long.

"Marie, you know why I am here. I have felt compelled to come to you, for you seem to have a sort of magic for me that I cannot ignore. You have accepted the idea, so I'm thrilled that we are here together. There is much that you don't know about me and me about you, so I think we will have a lot to talk about."

"Yes Dr. Eberts. I am pleased that you are here. I must admit I am flattered by your attentions."

After a brief, embarrassed silence, Herman started by asking her about her music, and she replied with great enthusiasm. She was pleased that he seemed to know a lot about her favorite composers, and that he would like to hear her play. They moved on to her other studies until, at just the right moment, he asked her if there was anything she would like to ask about him.

"There is, Sir, for I know little about you beyond what my father has told me. He says that you are a fine man and a fine doctor. He's grateful to you for helping him with his leg, and he has told me something of your military career – that you came to Quebec from Austria, and fought with the British against the Americans. But then you left the army and came to Montreal to settle. I know little more than that."

"That is a good start. Yes, I did come here from Austria. When I was a boy I always wanted to be a doctor. I believed that healing people who were sick or wounded would be a good and honourable way to spend my life. It was natural to join the army when I had learned my profession, for I am sure you know that there are always wars going on in Europe, and doctors are always needed in wars."

He spoke lightly, watching her face, and was pleased to see her smile at this simple jest. "So I joined the Hanau Regiment, which is famous in Europe, and almost as soon as I did we were engaged by the British to come over here and help them put down the American Revolution. I must admit I was rather set back by this, as I had a number of interests that were important to me in Austria, not to mention my family. But once you are in the army you must do what they tell you, so I soon found myself on a ship tossing on the Atlantic Ocean. As you can imagine, I spent a number of my early days as a military doctor caring for seasick soldiers, including a number of fellow officers!"

Marie was wide-eyed at this remark. "Oh but Doctor, were you not ill as well? Was it a rough crossing? Was it dangerous?"

And so the conversation went on, with Herman providing some detail to the story sketched out to Marie by her father in the market last fall. His explanation of why and how he managed to leave his regiment on good terms while they were on campaign to the south was intriguing.

"It's a good question. You see, during the time I had spent in Montreal, it seems that I had impressed the British officers and others in the community with my medical work. There was a lot to do, with the military work of caring for the wounded as well as dealing with the many diseases that seem to trouble people in this climate. As a relatively senior officer, I befriended some of the British officers at their headquarters, and even dined at their mess several times.

"When General Burgoyne's campaign to Ticonderoga was launched in June of '77, I was assigned to go with them to work with the other doctors on the campaign. It seems, however, that the senior British officers remaining in Montreal were not happy to see me go, and I must say I did leave a large amount of quite urgent work behind me. So, just as we occupied Fort Crown Point at the end of June, preparatory to taking Fort Ticonderoga, the commander of our unit, Colonel von Gall, received orders to give me an honourable discharge from the army on the condition that I return to Montreal to serve both the military and civilian populations.

"I was pleased with this turn of events as I was not satisfied with the management of the campaign nor even, in fact, with its very objective. Defending our own territory made good sense of course, but chasing the Americans back into their mountains and lakes seemed to me to be madness. And as you probably know, Marie, that is how it proved to be, with the terrible defeat at Saratoga. Colonel von Gall was aware of my feelings, and I believe the poor fellow was quite pleased to be rid of me! So back here I came, accompanying several injured and sick soldiers.

"I found lodgings in Montreal, and have established a good practice here. Indeed, I have managed to arrange the best of both worlds. I am no longer in the army, but am contracted directly by them to provide my services. I give priority to the military, but I do have a considerable list of private patients as well."

Marie smiled. "What an interesting story!" She then asked an undiplomatic but important question. She said that with his fine background in Europe, surely he would plan to return there sooner rather than later. Was this true? Could he be content to live his life in this relatively primitive colony?

"My dear Marie, you do have an eye for the important question! Well now, let me just say that there are different ways to view this colony. One is as you have mentioned, that it is 'relatively primitive', or perhaps 'backward', and certainly not as polished or sophisticated as the societies in Europe.

But there is another view that I share, and that is that Europe is stuffy and rigid and stifling, whereas here it is fresh and exciting, with almost unlimited opportunities for those prepared to work for them. I find every day an adventure. I have no intention of returning to Austria."

The conversation proceeded pleasantly for precisely one hour, when Marie's parents appeared at the door of the parlour and asked, with great politeness, if the doctor would care for more tea. He responded, equally politely, that he must not test their hospitality too far, and took his leave, placing a wonderful kiss on Marie's hand as he did so.

While Gregoire was still waving Herman away, Judith tumbled Marie back into her chair in the parlour, sat down opposite her, and pumped her for her reactions to that first meeting. Even before Marie started to answer, however, the mother knew what the answer would be, for her daughter was glowing with a warmth and sparkle never before seen. She spoke slowly and softly, saying how much she had enjoyed their conversation; what an interesting man he was; so enjoyable! So amusing!

By the time Gregoire came into the room, rubbing his hands from the cold and asking how it went, Judith was able to compress her reply into one statement: "Gregoire my love, I believe we will be seeing more of the good doctor in the months ahead!"

The Hucs knew that there were drawbacks to this relationship that had come upon the family so suddenly. They were members of a close-knit, Catholic community. The culture in the community was strong – the sense of history and solidarity, the joy and discipline of their church, the respect of the families for each other, the general unease with their English masters. A substantial number of Canadians had even sided with the Americans during the American invasion just ended, showing that the relationship with the English was still an uneasy one.

Mind you, the English had actually been sensible conquerors. They had taken over the governance of the land, but had left most of the day-to-day running of affairs to the French community. But there still did linger a sense of being wronged, and a right to the freedoms that had been granted them. The arrival of the Hessian mercenaries had been confusing and not well received. If the English were strong enough to defeat the French at Quebec, why did they now need these Germanic tin soldiers to help them out?

This handsome man who had entered their lives was not English, but he had come with the English. He was a welcomed member of the English community itself, and even of the English military headquarters in Montreal. Thus although respected for his professional skills and his excellent manners, he was a Hessian tarred with the English brush, so still an outsider to the people of Boucherville. A confusing mixture, indeed.

In Marie, the Hucs had a beautiful gem that could be of great value to them if she were to marry well. Now their gem was being courted by an outsider! They discussed the situation endlessly, for this was no mere drifter or poor but handsome soul seeking to improve his lot in life. Marriage to Dr. Eberts would be a solid, highly respectable match, and would likely have benefits for them too. But it would also come with costs, for their friends would not be amused.

Word of the doctor's interest in Marie was spreading (heaven knows how!), and noted by a number of families who made casual enquiries of the Hucs after church and at other gatherings. Their reactions to the news that yes, the doctor had shown an interest in Marie, were almost always variations of a cool statement of interest, and then some form of assurance that it would likely not last. A few actually said 'hopefully', always with a knowing and sympathetic smile.

The Hucs tried to calculate the balance of benefits and costs of different courses of action. If it turned out that Marie learned to love the doctor, then that would be wonderful for her, and therefore a real benefit. Concerning their own interests, they felt that a connection to a man of the standing of Dr. Eberts might well do them good in the larger community of Montreal and its surrounding areas. He himself must have at least reasonable resources, and was well connected to the English community and to the senior Francophone people in the area as well. This would surely be good for Gregoire's business, and that possibility could not be ignored.

So while they could, if they wished, ask the doctor to withdraw, in the end they decided to let the courting continue and just see how everything turned out.

The doctor's second courting call was in the first week of May. Marie had waited patiently for the exchange of notes between her father and Herman, taking every available minute she could to read about Europe and the military and other great subjects. She looked forward to their next meeting with great anticipation and not a little impatience, for Herman had already begun to dominate her thoughts. She was still too young and inexperienced to know what love was, or how it would feel to be in love, but she did know that he fascinated her in a new and exciting way, a way that she had never felt before. She wanted to sit with him and talk with him, to learn and yes, to make him see that she knew some things too! His dashing good looks naturally added to the attraction.

His second call went as had the first – tea with the parents, an hour of pleasant conversation, and then polite departure. The parents were more relaxed this time as they had made up their minds to let the relationship proceed as it might, and they continued to be impressed by the doctor. In fact, Gregoire admitted to Judith as they hid in the kitchen that he really did like Herman. He found the doctor to be a man of quality, polite and friendly, and respectful of the parents even though they were somewhat lower on the social scale than was he with his profession and high-level contacts. He also was pleased that the doctor recognized and respected him as a former soldier, known for his bravery and energy. He smiled to think that it was his damnable leg wound that had been the catalyst in starting the relationship between this distinguished surgeon and his young daughter.

As spring turned into summer, Herman's visits continued on a regular basis. He would always send a note in advance seeking permission to visit, and the parents would always reply that they would be delighted. The nature of the visits evolved sensibly. The parents soon left it to Herman to decide when he should depart, so the visits became somewhat longer, but never inappropriately so. In the warm weather the couple started to take walks along the country roads in the area. Judith accompanied them as chaperone the first two times, as seemed only correct, but that soon seemed silly in light of Herman's maturity and status, so from then on the young couple walked on their own.

As Marie became more relaxed with Herman her perception of him changed. From a rather formal and worldly-wise older man showing interest in her, he became a delightful friend who was eager to share stories with her, to laugh with her, perhaps just to be with her. There were several occasions during that summer when Herman met other members of the Charbonneau family and some close friends, invited by Gregoire and Judith to take lunch or tea when the doctor would be there. The relatives all took to him personally. Marie's Aunt Josie's description of him as a 'fine, accomplished man' was widely shared, as was only natural.

Josette Cecile Charbonneau had married into the Charbonneau family back in the late 1750s, and had four children of her own. Her husband Jacques ran a clothing shop in Montreal, and obeyed his forceful wife in all matters. Josie was the brightest of lights in a substantial family, and everyone adored her. She carried considerable social force in the community so that nobody, the clergy included, wanted to cross her. As a friend once had said of Josie, "it's really quite simple – you obey her. Period."

Josie's daughter Yvette, two years older than Marie, found the romance exciting, and always had questions about Herman, and what they talked about, and how Marie really felt about him.

There was always, however, that sense of concern about his situation of being older, a Hessian and not a Catholic. People made their feelings known to the family in subtle but definite ways. Gregoire ignored the comments that were made. Judith was more diplomatic, generally deflecting them with "well, we shall see", or words to that effect.

Marie was aware of these concerns, for she observed people's reactions when they met the couple on their walks and during visits with family and friends at home. Judith had discussed them with her, but Marie refused to concern herself, for her feelings for Herman had grown steadily from that initial fascination in the spring to the warm glow of love in the bright September sunshine.

In mid-September, as they walked arm-in-arm down a quiet country lane, Herman finally expressed his true feelings for her. They had just completed a chat about fall colours and were walking in contented silence when he stopped and turned to her. Taking both of her hands in his, he looked into her eyes. "My dearest Marie, I cannot continue with you for a minute longer without expressing to you my true feelings. You may well have sensed it, but it must be said. My darling Marie, I love you. You have captured my heart and my soul. You are with me always, in my every waking minute and in my dreams. My darling, I have hopes that we might spend the rest of our lives together."

Marie gazed into his eyes. She had known that it would come to this, and she had wanted it and waited for it.

"Oh Doctor, what you say gives me the greatest pleasure, for I have learned to love you too – to like you and to respect you and yes, to love you. You make me so happy!"

Herman drew her to him, bent and kissed her softly on the lips. It was her first kiss, but she responded naturally, as if she had been practicing over these past few months. He then pulled away and once again took her hands in his.

"Marie, my love, this is the most wonderful moment of my life. You make me happy too – so happy now, and with hopes for the future. When we are ready, I shall speak to your father to ask for your hand."

Marie hugged him hard, unable to speak. To her surprise she found him laughing quietly while he hugged her back. She looked up into his smiling face with a mischievous frown and asked "...do you find this situation amusing?"

He stole a quick kiss before replying "my darling, I just thought it amusing that you called me 'Doctor'. It seems rather formal with us in each other's arms. We must do something about that!"

Colonel Murray was in great spirits as he and Herman met in his office at the British military headquarters to discuss the October medical report. It was an excellent report. Herman's advanced European training was contributing to a visible improvement in the health of the British forces, their families, and many other citizens in the region as well.

"You have done well, my friend – as always, I must say. We are grateful, and I trust that our payments prove it."

"They do, Colonel, of course. You are most generous, and I trust that I will continue to meet your expectations."

"I am sure of it. In fact, this brings up a point that I've been meaning to raise with you. As you know we have a garrison down at Sorel. It's a busy place, and becoming more so every day. It's in need of more and better medical services to deal with an unfortunately heavy load of injuries and disease. Our medical staff there is woefully inadequate for the task, and I have had it in mind to ask you if you would be prepared to move there for a while. You would do there what you have done here – sort things out, heal, train people and so on. You would, of course, have my full support. It should take a year or two, and then you could move back here. Sorel is not as comfortable a place to live as here, but with your spirit you might find the challenge to your liking."

Herman leaned forward in his chair. He was alert; he sensed adventure in the air!

"How intriguing, Colonel Murray. I was in Sorel not six months ago to visit several old patients. It was certainly busy, but seemed to be reasonably well served by the hospital there. You indicate that it is changing, presumably quite rapidly. What's happening?"

The Colonel explained that with its strategic location between Montreal and Trois-Rivières, where the St. Lawrence meets the Richelieu River, Sorel was protected by five companies of British troops, comprising three hundred men. Then there was the growing influx of Loyalists flooding north as a result of the American Revolutionary War. Already almost nine hundred Loyalists had come through Sorel, and around ninety had settled there, and to this should be added the Loyalists settling in nearby communities such as Yamaska and Yamachiche. Many of these people were in a very bad state.

"And to add to this, we will soon be sending to Sorel a large contingent of old soldiers and their dependents. These old people – we call them 'Military Invalids' – will number over two hundred in all. They exist on pensions allowed by the government, and will be provided with small cottages. You can imagine what that will do to the medical staff already there! We plan to send Dr. Christopher Carter – you know Carter – to look after them, but he will need a lot of support."

Herman laughed and held up his hand. "Please Colonel, enough! You've made your point most admirably." He rose and walked to the window, gazing out while he thought for a moment before responding.

"I see, of course, why you want me there. There will be a great need for surgery, not to mention efficient general medical services. And providing those services in such a rapidly growing situation is by no means an easy task. I appreciate it that you would put your trust in me in such circumstances. But there is a complication that I must mention. As you may have heard, I have been courting young Marie Huc, the daughter of the brave Sergeant Gregoire Huc of Boucherville."

"Ah yes, I have heard of it. I also understand that she is an uncommonly attractive young woman, and I congratulate you on your good taste."

"Thank you Sir. But you see, the issue arises in that I am about to approach her father to seek her hand in marriage. I have every reason to think that my proposal will be accepted by him, and by her. It's just that... well...the prospect of an early move to Sorel may cause them some concern. I'm not saying that it will, for she is a spirited girl and may welcome the challenge, but I suspect that her family will not be happy to see her so far away from home." He paused, uncertain where this was leading him.

Colonel Murray filled the pause quickly and effectively. "I say doctor, well done! I wish you every success in your campaign to win her hand. As to the unhappiness that might accompany your move to Sorel, let us see what happens. The move might in fact be welcomed by a young wife ready to leave home and start her new life with you. Mind you, I think that there are other clouds on that family's horizon that may be more immediate. My sources tell me that Sergeant Huc is not faring too well in his business. We have had occasion to place some small orders for swords and the like with him and he has done a fine job, but I am told that his shop has an unhappy air to it, a sense of creeping failure, if you will. What a blow it would be if he were to fail, and one must wonder if his daughter would wish to leave her family in such circumstances."

"You are most observant, Sir. I have sensed the situation, although dear Marie has never spoken of it. She would not, of course. Well, perhaps the upcoming Christmas season will see a change in his fortunes. We must encourage all of our friends to purchase new sets of knives and forks for their tables!"

They laughed, but then Colonel Murray changed in mood swiftly, focusing on a new thought. "You know Doctor, this puts me in mind of a discussion I had with my Quartermaster not long ago. He was complaining about the condition of our cutlery here at the garrison, most of which came over with the invasion forces twenty years ago. This could prove to be a happy coincidence. Purchasing a supply of new utensils would not be of the highest priority for us, but the idea certainly has some merit. Please do keep me informed of the situation with our friend Huc."

"I will Sir, and I thank you for the thought. As to the move to Sorel, if it can wait until next summer I am certain that we will be able to work it out."

Herman's formal call on Marie's family took place in November. The day was pleasant for that time of year, with a warm sun glowing down on a land hardened by frosts and prepared for the first snows. The visit was a well-rehearsed ritual dance, for ever since that day when Herman and Marie had declared their love they had used his regular visits to talk about their future. He had not yet mentioned the prospect of the move to Sorel, but they had covered many other topics including a more general discussion on the joys of travel. He had been relieved that Marie showed great interest in the subject.

Marie had also warned her parents that a proposal might well be coming, and sooner rather than later. As usual she told Judith about it in one of their private talks, and Judith passed the message on to Gregoire. The parents were determined to stick to their agreed policy of letting the relationship continue its own course, so they reacted positively to the news. They did not mention it to their friends or extended family members, preferring not to cross that bridge until absolutely necessary.

Thus when Herman drew up at the house in his carriage and Gregoire went out to greet him, it was like the curtain rising on a familiar play. After the tea session with its hesitant conversation, Herman asked Gregoire if he might have a word with him in private. The women rose immediately and took the tea things out to the kitchen.

Herman then made his request for the hand of Gregoire's daughter in marriage. Gregoire acted surprised, then appeared delighted and said that he would be pleased to approve the match, and was certain that Judith would agree. He noted that, of course, it was up to Marie herself to make the final decision. They rose and shook hands, and then Gregoire called Judith into the room.

"Judith my love, Dr. Eberts has asked our permission to marry our dear Marie. I have told him that this has come as a great surprise, but that I welcome it, and that I was certain that you would join me in accepting his proposal. Is this not good news?"

Judith was up to her part. She smiled and blushed at the same time, said "oh my yes, it certainly is", and turned to Herman. "Dr. Eberts, this is a most moving moment for us. Marie is our only child and, as you know, we do love her dearly. So in accepting your proposal we are taking a bold and important step. We do so with the confidence that you will treat her well, even as we do ourselves. On that assumption we will be delighted to welcome you into our family."

Herman completed this act of the play by approaching Judith, thanking her "with all my heart" for her kind words, and giving her hand a classic Austrian kiss.

Judith then said that she would go and consult Marie to ascertain her response to the proposal. Marie had naturally been listening to the whole procedure from the top of the stairs, but to preserve protocol she and her mother withdrew into her room and closed the door before speaking. They dissolved into a tearful embrace for, although totally expected, the small ceremony had affected them both far more than they had anticipated. Then they parted and, dresses smoothed and tears dabbed away, went downstairs where Judith announced to the waiting gentlemen that Marie had accepted the proposal.

Herman closed the proceedings by shaking hands with Gregoire once again, noting that he would be in touch concerning a meeting to make arrangements, kissing both women's hands, and departing in good form.

4

MARRIAGE – 1780

The meeting in December concerning arrangements for the wedding was a delicate affair. This was not, fortunately, because there was any disagreement on the prospective marriage, but rather because there was such a wide difference between the fortunes of the two men. Herman was at the top of his game – a successful surgeon much in demand in the area, free to do what he wished and with great prospects. Gregoire, on the other hand, was a craftsman with a business that was slowly failing – desperately anxious to do what was best for his daughter, but not sure how he could do so; indeed, how he could continue to hold his head up in his community. Colonel Murray's observations about Gregoire's business had been accurate. These were tough times, and the Christmas season that had already begun was not looking to be of much help.

As to the arrangements for the marriage itself, Herman made it clear from the outset that he was not prepared to go through the normal Catholic system of the publishing of bans. He was not a Catholic, so to do so would be inappropriate, and in any event he knew that the Huc family's Catholic priest would be reluctant to perform the ceremony. That was fine with him; they would be married under contract, and by a Protestant minister. This would disappoint Marie and her mother, who had looked forward to the ceremonies of their church that surrounded marriages. But Gregoire had no way to counter this idea, and in any event he was not a keen churchgoer so didn't really care. What he did care about, however, were the financial arrangements.

The normal procedure for marriages was that the bride's family would offer a dowry to the groom's family, in effect showing their gratitude for the other family taking on the care and protection of their daughter. This did not seem to apply in the strict sense in this case in that Herman had no family in Quebec, and was actually better off than were the Hucs. But the formality had to be observed, and they agreed that the dowry would be a reasonable forty-eight hundred livres. This amount may be reasonable, but even so Gregoire was clearly uncomfortable as they discussed it. Herman knew that the man would have great trouble coming up with that much money.

The delicacy of the situation was exquisite. Herman liked the man for what he was, a brave, honourable soldier, forceful and yet thoughtful and kind. But he was also a proud man, so the situation must be handled carefully. Herman had thought at length about this moment, and after his very satisfactory second meeting with Colonel Murray just a week ago, he knew what to do.

With the dowry question settled, Herman turned the conversation in an unexpected direction. "Now that we have decided the essentials, I should raise another topic that will be of some interest to you. The other day I was at the British headquarters, dining with the officers. I noticed how shoddy their cutlery was, and asked jokingly if it had come over with the troops engaged at Quebec, for it seemed to be of a considerable vintage. They replied that I was indeed correct; that they had begged the Quartermaster to find some new cutlery before they were poisoned by these old weapons!" Herman laughed deliberately; Gregoire smiled hesitantly.

"Well Sir, I then took the liberty of telling them that my future father-in-law knew a thing or two about cutlery, and perhaps he could be imposed upon to produce some new pieces for them. They had been joshing me about my forthcoming marriage, so this followed up rather nicely. Colonel Murray said that he had not had this idea in mind, but now that it was raised he would look into it."

Gregoire was now smiling. "My dear Doctor, how kind of you! Why, an order from the British headquarters would certainly be most welcome. I must say, when I had occasion to deliver some blades to them several months ago I was permitted to visit their kitchen, and I was surprised at the condition of their pieces. The cutlery is of the type used in warships and war situations, often by the troops as well as the officers, and it has been hard used these many years. Oh yes, I could do them proud if they would let me."

"Now Sergeant, I hope that I have not overstated the case. If anything comes out of that conversation it would certainly be a good thing, but you must not, I beg of you, hold your breath."

In fact Herman had not had that conversation at dinner at the mess. He had, however, visited the Colonel and reported that Sergeant Huc's business was now in desperate straits, and that anything the Colonel could do for his future father-in-law would be welcomed. He closed the conversation by assuring the Colonel that he would be in a position to move to Sorel in mid-summer next year.

In the first week of January 1780, Gregoire received a note from the British Quartermaster inviting him to visit the headquarters to discuss business matters. The day following that meeting, Gregoire left his shop and paid a call on Herman at his office in Montreal. He was beside himself with joy, for the Quartermaster had given him such an order for cutlery and other pieces that it would pull him out of debt, save his business, and in doing so place him in front of many well-heeled families who would wish to deal with such a well-known craftsman.

Herman shook hands with him, warmly and with great smiles. "I am delighted that such an innocent conversation should have turned out so well. But incidentally, I should tell you of another conversation I have had at the headquarters."

He went on to describe Colonel Murray's request that he move to Sorel for a while, describing it as having been made only recently. He said that he knew this would likely upset M. and Mme. Huc as it would take their daughter out of the range of day-to-day visiting. They would, however, be within easy reach of longer visits and stays, and the adventure of such a move might even prove stimulating to his young bride.

Flushed with good humour, Gregoire said that it sounded like an interesting opportunity, and he had no objection to it. He was certain that he could convince his wife accordingly.

The wedding took place in the large meeting hall of the British headquarters in Montreal on Saturday, April 8, 1780. Marie was fifteen years old; Herman was twenty-seven. The Rev. David Chabrand Delisle, who presided, was surprised that there were just around fifty guests at the ceremony, given the status of the groom and of the Charbonneau family. But he was a man who kept his ear to the ground, and he knew that there were mixed feelings about this event. The Catholic community in Boucherville was not in favour and in some cases openly hostile, so that it was just family and a few close friends from that area who attended. Fortunately there was a sizeable group of officers from the British headquarters and some of the other military units where Herman practiced, so the gathering was large enough to be acceptable.

Herman was handsome in his finest formal dress, and Marie drove him almost to tears of joy as she came down the aisle on Gregoire's arm, so lovely was she in her simple white gown. After the ceremony they left the hall under a canopy of crossed British swords, and walked to the officers' mess where Colonel Murray had kindly consented to hold the reception. Soon the wine was flowing and it became a happy affair, with a fine meal and brief speeches and toasts. At 9pm the happy couple said their goodbyes and departed in their carriage.

Herman's rooms in Rue Ste. Therese, in the heart of Ville Marie, were pleasant and comfortable, but he had decided that they would honeymoon for two nights at the Hotel St. Pierre, a fine establishment not far away. Marie was shaking with a mixture of excitement and fear as they entered the hotel, were greeted by the manager and then shown to their suite. The door closed, and they were finally alone.

They came into each other's arms and kissed. Then they had a long embrace while their hearts pounded, for different reasons. For Herman this was the moment for which he had waited so long, the moment when he could make love to this young woman who had captured his heart so completely. He longed for her.

But for Marie it was a moment of fear, mixed with embarrassment. Her mother had told her about sex, warned her about the problems and pain of the initial act, but assured her that she should eventually find it enjoyable, a chance to express fully the feelings that she had for the man she loved. But now that the moment had arrived she felt a panic, a fear of exposing her body to this man, of the pain that would happen, of not pleasing him and having him disappointed in her. Oh, she had loved Herman through his looks and his wonderful kindness and attention, and his words had caressed her and reassured her and drawn her to him. But now…well, now they were on the threshold of a new and far more complex relationship. Her confusion and fear combined with her happiness at being with her man put a look on her face not unlike that of a scared rabbit.

Herman saw this as he gazed into her eyes. How very young she was! Young and inexperienced, and clearly afraid of what was to come. He relaxed the embrace, stepped back and suggested that they retire to the chesterfield in front of the fireplace, enjoy a glass of wine, and talk about the wedding and their plans for the future. Marie's effort to hide her relief at this reprieve was so unsuccessful that Herman almost laughed out loud. But he did not, and they had a wonderful chat as the wine and the fire relaxed them.

Herman finally introduced the subject that was foremost on their minds. "You know, my darling, as I sit here and gaze at you in the firelight, you are the loveliest thing I have ever seen. I am totally entranced with the very thought of being your husband. You know how I love you and, well, you must also know that sometime soon I would like to make love to you. I wish to express my love for you completely; to possess you, and to have you possess me."

He stopped, and watched her face go through a swift series of emotions. After a pause, she smiled at him and replied in a quiet tone, almost a whisper.

"Yes my darling Herman, I do know that. My mother has instructed me, so I am aware of what you wish and indeed, what I wish as well. It's just that, well…"

"I understand, my love." Herman leaned forward and placed a soft kiss on her lips. Then he sat back and looked her straight in the eyes. "I have no wish to rush you into anything. I desire you greatly, but I know that the decision of when we should begin must be yours. You must be absolutely certain that you wish to give yourself to me. Then and only then will I obey you and make you mine."

Marie sat back and gazed into the fire. "You are sweet, my love. You are so understanding!" After several more minutes of silent contemplation she said that she wished to wash her face, and went into the bedroom, which had a washstand. Herman waited quietly in front of the fire, sipping his wine and wondering what would happen next. Had he scared her off? As the minutes ticked by he began to fear that he had done so. He had been too sudden, too rash, and she was withdrawing from him, for now at least.

But then she returned to the room and stood before him, and he knew that he had not scared her off. She wore a blue negligee that was tied loosely at the waist, but still offered tantalizing glimpses of the body beneath the silk. She reached out for him with one hand, beckoning with the other towards the bedroom.

"Come with me, my darling. You are my love; be my lover."

5

SOREL

After their brief stay at the hotel, Marie and Herman moved into his rooms in Ste. Therese Street. He introduced her to his landlord, and then took her up the stairs to the door, opened it, and swept her off her feet and carried her over the threshold. It was wonderful! He carried her into the parlour and placed her on the love seat. Then he sat down next to her, took her into his arms and kissed her soundly on the lips. "Welcome to our first home, my darling" he declared, his voice first strong and firm, but then growing somewhat loose as he felt the warmth of her in his hands, and pressed his kisses.

Marie was warm as well, in the most delicious way. The two nights at the hotel had dispersed her fears. Her soreness after that first night had settled down, and she foresaw only pleasure and satisfaction in the arms of her handsome man. So she knew where things would lead if she didn't ask to, at least, see the rooms. And so they had a tour of his suite, which had a parlour with dining area, a small kitchen, two separate bedrooms and a washroom. One of the bedrooms was theirs, with its sizeable bed, chairs and wardrobe. The other was Herman's study and dressing room.

Sensing Herman's excitement, his glowing face, searching hands and firm trouser-front, Marie begged for a chance to wash up, and took several minutes in the washroom. When she emerged her husband was sprawled on the bed, coat off and arms reaching for her. It was only much later that they managed to sip the wine that he had brought in to toast their arrival.

For six wonderful weeks Marie knew the exquisite joy of love and new marriage. Herman was everything she had dreamed of, and much more as well. Their lovemaking was beyond her previous dreams. It became a most precious part of their time together. It changed and grew and flowered into a myriad of new sensations and pleasures. Herman had to be out a good part of most days to see his patients, and his homecomings were exciting and joyously happy and, as often as not, gloriously sexual.

She planned and prepared their meals, using her considerable cooking skills to good advantage. Herman always enjoyed the meals, and would often even applaud a particularly good dish. Dessert and sweet wine were often times when meals turned into hand-holding and kissing, and even urgent passage to the bedroom.

They had one visit to Gregoire's shop, where they found him and his assistant hard at work. Her father had explained to Marie what Herman had done to help his business, and she was happy to see him so busy and, for once, not beset with worries.

But then, of course, it had to end, for as May turned to June it was time to move to Sorel. As Herman had predicted, Marie was excited with the prospect of moving there. It would be away from her parents, but not so far that there could not be visits each way at reasonable intervals. Before they departed they spent three nights with the Hucs, sleeping in the guest room. Marie blushed a sweet shade of pink when, the first evening there, it came time for them to retire to their room. Judith actually grinned at her and gave her a sly wink as she and her husband went to the stairs, and Marie almost fainted with embarrassment.

As they entered the bed Herman whispered to her "well my love, this is the first time we will make love under the family roof. How exciting!"

"Oh Herman darling, we can't. We simply can't! What if they were to hear us?"

Herman would have none of it. "If they do, it will be to their pleasure to know that their sweet daughter is so happy. Now come here!" And she did.

Sorel began its life around the year 1642 as Fort Richelieu at the mouth of the Iroquois (Richelieu) River. The French authorities had strengthened the fortifications at Quebec and Trois-Rivières, and built the fort at Sorel to secure the route up the St. Lawrence River to the island of Montreal. Those were dangerous times, with the Iroquois newly on the warpath, breaking the 'eternal' treaty of peace they had signed with Samuel de Champlain.

The town and its fort grew slowly. With poor, sandy conditions for agriculture, a significant proportion of the men of Sorel were involved in the fur trade as voyageurs, transporting the pelts from the wilderness of the north and west to the exporting centres of Montreal and Quebec.

Until 1776 there was almost no English spoken in Sorel. In that year it started to undergo substantial change, for while just a small village, Sorel was the scene of much activity. Large numbers of troops passed through, and at times were stationed in the area. German auxiliaries employed by England were quartered in Sorel as they arrived in the country. Loyalists started to arrive, fleeing the war to the south.

The flow of Loyalists continued and grew throughout 1777, and in the following year the troops began to build storehouses, barracks and a hospital to handle the growing population. The situation in 1779 was, as described to Herman by Colonel Murray, desperate. The troops stationed in the town and nearby were taken care of adequately by their own internal medical services, but the growing tide of Loyalists was threatening to overpower the few services available to the population, which now had a significant portion of English speakers.

The Eberts' carriage drew to a stop in Sorel's market square in the late afternoon of Tuesday, June 20, 1780. It had been a long drive from Boucherville, the carriage and accompanying luggage cart jogging in the dust through the hot, humid sunshine. After a tearful farewell with her parents, Marie had dried her eyes and enjoyed the adventure as it unfolded – the long drive beside her talkative husband, the welcome relief of lunch beside a stream in the shade of huge trees, and finally their arrival in tiny Sorel. They were damp and dusty, happy to be there.

The square was of modest size, open on one side and with rough wooden buildings on the other three. A street somewhat wider than the rest went past the square where it faced the Richelieu River, with supply buildings, a store and an inn on the far side of the street, backing onto the river itself. To their right as they looked towards the river was a small church, and beyond that, along the banks of the river, was a grouping of military-looking buildings. They saw just how small Sorel was, yet it had a sense of energy and purpose. Men in uniform were everywhere, the few shops in evidence looked busy, and there were numerous horses and carriages plying the streets.

A soldier who had been lounging in the shade of a storefront saw them arrive and approached them. He smiled first at Marie, showing a soldier's natural inclination, but then came to attention, saluted Herman and said "Welcome to Sorel Doctor Eberts, Madame Eberts. Please wait here."

He turned and dashed towards the military buildings up the road. Five minutes later he returned, following a young officer who approached, saluted and introduced himself as Lieutenant Robert Maxwell. "Dr. Eberts, Madame Eberts, on behalf of Colonel Ebenezer Jessup, and of our entire establishment here, I welcome you. Colonel Murray has sent us explicit directions as to your placement, your duties and your privileges, and I can assure you that we all welcome you personally as well as officially."

He came to the carriage and shook hands with Herman, then smiled and bowed briefly to Marie. "We have your house ready for you, but it's growing late and you must be tired from your journey, so I have taken the liberty of reserving a room for you at the inn for tonight. Your movers" he waved at the luggage cart "will be housed at our barracks as long as they are of service to you."

The Lieutenant led them the short distance to the inn. He told them that they would be welcome to dine with him at the officers' mess, or even at his own residence, but that he had assumed that they would prefer the informal arrangements at the inn after their long day. They agreed happily, and he departed with a salute and a farewell smile at Marie.

As they were finishing their breakfast next morning, Lieutenant Maxwell came to their table, shook hands with Herman and welcomed Marie with one of his generous smiles. "Good morning Doctor, and to you Madame. I do hope that you have had a restful night?"

"We have indeed" said Herman. "The inn is comfortable and the food is excellent. Sorel seems to be well prepared for visitors. Please Lieutenant, do join us for a cup of tea."

"That we are" said Maxwell as he seated himself across from Herman. "As you can imagine we do frequently have important visitors to our town, so we have made certain that we have the facilities to welcome them. Mind you, this is not the luxury of Montreal!"

As they sipped their tea, Maxwell briefed them on the plans for the day. Colonel Jessup would greet Herman formally, and then there would be a briefing for him at the barracks, to be attended by the senior medical staff in Sorel. He said that while the medical situation in the town was not desperate, it was certainly serious. "The local doctor, French of course, is a nice fellow and hard-working, but he has very little formal training. Our military doctors are better trained and help him with his local practice when they have the time, but they are badly understaffed, and do not have the level of training required for a place with such a substantial military establishment. As you may know, we have five companies here, with over three hundred men, and there has been a constant flow of other units passing through. And of course, they all have their problems to be seen to.

"And now we have the civilian Loyalists flowing through as well, and many of them are staying on and settling down here, or at least trying to do so. Some of them are robust, but many have clearly suffered from their handling down south, and their long travels from there. They're in temporary housing while we try to sort them out. It's not a good situation, and this adds to the burden on our medical people."

Herman intervened to ask about the proposed arrival of retired soldiers and their wives – the Military Invalids that Colonel Murray had spoken of.

"Ah yes, Doctor, so you know about that as well. You are well informed, Sir. Yes, we expect to start receiving them early next year. We're told that there will be at least two hundred of them, and possibly more. We've started construction of cottages for them; you may have passed the construction site when you entered the town. There will be a doctor sent along with them, but those old people usually need a lot of care, so there will be more to do."

Maxwell leaned back and smiled broadly at Herman. "So you see why I have told you just how welcome you and Madame Eberts are to our community. Your reputation has preceded you Sir, and I can assure you that you will have much to do, and many willing hands to support you."

Turning to Marie, he bowed his head slightly and continued. "Which brings me to .the activities planned for you today, Madame. We have assumed that you would like to see the town, and also to direct your movers to install your furniture in your house. Is that a reasonable assumption?'

"It is, Lieutenant Maxwell" replied Marie.

"Excellent. So, when we leave this inn after breakfast I will introduce you to my wife Ginette, who will be waiting for you with the carriage. She will take you around, and to your house where the workers have already been directed. At lunch she will bring you to our cottage where you will meet several of our friends, wives of other officers stationed here."

Ginette Maxwell was a young French woman two years older than Marie. She had met her husband in Montreal when he was stationed there three years before. They had been married within the year of meeting, and Ginette was now the happy mother of a one year-old daughter.

She greeted Marie at first with some formality, as was appropriate for the wife of such a distinguished newcomer to the town as was Dr. Eberts. Very quickly, however, she relaxed as she found in Marie a woman of similar age, background and interests, and potentially a good friend. They were soon on a first-name basis, chatting happily about life in Sorel, their families back in Montreal, and the people Marie would be meeting over the next few days.

Like Marie, Ginette had learned to speak English through her relationship with her husband, and was now fluently bilingual. She naturally preferred to speak French, as did Marie, and she told Marie that she could expect to do so in all of the shops and other facilities in Sorel, and in fact with all of the residents who had been here prior to the arrival of the British forces. This rather strange situation in which all newcomers, army and Loyalists, both military and civilian, were English speakers, and all older residents French speakers, had caused some problems, but now seemed to be settling down. The French populace was quick to learn enough English to deal with their new customers and neighbours, and many of the new Anglophone residents were learning some French for the same reason. It would never be a perfect situation, but at least it was peaceful.

They drove around the town viewing its rough wooden houses and shops, the small Catholic Church and the substantial construction site where the Military Invalids were to be housed. Marie was distressed to see the places where many of the Loyalists were camped. The women and children appeared to be in rough shape, and their tents and shacks were anything but healthy. Over-all, however, she found Sorel exciting – small but lively. It was here that she would, for the first time in her life, be recognized as a mature married woman, independent from her parents.

After their tour of the town they came to the house which had been allocated to the Eberts. It was two blocks away from the square, one of a group of houses that had been constructed for officers and their families. The transport wagon was sitting near the front door, with half of its contents already moved into the house. The two workers came out of the house as they approached, saluted the women politely, and the older one said that they had moved in pieces of furniture which would clearly be in certain places. For the rest they were pleased that Madame had arrived and could direct them.

The house was a pleasant looking, simple house, not large but certainly adequate. It was painted white and had an unfinished, almost wild yard surrounding it. "As you can see Marie, our brave soldiers like to leave the gardening to us" laughed Ginette as they lifted their skirts and strode over the dirt up to the house. Inside they found that the army had placed the major furniture and a number of smaller pieces in their obvious places, and the workers had added to them in a logical manner.

Marie told them where to put the remainder of the items in the cart, which included their clothes cases, some kitchen equipment and utensils, small furniture pieces and Herman's books. When they were done Marie thanked them and sent them on their way. She and Ginette then sat in the parlour, happy in each other's company, and talked about the house and its potential. The place was spotless, and Ginette explained that the army had engaged a cleaning woman to prepare it for their arrival. She would be available to them in the future should they wish it.

"Oh Ginette, this is so exciting" exclaimed Marie. "This is my first house, you know, and it really is quite pleasant. It was nice of you and 'the brave soldiers', as you call them, to have it so ready for us. Thank you, thank you!"

Ginette chuckled. "You know Marie, with three hundred soldiers here, all bored and lonely over in the barracks, it's not difficult to find willing hands to help poor young women like us to fix up our houses. They are most polite, of course, but they do enjoy an occasional escape from their own quarters. And then we have the local tradespeople, who appreciate very much the payment that comes with helping us. I must say, my husband has told me that the orders from Montreal were to give you every assistance to make your arrival here as easy and pleasant as possible. You must be very important!"

Marie smiled. "Not me, but certainly my dear Herman is. He's a wonderful doctor you know, a surgeon. He is well known in Montreal for his skill, and that is why we are here."

"Is he German, Marie? He speaks with a very soft accent, but somewhat familiar, as we have had a number of German units come through here."

"He's Austrian, but popular with the English. As I mentioned, he was attached to one of their regiments that came out here. It's interesting. He's Austrian and a Lutheran, and the English like him and have no problem with his religion. Yet the French people in Montreal, including in my own town of Boucherville, who need his services so badly, dislike him because of that very fact. He is not a Catholic, and we were not married in a Catholic church, so they dislike him."

Ginette laughed. "How familiar that is! I've had the same experience with my Daniel. My own parents tried to talk me out of our marriage, but I loved him so much that I defied them and they had to give in. I regret that he's not Catholic, as I am and so wish it. But he really doesn't care about religion at all, and dislikes it when he has to attend services given by that horrid Chaplain Scott over at the barracks. Most of the soldiers there are Anglican, of course, and so are most of the civilian Loyalists."

"How interesting! Tell me, have you discussed this religious issue with your husband as it relates to your daughter?"

"Oh yes, and it's a great relief that, as I have said, he really doesn't care about it. So we are agreed that Celine will be brought up in the Catholic Church – she and all the other children we intend to have."

Marie blushed at this, but had to comment. "It's such a relief to hear you say that. Herman and I have not yet discussed this issue, and I've been afraid of it. You know, he refused to have us married in the Catholic Church, and I've thought that he might also insist that we avoid our church with the children as well. I believe that your example will be a good one to follow!"

"I think so. But now then, perhaps we should go to the shops so that you can have some food in the house? Oh, but not for this evening, I should say. Colonel Jessup and his wife have invited you to their home for a welcome dinner this evening. It will give you a chance to meet the other senior officers and their wives. I'm happy that Robert and I have also been invited."

"How wonderful Ginette. Why, it's almost as if we were best of friends already! So yes, let's visit the shops."

After that warm welcome the Eberts' settled down happily in their new home. Herman told Marie that he had much work to do, not just dealing with patients, but also organizing the medical services that were already in place. He said that there were three doctors active in the town, but their combined skills were inadequate to the growing demand, and they had welcomed him with obvious relief. Herman did his surgery, worked to organize shifts of work and patient care systems and routines, and provided training wherever needed. His days were full; he would arrive home late in the day, tired and either happy or frustrated depending on how things had gone in the previous hours.

With Herman so occupied, Marie was in full charge of the house and their social and personal lives. She found that she liked the responsibility of her new position, which placed her on a more equal footing with her older and more experienced husband than she had anticipated. She was not just the sweet young wife of an important man; she was a real person in her own right – an interesting and popular member of Sorel's community. She engaged the cleaning lady Mme. Lortie to come in once a week, but otherwise she tended to the chores on her own. The cooking she had done at home in Boucherville stood her in good stead here in Sorel. Herman praised her consistently for the fare that she served. When she had people in for a lunch or dinner she would ask Mme. Lortie to help, and that redoubtable woman was good at cooking and, of equal importance, washing up.

Aside from their personal life and social life with new friends, they were almost always invited to official functions hosted, generally, by Col. Jessup and his wife Elizabeth or other senior officers, either at the garrison's officers' mess or at their homes. Marie found these events enjoyable. There seemed to be no petty politics at play. Elizabeth Jessup in particular, who was the same age as Marie's mother, took a personal interest in Marie, and her attention rubbed off on the other women in the group. Marie started on the required round of visits for tea, ensuring that Mme. Lortie was always in her kitchen when the ladies came to call at her house.

Ginette Maxwell was Marie's closest friend, and Robert and Ginette often shared a pleasant evening with the Eberts'. Marie particularly enjoyed the times when the Maxwells' daughter Celine was there. She was such a sweet child.

In spite of his long days of work and their moderately active social life, Marie and Herman took advantage of their pleasant, private home to pursue the passionate sexual love that had commenced on their wedding night back in Montreal. As before, the event would often start with some casual handholding at the dinner table. A kiss would be next, a caress, and then a swift flight up the stairs, clothing strewn in their path. Their howls of laughter, gasping and exclamations of joy were often heard through the windows during the warm summer evenings, bringing blushes and secret smiles to the faces of passers-by.

Soon after their arrival in Sorel, Ginette introduced Marie to the Catholic priest, and Marie began to attend the church on Sundays. As she had discussed previously with Ginette, Marie was not able to convince Herman that he should join her at the church. He stated his case simply and firmly. "My darling, you have told me how the Maxwells are dealing with the religious issue, and I find it most sensible. You are welcome to attend your church, and to raise our children in that faith. And don't worry, I will not be a religious rival to you. The Anglican Church here is very poorly served, so I intend to spend my Sundays studying medical texts rather than religious ones. If there is eventually a proper Anglican church established in Sorel I might relent on occasion, but I must admit I'm in no rush to do so."

In early September Marie realized that she was pregnant. She felt that it was perhaps too early for them to have children, but when she told Herman he did a splendid dance of happiness, followed directly by an unusually gentle but nevertheless definite trip up the stairs. Their lovemaking became slightly less vigorous than it had been in deference to her 'glorious condition' as he liked to put it, but continued its joyous course as the months went by and she grew in girth.

She had a regular exchange of letters with her parents back in Boucherville, telling them in great detail of the wonderful life she was having in Sorel. In early October Gregoire and Judith came for a week's visit. They arrived late in the day, tired and dusty after their long carriage ride. Judith noticed immediately the tightness of the dress around Marie's waist, and the revelation of her pregnancy led to a furious burst of tears by mother and daughter, and a brave throat clearing and nose-blowing by Gregoire. When they had calmed down, Marie showed them through the house, and then sat them down for tea, to await Herman's arrival.

The doctor strode into the house an hour later, apologizing for being late, and saying that the poor fellow upon whom he had been operating simply couldn't wait another moment for treatment. "He's one of the Loyalists who have been streaming through here, and he was in terrible shape, I'm afraid – an accident on the road just outside Sorel! But now – my dear Judith, how are you? And Sergeant Huc, how fares the leg?"

And so went the visit, through happy days of walks and teas, quiet conversations and several enjoyable social events where Judith and Gregoire were greeted with great respect. They glowed when people told them how pleased everyone was with Herman and their lovely Marie being here in Sorel. She was so sweet and friendly, and he was a wonderful doctor and such a distinguished man! At their tearful farewell at the end of the week it was agreed that Marie and Herman would come home to Boucherville for at least a week at Christmas.

6

IGNACE – 1781

Christmas of 1780 was the usual cold, snowy time in Sorel, and in Montreal and its surrounding communities. Herman exchanged the carriage for a sleigh, and three days before Christmas they took advantage of a break in the weather and travelled easily and quickly to Boucherville.

Marie felt mature with her handsome husband and her growing waistband, but coming into her old home made her glow with youthful pleasure as all of the joys of a good home and kind parents rushed back to fill her life for this brief period. She had endless gossips with her mother and her old friends, enjoyed the church, and helped her mother preside over several social gatherings at their home. Judith presented her proudly as the mother-to-be, and most visitors responded positively. But not all; there was still evident a feeling that Marie had done the community a disservice by marrying an outsider, no matter how distinguished. A few friends simply did not show up, making excuses that were clearly lame and meant to send the same message. It made Judith and Gregoire angry and frustrated, but they kept their feelings to themselves, refusing to spoil the festive air that pervaded the house.

Herman left the house on several occasions to visit friends and contacts in Montreal, including a few important patients who had heard of his visit and begged for a consultation. He made courtesy calls on the various military offices, and had a particularly pleasant visit with Col. Murray, who invited him to lunch at the officers' mess, and then a private chat in his office.

Murray opened the conversation. "Well Doctor, it seems that you've started your time in Sorel in fine form. I've received some glowing reports from Colonel Jessup about your work there. He says that things are running far more smoothly than they did before, and there's a new sense of confidence in the medical services on offer. Well done, I must say!"

"Thank you Sir. Yes, I am pleased with progress so far. We could always use some more help, of course, and if this flow of Loyalists continues and even grows, we will definitely be calling on you. I believe you mentioned before that you would be sending Dr. Chris Carter to help with the military invalids when they start arriving this summer?"

"That is correct. As you may know he's been tossed around a bit down south, but seems quite happy up here now, and I think the posting in Sorel will be good for him. And of course, that will take a considerable load off your hands."

"That will be most welcome, Colonel. Now then, if I may, I would like to raise another issue with you to see if anything can be done about it. I'm speaking of the law against the dissection of cadavers. In my studies in Austria this was a regular part of our medical training. It's obviously the best way to learn about the human body so that we may better know how to deal with its ailments. Yet here in this Catholic environment it's considered a sin, a sacrilege, with dire penalties for those who practice it."

Colonel Murray held up his hand. "I do indeed know about this law, and I fully understand your frustration with it. It is, of course, an issue in many places. Many people in England, and even in the United States, have an abhorrence of it, and of the profitable body snatching that's at the root of so much of it. On the one side there are your very practical concerns, but on the other there are the strongly held feelings about the sanctity of the body. These concerns often have a religious basis, as they do here in Quebec, but sometimes just the thought of pulling bodies out of graves to cut them up is too much for some people to bear. As you well know, it is considered important to people here, and we have not seen it as enough of a problem to seek to change it. We don't wish to have a battle with the church, at least not on that subject."

"Ah but Colonel," cried Herman, "it's extremely important. I'm finding in Sorel that there are injuries and diseases that I have not seen before, and am having trouble treating effectively. It would be of great benefit to me, and to my colleagues there, if I could open up certain cadavers to learn about their afflictions so that I can deal with them when I come across them again. It's terribly frustrating having a religion-based law interfering with our medical work. Is there really nothing you can do?"

"I'm afraid not. This issue was raised not too long ago, and a decision taken on it – with regret, I admit, but there it is."

Back in Sorel the Eberts' settled into their routines, with Marie growing rounder with every passing week. The older women in her circle spared no opportunity to give her advice on birthing and child rearing, seeking to divert her and give her confidence, but as her time approached she grew steadily more nervous. Her chats with the midwife Mme. Richard helped somewhat, for she was so calm and organized, and exuded confidence.

On April 5, 1781, with early spring winds blowing the light snow that still persisted on the roads, Marie awoke early with her first labour pain. Her waters had broken the previous day. She had not expected the pains to come so soon, but they had, and Herman held her hand through several hours of intermittent pains. When a nurse from the hospital dropped by to see where he was, he asked her to fetch Mme. Richard, and soon the team of doctor, midwife and nurse were attending her.

It was a hard, painful time, but in mid-afternoon, with great noise and commotion, Ignace Herman Eberts burst forth into the world. He was a perfect, healthy boy, and the parents were ecstatic. His loud cries brought smiles to their faces, and Marie soon forgot the pain that she had suffered. Three days later the proud parents had Ignace baptized at the Catholic Church, presided over by Father Martel. Herman chose to ignore, for such an occasion, the fact that he did not want to be in a Catholic church.

Marie was captivated. The very sight of Ignace, or just his scent or the sound of his clucking, sent waves of delight coursing through her. She would hear nothing of wet nursing, preferring the quiet satisfaction of the baby at her breast. Only reluctantly did she let Mme. Lortie change or hold him, although this became easier and more natural over time. Lortie was the mother of six children so had great experience, and she and Marie had useful conversations about dealing with the noisy little fellow.

For his part, Herman stayed clear of the changing process, bathing and other womanly duties, but loved to hold Ignace and play with him. He was the picture of a proud father, bringing a smile to Marie's face with his prancing and boasting. It was he who greeted Gregoire and Judith Huc on their first visit to see the baby, holding Ignace for them to admire. This left Marie free to greet her parents with great hugs and the usual tears, and to start the process of their happy one-week visit in the warm June weather.

7
THE GROWING FAMILY

Herman took good care of Marie as she recovered from the birth of their first child. He gave advice on her diet, helped occasionally with chores around the house, and took her for increasingly long walks to build up her strength. She was young, and soon felt back to good condition. It was in mid-August, on a warm, almost steamy evening that he, for the first time, took the step to start the family process again.

They lay on the sheets lightly clothed, gazing at the ceiling and staying perfectly still in an attempt to cool off after a hot day. Ignace was sleeping in the next room. Herman turned his head to gaze at her through the gloom.

"Tell me darling, would you like me to kiss you?"

She chuckled. "My love, since when have you had to ask me for a kiss? Why, you kiss me every day, and even this evening after dinner you did so. What is it?"

"Well" said Herman, clearing his throat, "I was thinking of a real kiss this time. You know, a real one."

He paused, unusually embarrassed. Then he sensed a movement on her side of the bed, and suddenly she was on him, rearing over him and kissing him hard on the lips. With mouths open and searching, with hands tearing at their flimsy clothing, they launched once again their passionate sexual life.

Marie felt complete – satisfied and happy as her life with Ignace moved on through that summer and into the winter cold. Herman's work was demanding as the stream of Loyalists persisted. The authorities were working on laying out the town in a sensible pattern, with a large square and well-formed grid of streets. They also were allocating farm lands to the newcomers, and in the midst of it all the wave of Military Invalids started to arrive from Montreal and Quebec, taking up the recently-completed cottages. This added further burdens on the medical staff in the town, and kept Herman hard at it.

With these increasing responsibilities, complicated by the arrival of so many older people with their own range of medical issues, the inability to dissect cadavers continued to cause Herman concern. It was so frustrating! He mentioned it to Marie one evening when they were enjoying their glass of wine, and found that she was sympathetic to him as she loved him so much, but was repelled by the idea. Her church had always treated the body as a sacred vessel, not to be torn apart as it left the earth and started its journey to heaven. She expressed herself gently so as not to annoy her husband, and they soon moved on to safer topics.

Life was full, but left them plenty of time to enjoy their love together. Their second child Marie Thérèse Eberts was born in Sorel on August 30, 1782. Marie and Herman soon learned the lesson that having two young babies can be considerably more work than just one, and in November they engaged the services of a young girl from a nearby town to help with the children. Natalie Laberge was just thirteen years old, but mature due to her hard-working upbringing on the farm with her three siblings. Marie and Mme. Lortie quickly came to like young Natalie for her common sense and constant good humour, not to mention her attractive looks and farm-born natural strength, both physical and emotional. Herman was pleased that it worked out so well, but had little to do with Natalie himself. She held him in such awe that she could barely look at him or speak in his presence, so he left it at that and simply appreciated the usefulness of having her in the house.

Their second son, Philippe Jacques Eberts, was born late in the morning of April 17, 1784. The baby was tiny, but still caused considerable pain and bleeding as he emerged. Marie recovered well, but the baby did not seem comfortable in the world. He was smaller than the others had been and seemed sickly, spitting up his milk and crying often.

The family did everything they could, but the infant seemed to be floating beyond the reach of the loving care and the medical prescriptions that were lavished upon him. On July 12, on a hot and humid evening that hinted at thundershowers, Philippe died in his mother's arms. Marie and Herman sat in the dark in stunned silence until, just as the first heavy drops of rain slapped on the window sill, they both burst into uncontrollable tears. Natalie, in the next room with Ignace and Thérèse, heard them and did the same. Ignace knew what had happened and bawled, and Thérèse followed his lead.

They had all lost a baby who had been the focus of their loving attention for three months. For Marie there was an even deeper concern to deal with. Her idyllic life, so full of sunshine and laughter and success, had been found out and stopped. God had sent her the message that she had no right to unblemished happiness. What had seemed easy before – the producing and caring of children – now was exposed for what it really was: a delicate, perilous venture that could turn upon you in an instant. Life was still good and this tragedy would be put behind them, but there was a shade of fear in their lives now where there used to be simply confidence.

Their next child was born in Marie's parents' home at Boucherville on March 15, 1785. They gave him the formal name 'Joseph', but immediately dubbed him 'Joe'. With Joe's arrival they realized that now, definitely, their house was too small and crowded for their growing family. If they were to stay in Sorel longer, they would have to move to a larger house.

But Herman had another idea. He had accomplished the basic organizational and training tasks that had faced him on arrival, and another doctor and two more trained nurses were scheduled to arrive in the fall. Although Sorel had been a good place to start their family, he and Marie were now feeling its limitations socially and culturally, and were ready to move back to the larger environment of Montreal and its surrounding towns. They also wished to be closer to the comfort of the Huc residence in Boucherville. On a consultation visit back to Montreal, Herman received Col. Murray's agreement that they would move the following year, once the new people had arrived.

After several farewell parties and visits, the family left Sorel in June 1786, just after Marie had confirmed that she was pregnant again. Natalie begged to come with them, and they were happy to agree.

Gregoire and Judith Huc were thrilled that the Eberts family was returning to the Montreal area. They hoped that they would move into a house in Boucherville, but were not really disappointed when the young family found a suitable place in the nearby village of Longueuil, just up the river, on the south bank opposite Montreal. It was easily reached, so there could be frequent family visits, and it was the ideal location for Herman as the ferry from Longueuil went directly across the river to Montreal itself.

The house was large, with two full stories and four bedrooms. Its parlour was big and bright, the kitchen well laid out and warm. It had been built a few years before by a British Major who had been married just a short while before being sent with his new bride to a post in the Caribbean. In their haste to depart the couple had left most of the furniture intact and the house spotless. The large garden and stable were also in good shape.

Having said a tearful farewell to the redoubtable Mme. Lortie upon leaving Sorel, Marie soon found a good replacement in Longueuil. Mme. Cecile Cloutier was the wife of a local farmer. Short and very strong, she cleaned the house with amazing vigour, and had an interesting list of dishes when called upon to cook.

Antoine Henry Eberts was born on December 16, 1786 at Boucherville. It was so wonderfully convenient having the Huc family nearby, and Herman and Marie convinced her parents that once again it would be best to have the birth at their house.

Antoine was a fine, sturdy young fellow, and his arrival signalled the start of the happiest years of Marie's life. She had four adorable children, a nice home in a small but lively community, and a handsome husband who pursued his valuable profession with energy and pride. Ignace was now a sturdy five year-old who worshipped his father and adored his mother. She loved to read to him, often with young Thérèse listening in. He had an insatiable thirst for knowledge, for stories and wisdom and excitement, and Marie doted on him.

Herman's practice in Montreal picked up where it had left off when he departed for Sorel. The military welcomed him back, and he was once again a welcome guest at the officers' mess. His friend Col. Murray returned to England in early 1787, but his replacement, Colonel Jonathan Thorpe, was equally friendly and supportive. Word spread quickly that the doctor was back in town, and his civilian practice quickly filled to overflowing.

In September 1788 Herman was on the first list of those licenced to practice surgery and pharmacy in Quebec under the new *Medical Act 28, George III*. This confirmed his standing as a medical practitioner, but he still had two concerns that floated like distant clouds on the generally happy scene. One was his continuing concern over the law forbidding dissection of cadavers. The other was the continuing hostility that he felt emanating from a substantial part of the French community in and around Montreal. His patients liked and respected him, as did their families, but many others did not. He continued to accept this situation as the reality of the moment, hoping that it would pass as time went by. For Marie, however, it coloured her relationships with some of her neighbours and friends, so it bothered her.

After a welcome break from birthing she found, in early August of 1788, that she was pregnant again. Guillaume Jacob Eberts was born at Longueuil on February 1, 1789, and added to the din of her young family which now numbered five, ranging in age from newborn to Ignace's sturdy seven years. There was another break, and then in November of 1790 she announced to Herman that she was, once again, 'in the family way'.

8

DISASTER – 1791

The Christmas season of 1790 was filled with family gatherings and colourful festivities to warm the cold winter weather. Marie was so used to being pregnant that she hardly felt its effects as she gave her time and attention to her family and the small circle of friends who had taken her and Herman into their hearts. This circle included two of Herman's associates, the English army doctors Henry Brand and wife Martha, and unmarried James Cunningham. They lived in Montreal, but found their ways to the Eberts' door on numerous occasions. The Brands had yet to produce children, and Mary Brand was captivated by the Eberts brood. She always brought books and toys when she visited, thereby becoming a favorite of young Ignace.

In early April of 1791, when warm winds had brought a welcome sense of spring to the countryside, Herman had a conversation with Marie after dinner that she would always remember; always regret. The children were all asleep, Natalie had gone up to her room, and they were enjoying a late evening fire.

"I have decided" said Herman, gazing into the fire with a strangely stubborn look on his face, "that I simply must do something about this problem of not being able to research through dissection."

Marie stiffened. She put her knitting down into her lap and turned to face him. "Oh?" was all she was able to say as a bolt of fear went through her.

"Yes" he said. "I know it makes you nervous, my dear, but I really must try something. I'm working in the dark in so many cases where even a small amount of such research would allow me to do my work more effectively. As you know, I think that the law is wrong in this business, but of course we must be cautious so as not to be found out. But we really must try."

"You say 'we', Herman. Are there others involved in this – whatever it is?"

"There are. I've been speaking with Brand and Cunningham for some time about trying something, and they are prepared to join me. They have the same concerns as do I, and Cunningham in particular is keen to do something about it."

Marie sat back in her chair, her mind racing. Even without knowing what they were planning, her intuition was sending her violent warning signals. They were a mixture of fear over what might happen if anything went wrong, and a more fundamental concern that this dear man, her wonderful husband, was not as wonderful as she had thought. For the first time she saw in him a stubbornness that would not be brooked, even when the safety and feelings of his family were in danger. What might this mean for them in the future? But that was for later. For now she must try to convince him not to carry out this outrageous idea.

"Oh my dear, you know this is not a good idea. It would be so easy to make a mistake, and if you are caught at it we'll be ruined. We all will be. Think of the children! Oh Herman, surely it's not necessary to pursue this idea!"

"My darling Marie, I understand your loathing for the very idea of dissection, and I respect you for it. But you must – please, you must – remember that I am a surgeon, and I simply have to do everything that I can to prepare myself to provide the best service possible for my patients. I did some dissecting during my training back in Austria, and I know how powerful it is for the doctors involved. We should be doing it here, and I intend to try. But you need not worry. We've planned it carefully, so there should be no problems.

She frowned. "What do you intend to do?"

"It should be quite simple, really. I've told you about Mlle. Parent, the spinster who contracted food poisoning a few weeks ago and died last weekend. We know precisely where she is buried. Our plan is to fetch her body in the middle of the night this Wednesday and bring it here, to our basement. We'll have one day to do our work, and then we'll dispose of her remains. Nobody will suspect anything, and we will be much wiser."

Marie felt ill at the thought of such an event taking place in her house. She gasped and covered her face with her hands. When she was able to speak it was in a low, hopeless monotone. "And we, your family, will sit upstairs while this terrible thing is taking place beneath us?"

"Good heavens no! My plan is that you will tell your parents that I must be in Montreal for three days, staying there overnight, and so you wish to bring the family to visit them at their home. They will agree, they always do, especially when you have Natalie to help out. You will also tell Mme. Cloutier that we will be closing the house for three days, so she should not come during that time. So we can do the whole thing while the house is empty, and by the time you return it will be as if nothing happened. We will, of course, move the body only at night."

Marie was horrified and terrified in equal measure, and begged her husband to forget this insane plan. But he would not, in spite of her tears and pleadings. For the first time in their marriage he became the stern head of the house, issuing his orders and not accepting any excuses or alterations.

And so the plan proceeded. Marie told Mme. Cloutier to take the next few days off, and the good woman seemed pleased with the prospect of a brief rest. The family left in mid-afternoon on Wednesday, the children excited at the prospect of two nights with their grandparents, Natalie resigned to the extra work involved, and Marie strangely silent. That night the three doctors drove to the graveyard, which was well away from the church, hidden amongst trees. They dug the coffin out, extracted the body from it and wrapped it in a blanket, re-buried the coffin, and brought the body back in a carriage to the house. There was not a soul stirring on the quiet, heavily wooded street as they removed the body from the cart and carried it into the cellar of the house.

With doors locked and lamps lit in the basement, and with darkened house above them, they rolled up their sleeves and went to work with their instruments and their notebooks.

Mme. Cloutier was not just a good cleaner and cook; she was also a conscientious and thoughtful person. She enjoyed her work away from the farm, and the Eberts family was a favorite client. The doctor was so attractive, and Madame so sweet and friendly! She adored the children, and had good fun joking with Natalie, exchanging stories of their own families.

On the morning that the doctors were carrying out their illegal scheme in the Eberts basement, Mme. Cloutier was happy enough to have some rest time on her hands, but her work ethic told her that if there were things to be done, now was the time to do them. One of them was to do some cleaning in the Eberts' cellar, a task that she never seemed to get around to due to the heavy load of work upstairs and in the kitchen. She knew that the house would be empty, but the Eberts' had always entrusted her with a key. Mme. Eberts would be so pleased that she had taken this extra effort!

She arrived at the house in the late morning. It was a pretty sight, with the sunshine glowing warmly through the trees which sported the buds that would soon bloom into leaves. She left her buggy on the street and walked up to the front door. She opened the door and stepped inside, noticing as she did that the house was somewhat warmer than it might have been, having been empty for a day or so. However, they did have ways of stoking fireplaces to keep them going for a long time.

But there was also an unpleasant smell in the house. It was faint, but only too familiar to a farm wife. It was the smell of death, of a decaying carcass. This bothered her as she thought that it probably resulted from a dead rat in the cellar – the cellar that she should have cleaned better some time ago. Well, she would make short work of that problem! She walked straight to the cellar door, opened it and headed down the stairs.

The air of death in the basement was horrifying, as was the scene that greeted her. On a table in the middle of the cellar, lying in the full glow of an array of candles, was the naked body of a woman slit from collar bone to naval, and with the sides of the wound held back with clamps to display her innards. Her scalp had also been cut open, and one of her arms had been flayed. There were three men standing over the body, all with masks over their mouths and noses, their sleeves rolled up and with bloody hands and forearms, and blood on their aprons. They had obviously heard her as she came down the stairs, but were too shocked to move. They just stood there, dripping blood and staring at her. She recognized one of them as Dr. Eberts.

Mme. Cloutier was terrified beyond reason, for this, surely, was Hell! She had seen pictures of this in church literature – visions of tortured people, cut up and screaming, in pits of fire or pots of boiling oil. This is what happened to people who sinned! But who was this poor woman? Why was this happening, here in this calm house? Was the doctor, in fact, the Devil? She felt the edge of madness coming at her as she turned and bolted up the stairs and out of the house. She ran to her buggy and lashed the horse into a gallop, careening along the street towards the town where the constable was stationed.

Hours later Herman sat in Colonel Thorpe's office, filthy, exhausted and thoroughly scared. It had been a madcap six hours in which some things had been resolved, but his own fate was still unknown.

When Mme. Cloutier fled the house, the three doctors knew that they had no option but to clean things up and prepare for whatever might happen to them. They sewed up the woman's open wounds, wrapped the body in a blanket, and lifted it out of the cellar. They were laying it on the front porch when the village constable rode up to the house, supported by five local militia members armed with muskets. The constable was a recently retired French soldier, a man with strong religious convictions and, along with his colleagues, a dislike of Dr. Eberts. He could scarcely restrain a grin behind a serious face as he ordered his men to take the doctors prisoner.

"Dr. Eberts, Sir, it seems that you and these other two have been breaking the law, and in a most disgusting and sacrilegious manner. I am appalled that a citizen of your standing should do such a thing. You have driven poor Mme. Cloutier almost mad with fear and disgust, and we all share her feelings. You are well known for your dislike of our laws and our church, Sir, but this is too much. You shall suffer for it, I can assure you."

He ordered his men to place the body on Herman's carriage, and to accompany the doctors in their carriages to his tiny office and holding cell at the other end of Longueuil. As they drove through the town it was clear that Mme. Cloutier had spread the word of the terrible crime that had been committed. Several groups of citizens stood by the roadside, watching silently with grim faces as the procession passed by. The people were truly aghast that such a heinous crime had been committed in their town, and by such an upstanding (if unpopular) citizen. They did not know who the other two criminals were, but simply looked at them all as sinners of the worst sort.

For three hours the doctors sat in the tiny cell while occasional visitors came to look at them, frowning or sneering or just showing signs of disgust. They heard the sounds of a growing number of conversations, some muttered and angry, in the street in front of the office. It had the ominous sound of a growing mob, building their courage to take the law into their own hands. The local priest came, but as they were not Catholics he had nothing to say to them. He simply gazed at them with a mixture of disdain and triumph, graced them with the sign of the cross and turned on his heel. Their appeals for water and perhaps some bread were ignored.

In mid-afternoon a British military wagon arrived at the gaol, accompanied by soldiers on horseback. There was a brief conversation in the outer room, and then the door to the cell area opened to admit a British officer in full redcoat uniform, accompanied by three privates also in full dress. Herman recognized the officer as Lieutenant Ryland, a tough but amusing member of the officers' mess in Montreal. But there was nothing amusing about him today.

"Dr. Eberts, Dr. Brand, Dr. Cunningham, you appear to have committed a crime under the laws of Quebec. I am ordered by Col. Thorpe to arrest you and to take you immediately to British military headquarters. As the three of you are medical staff of the British army you will be subject to punishment as decided under British military law. Men, take them away!"

They were hustled unceremoniously past the gathering of angry citizens and into the wagon, ferried over to Montreal and, upon arrival at headquarters, placed in a cell and given some water. Lieutenant Ryland spoke to them briefly, saying that he and his men had rescued them from a very ugly situation that was developing in Longueuil. Their attachments to the British military had saved them, but Col. Thorpe was not sympathetic in any way, and would be dealing with them personally.

While waiting in the cell, Herman apologized to his colleagues for bringing them into this sad affair. Over their protests he told them how they should proceed. "I have full responsibility for this disaster. It was my idea, I have directed it, and it took place at my house. You have gone along with me, but reluctantly. You are not hostile to me now, but you sincerely wish that you had not given in to my suggestion."

They argued with him, but not energetically. They realized that there was nothing to be gained by showing a brave face in such circumstances, and possibly receiving heavy punishment. They had their pride but it was, after all, true that Dr. Eberts had been the moving force. In the end they agreed that he should take this line when he was interviewed by the Colonel, and they would take a consistent line when it was their turn.

Now Herman sat facing a thoroughly annoyed Col. Thorpe.

"Damn it Doctor, how could you do such a stupid – no, idiotic – thing! You know the rules here in Quebec. Surely to God you have the brains to stay away from such a hot topic. That law may not seem sensible to you, my friend, but it's the law here, whether you like it or not."

"Of course it is, Colonel Thorpe, but..." interrupted Herman, hoping to interject a word in his defense. But the Colonel would not be mollified.

"No damn 'buts' about it. Oh I know, you've been frustrated with this law, and it has impeded your professional ways. But God damn it man, it has almost cost you your life! Why do you think Lieutenant Ryland arrived there so quickly? Do you know? Do you realize that there was already a movement afoot to lynch you and your colleagues, and to pass it off as religious fervor? Which would of course have been accepted by our Catholic friends, and even if we would have condemned such a move, which we would have done, of course, it would have been too late? Don't you know anything about this community? How it operates? How it thinks? You've trampled on their church and their feelings and their laws, and why? Are you so damned important that it doesn't matter? Well Sir, it does!"

The Colonel leapt to his feet and began pacing across his office, back and forth like a soldier on parade. Herman recognized this as a cooling off gesture, so he kept silent. When Thorpe returned to his chair and started in again, Herman felt a momentary feeling of relief.

"I've decided to cast this affair as your fault entirely. Although you no longer have an official rank in the army, you are generally considered to be senior to Brand and Cunningham with your work in our military, so my report will say that you ordered them to be your accomplices. I shall admonish them as the fools that they are, and fine them enough that it hurts, and order them to restrict their work and other activities to our army community. They actually have little exposure to the French, and the English community will, in general, have no concern about what they have done. And of course, we do need them here."

But the relief did not last long.

"We also need you here, Doctor, but you are a different matter. I am aware of the ill-will towards you that exists in at least parts of the French community. I personally don't understand it, for you are a good doctor and a fine fellow as well. I also understand why you felt you had to do what you did. But this event has sparked an anger in your community that is bound to spread, and will cause all sorts of problems for you, and for us as well. The Catholics will be howling for your head, literally I dare say, and it will take a considerable effort on our part to save you. The fact that you are no longer a serving member of the military, in spite of your work for us under our agreement, is a complicating factor that could be used by them to protest that you should be subject to their court, not ours. We can force the issue, but it will inevitably damage our relations with them.

"And then there's the question of your personal safety, yours and your family's. No matter what we do there are bound to be people who will wish to do you harm in one way or another. You will be the prime target, but your family, your house, anything can happen. So I have decided, with infinite regret I can assure you, that you must leave Quebec at once. Just disappear. Be gone, so that there will be no target for their anger. I want you away from here by sunrise tomorrow and out of Quebec as quickly as possible."

Herman was stunned. "Good heavens Colonel, you can't be serious! Why, that would be quite impossible! My family is away at Boucherville, and …"

Col. Thorpe held up his hand to interrupt Herman. "It is absolutely possible, Sir, and you will do it. I have already sent a messenger to Boucherville to summon your wife home this evening. She will be there when you return, or shortly thereafter. You may, of course, wish to leave your family here for now. That should be alright once you are away. It's you that the wolves want, not them. But if you stay even one more day I cannot guarantee your safety. So this is an order."

Herman's mind was racing, moving quickly from anger to resignation to practical matters. Where would he go? How would he travel?

"I understand Sir, and will of course obey. But, well, where do you suggest I should go? I would be most grateful for any advice you may have for me."

Col. Thorpe leaned back in his chair and stared, not unkindly, at Hermann. He took his time in replying.

"It's a hard question, I grant you, and I have in fact given it some thought. It's your decision, of course, but I would suggest that you consider going to Detroit. It is now formally in the United States of America, but is still in British hands. That will change over time, but for now it's a friendly place for us. It's far enough away from here that your crime will not be known there, and even if it is they will not likely care. It's a frontier place, and the people there, both French and English, will have more urgent concerns on their minds than a professional indiscretion committed far away. It also has the benefit of being just across the river from our colony, so that it should be a simple thing for you to return after some time has passed."

Herman knew that the Colonel made good sense, but the idea naturally raised a host of questions in his mind. Thus even as he thanked Col. Thorpe for his suggestion, his consternation showed on his face.

The Colonel understood completely and went on, now in a softer tone.

"Dr. Eberts we are not, as you know, ungrateful to you for all you have done for us – for the army and for the community as a whole. We do not intend to desert you entirely. On the assumption that you would likely accept my suggestion, I have ordered that the packet *Adventurer*, that was scheduled to depart for the lakes this afternoon, be held for departure at dawn tomorrow. A carriage with armed guard will pick you up tomorrow at 5 o'clock and deliver you to the Longueuil dock. I have assumed that you will not take your family at this time, given the young age of your children and your wife's condition. You'll be living rough for a while at least.

"I have also prepared this for you." He handed Herman an envelope. "It's an official letter from me introducing you to His Majesty's forces. It gives you a good character and fine professional skills. I believe that it may be helpful to you in your travels."

Herman took the letter and thrust it into his pocket without glancing at it. He was exhausted and distraught, but he managed a smile at the man who was saving him from violence and even death. "Thank you Colonel Thorpe. I am most grateful to you for what you have done. I regret any inconvenience or embarrassment that my actions may have caused you. My apologies, Sir."

They rose, and the Colonel came around his desk to shake Herman's hand. "My regret is equal, Doctor, in that we are losing you. But so it must be. Our carriage will take you home, and we will leave two guards at your house for protection. Now then, good-bye Sir."

Marie was sitting with Judith and Natalie, watching the children play with their supper, when she heard a loud knocking on the front door. Gregoire went to answer it, and she heard a brief conversation before her father came and called her out, taking her arm and leading her into the parlour. Her heart sank when she saw that the man waiting for her was an army dispatch rider.

"Madame Eberts, your husband Dr. Herman Eberts has committed an act that is considered criminal under the legal code. He has been discovered, and as punishment to him, and to protect the safety of you and your family, Colonel Thorpe has ordered that he leave Quebec immediately. Specifically, he is to take an army packet departing from Longueuil at sunrise tomorrow. Colonel Thorpe has sent me here to inform you of this, and to accompany you, if you wish, back to Longueuil to assist the Doctor with his arrangements for departure."

With desperate thoughts and angry tears, Marie left the Huc residence in her carriage, with the despatch rider beside her, his horse tied behind. At 10:30pm she walked past two British guards into her home. Herman was in his study, sitting over a pile of papers on his desk. He did not move when he heard her come through the door. She stopped and stared at him, her face expressionless, as he turned to her. His face was a mask of grief.

They stared at each other for a full minute. For Marie it was a minute of fleeting emotions: first anger, then confusion, and then plain, violent grief. She rushed into his arms and his fierce embrace. With her arms around his waist, she could feel and hear the sobs that wracked his body. It frightened her, for this was her strong, wise Herman! But now he was being punished, and he was dragging them all down with him. She shared his grief and his tears as they stood motionless for several minutes. Then they parted to sit in the two reading chairs, exhausted with emotion, eyes streaming and hands clutched together. Herman found his voice first.

"My darling Marie, I am so sorry, so very, very sorry. I have been a fool and followed my own idea. Oh, I should have listened to you! You were the voice of reason, of calm. You understand this place so much better than I, but I could not see it. I am ashamed, my darling. I have ruined us! Yes by God, I have ruined us!"

He clutched his face in his hands as a new round of sobs burst from him. Marie sat back and waited. Her anger had not disappeared, but it had moved to the back of her mind, hidden behind a raft of practical considerations. She loved this dear man, even if he had been a fool. But he had been sincere in his quest for knowledge. There had been no sinful intent, no wish to harm! Oh, she loved him so! As Herman calmed down, Marie turned the conversation to the practicalities.

"We are not ruined, my love, but it will be hard. Where do you plan to go? When can we join you?"

Herman told her about the decision to go to Detroit, and the British packet that would take him away to safety. It was heading up the river, across the great lake to Fort George on the Niagara River. From there he would travel either by boat or land to the far end of Lake Erie, to Detroit. That would get him away from Quebec, but into territory that was still controlled by the British. He wished to be as far away as he could safely be, hopefully outstripping his shattered reputation in Montreal. He was certain that his medical services would be in demand at Detroit.

"As to when you can join me, oh my darling, I wish I could say 'soon'. But of course I cannot say until I'm established and able to bring you and the children there safely. I hope that you will be able to live with your parents until then. I'll write you as often as I can, and send you money when possible. Until then we have substantial savings with our bankers, so you'll be well taken care of."

Marie put together a cold supper for them and for the guards outside, and they worked on the details of their separation as the night wore on.

Herman had what seemed to be an endless stream of work to do at his desk: instructions and advice for Marie, notes to other doctors to reassign his patients, practical issues concerning the house and business affairs. Marie helped him sort his clothes and pack the one case that he felt he could take on his voyage.

At 5am next morning, just before the first light of dawn, the British army carriage drew up in front of their house. They embraced in a silent, tearful farewell, and then she watched her husband climb into the carriage. It turned in the road and was gone.

9

A TIME FOR TEARS

Tears flowed from Marie's eyes as the carriage carrying her husband away disappeared into the pre-dawn mist. She was in a position so confusing and troublesome that she scarcely knew what to think or do. In just a few days her life had plummeted from its pinnacle of happiness and warmth to a pit of despair – of guilt, anger and loneliness.

How could he have done such a thing? How could he be so stupid? She had lost the driving force of her life. Herman was gone, leaving her with a large and still growing family to care for in the midst of a hostile community. He was such a strong-willed man, sure of himself to the point that he was often stubborn and impatient. This was all well and good in the normal course of daily life, but when such major, important issues were at play, it was dangerous and showed a lack of judgement.

The house was cold, so she wrapped a blanket around her shoulders. Sitting in the parlour, she gazed out the window at the budding trees. They instilled a sense of calm and growth, and she finally stopped weeping and tried to organize her thoughts. She knew that her parents would be shocked by the turn of events, but they loved her and her family, and would help her. She could move in with them; it would be crowded, but they could make do for the time being. She had sufficient money to pay her way.

Dealing with the community would be the most complex challenge. The British had left the two guards at the house to ensure its safety over the next few days, so she was physically safe being here. She knew that the people of Longueuil were angry, but that anger would dissipate as word got around that Herman had been banished. The longer-term effects of Herman's actions would, however, be difficult to deal with. She was, after all, the wife of a man who had offended many in the community just by being who he was, and who was now a banished criminal as well. How could she possibly hold her head up in society? Who would speak to her? What would her priest think? Would her parents suffer with the shame of it all?

These thoughts were coursing through her mind when she heard a carriage draw up in front of the house. She was relieved to see her father climbing down from his carriage, helped by her son Ignace. She rushed to the front door to warn the soldiers who the visitors were, then down the steps and into Gregoire's arms. As never in her life before she needed the strength of the arms of the Sergeant. She wept on his shoulder as he held her in his bear-hug. He knew what had happened, based on what the messenger that told him the previous evening, and knew where he was needed.

Ignace was a different matter. He too knew what had happened, for he was very close to his grandfather, and Gregoire had told him about the situation. Ignace was now a sturdy ten year-old boy, intelligent and with a strong mind of his own. He loved his mother and his father, and was aware of the antipathy that existed in the community towards Herman. His response was always pride in his father and disdain for his detractors. Like his mother he was a strong Catholic.

Herman's action had shattered Ignace's world. His father had committed a sacrilegious crime! He was an outcast and had been banished! He had obviously done this without thinking about what the effect would be on his wife and their children! Ignace's love and respect for Herman had moved from love to hate, even revulsion, in that short space of time. He would never forgive his father for what he had done.

Ignace followed Gregoire into his mother's arms. He wept with her, and they rocked back and forth, moaning over their loss. They shared their anger and their sorrow, and in that embrace they confirmed the fact that the two of them must now manage the family together, without the help of that strong but foolish man. After their moans had ceased, Gregoire swung into action, ever the Sergeant ready to solve problems.

"Marie, my darling, we are all distraught over this terrible thing that has happened. As you can imagine, your mother is in tears. But we must take action now. You may not be safe here. The soldier told us yesterday evening that some of the people here in Longueuil were very angry, and might cause some trouble for you. I hope that won't happen now that Herman is gone, but we must not take chances.

"You will, of course, come and stay with us. It will be tight, but we can fit you all in, even if it means furnishing the room at the back of the stable. We must go there now. So come, let us fetch some of your clothes and other goods from the house and take you back home. We will take our carriages together, and perhaps Ignace will drive yours for you."

Marie and Gregoire headed for the house, but Ignace hung behind, staying with the carriage. Marie called to him to join them, and was shocked with his reply.

"No Maman" he shouted, "I will not come with you into that house. It's a place of death and sacrilege, and I will never go there again. We should burn it down! I hate it! I hate him!" With that he burst into tears once again, turning away from them and leaning on the carriage. Marie longed to go to him, but Gregoire was firm.

"Come Marie, come with me. The poor lad must live through his sorrow and anger. Leave him for now."

Gregoire saluted the two soldiers keeping watch on the porch. They saluted back, and the older one said "Sergeant Huc, we regret this inconvenience to you and your family. Our orders are to remain here until tomorrow at least to be sure that the house is not attacked."

Gregoire smiled at him. "We are most grateful, soldier. We will put some food out for you and your partner. We will be coming back over the next few days to collect things. I doubt that people will cause any harm now, but you never know. Please pass on my regards and thanks to your commander for the help you have given us."

"We will, Sergeant."

10

EMPTY YEARS

Marie and her father performed the practical work of loading the carriages for the return to Boucherville. Ignace was of little use, lost in his own world of loss and anger, but at least he took the reins of Marie's carriage and followed his grandfather along the rough road. He had no words for his mother and she, understanding, sat quietly beside him. The sound of their arrival brought Judith hurrying out of their house, and Marie ran to her arms for another tearful embrace. Her mother was sobbing, torn between love and concern for her daughter and anger at her departed son-in-law. Marie tried to calm her mother down, but it took some time.

"Oh Maman, please don't cry. It's a terrible thing that has happened, but we will come through it. I know how you must feel. Papa has been so strong and so good, and I need you both now, more than ever before. Please Maman."

Judith slowly relaxed, finally just standing there holding her daughter in her arms. She knew that she must be strong. She felt as she had many years ago when Marie lived at home and needed and received constant loving attention from her parents. So it must be again.

And it was, but it stretched Judith and Gregoire to the limits of their energy, patience and resources. The family fit tightly into the large house. Marie shared a room with Thérèse, Ignace and Joseph had the attic room, and Natalie slept with the two youngest, Antoine and Guillaume. With the extra burden on them for an unlimited period of time, the Hucs were obliged to engage a full-time maid named Emily to help with the cooking and cleaning. Emily lived on a farm not far away, so did not need sleeping quarters.

Marie was now heavy with child, and on May 5 she went into labour. Marie Françoise Eberts II was borne into this overcrowded situation on May 6, 1791. Marie hesitated to name her after herself, but was too tired and distracted to think of another name that would suit her. From the start the baby was called 'Françoise'. She was a cheerful baby who, fortunately for all concerned, caused very little fuss. Her crib was in Marie's room, watched over by her older sister Thérèse.

The financial resources left by Herman were a comfort to Marie. She could afford to pay her share of the expenses, to the relief of her parents. But the future, for now at least, looked bleak in other ways. The members of the community who had been so negative about Herman before, and they were in the majority, now sneered in smug self-righteousness. They had been right; the man was no good, and now it was clear that he was actually evil! They had little chance to say this to Marie's face as she shunned society almost completely, but they made life difficult for her when she did appear, and even unpleasant for her parents as well. On several occasions Judith had to restrain Gregoire from lashing out at people as he defended his family. He detested their conviction that they held the high moral ground, and could not forgive them for forgetting completely the many benefits that Herman had brought to the community.

Judith avoided the stores whenever possible, sending Natalie or Emily in her place. Marie also kept to home, ostracized by so many people who used to be friends. Fortunately, a small group of family and close friends stuck by them, visiting their home and putting a brave face on the situation, but even the redoubtable Aunt Josie seemed uneasy during these visits. The situation was still too raw. It needed time. Only Josie's daughter Yvette shrugged off the incident completely, supporting Marie without hesitation. In one of their private conversations she told Marie that "...it's about time we stopped letting the church tell us how to run our affairs. You know, I would rather have a doctor who knows what he's doing than a religious one who does not!"

The children suffered along with the parents, having to stay close to home when they would normally be visiting with friends for play. Young people can be cruel, and there was always the potential for bullying and fights as their supposed friends turned on them for being the children of a sinner.

Gregoire managed the sale of the house in Longueuil. His visit to the local agent showed him that the sale might take some time, for at present it was viewed by many as a place of sin, almost a haunted house. He consulted with the priest and another senior citizen, an old colleague of his, and they decided on a plan. Gregoire's family would pay for the church to carry out an exorcism of the house, banishing any evil spirits that might be lingering there. They would also pay some compensation to the family of Mlle. Parent, who were seriously and vociferously aggrieved that the body of their dear departed had been vandalized. Finally, they would put the house into pristine shape, have it watched over by a caretaker, and then just wait long enough that the event would pass out of the minds of most citizens. It should then be salable.

Marie attended Mass every Sunday, bringing the older children with her, and accompanied by her parents for support and, in Gregoire's case, protection. She also went into Montreal on occasion to visit shops and her bankers. On a visit there in July she went to the British military headquarters, answering an invitation from Col. Thorpe to call upon him.

The Colonel was polite and friendly as he showed her to her chair and offered her tea.

"Mme. Eberts, it's good to see you looking so well. I understand that you now have another child, and that the birth went well?"

Marie blushed. "It did Sir. Thank you. Yes, I now have six children to take care of, unfortunately without their father to guide them. I am just happy that my father adores them and is most helpful. And my mother too, of course." She came to a stop, uncertain how to proceed. The Colonel took up the conversation.

"I'm informed that your house is being kept in good order, and has even been exorcized to free it of any evil spirits that might be hovering around." He said this with a smile, showing that he did not take the idea seriously. "I've instructed my people to keep an eye on the house, just to be sure that there is no mischief. I doubt that there will be, but we can never be too careful."

This surprised Marie. She thought that she and her family were now totally separated from the British headquarters; in fact, that the officers would be pleased to have it so, in light of the trouble that Herman had caused.

"You are most kind, Colonel. I must admit I was terribly afraid at the beginning that there would be trouble, but your prompt action seemed to deflate the people who were angry. You took away their target, and fortunately they seem to have no dispute with me and my family beyond a sense of superiority that they feel they deserve. And I must say I can't blame them. Like them I was very unhappy with Herman for what he did. I even told him so when he was planning it, but then it was done, and we had no time to discuss it before he was away." Tears came to her eyes as she thought of Herman in hasty retreat up the river to the lakes. "Oh Colonel, I am so grateful to you for what you did. If only…". She had to stop and dab her eyes, and Col. Thorpe rose and walked over to the window, giving her time to recover.

He turned when he heard her sobs diminished. "Madame, please be assured that the British army does not condemn your husband for what he did. He is a superb surgeon, and he felt that he had to do it to support his very complex work. We naturally are saddened that it has ended this way, but all is not lost. I have given him an introduction to our forces wherever they may be stationed, and it will guarantee him a welcome, and assistance when required. Our posts are always in need of medical services, so he will be able to help them. He continues to be important to us. We have offered him the use of our courier system for his letters to you and to his bankers, and we can assist you should you wish to correspond with him. It is, of course, impossible to know when and where he will be established and can send for you and your family, but let us just hope that it is sooner rather than later. I am certain that he misses you all terribly."

Marie smiled at him. For the first time in almost three months she felt a sense of community. She had the support of some very important people, and she was not really totally separated from her husband.

"Thank you once again for everything you have done for us, Colonel Thorpe." Marie rose as the Colonel came around his desk and led her to the door.

"You are most welcome, Madame."

The efforts by Marie and Gregoire to turn Ignace's feelings for his father from hatred to acceptance and even, eventually, love and respect, were totally unsuccessful. The end of one attempt by Gregoire to talk him around was typical.

"I don't care about him, Grand-père. I no longer think of him. What he did...what he has done to Maman. I will never forget it, and I will never forgive him." He stopped speaking as tears spilled from his eyes.

In early September a British soldier rode up to the house and delivered a letter addressed to 'Mme. Marie Eberts, c/o Sergeant Gregoire Huc, Boucherville'. Gregoire took the letter from the soldier, thanked him formally, and brought it into the house. He handed it to Marie who was sitting in the parlour knitting and chatting with Judith. The women stopped talking and stared at the envelope, which was of rough yellow paper. Then Marie rose without a word and rushed upstairs to her room.

Detroit *August 5, 1791*

My Dearest Marie,

I am in Detroit, finally settled into rooms in a small house near the river. It is rough compared to Montreal, but acceptably comfortable. Fort Lernoult stands above us, away from the river, and I have been fortunate to strike up a friendly relationship with Major John Smith, the Commandant. He has several hundred troops under his command, and reasonable medical services. I have been welcomed at the fort thanks to the letter from Colonel Thorpe, but they have as yet no need of my assistance. Maj. Smith wishes to continue showing full confidence in his military doctors, but says that as things proceed he may well need more hands, so he is pleased that I have come to Detroit. I made it clear to him why I have been banished from home, and he said that it was ridiculous!

The situation in the town is quite different. There is some competent medical service to be had, both in the town itself and the surrounding area, but severe cases must often be referred to the fort, where they must take their turn after the military. Thus my services have been welcomed, and my fees are already covering my rent for lodgings and food. I am confident that in short order I will be nicely independent, and ready to start sending you money. I have even noticed that I could do some good work in trading and other businesses, for these activities are at a very low level of competence at the present time. Most of my fellow inhabitants are more comfortable hunting, fishing, farming or fighting than doing business, yet there is much that could be done, I am sure of it.

Oh my darling Marie, how I miss you! You are so precious to me, and I continue to regret most sincerely the events that led me away from you to this distant, primitive place. How are you? How are our children? How is dear Ignace? And the baby? I do not know how you fared after I departed! Do we have another fine boy, or another sweet sister for Thérèse? It is hard to be so far from you!

Through my work I have met a fair number of people here. They are a rough group, but strong and proud. They are very direct in their dealings. There is no sense of privilege or special status in them. Mind you that does exist at the fort, with its military protocol, but that is to be expected. Nevertheless the officers are most kind to me, so I do not lack for company.

It is strange being in a region that is now part of the United States, yet still seems British, and is run by the British army. This will of course change as time goes by. Indeed, as I understand it from the Commandant, our two governments are busy negotiating how to deal with the changeover of all this territory, all these lands and forts and settlements. It's fine to have a treaty, I suppose, but the details take a lot of time to work out. Mind you, the natives are playing their role in this. They dislike the Americans, who do not wish to recognize the Indians' claims to the land in this region. So a number of tribes have joined forces to fight them and keep them away from these western areas. The British are supporting the Indians as a way to slow the Americans, and their efforts have so far been successful. It will take some tough fighting before the issue is settled.

I try to envisage you living here with me, and it is still troubling. I would worry about you and the children in such an isolated setting, with its frontier dangers and unsettled political picture. The town itself is very rough, with narrow, dirty streets and few amenities. Should the Americans make a sustained effort to control this territory it could mean war not just with the Indians, but with our troops here as well, and I would not want to have my family exposed to such dangers. I will not summon you as yet, but will do so as soon as I feel more secure, and able to deal with all contingencies.

I should tell you about my voyage to this place. The boat that took me away from you – the 'Adventurer' – was most efficient, and the crew extremely polite and helpful. The Commander, a Lieutenant Forsyth, said that they knew all about my exploit, and were amazed at the trouble it had caused. Forsyth himself said that he always assumed that dissecting was the way surgeons learned their trade. He could not see it any other way!

He was a fine young fellow, and I was pleased to be able to help him and some of his crew with minor medical problems.

The voyage up the river was peaceful, but Lake Ontario gave us an unpleasant time. We had some severe weather as we sailed across to Fort Ontario at Oswego, and were pleased to set our feet on land. From there we sailed on to Fort Niagara, at the mouth of the Niagara River. The fort is large and impressive, and the officers there gave me a warm welcome, as well they might, for they had several cases requiring my attention. I stayed there for several days, and said farewell to my friends from the Adventurer. Then I accompanied a troop of soldiers riding up the Niagara River to Fort Erie. We passed the amazing falls on the Niagara. They are quite the largest I have ever seen!

Fort Erie is on the river's edge, on the eastern shore. It used to be an impressive structure, but has been harshly dealt with by the weather as well as various actions during the American Revolution. My reputation had, it seemed, preceded me, for I was met by a very jolly Commandant and a relieved doctor. This place has been a supply base for many years for the army as well as Loyalists and even Iroquois allies (as tough a group as I have ever laid eyes on), and is still actively involved in moving goods up the lake system. They had a number of complex cases for me to look at, generally related to shipping accidents.

From there I boarded another packet, this time the 'Valerie', which was heading for Detroit. We stopped in briefly at Port Talbot, but from then on we had smooth sailing right up to the dock here at Detroit. I must say it was nice to be able to come ashore and settle in.

I am certain that you will have moved in with your parents by now, and will be anxious to sell our house. Those ruffians in the town will make it difficult for a while, but it is a good house, and will sell at some point.

I shall send this with the next packet, which departs tomorrow morning. My darling, I miss you so, I long for you. This is a hard time for us, but we will see it through and be together again before too long. Please pass on my regards and love to your dear parents, and to you, of course, my very dearest love.

Yours affectionately,

Herman M. Eberts

She read the letter several times, drinking in every word of love and encouragement. He was well! He had escaped with his reputation intact, at least away from here! He was established, and it might be possible to join him reasonably soon! She felt a wonderful sense of calm, of relief. And behind those feelings lurked a sense of anticipation – of excitement, of adventure.

She gave the letter to her parents to read, and while they were doing so she called the older children – Ignace, Thérèse, Joe and Antoine – into her room to tell them about the wonderful news. The three youngest were thrilled and pummelled her with questions, but Ignace stood in stony silence, gazing out the window.

When she could finally join her parents downstairs, she found them in a strange mood. They professed to be happy with the letter, but there were clearly questions in their minds. Marie could not let it rest on that note.

"Maman, you do not seem overly happy with the news. What is it that concerns you…and Papa as well?"

There was a long pause, and Marie saw that her mother was perplexed.

"Well, my darling, well…we are confused. We don't know what to think. We…oh, I don't know."

Gregoire moved away from the window where he had been standing, and came between his wife and daughter, cutting Judith off. "That is, we don't know what to think about this situation. We've become comfortable here with our large family, having you with us all of the time, sharing the children as they grow. We miss Herman, of course, but the thought of you joining him in that violent backwoods place is upsetting to us. What if you go to him and you are caught in one of those Indian battles? Or perhaps captured by American soldiers? You are our precious girl Marie, and your children are our precious grandchildren. We are afraid. That's it. We are afraid."

He turned away and strode back to the window, leaving the women to look forlornly at each other. For it seemed to be a hopeless situation.

Boucherville *October 6, 1791*

My darling husband,

I was so happy to receive your letter from Detroit. It was a joy to know that you arrived safely, and are well. I think of you always, and miss you more than I can bear. We all do, my darling. We miss you and need you.

We moved back to my parents' home immediately after you departed. Papa felt that it would be dangerous for us to stay on in Longueuil, and I learned somewhat later from Colonel Thorpe that this was in fact the case. We had the house cleaned, and the priest performed an exorcism to cleanse it of any evil spirits. I know that you will laugh at this, but it pleased me, and also helped the community accept the fact that it is really just a house that can one day be sold. We will look into that next year.

On May 6, so soon after you left, dear little Marie Françoise was born. She is a fine, healthy little soul, full of great noise, but also smiles and laughter. I gave her my name as I was too tired to think of anything else. We call her 'Françoise'. Needless to say Thérèse dotes on her, and is already almost a fine little mother. She and all of the other children are well. Joe is a good boy, big for his age (he is now six, remember?) and very strong. He adores his grandfather, who is teaching him how to ride. Antoine is also doing well. He is smaller than Joe, but he is full of energy, and even sings with his grandmother sometimes! Baby Guillaume is well.

My one concern is Ignace. He has taken our problem to heart, and continues to be upset. He feels that what you did was very bad, in spite of Papa's attempts to make him understand. He refuses even to talk about you. He did not read your letter, and leaves the room whenever the subject is raised. I am certain that he will come around in time, but he is a strong and stubborn boy, soon to be a man. I pray for him. Papa is teaching him to ride and shoot, and says that he is good at both.

Maman and Papa have welcomed us into the house, and it is working well. There is not a lot of spare room, but we seem to manage, especially with the woods and fields for the children to play in. It is wonderful having Natalie with us. I could not do without her. She was afraid at first, and I thought that she might leave us, but she is wise beyond her years, and knows that this is a good place for her. Maman has also engaged a woman named Emily to help with the cooking and cleaning. She lives on a farm nearby, so does not need living quarters here.

Many in the community still have not accepted our situation, continuing to be critical of you, and not friendly to us. Thank heavens for Aunt Josie and her family, and of course the usual friends who will stick with us, no matter what. Yvette is very kind and understanding, and has become a dear friend. The older children are taking some lessons at the church, but I stay home most of the time.

Col. Thorpe has been most kind to us, offering us this mail service. He also has his men keeping an eye on us. I am not sure what that means, but I think he is being protective, and we have expressed our appreciation to him. Papa's business continues well.

You seem very cautious about sending for us to join you. We hear little about what is happening there, except that the Indians are unhappy with the Americans, and are fighting with them (it is always war, is it not?). I would not want to bring the children to such a dangerous place, and trust your judgement about when it will be safe to come. Let us pray that the issues will be settled quickly.

My darling, do take care of yourself, and write to us as often as you can. We pray for your success and happiness, and for the day when we will join you and become a whole family once again.

With all my love,

Your

Marie

The Hucs' extended family had a quiet Christmas, staying for the most part at home. Yvette visited frequently and became a special, valued friend to Marie.

As the year turned to 1792 there was important news from the government. At the very end of 1791 the British government had passed the Constitutional Act which divided the Province of Quebec into Upper and Lower Canada. The names Upper and Lower Canada were given according to their location on the St. Lawrence River. Upper Canada received English law and institutions, while Lower Canada retained French civil law and institutions, including land tenure and the privileges accorded to the Roman Catholic Church. Representative governments were established in both colonies with the creation of respective legislative assemblies. This Act made no difference to Marie's family, but would clearly have an effect on the Upper Canada region, across the river from where Herman now lived.

But these affairs of state were of little interest to Marie, for as the icy winds of January 1792 swept past the Huc residence young Antoine, who had just turned five years of age, was taken to his bed with a raging temperature. He was a happy little boy, full of mischief and music. That made him a special favorite of Natalie's, who taught him songs and poems, and then listened to him perform them for the family, often in duet with his grandmother Judith.

The boy stopped singing half-way through the month, complaining of hot sweats, a sore throat and painful ears. Marie put him to bed, and as the days progressed and he showed no signs of improving, they sent for the doctor in Boucherville. From the very start Dr. Levesque showed great concern for the boy. He did what he could, urging Marie to keep Antoine as cool as possible, and prescribing a variety of medicines. But nothing worked, and the boy's condition continued to worsen. Finally, late in the morning of January 27, 1792, Antoine succumbed to his fever and died in the arms of his stricken mother.

It was the cruelest of blows. Little Antoine had been a pet for the entire family, and now he was gone. It seemed so senseless to Marie, who had great trouble clinging to her religious convictions in the long nights of grieving that followed. The entire household mourned the loss. Stern-faced Judith kept the household going while the rest of them worked through their grief. Yvette spent precious hours sitting with her cousin, comforting her with soft words, holding her hand.

The priest seemed kind and even solicitous when he visited the aggrieved family, but he warned Judith privately, with a hint of satisfaction, that in the community there was a widely-held feeling that this sad event was just payment for the crime that Herman had committed. This drove her almost mad with anger. She rose to her feet and with barely controlled voice told him to leave immediately. She did not dare to tell Gregoire about this conversation for fear of what he might do, but several days later she told Marie and Aunt Josie about it. She was not surprised that Josie rose to the occasion with a most amazing outburst of curses.

Boucherville *February 7, 1792*

My darling husband,

We have lost Antoine! Oh my dearest, we have lost that wonderful little boy. He came down with a terrible temperature and cough in the middle of January. The doctor was not certain what the problem was, and gave him all sorts of medicines, but nothing seemed to work and he died on January 27.

He was such a sweet child, so full of music and laughter. Remember how he used to make us all laugh with his songs and play-acting? Well, Natalie kept on teaching him, and he loved his music so much, and was doing very well with it. It is such a tragedy. We are all terribly sad. Even Papa cannot seem to lift his spirits. Ignace is a great comfort to me, and Maman has been brave and kept the house functioning while the rest of us sit with our thoughts.

Father France came to the house to pay his respects, but Maman told him to leave after they had a private conversation. She told me that he mentioned that this terrible thing was viewed by some (probably including himself, although he would never admit it) as just payment for the 'crime' that you committed. Oh, what a terrible, ridiculous thing to say! I have never seen Maman so angry.

Aunt Josie has been wonderful (as always). She brought some special little gifts for the children to divert them, and I have appreciated her warm embraces and words. She is such a treasure! I hate to think what she will say to people who hold that terrible opinion expressed by the priest. And Yvette has been here often, and is most comforting. I do love her!

Colonel Thorpe has sent me a note expressing his condolences most kindly, and has asked me to pass them on to you as well.

I have no other news. The other children are fine, but I simply cannot think beyond today. I long for you, my darling. We all need you with us, to comfort us in this cold, sad time. I long for your arms and your strength.

With love, your

Marie

Detroit *March 17, 1792*

My Dearest Marie,

I received your letter of February 7 a week ago, and have been adrift ever since. I don't know what to think, much less to say. I am so sad, and then so angry!

Poor little Antoine! He was such a blessed boy, such a joy to us all. I think of him as our family delight, our toy. It was Antoine who could make us all laugh when times were difficult. He always had a smile for us, or a laugh, or a song. Oh my darling Marie, I know how you must be suffering, and I am devastated that I am not there to comfort you, and to have you comfort me!

But there can be no real comfort, I suppose. All we can ask for is time to heal the wound in our hearts. And you can certainly not ask that fool of a priest to help you. I am glad I wasn't there for his visit. Had I known what he said, and the inference of his own feelings, I would have had him out on his ear, I can assure you. That smugness, that self-righteousness is appalling. Please forgive me for saying this, but I must.

As this winter progresses I find myself increasingly involved in the business life of Detroit. It is such a small place, not yet well served as it would be were it more substantial. My medical services are very much in demand in the town. This led me to realize that nowhere is there a reliable supply of medicines and ointments and other useful products. Thus I have joined with a trader from New York to bring in supplies, which I sell through a small shop right next to my examining room. It is already proving to be a profitable enterprise, as well as of great assistance to my medical practice.

Other opportunities present themselves, particularly in the trading line. It seems that once you are in the business it can grow and develop almost on its own in this frontier place. I have already been asked to help place some shipments of furs into the New York market, and may well become involved with a portion of the capital gained from the sale of medicines.

This business has helped me to meet many people, including the most important people in Detroit. They are not an inspiring lot, but there are a few bright lights, and fortunately I have my welcome at the fort, so I have no lack of social occasions. I only wish that you were here to join me in the events and activities.

But the hostilities between the Americans and the Indians continue, and so it is not yet safe for you to bring the family here. I just hope that the issues are settled soon! At any rate I have been able to send my first draft of funds to our bank in Montreal, so you can feel secure on that score.

My darling, please pass on my love and condolences to your dear mother and father, and to Aunt Josie and Yvette and the others, and to Ignace, Thérèse and Joseph. Kiss little Guillaume and Françoise for me, and keep in your mind and your heart that I love you dearly, and share with you the grief in losing Antoine.
With great love,
Your husband
Herman M. Eberts

Those first months of 1792 set a tone in the lives of Marie and her family that was to continue throughout that year, and then for the next three years. Marie and her five surviving children lived as welcome, much loved guests in the home of Gregoire and Judith Huc. They continued to be looked upon with condescension and, in some cases, derision by many in the community, although that feeling waned as time went by, only occasionally lifting its head in the form of taunts by children or snubs by adults.

Ignace performed well in several fights occasioned by insults directed at his mother by careless boys who, over time, learned that the Eberts boy, tall, strong and serious, did not take lightly to such things. Antoine's death left a shadow over the family, a legacy of caution and even fear. The children seemed so healthy, but then so had Antoine, and he had been taken in a very short time by illness that seemed to have come out of the blue.

As the months went by Gregoire and Judith realized that in a very real sense Marie had brought to them the family of children that they had so yearned for in those early days of their marriage. They found themselves in a situation of conflicted feelings with respect to Marie and her husband. While they sympathized openly with Marie for her separation from her husband, they were secretly pleased with the situation, and even hoped, to their embarrassment, that it would continue forever.

Marie's feelings were much more straightforward. Although she appreciated the love and attention that she received from her parents and other family members and close friends, she disliked her current predicament, and longed to join her husband wherever he might be. Fortunately her financial situation was comfortable. They sold the house in Longueuil in July 1792, and with that money plus the funds coming from Herman she was financially secure.

Her greatest joy was always the arrival of letters from Herman. He was doing so well in Detroit; if only she could be there with him! Unfortunately the situation continued to be too dangerous. "It seems so ironic" said Yvette one day over tea. "There is not a real war going on at present between our two countries, but still you are kept away from Herman by fighting that involves our two countries! Our lives are controlled by war, by military things, even when there is no war!"

Detroit *October 12, 1792*

...It is so strange, is it not, that the Treaty of Paris was signed nine years ago, setting out the border between the United States of America and British North America, and yet this part of the United States is still in British hands! It seems that it is one thing to sign treaties, but quite another to carry them out. There is no love lost between the two countries.

The Indians continue to attack the Americans and keep them from controlling these western areas. Our British friends are supporting the Indians, and the Americans are not yet taking the situation seriously enough to forward their own cause. The efforts they are making to subdue the Indians have so far been defeated. This is bound to change, but as long as it persists, this is a dangerous place.

I continue to prosper. We have a new Commandant at the fort, Captain Richard England. He is most friendly and courteous, and has taken a lively interest in my medical skills. It seems that he is not satisfied with all of the medical work performed at the fort, and has recently had me called in to consult on several cases. It has been interesting to see that, although the army doctors were initially quite annoyed at my intrusion into their affairs, they have actually been relieved to have some outside assistance, and I have now been nicely welcomed.

My practice in town is flourishing. I am making calls not just within Detroit, but in the surrounding area, and even across the river in Upper Canada. Some of my work I do on a charitable basis, with patients who have no way of paying for my services, but are in need. This seems to have made me quite popular in some quarters, and certainly at the fort.

I am also becoming quite an accomplished trader. The medical products are doing well, and I am now handling some shipments of other things such as furs and clothing, and even some wines and spirits. I have had to engage a local man to assist me...

Detroit *September 14, 1793*

...the Indians have repelled the offers of the Americans to settle their border claims, and I am informed that the Americans are now intending to take serious action. I think they are afraid that, should war break out once again between the two countries, these western areas might well be lost to them. Word has it that they are planning a major initiative for next year. Col. Richard England, our new Commandant here, is cautious in his assessment of the situation...

In the early spring of 1794 Colonel Thorpe sent Marie an invitation to call on him during her next visit to Montreal. The invitation came along with a letter from Herman saying that things continued to go well from his perspective, but that the situation with the Indians was uncertain. In other words, it was still not wise for her to take the family to Detroit. She hoped that Col. Thorpe would have a more positive viewpoint.

The Colonel was his usual friendly self as he welcomed Marie to his office.

"My dear Mme. Eberts, how nice it is to see you again! It has been a long time since last we met. Do come and sit over here, and we will have some tea." They settled in chairs around the small side table, and paused while the servant set out the tea things. As he was leaving, Marie smiled at the Colonel.

"It's good of you to invite me here, Col. Thorpe. I trust you have some good news to tell me?"

Thorpe laughed politely. "Well now, I do have some good news, mixed in nicely with the usual caveats and concerns." He sipped his tea.

"But to begin, I understand that you have been hearing quite regularly from Dr. Eberts, as have we. As you know he is nicely settled in at Detroit, and I have good reports on his medical work. Indeed, I was prompted to invite you here after receiving the latest report from Captain England, our Commandant there. England speaks most highly of the doctor, for his medical work, of course, but also more generally for the role that he is playing in the town, and even with the soldiers posted at the fort. He is somewhat older than most of the people at Detroit, and certainly than the soldiers. Perhaps I should say 'more mature' rather than 'older'?" He said this last with another smile, which was matched by Marie.

"His maturity, his fine training, his experience, all have contributed to his becoming a sort of mentor to many people there. He is well known, and indeed, looked up to. I wished to pass on these judgements to you personally. You can be proud of him."

Marie blushed and looked down at her cup. "You are most kind to tell me this, Sir." Then looking up at him: "but tell me, you mentioned caveats and concerns. What of them?"

Thorpe sat back in his chair and glanced out the window. "Ah yes, of course. There is much that I cannot tell you, but I can give you the gist of the situation. We have been aware for some time that the Americans have been preparing for a substantial offensive to deal with the Indians, who have been on our side and making it difficult for the Americans to control the western areas. Governor General Lord Dorchester addressed a great gathering of the Indians at Quebec earlier this year, telling them that war with the Americans was imminent. He found them thoroughly annoyed with the Americans, and ready to cause more trouble.

"He has ordered Lt. Governor Simcoe to build and garrison a fort near Detroit, on the Maumee River, as further protection of Detroit. I believe it is to be called Fort Miami. In other words, we plan to protect our interests in the west, whether in Upper Canada or across the border. We are taking steps to establish militia forces. I tell you this so that you can see two things – that your husband is safe and well protected, but that the situation remains volatile. I therefore continue to share his view, which he has stated to me in a recent letter, that you are best to remain here for the moment. It's trying I know, but it cannot be helped."

Marie gazed out the window for a moment, reflecting on this seemingly endless impasse. There were so many questions, but she knew she had little time.

"Tell me Sir, what would happen if the Americans were to defeat the Indians and take over Detroit and the other forts and communities that are on their side of the border. Would it be bad for the people living there now, or would their lives continue as before, but with new rulers?"

"That's a good question. We can only conjecture, of course, but we believe that little will change. The Americans will take over the forts, and our troops will have to withdraw back to Canada. I'm certain that we will be adding some new forts on our side of the border to maintain our defenses. But we doubt that there will be any serious consequences for the people living there. Mind you, over time they will likely be asked where they loyalties lie, and those loyal to the Crown will want to move across the border to Canada. There will be another wave of Loyalists, in fact. But as I say, we do not see any danger in it. I should add, however, that if our two countries were to go to war again it would make a difference, as the Americans would probably have to use force to take back the forts. That would, in turn, endanger the populations there, and certainly make it hot for the Loyalists still living there. But as I have said, Madame, we do not expect that to happen. Our sources tell us that President Washington does not wish a war with us, for the time being at least."

They discussed Marie's family situation for a few more minutes, and then Marie departed after thanking the Colonel once again for his kindness to herself and Herman, and also to her father who continued to benefit from his contracts with the British headquarters.

Gregoire Huc kept Marie up to date on the situation during that summer and fall. Through his contacts at the British headquarters and his trade contacts and regular scanning of the local news sheets he was able to follow the course of events with a delay somewhat shorter even than the letters from Herman. Between the two sources, Marie was well informed.

Gregoire spoke of the appointment of U.S. General Anthony Wayne to head a force to crush the Indians. In a subsequent letter from Herman she learned that General Wayne had defeated decisively the Indian Alliance at the Battle of Fallen Timbers on August 20, 1794.

"Fallen Timbers?" said Marie. "What a strange name for a battle!"

"Not really" replied Gregoire. "It was called 'Fallen Timbers' because it took place in an area that had earlier been hit by a tornado, leaving so many trees uprooted that it affected the course of the battle. As I understand it, the troops on both sides could use the fallen trees for protection."

He went on to explain that the battle took place across the Maumee River from the new Fort Miami, and the British Commandant there refused to help the Indians. One member of the Indian forces was a Shawnee leader named Tecumseh. Britain was not at war with the United States, so the decision by the British not to join the battle was justified, but the Indians were furious with their supposed allies for not helping them.

For his part, General Wayne did not attack Fort Miami because he knew that President Washington did not want war with Britain just then. The Chief Justice of the United States Supreme Court, John Jay, was at that very time in England negotiating with Foreign Secretary Lord Grenville on a broad number of issues in the hope of avoiding war. The issues under discussion included the evacuation by the British of forts on the American side, so it was not the right time for an attack. Wayne approached the fort the day after the battle, hoping that the British would fire on his troops and he would then be justified in taking the fort, but the British held their fire.

With the defeat of the Indians at Fallen Timbers, and their annoyance at the British for not assisting them, the situation was, as Gregoire put it, 'fluid'. Herman agreed.

Detroit *January 27, 1795*

...There seems to be great confusion here, since the debacle at Fallen Timbers. I am told that the Indians are furious with us for not helping them, and our contact with them has become confused. That being said, a large number of Indians, well over one thousand I think, have come here for protection, and many of them are wounded. The Commandant has established an additional hospital to accommodate them, and he has appointed me under agreement to assist with the medical

work. So I am once again working directly for the British military, as I was back in Quebec. I am naturally pleased, as this helps me to maintain my good relationship with them.

General Wayne has not yet taken further action against us or our Indian allies. He is probably awaiting orders from Washington. The action, when it comes, will of course be the taking over of forts such as ours, and it would be good if that could be done without open warfare. The Commandant tells me that there is word that Judge Jay has signed an agreement with the British government, so perhaps this will all be settled this year.

These changes affect some of us more than others. For you and me, of course, it is vital to have such peace so that we can be reunited. For others, it depends on their situation. I have told you about my friend William Baker, the British ship-builder who came here from New York in 1789 to work for a company here. Back in 1792 he re-entered the British service here, in which he had served in New York, and is in charge of the dockyards where they are building ships to help ensure that Britain continues to control the lakes. He is a fine fellow, and he and his wife Effie are great friends of mine. Late last year he was told that he would soon be ordered to move over to the Canadian side, to assist with the development of the new Fort Amherstburg, and its navy yard where they will be able to build ships outside of the American jurisdiction. He has also been assigned to a special project on the Canadian side, to construct a blockhouse and shops at a site up the Thames River for building gunboats for use on the lakes. The site is to be called Chatham, and will inevitably grow into a town. He has already started work on the projects. I don't know when they will actually move.

So you see how things are progressing. We are still busy here on the American side, but steps are being taken to ensure our continued survival (prosperity?) if we are forced to abandon these many facilities now located in the United States. In light of these various agreements, it appears that will happen, if not this year, then certainly next...

Jay had in fact signed the *Treaty of Amity, Commerce and Navigation* in London on November 19, 1794. A key term in the treaty was that by June 1, 1796 Britain would withdraw from the northwest posts on United States territory: Michilimackinac, Detroit, Sandusky, Presque Isle (Erie), Niagara, Oswego and Oswegatchie (Ogdensberg). The treaty squeaked through Congress and President Washington signed it on June 25, 1795.

With the British having seemingly abandoned them, in spite of protests to the contrary, the Indian Alliance decided that they must make their peace with the Americans. They accepted the Peace of Grenville offered by the United States on August 3, 1795, giving up a huge tract of land comprising most of present-day Ohio in the process. In the following two years they gave up an additional thirty million acres of land in order to survive.

These events strengthened Marie's resolve that had started when she received Herman's letter of January 27, to move to her husband's side as soon as possible and certainly within a year. In the fall of 1795 she started to speak openly with her parents and family about moving with her children to Detroit next spring. Indeed, the only thing stopping them from leaving immediately was the approaching winter. It would not be wise to travel such a distance over the stormy lakes and through snow-covered forests of winter; better to wait for the calmer conditions of spring.

II

TO DETROIT! – 1796

Judith and Gregoire Huc clearly disliked the idea of Marie and the children leaving them for the western wilderness. They felt a sense of near panic at the thought of them subjected to the dangers of that far-off region. Marie knew what they were thinking, and she treated them with gentleness and tact. She was so grateful to them for the shelter and support they had given to her and the children, and she hated to hurt them or appear to be ungrateful. But she had grown strong during those long, testing years, and she knew full well wherein her future lay.

It was Aunt Josie who calmed the situation down. She knew that Judith and Gregoire were in turmoil over the situation, and that the atmosphere in the house was growing more charged as the weeks progressed. Marie kept insisting, in her gentle way, that spring would see them on their way to Detroit. Her parents, on the other hand, refused to accept this as a *fait accompli,* counselling patience and a 'wait and see' attitude. The tense moments and occasional angry words that were caused by this stand-off were not lost upon Josie, who visited the Huc residence frequently.

On one such visit in mid-January of 1796, as they sat having tea following a concert given by the children, she heard some provocative words coming from the normally calm Judith, and sat red-of-face as the room fell silent and the Hucs and their daughter examined their tea cups with unnecessary interest. Judith had said words to the effect that such delightful music from the children would likely be dulled and even muted under the harsh conditions of the backwoods. This was too much for Josie to bear.

"I would think", she began, "that children's voices are as welcome in cabins in the woods as they are in houses here in the civilized world. They are always seen as an expression of joy, and so it is wherever it is. But my dearest Judith, that is not, I know, the real source of your concern. You have all tried to hide from me your disagreement over Marie's wish to depart in the spring to join Herman in Detroit. But you have failed miserably, I can assure you!"

They waited for Josie to continue, for they all knew that they needed some wisdom to calm the tension in the house.

"I understand it, of course. Marie my darling, I will miss you and the children terribly when you leave. You are a joy to me, and their concerts are my favorite form of entertainment! But I know how you must yearn for your husband, and it is to him that you must owe your ultimate loyalty."

She rose from her chair and walked over to Judith. Taking her hand, she looked into her eyes, her own eyes slowly filling with tears. "Dear Judith, I do understand how you feel. But let me ask you a question – not a diplomatic question, but an important one. If it were Gregoire who had been banished, for whatever reason but certainly for a reason that you did not accept, would you not go to him if you possibly could? Would your life in this community, your standing with your friends, be more important to you than the love of your husband? Would you not take your child with you, protecting her on your journey with all of your energy, until you were back in the arms of the man you loved?"

For a moment Judith just sat with eyes closed, gripping Josie's hand. Marie and Gregoire looked on from their chairs, holding their breath. Then Judith stood up, eyes streaming, and embraced Josie so that they wept together. Gregoire reached over and took Marie's hand, and they sat in silent understanding. Then, in a sort of ritual dance, Judith left Josie's arms and came to embrace her daughter, while Josie came to Gregoire for the bear-hug she so richly deserved.

From then on the idea of Marie taking the children to Detroit in the spring was accepted by Marie's parents, and they turned their energies to preparation for the departure and, at the same time, enjoyment of these final months together. The children were told of the plan, and all but one were excited by the prospect of such an adventure, and of seeing their father again.

Ignace was the exception.

"I will not be going with you, Maman. It hurts me to say that to you, but I must. I simply cannot come to Detroit to be with Papa, who has caused us so much pain. And besides, I wish to stay here. My studies are going well, and I have Grampa Gregoire and Gramma Judith to help in the house. And they will need me even more as they grow older. Oh Maman, I hate the thought of you leaving, and Thérèse, and the others. I just hate it! But I will not leave our place here just because that man calls us away."

Back in March Marie had sent a note to Colonel Thorpe informing him of her plans to go to Detroit in the late spring or early summer. She also sent a letter to Herman with the same news. In both cases she asked for their advice concerning their mode of transport, and any issues concerning timing.

Colonel Thorpe had been away at Quebec when her letter arrived, so had not replied immediately. On his return, however, he invited her to visit him at his office.

The Colonel's first words were congratulations on taking such a daring step. "All of the required agreements are in place to create a peaceful situation for your journey. We can only hope that things progress in light of the agreements. By this I mean, of course, a peaceful passage through country patrolled by the Indians, and a peaceful hand-over of Detroit to the Americans when they get around to taking such action. In his recent note to me, your husband expresses confidence that this will happen, and probably quite soon. He does not think that either side wants war, at least for the time being, so this spring will be as good a time as any for you to join him. I tend to agree with him. Hopefully you will arrive there while Detroit is still in British hands. Tell me Madame, how are your preparations proceeding?"

"Quite well, thank you Colonel. As you can imagine, our main preoccupation is with the clothing we will require for the trip, and for when we arrive there. It will likely be a rougher existence than it is here, so my mother and I are sewing all sorts of warm clothing for the children. Oh, but I should tell you, not all of the children will be going with us. Our oldest son Ignace has decided to stay here with his grandparents. He continues to be unhappy with his father over what happened in the past, and would rather stay here."

"Oh, but what a sadness for you, Madame!" The Colonel looked down at the table, uncertain of what words of consolation to use. "I am so sorry..."

"Thank you Sir" said Marie, interrupting in an attempt to control her own emotions. "But it has been decided, and my parents are more than happy to have him stay with them. The doctor and I will still have four children to care for, so our home will not be empty!"

The Colonel looked relieved. "Quite so, Madame, quite so. Now then, concerning timing and mode of travel, in his note to me your husband says that he believes you can travel any time it is convenient. Conditions seem to be generally peaceful. I am sure that he has said the same thing to you in this letter, which arrived yesterday with his note to me." He handed her an envelope which she stared at greedily before placing it on the table next to her bag.

"Concerning transport, as he is still of such great service to us, now in Detroit, I am pleased to advise you that we are prepared to offer you transport in our official vessels. Indeed, our Commandant there has insisted upon it, saying that it is of great benefit to all that the doctor be in good spirits! This is, of course, highly irregular, but then so is the situation itself, and the times, for that matter."

"That is most kind of you Sir" said Marie, blushing in spite of herself. Use of official vessels would solve many problems that she had anticipated, from speed and reliability of transport through to safety from whatever hostile environments they might encounter on the trip. "Is there some official schedule that we should know about?"

"There is, and I suggest that we decide on a date of departure that suits you, and then we can fit it to our schedule of sailings. This will be helpful to us as well, as we will need to ensure that there is room for you and your family on board."

After Marie told him that they would be ready to depart in the last week of May, Col. Thorpe consulted a paper, and then they agreed that they would board the packet *Racer* during that week. It would take the family up the river and then across Lake Ontario to Fort Niagara, at the mouth of the Niagara River. From there they would travel by horse cart to Fort Erie, at the Lake Erie end of the river, and by ship from there to Detroit.

Marie agreed to this plan, and Col. Thorpe said that he would alert Dr. Eberts concerning their travel plans. He would also send a note to Marie at the appropriate time concerning arrangements for boarding the *Racer.*

Marie left the office with a rush of spirits. It was actually going to happen!

Marie and her mother worked hard adapting the family's clothes to the harsher conditions that awaited them in Detroit. They knew that it would be hot and humid when they arrived, but that the winters would be brutally cold. They purchased new boots for all, strong hats and leather gloves with wool lining.

Cousin Yvette was a great help in these busy days. Now married to a man named Francois Proulx, and with two babies, she still had time to visit with Marie and her family for tea, to show off her children or just to chat. Her lively spirits served to lighten the mood in the Huc residence, so that even Gregoire looked forward to her visits. In a private chat with Marie she went further, giving her assurances that she would look in at the Huc residence to see how Judith and Gregoire were doing, and to talk with Ignace. She doubted that Marie's parents would write to her often. Ignace might; she would do so often to keep Marie well informed. This earned her a warm hug of thanks from Marie.

As the day of departure approached they began to lay in supplies of food for the trip. They would be guests of the army so could probably count on army food, but Judith insisted, as did Gregoire with a knowing smile, that the children might appreciate some tastier fare. They stocked up on supplies that they could hand over to the cook to supplement what was already planned.

They also began to load their trunks for the journey. Gregoire urged caution as to the volume of their luggage as there would be limited space on board the *Racer*. So some choices had to be made and some treasured items sacrificed. But they did their duty, and on the morning of May 26 their luggage was neatly stacked at the front of the house, where Ignace helped them load it into the cart.

There, at the front door, they said goodbye to Judith and to the faithful Natalie. Both women were swimming in tears, as was Marie. Her children were braver, excited as they were about the impending trip on a real army ship! Marie thanked Natalie, hugged her hard and wished her well on her return to Sorel. She had the same hug for Judith, except that it was longer and completely silent. They had talked over everything so many times! Everything had been said that needed saying.

They travelled quickly through the town and out to the docks on the St. Lawrence River. Waiting for them was the fine looking, sleek *Racer*, crew at their stations and the commander, Lieutenant Archibald, pacing impatiently next to the ship. When they arrived his impatience turned to smiles as he handed Marie down from the carriage and ordered his crew to see to the children and the luggage.

While they were doing so Marie turned to face the occasion that she had been dreading. Ignace stood there, anxious and ill at ease, holding the reins to the cart horse. Her heart went still as she approached him, fighting back tears; she had to breathe hard to keep going. She walked straight up to him and put her arms around him, hugging him hard. She could feel his sobs at her shoulder, once again a little boy, saying good-bye to his mother. She whispered "good-bye dear. Take good care of yourself, and write to me."

Then she pulled away and went to her hug with Gregoire.

From there she turned and walked to the gangplank, where Lt. Archibald met her and escorted her onto the vessel. He introduced her to two young army officers who were accompanying them on the journey, but she did not hear their names as her ears had a rushing sound in them – the sound of sadness and of loss. She and the children gathered at the rail as the ship left the dock and headed up the river, waving at Ignace and Gregoire as they slowly disappeared in the distance.

They arrived at Detroit on June 29, 1796. As their ship approached the dock they could see Herman waving happily at them. The children crowded along the rail, frantic for the boat to dock so that they could run to him.

12

REUNION

The three older children ran down the gangplank ahead of their mother, while little Françoise followed behind, clinging to Marie's hand. They swept into their father's arms and hugged him tight until he was finally able to pull back a bit and greet each of them in turn.

"Oh my Thérèse, how lovely you are! Just like your mother...so beautiful! And Joe, you are a fine, big fellow, I should say. You look very strong; I think that you've taken good care of your mother? Ah, and little Guillaume. You were just a baby when I last saw you. Well, you're certainly not a baby now!"

Marie stood back during these greetings, gazing at her husband. He had not changed much, still wonderfully handsome. His face looked lean and strong, reflecting the vigorous life that he was living here in Detroit. He was well dressed in dark trousers, a leather jacket and grey shirt with blue cravat. He looked like the important man that he surely was according to the reports from Colonel Thorpe.

Herman turned to Marie as she approached, with Françoise now hiding behind her mother's skirts. He crouched down almost to eye level with the shy girl. "And who is this lovely girl? Come here my dear. You have never met me, have you? Well, I'm your father, and I'm very happy to see you at last!" She came to him slowly, and he gave her a quick hug before she turned away and went to her sister.

Then he stood up and turned to Marie, but in doing so glanced back over the ship, which was now being unloaded. He turned back to Marie with a worried look on his face. "And Ignace? My darling, is Ignace not with you? Surely he's still on the ship?"

Marie finally swept into his arms and hugged him firmly, kissing his neck and cheek as he buried his face in her hair. This was the moment she had been longing for all those years, and she savoured it. But she knew that she had to answer his question, so she pulled back out of his arms and looked him squarely in the face.

"Ignace is not with us, my dearest. He decided to stay at Boucherville with my parents."

"But will he be coming here soon?" Herman blurted out his question, his expression turning stormier by the second.

Marie was aware of her other children gathered around, and did not wish to involve them in the discussion of Ignace's future. "I hope so darling. I'm just not certain yet. But now then, here we are at last. We can't wait to see where we will be living in this town. May we go there now? I see that you have arranged for our boxes to be brought along."

Herman knew that there was a story to be told, but appreciated Marie's reticence at the moment, so he smiled and said "absolutely, my dear. Come along children, let me show you our home!" He turned and led them off the dock and up a street called 'St. Honoré' into the town. They passed one cross street and came to a second, more substantial street named 'St. Anne'. Marie saw that these street names were in French, and she asked Herman about it.

"You may know that this was originally a French fort called 'Fort Ponchartrain du Detroit'. It was somewhat smaller than it is today, right on the water's edge. Naturally, all of the streets had French names, and when the British took it over in 1760 they changed the name to 'Fort Detroit', but kept the street names."

"But how interesting" said Marie, smiling at him. "So, do people speak French here?"

"There's still a preponderance of French people in the town and the surrounding countryside, so many do. But English became more common as more English, Scottish and Irish settlers arrived, and of course, the British soldiers in Fort Lernoult speak only English."

"Oh" said Marie, "I have heard about the fort."

"Yes, the town was improved in the '60s when they built an addition to the fortification, which they called the 'Citadel', and the troops were lodged there. Then around 1779 the Commandant at the time, a Captain Lernoult, built the fort that you can see inland from here, connected to the town by the palisades. That is now called 'Fort Lernoult', and the town is still 'Detroit'.

As they walked along, the children stayed close to their mother, gazing around them with curiosity and a touch of fear. The town was not attractive. The streets were narrow and made of dirt. There were many people in the streets, with a few well-dressed merchants but, for the most part, poor looking people, some of them showing signs of habitual hunger. There were also Indians, fierce-looking men who seemed to have little interest in the town, but also were clearly at home there. Many carried sacks, showing that they were involved in trading activities.

Marie remarked on the poor state of the streets, and found Herman's explanation distressing. "Since the treaty back in 1783 placed this town in the United States, the British authorities have done nothing to enhance or improve Detroit, or even to repair its faults. In their view, as it will be handed over to the Americans sometime soon, there's no sense spending anything on it. So it has been decaying for over a decade, and looks it. Even the gates of the palisade have eroded and are not secure! So in that sense, it's a good thing that the Americans will soon be taking over."

They came to a halt in front of a tall, narrow house, one of the few houses with more than one storey. It appeared to be well built and maintained, with a veranda across the front and a white front door. "This is it, my dears" said Herman, and they all studied their new home.

"Oh Herman" said Marie, clutching his arm, "it's quite pretty. Or perhaps I should say, quite attractive. Well, whatever I mean to say, it looks like a very nice home for us. It looks like it has sufficient space."

"Well yes, my darling, it does. I admit it's not the most beautiful place you've ever seen, but it's not bad for here in the backwoods, safe inside palisades! I've worked to make it so, I can assure you. Most of the homes here have that crude look, being made of logs or rough timbers. It's a bit more refined inside. Come, let me show you!"

Herman led them across the street and up the steps, which were made of half logs. They entered the front door eagerly, and found themselves in a small entrance hall, with rooms going off on both sides and one straight ahead, and steep stairs leading up to the next floor. The children gathered around their mother, in silence or whispering to each other, gazing at the rough board walls. There was good light coming in from the windows in both side rooms, and they were relieved to see at least some comfortable looking furniture in the room to the right, which looked like a parlour.

Herman laughed. "Now then my dears, this is not Montreal, you know, or even Boucherville. You can't expect to find things quite as fancy as you are used to. But I can assure you that this is a sturdy house, and warm in winter. I'm certain that once you settle in you will find it quite to your liking."

Marie, like the children, felt her heart sinking as she could not stop herself from comparing this rough place to the warm comforts of the Huc residence back at Boucherville. But she knew that she had to help out. "Of course it will be, my darling. We will be just fine here. Come on children, let's have Papa show us the rooms!"

The house was sturdily built of logs, and practical. To the left of the front entrance hall was the master bedroom, opening onto a washroom and changing room at the back. To the right of the hall was the parlour, with its chairs and tables at the front of the room, and a dining table and chairs at the back. From there a door opened into the kitchen. Both the kitchen and the bedroom's washing room had doors that opened out to the backyard, with its privy, vegetable plot and wood shed. Both side rooms had windows and fireplaces, and the kitchen had a window and iron stove.

The second floor was divided into three bedrooms and a wash room with storage and changing area. Each of the four rooms had windows, so the whole house had a feeling of brightness. All of the rooms had solid, practical furniture in them, with little decoration. Marie saw that it would be her job to bring some colour into the house. In answer to her question about the source of water for the house, Herman told her that all water had to be brought up from the river. He had retained a local man who brought a supply for them every morning.

They finished their tour, and then Herman summoned them all into the parlour where they sat around the dining table to discuss who would sleep where. The trunks that they had brought with them were now resting on the front porch, so once these decisions were made they could settle in. After a brief discussion Herman announced that Thérèse would have her own room, the boys would have the other room at the front, and little Françoise would occupy the room at the back. There were two beds in that room, so lots of space for a maid should they wish to have one living in.

Marie agreed with this allocation in her mind, but hesitated to accept it outright. After over five years running the family on her own, she had a reaction to Herman taking charge quite so quickly, without seeking her agreement in advance. It was not a big issue for her and Herman was, after all, the head of the household. But still, she felt the need to exert her influence in this household decision. After all, she had been in charge of the house back in Quebec, and would be running the house here while her husband pursued his many interests.

"I think that's a good idea dear, at least at the outset. We will see how it goes, and perhaps make some adjustments later on. Oh, but one thing I should mention: the stairs are very steep, and could be dangerous, especially at night. Do you think you could install a bannister so that we will have something to hang onto?"

Herman looked at her with a surprised expression on his face. His years spent on his own in Detroit had made him forget how independent and responsible his young wife was. Her decisive comments showed that she had not changed. He smiled and said "of course, my dear. Joe, perhaps you can help me build that bannister?"

The family settled in with great confusion and rushing around, but with no arguments. The main decisions had been taken, so now each family member could take his or her own things and put them away or set them up. It was a happy house, with Herman wandering around to help wherever needed, and Marie doing the same. Whenever they came together in a hallway or a room they would touch or have a brief kiss, to the embarrassment of the younger children who saw them, but the delight of Thérèse.

In the early evening, just as Marie was starting to worry about dinner, Herman came to the rescue. "My love, I have foreseen this situation in which my dear family will be happy but also hungry, so I have made arrangements accordingly. There is a delightful woman, a widow, who lives over on St. Louis Street, whom I have engaged on a number of occasions to cook for me. She's a merry soul named Mrs. Plumley. She loves children, but all of hers have grown up and gone elsewhere except the one in the army, and she is looking forward to meeting you and the children. I have asked her to prepare a dinner for us this evening, and she will be arriving shortly with her supplies. The kitchen is well stocked with basic materials, as well as water and firewood, so she should be able to produce a fine meal for us."

"Oh Herman, how wonderful! Yes, I was just starting to think about making something, but I had no idea what!" They laughed together and then hugged, and five minutes later Mrs. Plumley arrived carrying a basket of food supplies. Herman introduced her to the family, all of whom found her wonderfully cheery. Marie felt her spirits lift, thrilled to have such a helpful person so near at hand.

With Mrs. Plumley's help they had a splendid family dinner and then the children, each in their turn, retired to their rooms, their books and their beds. As Marie worked with Mrs. Plumley to wash up after the dinner, they talked about future arrangements. Mrs. Plumley, whose first name was Agatha ("I know that Aggie Plumley sounds like a stew or a dessert, dear, but what can you do?"), was open to any sort of arrangement that would be convenient to Marie, from cooking to cleaning to minding the children. "I'm on my own, dear, and I do love to spend time with families and children. The doctor has been most kind to me, and I look forward to helping you. You just have to ask."

Marie agreed with Mrs. Plumley on terms of employment, which seemed more than reasonable after the expense of Montreal, and they parted on the best of terms.

With the children in bed, Marie was finally able to sit down with Herman in the parlour with cups of tea in hand, and talk about their situation. The air was warm and still and they would have liked to be out on the verandah in front, but the mosquitos and other pests made it more comfortable to be inside.

"Herman my love, here we are, finally, after five years. It's so lovely to see you, and the children are thrilled. If only Ignace were here."

Herman's calm expression darkened. "But, tell me, what has happened? I know he was upset with what I did, but that was years ago and anyway, most intelligent people think that it was the right thing to do! What is it? Why has he not come?"

Marie's eyes started to tear up. "It's so hard to understand. I've spoken with him many times about it, but he's adamant. He is a very strong Catholic, as you know, and he firmly believes that what you did was wrong – a sin, a sacrilege. Then he says that because of it you hurt your family, tearing us apart. Which of course is true, but we always knew that we could deal with that, as we have. But no, he will not accept it."

Herman leaned forward, hands clasped together. "But my darling, surely you and your parents could have calmed him down! Gregoire is such a forceful soul; did he not try to talk some sense into the boy?"

"Oh yes he did, but it didn't help." The thought of her parents' dilemma over Ignace leaving came into her mind, but Marie dismissed it as the wrong thing to say. "Maman tried as well, but to no avail. So he's living there in Boucherville, and heaven knows when we will ever see him again!" That was too much for her, and her silent tears burst into loud sobs. Herman took her in his arms to comfort her, and it was several minutes before they could resume their seats and sip their cold tea.

They discussed the other children, with Herman eager for details of the family that had become almost strangers to him over the years. By mutual, unspoken agreement they skirted completely the painful subject of poor little Antoine.

After refreshing their tea cups, Herman moved on. "Of course there's the whole matter of settling and schooling for the children, and friends and, well, our lives here. But before we start, I must tell you the most important news. There are big changes coming, and we must be prepared for them."

Marie sat forward, took his hand again and gazed straight into his eyes. "I believe you're talking about the political situation here, aren't you? Colonel Thorpe told me about it, but that was several months ago. So, what now?"

"Well, within a matter of weeks the British troops will leave Detroit, and the Americans will move in. We've been part of the United States for several years now, but soon that fact will be a reality for us. It will be American soldiers in the fort, Americans on the streets, and American laws to guide us. God help us!"

Marie was confused. "But my darling, is that really so bad? Are the Americans terrible people? Will they be cruel and, what else? Dirty? Dishonest?" Her voice rose. "Will their soldiers be a danger to our women? Will Thérèse and I have to hide in the house? What will happen Herman? Tell me!"

Herman smiled. "Shh my love, there's no need to shout. You'll wake the children. No, I'm certain that none of that will happen. But I know that the culture of Detroit will change. Our Redcoats and their officers are a disciplined, quite distinguished lot, but the American troops, many of them rag-tag militia, will be tough country boys. Nevertheless I think they will be polite to you and to the children, and in some ways it may be quite good, even quite amusing. But there will be changes.

"As it is now, I am well placed in this town. The British like me and rely on me at the fort, and I'm respected by the townspeople because of that, not to mention my reputation as a doctor who actually knows something about medicine. That will not likely change, but my standing with the Americans is an open question. My guess is that they will need my services and we'll be fine, as long as they are prepared to pay my fees, of course. But there will be many other changes. One example close to my heart is my dear friend William Baker and his wife Effie. I think I told you in my letters that he's involved with building ships here for the British navy, and is also working on some new facilities at Amherstburg and up the Thames River, where they propose to build gunboats for our navy on the lakes. Well, just two days ago he finally received orders to move with his family back to Canada. They'll be going to Sandwich, just across the river."

Marie nodded. "I can understand that. Obviously the Americans would not put up with him staying here for long, building ships to fight them!"

Herman agreed. "Precisely! So we will miss them. As far as we are concerned, we'll just have to wait and see. I'm certain that at some point we'll have to declare our loyalty to Canada or the United States, but that's not likely to happen for some time. So I think we should just stay here, greet the newcomers and see what happens. It doesn't hurt, of course, that they will probably need me for medical purposes."

Marie nodded again, but slowly as the cares of a very long day started to weigh on her. "Oh I do hope so darling. For if we were forced to return to Canada, would you not be in trouble?"

Herman laughed. "Oh no, for we would be returning to Upper Canada, where the laws are British and make good sense. I would be well received there, I can assure you. But..." leaning forward, he saw that Marie was almost asleep. "I think, my dear, that we've had enough chatter for today. Come, let me take you to bed. I must admit I had some interesting plans for tonight, but I can see that they must wait."

Marie was finally in the bed that she would be sharing with Herman, nicely kissed by him as he wished her sweet dreams and then left the room to read by the light of the fire. She was exhausted and longed for sleep, but it did not come quickly. She was unable to overcome the many thoughts that roamed through her head.

It was wonderful to be with her husband again, after all those years away. He seemed to be in good health and spirits, and doing well. Surely he had learned his lesson about rash decisions, and would be open to reason and common sense in his work as well as in their family lives! The children were fine. But, well, there was Ignace! No, she refused to open that door in her mind. The town was terrible: disappointing, dirty and small, isolated in the woods, and the people did not look very pleasant. She wondered about the children – how they would fare in this place. Would there be schooling available to them? Would they be healthy? The house was acceptable, just. Herman had done what he could to make it comfortable for his family, so she must be positive about it. Mrs. Plumley was certainly nice. Thank heavens for that. Oh dear...why did so many people in the streets look hungry?...

Next day the family completed its settling in. Mrs. Plumley came over in the morning to help out, and Marie sent her to the market to buy foodstuffs to stock the kitchen. At lunch time they marched in the summer sunshine two blocks over to the home of William and Effie Baker. Herman introduced Marie to his friends, who were pleased to meet the woman about whom Herman had told them so much. They greeted the children in the same warm manner, and introduced their own daughters Catherine and Ann. Catherine was a tall, slim fourteen year-old, and Ann was a pretty twelve year-old. Catherine and Thérèse Eberts took an instant liking to each other.

Over lunch they talked about Detroit, and the changes that were to come. A sadness descended upon the table when William Baker confirmed that he and his family would be leaving within the week, moving over to Sandwich on the Canadian side of the Detroit River.

"There was no way around it, I'm afraid" said Baker. "Once they are here and in control, the Americans will not permit us to build ships for the British. So we either build ships for them, which I will not do, or we move over the river. In any event, I have my orders so there's no question in the matter."

Herman added that much of Baker's work was already over there anyway, at the new dockyard and townsite at Amherstburg, and that project up the Thames. "And of course you will still be nearby, so we can see you as often as we wish."

The conversation continued while Effie and her daughters served lunch. Then the Eberts family said their good-byes and headed out for a walk around the town. They smiled as they passed people on the streets, and some smiled back and called greetings. Marie saw that Herman knew many of them, by name at least.

One of the families they met was a Mrs. Jennifer Black and her ten year-old son Jonathan. Herman said that the Blacks were great friends of his. Curtis Black was a surveyor doing work for the army as well as for the town, and they had been very hospitable to him. Jenny Black, a strong looking blond woman, greeted Marie warmly, and promised that she would visit soon to give a proper welcome to the family. Young Jonathan looked with cautious interest at Joe Eberts, who was around the same age and even looked quite similar. Eventually they smiled at each other, and Marie was pleased that Joe might already have a friend in the town.

Marie was impressed with the Catholic Church down St. Anne Street, and they were able to greet the Priest, Father Dufleaux, who was out in front tending the garden. He welcomed his new parishioners, noting with some humour that he had been less than successful in luring Dr. Eberts into the fold. But he liked Herman nonetheless, explaining that while the doctor was not a man of God, he was a very good doctor, and had been of great assistance two years ago when the priest had broken his arm in a fall on the ice. Since that time they had taken a glass of wine together on a number of occasions, and had enjoyed some good conversation.

The town had some pretty houses, but most were plain and in some cases rough. The streets were dirt, dry and hard at present. Marie noticed with interest the large military gardens located around the town. Herman explained that in these troubled times it was important for settlements to be as self-sufficient as possible. "We can't always rely on shipments of food and other supplies from distant ports. And with the tricky situation with the Americans and the Indians, there's always the possibility of siege. Unfortunately the farms in the surrounding areas are not very productive, so we grow as much as we can right here in town, and keep some livestock, and store and preserve whatever we can. So far it has worked acceptably. This effort is something in which you may wish to involve yourself, my dear."

As they stood in the military garden and gazed over the grand parade at Fort Lernoult, Herman said that he had been summoned to a meeting with the Commandant later that day. Richard England had arrived at Detroit as a Captain, and had progressed to his current status as a Lieutenant-Colonel. "Colonel England wishes to have my views on a few cases at the fort, and also to brief me on plans for the Americans when they take over. I would like to introduce you to him. He's a pleasant sort, and has asked after you several times."

They completed their tour with visits to the shops in St. Louis Street and the docks area, and then returned to a home that smelled wonderfully of freshly-baked bread. Mrs. Plumley had been at work, and they heard her rustling her pots and pans and whistling to herself as they came in the door.

At 4pm Herman and Marie left the children at home, watched over by Mrs. Plumley, and walked over to the fort. They were greeted by two friendly Redcoats who smiled and saluted them. The older one said "good afternoon Doctor. And I see this must be the missus. Good afternoon to you, Mrs. Eberts. Welcome to Detroit." Marie smiled at him as he turned to Herman and said "right on time as always, Doctor. Colonel England will be waiting for you in his quarters."

"Thank you Private Carter" said Herman, and they walked into the parade ground of the fort. Herman whispered to Marie "there's nothing like repairing a soldier's broken leg to make him a friend for life!" They chuckled as they walked across the ground, and came to the door of the Commandant's quarters. The sentry there was more formal. After an abrupt "good afternoon Doctor, Madame", he turned and knocked on the door. Responding to a shout of "come" from inside, he opened the door and stepped aside to let them through.

Marie was surprised to find the office room quite disorderly, with piles of books and papers strewn around, and some boxes along the walls either empty or on the way to being filled. The Colonel was at his desk, head down and writing furiously into what looked like a ledger. They stood politely for a minute before he looked up and saw them, bursting into a smile as he did so. "Ah, Doctor Eberts, there you are. Please forgive my bad manners; I simply had to complete that report before I went absolutely mad!"

Marie saw a middle-aged, good looking man with well-kept long hair and a trimmed beard. He was unusually tall and strong looking, evidently a man of action. He rose from his desk as he turned his attention to her. "And this must be Mrs. Eberts. Well I say, welcome to

Detroit, Madame. My, I can see why the doctor has been pining away all these years! It's good that you have finally arrived. But come, let me recover my manners. Corporal" he called towards an inner door, which was opened immediately by a uniformed aide. "Kindly have the cook send us some tea, will you, and then join us with your pen."

The Corporal disappeared briefly, and then returned with notebook and pen, and sat at a side table as the Colonel seated his guests around the main table in the room. Within minutes a servant arrived with tea, and then they settled in to talk.

"You are here just in time, Madame, to see us before we depart to make way for the Americans. They will be here within the week, and we are making arrangements to depart just as they arrive. We do not wish to leave the town unprotected for even one moment. I expect that it will be different when they are in charge of things. I can't know for certain, of course, but I believe that their troops are, shall I say, less disciplined than our Redcoats. They are tough fellows, with a lot of hard fighting behind them, but I'm hopeful that they will respect the townspeople. It will be a case of wait and see for you. Watch them carefully, treat them with respect and hope for the best. What think you, Doctor?"

"You know, Colonel, I'm tempted to say that 'soldiers are soldiers', no matter where they come from. Oh, some may be cruder or rougher than others when they come in contact with society, but I think that is generally the case when they are so-instructed by their superiors. If there's a reason to subjugate the citizens, or perhaps to punish them, then you will perhaps find the soldiers a bad lot to deal with. But in this case we have frontiersmen on the one side, and frontier people on the other. They'll understand each other very well indeed, and I believe that the Americans will have every reason to be kind and helpful, rather than the opposite."

"Well said Sir" said the Colonel, sipping his tea and smiling at Marie. "You are well settled in, Madame? I think the Doctor's house is comfortable?"

"It is, Colonel England, thank you. And yes, we are settled in and pleased to be here. We have already met several new friends."

"Excellent" smiled the Colonel. "Well then, let us get down to the business at hand so that you can get back to your family. Doctor, I have the medical reports from my physicians, but if you have any special cases you would like to mention, please do so now. Keep in mind that within a week we will be moving over to Amherstburg, so they may not be able to have the same level of care as they have received here, but at least you will still be nearby."

Herman mentioned three particularly complicated cases involving fractures with associated infection, and said that he would discuss them with the army doctors before they departed. "I believe that they are in good hands now, Sir, although two of them were touch and go for a while."

"Good" said Colonel England. "As for you, Sir, your status with us is excellent. We are pleased with your services, and only wish that you could depart with us! However, as you may find over time that it's uncomfortable for you to remain here in the United States, I have prepared letters to ensure that you continue to be well received by our authorities throughout Upper Canada. I am certain that you will be welcomed by the command at the new shipyard at Amherstburg once it is completed. There will also be a fort built there, which will in all likelihood have need of your services. It's so close to here, in fact, that you may be able to assist there while still living here. You'll also be able to serve people in the Sandwich area. I know your friend William Baker will be living there, working at the new naval yard, so undoubtedly you'll be visiting there frequently.

"I would add, in fact, that we may meet again there. I have already sent a large group of my men there, leaving me with the small detachment that you see around us. We will depart when the Americans arrive, and our first port of call will be Amherstburg. I have also taken the liberty of introducing you by letter to the American Commandant who will be arriving soon. He is Lt. Colonel John Francis Hamtramck. I'm told that he was born in Quebec, but went to the United States and has served their army with distinction. He was at Fallen Timbers under General Wayne, and has now been chosen as the first American Commandant of Detroit."

The Colonel handed Herman several letters. "These are the letters that you may find useful."

"Thank you Sir" said Herman. "You are most generous. I am pleased that you have appreciated my services, and I wish you well in your continued fine service to His Majesty."

They rose from the table, and the Colonel came around to shake hands with Herman and kiss Marie's hand. "Thank you Doctor, and to you and to Madame Eberts I wish good health and good fortune."

13

THE NEW REGIME

As the sun moved high in the hot sky on the morning of July 11, 1796, the citizens of Detroit were out in the streets to watch the extraordinary events about to unfold. Down on the river, several small British naval vessels were assembled. They had been loaded with munitions, baggage and supplies the previous day. They now awaited their passengers.

The people crowded around the edges of the Grand Parade, tense with excitement. Just before noon the gates of the fort opened and Colonel England led his small troop of Redcoats out, looking fine in their brilliant coats, with muskets at the shoulder and bayonets shining in the sunlight. They paraded smartly around the square, finally halting in front of the flagpole at the main gate of the fort. Colonel England, accompanied by an aide, strode over to the gate of the fort, which had been closed, and turned a large key in the lock of the gate. He then handed the key to his aide, who in turn handed it to a Negro – a freed slave, the servant of a local saloon keeper.

The Colonel then returned to his troops and faced the flagpole. When the aide said something to him, presumably referring to the time which was around noon, Colonel England issued an order and a Lieutenant lowered the British flag for the last time. He folded it neatly, turned and handed it to Colonel England, and then saluted and turned to face the ranks.

The Lieutenant gave the order to march, and the British unit moved smartly off the parade square and down through the town to the dock, where they boarded the waiting vessels. The event took place, at the beginning, in an atmosphere of shocked silence on the part of the watching crowd. Standing next to Herman, who had little Françoise on his shoulders, Marie felt the tension in the people around them as they watched their guardians disappearing from their fort, and then their town. But as the troops started their march off the parade square a ragged applause started up, breaking the tension, as the people sought to register their thanks to the troops who had kept them safe for so long. The crowd streamed through the streets, accompanying the troops to the docks, and then continued their clapping and calling as the troops boarded their vessels. When all were aboard the gangplanks were drawn, and the vessels headed out into the river.

The British boats turned downstream, aiming towards Amherstburg. Before they were even out of sight two American vessels passed them, coming toward the Detroit docks. The crowd clustered around the dock area, eager for a sight of their new protectors.

Standing with her family, Marie watched the arrival of the Americans with a mixture of excitement and trepidation. There were two vessels of fair size, laden with troops and some cannon and supplies. The first off the ships was a Captain, later identified as Capt. Moses Porter. Given the small size of this troop, it was clear to all that this was an advance guard, sent to secure the fort and the safety of the town pending the arrival of the main American forces.

Captain Porter ordered his men, sixty-five in all, to form up on the dock, having first offloaded three small cannon and some cartloads of supplies. The column was greeted by scattered applause from the surrounding crowd, and some cries of greeting. The Captain led them off the dock and the column came through the town in good order, and formed up on the parade ground in front of the fort. The crowd moved like a tide up from the dock, returning to its position surrounding the parade ground.

The American soldiers looked splendid in their blue and white uniforms – tough looking men, well-drilled and finely turned out. This was no motley crowd of backwoods militia; this was a real army, a proud army. As the American flag was raised the crowd broke into loud applause, and Marie could see that many of the soldiers, including the Captain, smiled with pleasure at this warm welcome.

Captain Porter stepped forward and, turning toward the main body of the crowd, made a brief announcement.

"Ladies and Gentlemen of Detroit, I bring you greetings from Colonel John Francis Hamtramck, Commandant of this fort on behalf of the United States of America. Colonel Hamtramck will arrive in two days time to take up his command and complete the manning of this fort. We are his advance guard, and we appreciate the warm welcome that you have afforded us. We wish you a happy and prosperous future under the government of the United States of America."

Turning, he called out "Sergeant, open the gate of the fort".

There was then a moment of confusion when the Sergeant went to open the gate and found it locked. He turned to face the crowd and, spotting some prosperous looking men nearby, asked where the key might be found. One of them pointed to the Negro who had received it earlier from the British. He came forward with a nervous stride and handed it to the Sergeant, who was clearly angered by this slight delivered by the departing British. The crowd turned silent, waiting to see what would happen, but the incident was quickly forgotten.

The Sergeant unlocked the gate and the American troops marched into their new home.

"What a splendid show that was, Papa" exclaimed Joe, his mouth full of the potatoes that Mrs. Plumley had cooked for their supper. "Didn't the American soldiers look fine? Why, they looked as smart as our Redcoats! Are they as good soldiers, Papa?"

Herman and Marie, enjoying a glass of wine while watching their children eat their early supper, could only smile at the boy's enthusiasm.

"Oh I think so Joe" said Herman. "After all, they've won several battles with the Indians just to get here, and that is hard fighting indeed. And of course, they won this entire country away from the Redcoats all those years ago. And yes, they certainly looked fine."

"That they did" said Marie. "And wasn't it an exciting day, with the Redcoats marching off to their boats, and then the Americans arriving so quickly? All of a sudden, in just a few hours, we are no longer in a British town, but an American one!"

Guillaume, with a perplexed look on his face, started his intervention with a squeak, as he always did to gain attention. "But, but Maman, is it really Canada just across the river? Can we just get on the ferry and go there? Is it that easy?"

"So far it is" said Marie, glancing at Herman for reassurance. "We are two countries separated by a river, and we can go back and forth just as we please. That is, of course, because our countries aren't at war with each other. Let's hope that it stays that way! Oh...Thérèse, would you please help Françoise with her potatoes? Thank you dear."

The excited chatter of the children filled the house as they finished their supper and went to their rooms to play. Marie and Herman finally had time to talk about the day in more detail.

Marie was excited and optimistic. "I do wish the Bakers had been able to stay here at least until today. I feel reassured having seen the American soldiers. There was so much talk about them being crude ruffians, menacing all of us as their conquered enemy. Now, not only did they look clean and decent, but according to their leader they're happy to be here, and we can feel welcome in this new country. Do you agree, darling?"

Herman was calmer. "I suppose so...I hope so. I certainly agree that they carried things off well today. And they had a right to be angry, I think. You saw the incident with the key? It was a nice slight, making the Americans take their key from a freed slave! And I was told by Judge Powell – I had a brief word with him on the way here – that they were even more annoyed when they entered the fort. Evidently the Redcoats had broken the windows in the barracks and even put stones down the well as a parting shot. It sounds childish to me, but there it is. We can just hope that the Americans rise above such behavior."

"Oh dear yes, let us hope so. I saw you talking to the judge. Did he have anything else of interest to tell you?"

"He did, yes. He's been requested to be the official contact between us and the American army. He is to gather a small group of important citizens to meet with Colonel Hamtramck soon after he arrives. They will be expected to brief him on local conditions in the town, and advise on his dealings with us. He said that I'm on his list."

"Oh Herman, how very exciting. I'm so proud of you."

Herman nodded. "Yes, thank you. I was pleased to be selected, if for no other reason than I will come to the Colonel's attention from the earliest time, which should serve our purposes. But you know, returning to the soldiers, I think that we should be very careful how we deal with them, particularly in the early going before we have a real sense of what they are about. It's true that they look splendid, but soldiers are soldiers, and can be rough characters out of uniform, and also in uniform on occasion. I would wager that they were looking for every tavern in sight as they marched through the town. A drunken soldier can be a dangerous animal. You probably also noticed that there were very few Indians around this day to welcome the Americans. They have made peace of a sort, but the Indians are far from trusting them. So I think we'll be seeing a lot of the Indians over in Sandwich and Amherstburg."

The conversation wandered along through their dinner, children's bedtime, and then their early trip to bed. Marie was shy at first, appearing at the bedside of this man from whom she had been separated for so long. But he was gentle and happy, warm and then passionate, and she soon joined in with abandon.

At 7:30am next morning there was a loud knock on their door. Herman opened it and was met by an officious looking American soldier.

"Dr. Herman Eberts?"

"Yes Soldier, what can I do for you?"

"Sir, Captain Porter sends his compliments, and requests that you attend a meeting at the fort at 10am this morning. He wishes to brief you and other citizens concerning the arrival tomorrow of Colonel Hamtramck."

"Of course. Yes, please thank the Captain and say that I will be pleased to attend."

"Thank you Sir." The soldier saluted smartly, turned and headed up the street.

At 9:30am Herman was at the front door, ready to leave for the fort. He was dressed in his most formal suit, and Marie thought that he looked wonderful. "Well my darling, you may no longer have your uniform, but you look very important and doctoral, if that is a word. I'm certain that you will impress the Captain."

Marie put the children to work tidying and cleaning their rooms, and then playing quietly until Herman arrived home just before noon. They rushed down to see him, and he drew them all into the parlour, where they sat around the table for Marie's soup and his description of the meeting.

"There were about ten of us there. This is the group that Judge Powell has put together to greet the Americans. The judge was there of course, and some others I might have mentioned to you. Angus Mackintosh, the merchant was there, George McDougall, Gregor McGregor the Sheriff, two lawyers, Walter Roe and Charles Smith, and three others. Captain Porter brought us in to gain any immediate insights that might help him deal with our people over the next few days, but mainly he wanted us to prepare for the arrival tomorrow of his Colonel and the rest of the troops.

"He wants their arrival to go off smoothly, without any embarrassments like the key incident yesterday. He said that the Americans will arrive at the dock in mid-afternoon. There will be around one hundred and fifty troops, with a lot of baggage and cannon and supplies. They will march up to the parade ground where they will join with the troops already here. We ten citizens will stand near the flagpole and greet the Colonel on behalf of the people. The Colonel will make some sort of formal speech, and then they will all retire into the fort. And that will be that."

Guillaume squeaked. "Will we be allowed to watch, Papa?"

"We certainly will, dear boy" said Herman. "Indeed, the Captain made it clear that he hoped for a big turnout to greet the Colonel, and he was sure that everyone would be welcoming to the troops. Now then, let's finish our soup. Then we can go and walk around the town and see what's happening."

The scene in the town was one of subdued excitement. Most of the citizens were pleased with the change of command. The French people, who were in the majority, were more than pleased that the British had left, and most of the others were at least accepting of the turn of events.

Mixed in with the citizens were small groups of American soldiers in uniform, sent out from the fort to familiarize themselves with the town, and to show the people that they were there as friends and protectors. Thus they were open and friendly, respectful to the men and courteous to the ladies. They did not enter any of the taverns, presumably due to strict orders from the fort.

The arrival of Colonel Hamtramck and his remaining troops went off precisely as foreshadowed by Herman. They arrived at the docks in a sloop and eleven bateaux, off-loaded efficiently and proceeded up to the parade ground through a crowd of applauding citizens. The troops joined the sixty-five already there on parade, and Colonel Hamtramck came to the front where Captain Porter saluted him and handed him the key to the fort. The Colonel, a short man clearly strong on military discipline and decorum, saluted the flag and then approached the ten citizens assembled by Judge Powell, who introduced them. Treating this as his formal welcome, he then ordered Captain Porter to move the troops into the fort. He followed them in, and the ceremony was over.

"It looks like he isn't a politician" said Marie. "I suppose the speech by Captain Porter two days ago was sufficient for the purpose of welcoming themselves to their own fort!"

"No, he isn't" replied Herman, "but he has the reputation of a fine soldier and leader. That should bode well for us."

14

LIVING IN AMERICA

On the day after Colonel Hamtramck arrived, everything in Detroit seemed about the same as it was before, with some important exceptions. One was the presence of blue and white clad soldiers walking around the town, in place of the old familiar Redcoats. They continued to be friendly and courteous to the citizens, stopping and chatting when it was possible to do so in English. Another was the absence of the many familiar faces of families who had moved across the river to Sandwich or nearby Amherstburg. There must have been at least one hundred people who had moved, and the departures continued, albeit with less frequency. At the same time a slow trickle of new citizens had started to appear.

The Eberts family continued their strolls around the town, and had several brief talks with soldiers. Marie saw that they admired her greatly, and also often gazed longingly at Thérèse. There was no doubt that these young, battle-hardened men missed their mothers, and also the company of young women. She would have to watch over her daughter carefully!

There was one change that affected the family personally and painfully. Cheerful Mrs. Plumley announced to Marie before the family left the house that morning that she would not be staying in Detroit. She had secured a permanent place with a family that had just moved to Sandwich, and would be moving over there in the next few days.

Marie was distraught. "Oh but Mrs. Plumley, it's so wonderful having you here! You've been such a help to me, and the children adore you. Surely we can come to some arrangement?"

Agatha Plumley had tears in her eyes as she replied. "And I adore them too, Madame, and you as well. And the doctor is a fine man. But you see, I'm British at heart, and I just cannot stay here in the company of the soldiers who have dealt such a blow to us. Oh, I know they are reasonable men, most of them, but this is a new country now, and it will change and be different, and not at all what I have come to admire, and indeed to rely upon for my peace of mind. It has not been easy, but I have made up my mind that I must return to the British side. The Murdochs, whom I have worked for off and on for several years, have made me a very kind offer to stay with them and help with their family, and I have accepted."

The two women stood looking at each other, and then embraced without another word spoken. Mrs. Plumley then left the house for the last time, and Marie went into the parlour to inform Herman of the situation. He was upset. "That is a hard blow, I must say. Mrs. Plumley was so good for us. She had everything that we wanted. Oh my, we will miss her!"

Marie nodded her assent. "That we will. Do you know of someone who might replace her?"

"No, I don't, at least not on the spur of the moment. You know, this is such a small place, and most women with those skills have families and homes to take care of, without adding to their burdens by helping us as well. Now of course, there would likely be some young French girls in the farms who could use some paid work, like the situation in Sorel. But they are generally a poor and uneducated lot, and would probably be more trouble than help." He fell silent, and they sat looking at each other.

Then Joe appeared at the door and asked if it was time for them to head out for their walk, so they left it there for the moment. But Mrs. Plumley's departure left a large gap in Marie's sense of comfort and security in her new surroundings. Unless she could find a replacement, she would have to watch over the children all the time in this very restrictive environment, and do all the cleaning and cooking and running of the house without any help. And she would have to do this in quite primitive conditions, with water that had to be fetched in pails, a chilly, small house, few stores with attractive products of any kind, and not even substantial schools for the children.

Marie's life had come down several notches – from warm and comfortable to cold and hard. She was determined; she would make the most of it. But it was a daunting prospect.

The next day Herman was summoned once again to appear at the fort, this time for a personal meeting with Colonel Hamtramck. While he was gone Marie took the children to the local market, which was small and not well supplied but the best there was on offer. She was still smarting from the loss of Mrs. Plumley, but that loss had her looking carefully at her two oldest children: Thérèse , who was just coming up to her fourteenth birthday, and Joe, a strapping eleven year-old. They were about the same height as her and each other, and remarkably well filled-out and mature looking for their ages. They could certainly be capable helpers around the house, including helping with the younger ones.

She managed to fill her string bag with vegetables and a questionable cut of beef, and then they dropped into a dry goods establishment that seemed to sell a bit of everything, from flour to muskets to fur hats. She asked Thérèse to order some sugar and flour, and watched with pleasure as the girl carried out the task with great efficiency. The young man behind the counter greeted the girl warmly and asked her name, and his fond looks confirmed once again to the watching mother that she and Herman would need to keep a sharp eye out for young Thérèse.

They walked home through the hot and crowded streets, stopping for a moment for a chat with Jennifer Black and her son Jonathan. Jennifer sympathized with Marie over the loss of Mrs. Plumley. "I'm afraid you'll have a difficult time replacing her, Mrs. Eberts. This is not like Montreal, with all those well-educated women just waiting to go to work for you. You may have some luck, though. There are new people arriving every day, so you must keep your eyes open."

"Tell me, Mrs. Black, changing the subject from my woes (they both smiled), does Jonathan go to school here? Are there good schools for the children to attend?"

"Yes and no. There are some schools, but whether they are good or not is another question. Jonathan goes to a small school for boys run in his home by a teacher named Brownlee. There are about seven boys there, all different ages, so it's a struggle for him. But he seems to have given my Jonnie a good start. I'll introduce you to him when you are ready. As to the girls, I haven't had to deal with that side of it, but I know that there's a small school for girls recently opened up by a teacher married to a local merchant. Her name is Campbell. I'm sure the doctor will know of the family."

Marie beamed. "Thank you Mrs. Black, you've been most helpful. But tell me – I should have asked before – how is Mr. Black's situation now, with the new administration at the fort?"

"He seems to be fine. It's too early to tell, of course, but there's a lot of surveying work to be done, and still only him and one other surveyor to do it. He's at work now, and so far he hasn't had to come home in a huff!"

They laughed, and then said their good-byes. Marie and the children continued home, arriving at the same time as did Herman, fresh from his meeting with the Commandant.

"Colonel Hamtramck is an interesting man, I can tell you. He's around my age, forty I think, short but athletic. He acts like a soldier in all aspects, in his speech and his walking and mannerisms. He's very direct, and clearly well-informed. I believe he has spent some useful hours with the judge. In any event, he knew all about me, and I was pleased that he seemed to respect me as a citizen of this place, and a useful medical man. He said that his army is sadly under-staffed in the medical area, so I could be of use to them.

"On that theme he sent for one of his army doctors, who joined us for a while, His name is John Plummer, and he seems like a thoroughly good sort. When he heard that I am a surgeon he was particularly pleased, for it seems that they have a serious need for surgery, and little enough capability to practice it. So once again, I'm in good standing at the fort!"

The family burst into clapping at this, and Herman smiled at them.

"I am to make an agreement through Dr. Plummer for the provision of services, but I will still be free to carry on with my private practice. The Colonel then made a point about trading, and especially about wines and spirits. He fears that his soldiers will soon become bored and restless, and will seek out liquor to drown their sorrows. That, of course, can lead to problems in the town. He mentioned it because he knows that is part of my trade. He did not suggest that I cease that trade, but it was a warning to keep a sharp eye out for excesses.

"Then he spoke about loyalty – I know that he's doing this with everyone. He stressed that we are in the United States now, and must be loyal to the American flag. If we are not, we will not be welcome for long. It's important that we all remember this."

Guillaume squeaked. "Are we Americans now, Papa?"

Herman beamed. "What a good question, Guillaume! My, you are a fine little fellow! I can tell you that under that treaty, Jay's Treaty, it was provided that people living here could become citizens of the United States, but I don't think it covered people living here who would like to remain British subjects. As I've mentioned, the Colonel did speak to me about loyalty, so I suppose that at some point the issue will become a lively one."

Thérèse raised her hand like a school girl, eager to ask a question. "But if this country is as free as they say it is meant to be, then surely they don't care if we are citizens, or foreigners living here! Is that not so?"

"Perhaps, darling" said Marie, "at least as long as Britain and the United States are not at war with each other. But if that should happen again, then…oh dear…that would be difficult would it not, Herman?"

"Yes it would" replied Herman and, turning to Guillaume who was sitting next to him, patted his head and said "there, you see my boy, you have thrown us all into confusion!" The boy looked as if he would cry at what he thought was criticism, but Herman took him onto his lap and gave him a hug while the rest of the family laughed, and the discussion moved on.

In the weeks that followed, life in the Eberts home started to develop patterns of activity and the predictabilities that are the hallmark of a happy family. Herman left early each morning to attend to his patients inside the town and in the surrounding countryside. Marie would give the children their breakfast, and then head out with them in search of things for the house, or activities to engage the family members.

Her first task was to look for schools, and she asked about and visited several small ones, all taking place in private homes. She soon decided on the schools mentioned to her by Jenny Black, and she was successful in finding places for all of the children except Françoise who, at five years of age, was too young to be mixed in with the older students. Joseph and Guillaume fitted in nicely with Mr. Brownlee, a scholarly man who was clearly thrilled to have two more paying students. Margaret Campbell's school for girls was well established, with nine students ranging from seven to fifteen years of age. Mrs. Campbell was a widow, having lost her husband in a skirmish with an Indian war party back in 1792. She was strong willed but pleasant, and the girls clearly liked her, which reassured Marie as she signed up for Thérèse. There were two other girls close to Thérèse in age, and they received their new schoolmate with welcoming smiles.

That accomplished, Marie paid more attention to the town itself. She liked the church, and made sure that she kept up to date on services and events in which she might become involved. She visited all of the stores that were of any interest. There weren't many, and the stock of goods was small and generally uninteresting, but she met more people through these activities. In the stores she found that people were curious to meet the newly-arrived wife of Dr. Eberts, and were generally friendly and helpful. A number of women said that they would be prepared to come and help her in her home if she ever needed it. Two, with small children themselves, offered to take little Françoise for play at suitable times. As her stock of friends and acquaintances grew, so the hurt of losing Mrs. Plumley slowly faded.

Herman occasionally dropped in at home during his working day when he was practicing in the town or working at his trading office. The town was so small that it was no chore for him to do so, and she loved it when he came striding in, generally hoping that there would be some soup on the stove. More often than not, however, he would not arrive home until 5pm or later. Visits to farms in the countryside would often keep him away until dusk, and once during the month he went over to Sandwich and stayed with the Bakers overnight. He told Marie on his return that Sandwich had been populated rapidly over the past few months, and the need for his services might take him over there on a regular basis, often overnight.

That was not good for Marie. She missed him when he wasn't home in the evening. It was nice to have him sharing the children with her. It was also very nice to have their private chats after dinner, and of course their loving on the hard bed. During those long years of separation she had all but forgotten the joy of his strong arms and lively body; now it came back to her in a rush, bringing with it that feeling of life and loss of inhibition that would set her blushing and smiling as she thought about it during the day.

His practice was flourishing as never before, for several of the British doctors had left Detroit for Sandwich, and there was a need for his services almost every other day at the fort. Dr. Plummer became a friend and confidante, giving him an entree to the situation at the fort almost as open as he had enjoyed when the British were there. In early August they invited Dr. Plummer to dinner at their home, and found him a jolly companion, full of stories and, of considerable importance, instantly fond of the children.

John Plummer grew up in Boston, studied medicine, and then entered practice in 1775. By that time he was also married to Rita Robben, who was of Dutch/British heritage, and they had one son. The doctor was involved in the revolutionary war, declaring himself on the side of the Americans whose cause was, he said, "a damn good idea, and about time too". As an officer in the United States army he continued to work out of his home in Boston, and they had two more children before he was called away to serve with General Wayne in his campaign to subdue the western territories.

"I miss my wife terribly, you know" he said over his wine, as Marie cleared the table with Thérèse assisting. "I know that the Colonel wants me to stay in Detroit for quite some time, so I've petitioned to have her join me here. It's a far cry from Boston, and I'm sure she will find it a challenge. Well", he chuckled, "I suppose you two know all about that!"

Marie entered the conversation with a question about life at the fort. "It must be quite difficult with so many young men living there without a lot to do. The British troops were used to that sort of life, I think, but how are the young American soldiers going to fare? They must be awfully lonely and bored."

"Yes Madame, they are, and you've put your finger on a real concern of mine. We already have a lot of soldiers at the fort, with more to come when General Wayne arrives in the near future with his own troops. It's going to be crowded, and it may prove unsettling for the local population. Of particular concern is the availability of liquor in the town. There are a number of taverns only too happy to serve off-duty soldiers, and that's bound to lead to trouble, especially in such a small town. Why, it's bad enough in the cities like Boston and New York. I know that the Colonel is keeping a sharp eye on the situation, but it's tricky. After all, these are tough, fighting men who have already served their new country well. They won't take kindly to being confined to quarters and fed milk and porridge!"

This reflected a concern that Marie had already discussed with Herman. Drunken soldiers had started to appear on the streets in the evenings, sometimes just boisterous and loud, but sometimes aggressive and fighting. On a night that Herman had been over in Sandwich, in fact, there had been a fight right in front of their house. The family had cowered inside, afraid to show a light or make any sound lest the soldiers decide to seek them out and cause some mischief.

This turned out to be a regular occurrence, and Marie was always relieved when Herman was home to help them deal with any problem. But he was not always there, and on one occasion when he was away fights did in fact lead to an angry knock at their door. She made certain that the children were all upstairs, and then stood guard silently, broomstick in hand, until she heard the soldiers move away.

Most of the citizens were concerned about this situation, and perplexed as to what to do about it. They dared not try to control the soldiers themselves, for obvious reasons, and they knew that the officers were aware of what was going on. All they could do was keep out of the way.

Detroit had no newspapers or other publications to keep the citizens informed. The word-of-mouth system of rumour and gossip made up somewhat for this lack, but a more formal response was the town crier. He would usually announce his presence by ringing a bell in the streets, although for important news he liked to have a drummer play a loud roll, if possible on Sundays as the service at St. Anne's church was ending. That gave him by far his largest audience.

During the week of August 8 he had, on two occasions, announced that the fort expected the great American General Anthony Wayne to arrive very soon. Citizens should be prepared to greet him with a high level of enthusiasm. On Sunday, August 14 his drum rolled loud and long as the worshipers filed out of the church. Marie was there with the children, and they stood on the steps and watched.

The town crier was a middle-aged man, large in the waist and with a huge baritone voice. He dressed in a strange sort of formal attire, with several different colours at different levels, topped off by a spectacular tricorn hat. Prancing and grandstanding were part of his act, making him a beloved character. On this particular day he was fluffed up with importance, for he had a major announcement to make.

"Hear ye, hear ye. Draw near and listen, good people, for there is important news that has come straight to my attention from the fort. Tomorrow, being Monday the fifteenth day of August, the grand and glorious General Anthony Wayne, hero of Fallen Timbers and many other important battles will enter the gates of our town with a large body of American soldiers in attendance. We will finally have this great man amongst us, giving us the opportunity to greet him and thank him for delivering us from the Redcoats.

"He will be accompanied by His Excellency Winthrop Sargent, who is Secretary and Acting Governor of our territory. We can, perhaps, look forward to many important events and announcements! I am instructed by Colonel Hamtramck to inform you that the General and the Secretary will likely look kindly upon a warm welcome from us all, such as he himself had when he arrived one month ago. Let us all take note of this advice!

Now then, on to other news..."

But the other items were almost lost in the rumble of conversations that arose around the square as the people absorbed this exciting news. What a thrilling summer it was – such great events in this small, dishevelled outpost!

The arrival of General Anthony Wayne, who had the nickname "Mad Anthony" due to his unorthodox exploits at the historic Battle of Stony Point back in 1779, was similar to that of Colonel Hamtramck a month before, but even noisier. A fine looking man in his fiftieth year, tall and soldierly in appearance, he was a hero of the revolutionary war and events thereafter, and the citizens of Detroit gave him the enthusiastic welcome that he deserved.

Stepping off the ship with the General was another man in senior military uniform: Winthrop Sargent, Secretary of the Northwest Territory, a post second in importance only to the Governor, Arthur St. Clair. He had served in the Indian wars of 1794-95, and carried both military as well as civilian responsibilities.

They strode through the town from the docks to the parade ground, accompanied by their officers and followed by a large force of troops. Marie and Herman and the children were waiting in a good position beside the parade ground, and watched as this procession entered, and the troops joined up with the force already located in Detroit. The combined forces looked to be around five hundred soldiers, and Marie smiled to herself as she thought of all those men squashed into the fort. Why, they would have to sleep in shifts!

Colonel Hamtramck came forward to greet the General and the Secretary, saluted them, and then stepped aside as the two important men inspected the troops. The tumultuous cheering that had greeted the procession at the dock had followed them up to the parade ground. It subsided slowly during the inspection, and there was finally just a light buzz of conversation as the people waited to see what would happen next. They were not disappointed.

The general mounted the platform that had been erected next to the flagpole, and addressed the crowd. He brought them the wishes and salutations of President George Washington, and declared that the liberation of Detroit from the British was a great thing for the United States of America. It was his fervent hope that the United States and British North America could continue to live in peaceful co-existence. However should this peace be broken, the citizens of Detroit could be assured that the army of the United States was ready and willing to protect them and their property.

After the cheers subsided the General introduced Secretary Sargent, who was at present Acting Governor of the Northwest Territory in the absence of Governor St. Clair. After introductory remarks, Sargent announced that as part of the development of the governing system for the Northwest Territory, the government had authorized the formation of the sixth county in the area. It would be the largest county in the United States, and the county seat would be Detroit.

"Its boundaries will begin at the mouth of the Cuyahoga River, go west to Fort Wayne, then to the southernmost point of Lake Michigan. From thence the boundary will go along the western shore north to the territorial boundary in Lake Superior, and then along the territorial boundary through Lake Huron, Lake St. Clair and Lake Erie back to the starting point.

"You will, I know, be pleased with this decision, and you will be even more pleased when I inform you that this new county will be named 'Wayne County.'"

His closing remarks were drowned out by the cheers of the crowd.

That exciting day was still ringing in her ears several days later when Marie sat down to write her first letters to Ignace and her family back in Boucherville. Herman was out with the children. She wrote the note to her parents first and then, sitting with pen in hand, she saw Ignace's wonderful face smiling at her in her mind's eye. It was all she could do not to weep. She finally began writing, telling him that they had all arrived safely and settled in. She described the town and the exciting things that were going on with the Americans taking over. She said that his father was doing well here, and missed him very much, as she did. She asked after her parents, and Aunt Josie and Yvette, and other friends back home.

> *...In closing, my darling son, I must tell you that I miss you very much. I am sure that you are taking good care of my mother and father, and that they are pleased to have you there. But I would love it if, someday soon, you would change your mind and come to us.*
>
> *With much love from*
>
> *Mother*

15

THE NOVICE OFFICIAL

Over a period of less than a month Detroit had changed from an unimportant outpost run by the British to the busy and important seat of the largest county in the country, and the home of some very important people and a lot of American soldiers. The word spread quietly and with considerable humour that Secretary Winthrop Sargent had not been authorized to declare the formation of Wayne County. He had done so as Acting Governor in the absence of Governor St. Clair, but the Governor had in fact been in the area, and was not amused that he had been upstaged illegally by the Secretary. But St. Clair was a reasonable man, and soon accepted the situation as a *fait accompli*.

The officials in Detroit had much to do to establish the workings of the new county. They knew that there would be changes in its shape and area as new counties and then states were formed, carving up the federal territory into more manageable-sized areas for governing. Adjustments would have to be made so that the governance at the different levels – federal, territory, state, county and municipal – could be aligned and coordinated. This Northwest Territory, which covered a huge area across the southern tips of the great lakes, and would eventually be divided into states (Illinois, Indiana, Michigan, Ohio, Wisconsin and part of Minnesota), was administered by the Governor, General St. Clair, Secretary Sargent and three judges.

"It's so confusing, Herman" cried Marie, as he started to explain to her about the new county that had been announced. "They have a federal government which is in Philadelphia, but may move to the new place called Washington. They have thirteen states and this Northwest Territory. Now they have Wayne County and several others as well, and also towns and cities. It sounds like an awful lot of government, and it must be difficult to have them all understanding one another."

He laughed, almost spilling his tea. "You are so right, my dear. I have some insights from Plummer, but even then it does seem like a bit of a mish-mash! Let me see now.

"The federal government is clear. They must have one, just as England has in London. Then they have the thirteen original colonies that were quite independent, but will now be governed as states under the federal government. I believe we could compare them to England's counties. So far so good?"

"I suppose so" said Marie, "although I wonder how they decide who does what, at what level."

"Hmm, yes, and knowing the way government works, that will probably take a long time to sort out. Anyway, let's suppose that they do work it out. But even the states can't do everything for the people. When you get down to local issues such as roads and tavern licenses and the like, you need more local authorities. So, in the larger areas they're establishing counties, which have courts and sheriffs and that sort of thing. They can do local governing when the towns in the area are small. When those towns become larger, they'll start to have governments of their own.

"So we have been in a large area run by the federal government – the Congress – that is called the Northwest Territory. It's all of the territory that's in this part of the United States, but has not yet been divided into states. The government has set up counties to run the areas as the populations grow. After they get to a certain level, I suppose, they will carve off parts of the territory and turn them into states, just like the original thirteen states. I don't know what will happen to the counties then. They may still have some use. We'll have to just wait and see."

"Thank you darling" said Marie. "That makes it clearer for me. So now we're in Wayne County, and it will be run by Detroit. My, that is a step up in life, isn't it!"

"It is indeed. Oh, and I should mention that there are still those enormous territories west of here, all the way out to the Pacific Ocean. Much of that land is disputed with Indians as well as other European countries, but as that gets sorted out I'll bet that the United States will grow and have many more states within its borders".

The feeding and supplying of the greatly expanded military force at the fort and in officers' homes in the town presented an opportunity to the local merchants, and the farmers and hunters in the surrounding areas. But it also posed serious challenges, for the area was not very productive, and many of the suppliers were struggling even before the newcomers arrived. Trading grew to fill the gap.

The taverns expected a wave of new business from the greater military presence, and were not disappointed. There was, fortunately, no noticeable increase in the incidence of drunken brawls in the taverns and streets. It was assumed that with General Wayne and Secretary Sargent in town, along with Governor St. Clair and many other important officials visiting frequently, the Commandant was giving stern warnings to his troops to restrain their warlike tendencies in the town, lest they embarrass him in front of his superiors.

Herman was involved in discussions at the fort concerning the creation of courts and court officers. The court system was to be similar to that in other parts of the Northwest Territory. There would be the Supreme Court, the Circuit Court, the Court of Common Pleas, Probate Court, Justice Court, and the Court of Quarter Sessions of the Peace. On September 29 the Court of Quarter Sessions and the Probate Court of the county were organized. Judges and officers of the courts were appointed at that time, including Louis Beaufait as senior justice and James May and four other men as associate justices, Peter Audain as Prothonotary, Clerk and Judge of Probate, George McDougall as Sheriff and Herman Eberts as Coroner.

At home that evening Herman announced his appointment to Marie in excited tones. "I was telling you a few days ago that I've had some interesting discussions at the fort concerning government and laws and appointments.

Well, one of the appointments for Wayne County is Coroner. And I have been named!"

"Coroner?"

"Yes, it's an official position, and should if possible be filled by a doctor. The job involves overseeing deaths in the county, establishing for the law how they came about, and issuing death certificates. It sounds gruesome but is actually quite an interesting function and will be a paid position. It won't take up nearly all of my time, but will be helpful."

Marie put down her cup and smiled at Herman. "Oh my darling, what an honour! Imagine, you're still a British subject, but even so you've been appointed by the government of the United States to an official position in this country! My, what an amazing country this is!"

"Well now" replied Herman, "I believe that they are assuming that I'm an American citizen, or at least plan to become one. There's a strong sense of patriotism in this country, and I don't believe that they would consider any other way."

Marie knew why he was so pleased with the appointment. It showed that he had been fully accepted by the Americans, and carried their respect. No longer was he just a surgeon and trader; he was now a recognized official in this new and exciting country! As the news of the appointments spread, she found that her status was elevated in the eyes of the community. People who knew her generally liked her; now there was a new respect in their eyes when they met her on the street or at functions. It was a nice feeling after those dark days back in Boucherville when her connection to Herman had made her almost a pariah in the community.

Over tea at the Eberts home some days later, John Plummer made a comment about the appointments that proved to be prescient. He congratulated Herman once again, but then said that he had some concern about the McDougall appointment. "There's no doubt that he's a strong man, and obviously liked by the authorities. But I'm told that he is known to have an unusually strong love of the bottle. In other words he loves life, but perhaps somewhat too much for the good of his important appointment."

Within a week this comment proved to be accurate. Herman told Marie that he had met with McDougall, who had admitted that he rather enjoyed his lifestyle, and would appreciate some assistance from the new Coroner, perhaps acting on his behalf when called upon. This would be done on an informal basis, with Herman called 'Acting Sheriff'.

"Have you agreed?" asked Marie, a worried frown wrinkling her brow. "It sounds strange to me. He's just been appointed, and is already asking you to do some of his work. Is it even legal?"

"Yes, it's legal. He is permitted to appoint others to act on his behalf if he so wishes. Of course, this is normally meant to be an occasional request for extra help, but he feels that it can cover this situation as well. He'll still carry out some duties, but has already mentioned several cases that I'll have to pursue on his behalf."

"Will you be paid for this extra work?" asked Marie, not yet mollified by his assurances.

"He will pay me something out of his own fees when I work for him. We have no formal agreement, but I'm certain that he will do so."

"Hmm. Well, let's hope so. So you are now Coroner and also occasional Acting Sheriff. You are an important man, my love!"

Several evenings later the Eberts family entertained at their home. William and Effie Baker were there, visiting from Sandwich. William was back in Detroit to speak with several of his old skilled workers to see if he could talk them into moving over to Sandwich to work at the new naval yard at Amherstburg. Effie had joined him to catch up with some of her friends. Also at the table were the Scottish trader Angus Mackintosh and his wife Archange.

Mackintosh was a lively, voluble Scot, well-known for his energy and resulting prosperity. He had come to Detroit from Scotland in 1789, and was employed by the merchant firm Forsyth, Dye & Mackintosh. In 1783 he married Marie-Archange St. Martin, and by 1796 they had seven children. He also worked as the agent in Detroit and Sandwich of the Montreal-based Northwest Company, the major competitor of the Hudson's Bay Company. He bought provisions for the company from local farmers, and also had the important responsibility of providing safe passage of the company's pelts and merchandise between the Canadian west and Montreal. Archange and Marie were almost the same age, and had become close friends.

In light of Herman's long friendship with the guests, they were all on a first-name basis, and this privilege extended to Marie.

Both couples congratulated Herman on his appointment as Coroner, but were guarded concerning the job of Acting Sheriff. "McDougall is a bit of a loose cannon, as you probably know" said Baker. "He enjoys the taverns, which is fine, but there's a rumour that he is somewhat indiscrete in his visits to the Indian villages. I hesitate to speak ill of the man, because I actually like him, but I'm just saying – be careful in your dealings with him." The women were too polite to ask what 'somewhat indiscrete' might mean, but Effie smiled at Marie in a way that indicated that she would provide more details when the women were by themselves.

As he poured more wine, Herman thanked Baker for his frank comments. "Yes, I know what you mean, William. I like the man too, but I will certainly take your advice and watch things carefully."

"If I may add my piece" said Mackintosh, "we all have our weaknesses, as does he, but he's a good enough man to have received his appointment as Sheriff, and that says a lot. Herman, if you can help him work his way through his difficulties, then well done."

Marie felt the need to lighten the conversation. "Tell me, what do you all really think about my husband becoming an official? I must admit it's flattering, but then I've never thought of him as being a government man."

Effie Baker laughed. "An interesting point, Marie! You'll certainly have to watch what you say in the house from now on. You never know what might get back to the fort!"

This set them all laughing. "Absolutely right, Effie" said Mackintosh, quaffing his wine and grinning at Herman. "You're a marked man now, my dear doctor. We must all start to keep our secrets from you!"

"Very well then" said Herman. "I shall make an inquiry right here and now. William, how goes your project up the Thames River?"

"It's only just commenced" replied Baker, embarrassed to be questioned about what he considered a confidential project. "I've visited the site with two of my men, and we've started cutting some trees. The location seems to be a logical one in that it's well away from the border, so quite secure, and yet the river is large enough there that we'll be able to float the boats that we build down to the lakes. But it won't be easy. After all, we're asked to cut a stockade and townsite and boat building facility out of the woods, which in itself is a challenge. And then we are finding that there are virtually no skilled workers available to move there. There's even a shortage at Amherstburg, so the people who have ordered me to start the project up the river are, at the same time, telling me to keep my hands off the skilled workers there. Oh, and another problem is that there's no supply of cured lumber up there for the boat building. We'll have to start from scratch, cutting trees and milling and drying and so on. It'll take time."

"Is there not a similar problem at Amherstburg?" asked McDougall.

"No, there isn't" replied Baker. "You see, over the past month or so, before the Americans arrived here, we managed to ship all of our lumber and other supplies from our operations here to Amherstburg. So we're well provided for, while the Americans here will have to start from scratch. This isn't a secret, I should add. The Americans are, of course, fully aware of it now, and the story is that they expected it and are dealing with it."

"What a clever idea" said Archange Mackintosh. "It just shows you how complicated this changeover of government is. And speaking of change, Effie, how is it moving to Sandwich? There have been so many people moving there over the past few months, it must be quite lively."

"Yes, it is" replied Effie. "Lots of people had moved from here before we did, and there are more coming in every day. We have all types over there, from lawyers to doctors to storekeepers, and some working men to help us all settle in. As William has said, there's no reason for working people to go up the Thames River to find jobs! I'm told that we'll soon have a post office, and even a gaol! But there's still lots of room for more, so please don't hesitate to join us."

The evening moved on pleasantly, with the talk ranging over many topics concerning the new status of Detroit. They talked at some length about the merits of the various American officers in town, and about the health of General Wayne. Rumour had it that he was not well.

As autumn turned cold, Marie felt more and more at home in Detroit. It was not a loveable place, but most people were friendly and even respectful to her and to Herman. The children were settling into their schools, and Marie had found enough playmates for Françoise that she could easily keep the little girl happy and well looked after if she had other things to do. She loved taking the children to church on Sundays, and started to become active in church affairs.

The town itself was confining. She was not ready to travel outside its gates on her own, nor did she feel free to visit over in Sandwich unless she was accompanying Herman on one of his business trips there. Her small group of friends, which included Jennifer Black and Archange Mackintosh, was a god-send to her. There were social events to attend on occasion, at the fort or the homes of important citizens. She enjoyed these events, always looking for new people who might become friends and help her to endure her confined life. She met General Wayne on two occasions, and found him charming but tired looking. Perhaps the rumours of his ill health were true?

Her major concern, however, was not the confining nature of her life, but rather the evolving personality of her husband. He was certainly still attentive and loving to her, whether in bed or out. He loved her, and she him. That was not the issue. What started to bother her was his changing face in public. His appointment as an official had given him a new sense of self-importance that did not sit well on him.

Back in Quebec he had been a respected doctor, but not well loved by the community at large. The dislike related somewhat to his personal traits which were seen by some as too Germanic and formal, but also to his background as a mercenary soldier and a non-Catholic. When he came to Detroit he was welcomed as an excellent doctor and interesting man in his own right. He was energetic, productive and friendly, and his trading activities, especially in medicines, were of real benefit to the citizens. He worked hard and was generally liked.

That was how Marie saw him when she first arrived, and she welcomed the change. But now he was gradually taking on airs and traits that threatened to return them both to the uncomfortable status they had endured in Quebec. His appointment to the group of ten eminent citizens to greet the Americans had been the start of the change. Marie noticed signs of arrogance showing through his normally friendly exterior. All of a sudden he was better than most of his friends and colleagues. He had been chosen. He was in an elevated class, perhaps reminiscent of past times in Europe when a fine name or title placed you securely above 'the people' and indeed, almost above the law.

The changes were subtle, and probably only she noticed them at first: a disdainful word about a friend, or perhaps expressed annoyance at some attribute or action by 'some people'. He started to dress more formally than before, with good reason of course as he was now dealing directly and frequently with the important people in the town, but it bothered her. She had liked the less formal man who had met her at the dock back in July.

Then came his appointment as Coroner, and shortly thereafter his duties as Acting Sheriff. He started to dress even more carefully, keen to have his clothes, though not an actual uniform, separate him from ordinary citizens. Friends started to notice the difference in him. "My but doesn't Herman look grand" said Archange Mackintosh to Marie one day over tea. "You must be proud of him Marie. He's an important man now."

Marie was disturbed by the tone in her friend's voice. It implied, in a mild but definite way, a distrust of people who take appointments so seriously. And this feeling did not rest with Archange alone. The tone in conversations they had with people in the streets was changed. There was nothing that she could easily say to him about this emerging problem, for after all, he actually was more important now than he used to be, so he did deserve some sort of recognition. It was just that he seemed to be going about it the wrong way.

Herman's work as Coroner was limited; his work on behalf of George McDougall was more active. McDougall was not interested in being Sheriff at that point in time, so Herman received a steady stream of requests for service. Marie saw that he enjoyed this work. She could feel his sense of importance as he said his good-byes upon leaving the house.

It started quickly but not well with a visit to the countryside on October 25. He arrived home late in the day looking thoroughly annoyed. He calmed down somewhat over dinner with the family, but after, sipping tea in front of the fire, he told Marie about his day.

"Yes, I was annoyed when I came home. I had a difficult time today, I can tell you. I rode out to the Raisin River area to serve some warrants, and presented my letter of introduction to the Justice of the Peace there, a man named Francis Navarre. He was a cocky fellow, head of the local militia and very sure of himself. I thought it would be helpful to have some support when I visited the various homes with the warrants, and asked him to call out some of the militia to help me. Well do you know, the man refused to do so! He told me that I had no right to ask for such assistance until I had made my visits first, and experienced resistance that would warrant the help of the militia!"

Marie kept her silence – she felt that Navarre's position was not unreasonable. But it would be unwise to interject when Herman was making his point so forcefully.

"I must admit I was annoyed at that, for surely the Sheriff has the right to ask for support. At any rate I did make my calls and delivered the warrants. I managed to do so without serious incident, but I did have to use some strong language in some cases. They're a surly bunch, and most of them were not happy with me, but then, what can you expect? They're ignorant people with no knowledge of the law, and little respect for it. Before coming home I dropped back to Navarre's place and told him what I'd done. He was still not pleased! Told me that I had been too rough on some of them! I ask you, what does the man want?"

Herman stopped and gazed into the fire, trying to calm himself. Marie also gazed into the fire, but her feelings were anything but calm. She could see Herman's point, but she could also understand what Navarre had done, and why. She knew that her husband had been high-handed in his approach to the Justice of the Peace, and certainly with the local people. They would not thank him for it, and this would fan the smouldering flames of dislike that his appointment, even in an acting capacity, had aroused in the community. But she dared not say anything along that line as he might not take it well, and if so it would only anger him more.

16

WINTER

In the first week of November, on a cold and wet Wednesday morning, Marie was cleaning the children's rooms, with Françoise helping out in her usual playful way, when there was a knock on the front door. She opened it to a young man from a family that had moved over to Sandwich three months ago. He handed her two letters that he said had come from the British camp at Amherstburg by way of William Baker, who had asked him to deliver them during his planned visit to Detroit. She thanked him and closed the door. Françoise was still playing upstairs, so she had some time to herself, and she needed it as she knew from the writing that one was from Ignace. His first letter! She put the other aside for the moment.

Boucherville *September 22, 1796*

Dearest Maman,

I hope this letter reaches you, so far away from us. I miss you, Maman. We all miss you. Grampa and Gramma were very sad when you all left. It is good that I have stayed here, for I feel that they need me.

I am sorry that I have taken so long to write to you. I received your letter three weeks ago, but then I did not know where to send a letter until Grampa finally told me to take it over to the British headquarters, and they would bring it to you.

We are all well here. My studies at the school are fine, and I am enjoying them. I like reading about history, and Grampa likes to talk about it with me. I have heard about the battle at Quebec many times! His leg is better, although he still uses a cane.

I do not know what I will do when I finish my school. I suppose I could go into the militia, or perhaps work in the town at a store or something. Grampa says that he would like me to work in his shop, and I suppose I will try that. I would like to continue my studies, especially in history, but I don't know how.

How is Thérèse doing? And how about Joe? I suppose Guillaume and Françoise are excited about being there. Have you found a school for them?

Please give them all my love. I will write again soon.

Your loving son,

Ignace

She sat there smiling, thrilled with the very thought of receiving the letter. It renewed the bond that had always existed between them. They were in touch! But she felt a shadow of sadness too, for he made no reference to Herman. He had not asked after his father, or sent him any message, or wished him well. She had hoped that the wound would have healed after their departure, but obviously it had not. She debated whether she should hand the letter to Herman when he came home. He would be hurt, but then, he would be even more hurt if he found out that she had kept it from him. Better to keep him informed and knowledgeable about the situation. He might actually have some ideas as to how to deal with it. So she decided that she would show it to him.

The second letter was from her cousin Yvette Charbonneau. It was just as Marie had expected – chatty, full of family news and gossip. Marie's parents were well, Ignace was doing fine, and her own family was a joy. She hoped that they were well settled in Detroit. The letter had Marie chuckling happily.

When Herman returned home at the end of the day Marie first showed him Yvette's letter, and he enjoyed it. Then she showed him Ignace's letter and, sure enough, he was hurt and angry. "The boy certainly knows how to carry a grudge" he said, before handing it back to her.

The following day provided another welcome experience. It was a chilly, windy day, with a promise of winter flitting through the trees, when Doctor Plummer called to introduce his wife Rita, who had just arrived from Boston. She was a friendly, motherly woman, perhaps ten years older than Marie. She was clearly in some shock at being in tiny Detroit after the bright lights of Boston, but she faced the challenge with great energy. She enjoyed meeting the Eberts family, and spent some time with the children, who seemed to love her on sight. In a side conversation with Marie she thanked her for the hospitality that they had shown John.

"John is proud of his work with the forces, as you have probably seen, but he does get terribly lonely. You've been of great service to him – to us, my dear Marie. Oh, may I call you Marie?"

Marie blushed with pleasure. "Of course you may, and I will call you Rita. We seem to be very informal out here in the wilds!" She knew instinctively that Rita would be a welcome addition to her circle of friends.

Over afternoon tea they talked about the town, and the fort, and all of the exciting things that were happening as the new country took shape around them. But Dr. Plummer had some bad news to impart as they discussed the amazing successes of General Wayne.

"This is still confidential, but I know that I can rely on your discretion. You may have noted that the General has not been seen much over the past few weeks. I'm afraid he's not well. One of my colleagues has been treating him for his gout. He's bearing up, but it's troublesome. It's a shame, I think, for he's a fine man, and having him here has been good for us, for our operations and also, of course, for our status. But I have to wonder how long he will stay with us."

On November 15 the town turned out to say farewell to General Wayne. He put on a good show for them, riding bravely down to the docks, followed by a large contingent of troops. He dismounted beside his ship, a fine new American sloop, waved farewell to the crowds, and then limped with the assistance of his aide aboard ship. Marie knew what pain he was in – Herman had explained the ravages of gout. She and her family joined the hundreds of voices calling out their best wishes to the departing hero.

Winter came to Detroit that year early, and in force. November proceeded with icy winds and snow flurries that came frequently and, at times, violently. As the temperature dropped, the Eberts house started to show its weaknesses: gaps around windows and between logs, a breeze rushing up the stairs as the warmth from the fireplaces and the stove ascended. Herman and Joseph did their best to shore up the gaps, and they all worked to keep the house reasonably warm through frequent stoking of the fires. Marie had brought some winter clothing for the children and herself from Boucherville, and had bought some more earlier in the fall, and she spent every spare minute now knitting more woolen socks and other items of warm clothing. After growing up in Quebec they were all used to cold winters, but there they also had the comfort of large, well-built buildings to protect them. Here most buildings were not well constructed for winter protection, so the town had a general feeling in it of chill and darkness.

She thanked the Lord every day that Herman was earning sufficient money that they were well provided for. Her heart went out to the many families in the town and the surrounding area who were poor, and not able to look after themselves properly in these conditions. She supported and donated to the work of the church as it reached out to help them.

The children enjoyed the snow, bundled up as they ran around. They generally went off to school in good spirits, although they soon found that their teachers were anxious to save money on their heating, so the pupils often went through entire days of classes almost fully bundled.

The cold weather and the departure of General Wayne combined to send the soldiers from the fort into the taverns of Detroit whenever they had time off. They warmed themselves with ales and spirits, grew loud, and often fought in the taverns or out in the streets. Fortunately they were careful not to harm the citizens of the town. The few prostitutes brave enough to live in Detroit did well by them, and there was little violence against them. The soldiers viewed them as a precious commodity, to be protected.

Marie shared the nervousness of her friends over this situation. Although the soldiers left them alone physically, they did eye the women in the street in a most wanton manner, making them afraid for their safety, and that of their children. She asked Herman if there was anything the Colonel could do, but he was not hopeful.

"Colonel Hamtramck has lectured his troops on the importance of peace and good citizenship, and warned them of terrible consequences should they cause trouble. But you must remember who they are – tough country boys, used to fighting and hardship, yet desperate for some love and some good liquor. They're cooped up at the fort, bored out of their minds, and with nothing to talk about except each other and their own problems. Yet they're serving their country, and feel that it owes them something besides their meagre pay. The Colonel's main responsibility is to keep them here as a fighting force, and he knows that if he's too tough on them they might well cause him trouble. So he treats them as naughty children when they cause trouble, but let's them off without the levels of punishment that would anger them and their friends."

Marie nodded. "Yes, I understand. But tell me, was it the same with the Redcoats?"

"There were some disturbances, but the Redcoats are long-term professional soldiers, quite used to these conditions. And the British army has a high level of internal discipline, which the rank and file disobey at their peril. So there was very little of it. And they certainly kept their hands off the citizenry!"

There was nothing for it but to live with the situation as best they could. They knew that they were probably safe, but there was always the chance of an accident stemming from an out-of-control fight near their house. In his role as Acting Sheriff, Herman was called upon several times to deal with incidents involving soldiers. There would be fights amongst soldiers, but sometimes with civilians drawn in as well, and Herman and his assistants, the gaoler and some part-time deputies, would have to work with the fort to sort out the disturbances and their consequences. He pitied the locals who had to spend time in the gaol which was a couple of rooms attached to a house, because it was a chilly, unforgiving place. But perhaps that very fact acted as a deterrent to more widespread violence.

With the town so small, the Eberts family lived close to friends. The Plummers had moved in just three doors away on St. Anne Street, and several other friends were also nearby, so help was near at hand should the need arise.

In early December William Baker dropped in for afternoon tea with the Eberts. He told them that the naval yard at Amherstburg was coming along well, but that the project up the Thames River was at a virtual standstill. Some planning was proceeding, but with the winter closing in it was proving impossible to start building anything, much less gunboats.

William had other news that was of great importance to them all, and warranted serious discussion. It concerned the tricky question of the nationality of persons living in Detroit.

"As you know, the Supreme Court in this area has decided that if a person resided in Detroit at the time Jay's Treaty took effect, and did not file a petition against becoming an American citizen, he became naturalized by virtue of the treaty. Nobody is certain about the timing, but it seems that if you do want to remain a British subject, you will have to take action at some point, and certainly by the end of next year. The details of what you do to declare your citizenship are unclear, so John Askin is taking action on his own initiative. Do you know him?"

"Yes I do" replied Herman, "and I have introduced him to Marie." He turned to Marie, who was looking unsure. "You met him at one of those functions at the fort. He's an elderly chap now, but still very bold and active. He came over from Ireland with the British army back in the late 1750s. After the British took over New France he left and went into business, mainly in the fur trade, and I think he had a post over at Fort Michilimackinac. He was involved in trading and shipping, and even some land speculation, and then for some reason he became involved in official life. He became a Justice of the Peace here in Detroit, under the British, of course. This year, with the Americans taking over, he was named by the British authorities a Justice of the Peace for the Western District of Upper Canada. But mark you, he still lives here in Detroit, and he and some partners are trying to buy up the entire Michigan peninsula from the American government! He's a substantial man. But William, forgive me. Please do go on."

"Not at all, Herman. Just let me add one more fact about Mr. Askin. He's a Lieutenant-Colonel in the local militia in Upper Canada, and a local magistrate. So you see, he has large feet on both sides of the border.

"But to continue, I've learned through my army contacts at Amherstburg that there is concern in Canada that France may be working to encourage an uprising amongst our French-speaking citizens, with a view to pushing the British out. And they may have the support of the United States. The orders have gone out for militias all over Upper Canada to arm themselves and be prepared to act, and our friend Askin has been involved in transmitting those orders. So as you can see, he's in a serious position of conflict of interest. In fact, his actions might well be seen by the authorities here in Detroit as treasonous if they were known. This is all strictly confidential, of course; I beg you to keep it to yourselves." Herman and Marie nodded, and Baker went on.

"While all of this is going on, Askin has decided to take action on the question of citizenship preferences of people living in Detroit. He's circulating a paper for the signature of people living here who wish to declare that they prefer to remain as British subjects. He claims to be doing it as a service to people, but there's a suspicion that his real motive is to retain as large a population of British sympathizers as possible here in the United States. Have you heard of this? Has he perhaps approached you?"

Marie turned to Herman for the answer. "I've heard of it, but he's not approached me as yet. I suppose my position with the government has kept him at bay. And well it might, for I surely could not sign that paper and retain my positions here. The authorities would not stand for it. But I have heard of Askin's activities, and I know that he's not well thought of at the fort. But tell me William, have you signed it? Have many others?"

"Oh yes, I have done so. Of course I have already moved over the line back to Canada, but I still retain some property here, so I have wanted to keep my situation absolutely clear. As to how many have signed, I don't know for certain, but I think that Askin has been quite convincing. Keep in mind that people who are still uncertain will be likely to sign, as they will hesitate to receive the blessing of American citizenship without giving it due consideration. The only other person who has told me that he has signed is Angus Mackintosh, and that comes as no surprise. His attachments are for the most part into Canada, and I expect to see him moving there very soon. I don't know if Askin has handed the papers in to the authorities yet."

Marie turned back to Herman. "It seems strange to think of it, does it not? We and our children becoming American citizens! When I think of my father fighting for the French at Quebec, and then us so involved in English Canada as it has grown. And now we are to change our loyalties again! I suppose it's necessary, as you say, but, well, let me say that I wish someday to return to Canada. Perhaps when your appointments are finished. What will we do then? Will we be forever foreigners to our family and old friends back in Canada? Oh Herman..."

Herman took her hand and reassured her. "My darling Marie, this situation will be changing and flexible for years to come. If we choose to go back to Canada, I can assure you that William and our many other friends will welcome us back. Keep in mind we have not had to actually declare ourselves Americans, and that will mean a lot if we wish to return to British territory one day."

On December 23 Herman told Marie at breakfast that he had a meeting arranged for that day with Sheriff George McDougall. "He seems anxious to see me. My guess is that he would like to step back formally from his duties as Sheriff for a while. His personal life seems to be an impediment to his duties. Or perhaps he has other work, his former work that is keeping him too busy. I don't know, and don't care to speculate. One way or the other, we'll see how it relates to me."

Marie replied easily that it would be interesting, but her mind was racing. Was this the occasion to raise with him her concerns about his arrogant official 'face'? What if she suggested that he reconsider, and go back to his private life of medical practice and trading? But of course, he would say that he was still doing all that, and that this Coroner and Sheriff work was simply an interesting and valuable sideline. And that would push her into a direct confrontation with him about his attitude, his arrogance (how she hated to even think that word). There would be hurt and anger; probably some sort of difficult scene, with the children still at home. Well...

It was too late. Herman left the table suddenly, in a rush to start his day.

Marie's day passed with the usual mix of activities: cleaning the house and keeping the fires stoked; looking after the children; enjoying a pleasant cup of tea with Rita Plummer, who was now a fast friend of little Françoise Eberts; visiting the church to assist with arrangements for a church supper; and shopping in the town's forlorn market. Through it all her thoughts kept straying to Herman and the possible outcomes of his meeting with the Sheriff. You never know. Perhaps the Sheriff would say that he wished to take on the office full time, and thank Herman for his past help. But the more likely outcome would be more official work for Herman, and that worried her.

Her concerns were realized when he bounded in the door later in the day, kissing her and smiling with triumph. "My love" he cried, taking her hand, "you are looking at the official Acting Sheriff of Wayne County! Actually, I am to call myself 'Acting High Sheriff'. And of course, the Coroner as well!" Marie had to smile at his exuberance. He took this as a sign of her joy at his appointment, and gave her a hug.

Marie was used to putting on acts to protect Herman from hostile gossip. Now she had to put on an act to support him in his happiness. "Oh Herman, I'm so pleased for you. You must be very proud of yourself." She said this last carelessly, without thinking, and blushed immediately at its possible interpretation. To her it was an indiscretion, but he took it as a compliment, and continued to smile as he moved to the sideboard to find a bottle of wine for a celebratory toast.

As they raised their glasses to each other, Marie asked him about the specifics of the arrangements.

"I've agreed to perform all of the duties of Sheriff for one year. I'll have full responsibility; McDougall is relieved for that time. And you know, this really is a substantial position. I'll have officials such as Justices of the Peace in the various communities, and aside from delivering summonses and warrants and the like, I'll have to appear in the courts for criminal cases. And you'll be delighted to know that I will preside over the criminal facilities in the County, which include the courthouse, gaol and pillory, whipping post and stocks!"

Herman laughed at his jest, but Marie's heart fell as she realized that her wonderful husband, the respected surgeon, was becoming the proud, somewhat feared and disliked Sheriff, official of the County. But what could she do?

"That sounds fine, dear. But...will you have any time for your medical practice, or for trading? I do hope that you won't have to leave them entirely."

"Oh yes, I'll have some time for them, but not much. Wayne County is a large area, so there's a lot of territory to cover. I'll have some help in communities, of course, but I'll have to take the responsibilities seriously. But I can assure you, my dear, that I have no intention of deserting my profession. It will be with me long after the government people tire of me, as they inevitably will. As for the trading, I already have Preston doing a lot of the work on it anyway. I'll meet with him regularly, but won't spend much time on it. Mind you, it won't hurt to make connections all over this county as I ride around as Sheriff. Good for the future, anyway!"

So that was that. Marie was now the wife of an important official in a vast new county of the United States, and she hated the thought.

That same week they heard of the death of General 'Mad' Anthony Wayne. When he left Detroit back in November he was not well, but determined to complete his visit to the northwest before returning to his family seat at Radnor, near Philadelphia. On his final stop, at Fort Presque Isle on the south shore of Lake Erie, he had a serious attack of the gout that had worried him for some time. The officials at the fort sent to Philadelphia for doctors who could treat him, but he died there on December 15, before they arrived.

The flag at the fort at Detroit flew at half mast, and there was a feeling of sadness throughout the community. General Wayne had opened the way for the 'liberation' of Detroit with his victory at Fallen Timbers. His arrival in Detroit had been symbolic of the power and influence of the new country. Few of the citizens had met him personally, but most of them were proud that their town had been the host of the great general. It was an honour; it gave Detroit prestige.

The 1796 Christmas season saw a small but determined display of celebration in the town. It centred on the church, but spilled out into the community where there was some partying in the snowy streets. Colonel Hamtramck held a large gathering at the fort for his officers and the important citizens of the town, and Marie enjoyed the opportunity to wear her one warm yet pretty dress. There was also some visiting amongst the homes of their friends, always involving the children.

But there was a general air of desperation that haunted Detroit, and was particularly cruel in the outlying communities. Their low agricultural productivity meant that they were stretched in the best of times. In the freezing temperatures and snows of that winter there was cold and hunger. There was little that Herman could do in his medical rounds outside the town. The people did have colds and flus and other diseases that he could attend to, but what they all really needed were warmer temperatures, more fuel for their fires and more nourishing food. The one consolation was that with most people huddling at home for warmth, the demand for his Sheriff services was limited.

Three days after Christmas Marie received her second letter from Ignace, delivered by a very chilled British army messenger. It had with it a letter from her mother Judith Huc. To her surprise she opened Judith's letter first. It was a natural motion – the daughter longing for her mother's words. But it surprised her because her initial feeling of joy at receiving mail had been thoughts of Ignace.

Judith gave her a straightforward account of life back in Boucherville. Gregoire's business was going well, and Ignace was now working there when not studying. They had been forced to do major repairs to the stable, and Aunt Josie had the flu but was on the mend. Yvette had visited several times – my, what a nice girl she was! And her children were so sweet! She hoped that Marie and Herman and the children were well, and sent them all her love.

Marie turned to Ignace's letter, and as she did so, felt a strange feeling of...what? Anger? Annoyance? Frustration? Before reading it she turned in her chair and looked out the window at the falling snow. The children were all out playing with friends, except for Françoise who was having a baking visit with 'Auntie Rita' Plummer. Dear Rita had all but adopted the girl, taking her out for visits and play whenever she could, and thereby helping Marie immensely.

Alone with her thoughts, Marie could not shake the negative feeling that was so alien to her with respect to Ignace. Herman refused to even talk about him, but that was only natural. She had held out for her first-born son, understanding his sensitivity and sympathizing with his loss of love for his father. But what now? She still loved him, of course. She would always love him. But seeing his letter come along with Judith's seemed to have changed something for her. In his letter he sounded happy. No mention of Herman; no reference to his father at all. It was as if Herman no longer existed.

Marie was a soft, loving person most of the time, but she had a tough streak in her when she needed it. It was that quality that had kept her going through those lonely years back in Boucherville, and it had helped her to settle reasonably well into the rougher life in Detroit. Now it rose in her again, feeding her with a negative reaction to Ignace's letter. She knew that her anger stemmed not just from Ignace's stubbornness, but from the happiness in Judith's letter that she had Ignace there with her and Gregoire. It was nice that the boy could be back at home to help her aging parents, but that was not fair.

...Ignace, my son, I'm pleased that you are well, but I do not understand why you have not come to understand your family. I know that you feel strongly about what your father did, but surely you are old enough to realize that it was necessary for his profession and quite acceptable in many places in the world, including in Upper Canada. The British have no objection to it, and I doubt that the Americans do either.

Oh Ignace, you should be here...

1797 opened with a heavy snowstorm that kept most of the citizens of Detroit cooped up in their houses for two days. Soldiers were sent from the fort to clear away some of the worst drifts, and life returned to normal for this time of year – functioning but slow and restrictive. Food supplies started to run out at the shops and Marie was, like many others, pleased that she and her family had put supplies away in the cold cellar against just such a situation. The dried meats and pickled vegetables and potatoes became valuable commodities. The traders were desperate to bring in more supplies, but were more often than not frustrated by the terrible conditions on the frozen river and the lakes.

17

REALITIES – 1797

With the family so confined by the weather, Marie had lots of time to spend with each of the children, and she found that aspect of her life thoroughly enjoyable. They were all so brave, adapting with determination to their restricted life in Detroit.

Thérèse, a lovely fourteen year-old going on fifteen, accepted with energy her role as assistant manager of the house. She was somewhat bossy at times, pushing the younger children to keep the upstairs at least reasonably tidy. She enjoyed her school, and visited back and forth with the two new friends she had made there. At the youngest end of the family, Françoise continued to play her role as the 'little doll'. She had curls to show off, along with the frilly dresses that she adored. She was a sweet child, and everyone in the family, and most visitors, babied her and spoiled her. To her, house cleaning was an opportunity to do things with her mother.

As Joe approached his twelfth birthday in March he was unusually tall and strong for his age, good looking in a rugged way. Like his baby sister, he ignored the cold weather. He reminded Marie of her father Gregoire, the soldier. He worshipped his father, often begging to accompany him on his trips away from Detroit. He did reasonably well at school and had several good pals, including the equally strong but more serious Jonathan Black.

And then there was little Guillaume, nicknamed 'Squeaky' because of the tone of his voice, and the way he entered conversations with a mouse-like squeak. He was a quiet, intelligent boy, small for his age of seven, turning eight in February. He had bright, inquisitive eyes, a kind, almost pretty face, and an amazing level of articulation for one so young. He was hopeless at chores but, fortunately, neat and tidy in his habits. He hated the cold weather, dressing dramatically in as many layers of outdoors clothes as he could find.

The children were remarkably free of colds and other diseases as the winter progressed. Their home was warm and dry, and Marie kept her ears open for news of problems in other homes and the schools, and made sure that her brood stayed clear of trouble. This was by no means the typical story in the town. Herman was kept busy on the medical side with visits to homes, sometimes very chilly homes, where disease problems were serious.

Ironically it was at the fort where problems seemed the most serious. With their drilling and guard duties out of doors, the soldiers were constantly placed in chilly, uncomfortable positions for extended periods. The results were predictable: colds, influenza, and a number of cases of pneumonia, some ending in death.

Françoise was finally down for her sleep after lunch, and Marie and Rita were enjoying a quiet cup of tea. It was a bitter day in February, and they sat close to the fireplace in the parlour. Marie started the conversation. "Well, my dear, you'll never guess what has happened. I'm pregnant! Herman confirmed it yesterday!"

As she expected, Rita was happy for her, giving her a hug and a kiss on the cheek. "Oh Marie, how lovely! You'll have an American child!" They talked excitedly about how a baby would fit into the family, where it would sleep, what it could eat here in Detroit. As their conversation moved on to other topics, Rita mentioned that John was feeling satisfied with his work at the fort. There were few wounds to deal with in the middle of winter and in peaceful times, and they could spend more time on illnesses and long-term recoveries.

"And I must say, Marie, he does appreciate the chance to do some dissecting with such a fine surgeon as Herman. He's learning so much!"

She paused when she saw the shocked look on Marie's face. "Why Marie, what's the matter? Are you unwell?" She moved towards her friend, but Marie waved her back to her chair.

"I'm fine thank you Rita. It's just that…well." She paused for thought. "I take it you don't know the full background of why we're here in Detroit?"

It was Rita's turn to look surprised. "No, I don't. I've just assumed that Herman came out here to pursue his profession with the British forces, and you decided to join him. Why?"

Marie smiled. "No, I'm afraid there was more to it than that." She went on to describe the situation in Boucherville, Herman's rash experiment, his banishment, and the five years of isolation before they had been re-united. When she had finished they sat for a moment in silence, Rita staring at Marie while Marie gazed into the fire. Marie did not know how her friend would react to the story. She hoped knowledge of that sorry affair would not harm their friendship.

The effect on Rita was, in fact, quite the opposite. She leaned forward, her hand at the side of her face, and cried out in exasperation. "Oh Marie, my dear, dear Marie, what a terrible thing to happen to you! Oh dear. I really must say, that law against dissection is so primitive! So silly! No, I must not speak ill of your church. Please excuse me, but I'm horrified that Herman should have been banished for doing something that is such an important part of his profession. Oh my dear, and it has caused you all that time apart. So much pain for you!"

Rita burst into tears, overwhelmed by the news, and by sympathy for her new friend. Marie stood up and came over to her, hugging her as tears flowed down her own cheeks. Rita's reaction to the story flowed over her like a healing shower, freeing her from any sense of guilt, or even anger.

As they recovered from their tears and Marie poured more tea, Rita delivered a lecture on the importance of the medical profession, and of dissection as a learning tool. She knew that there were religious objections about it, and some legal questions to be sorted out, the body being a sacred vessel and so on, and many people considered grave-robbing a terrible thing to consider. But civilized societies (as she put it, rather carefully) were moving on from such beliefs, and finding practical ways to make ample supplies of cadavers accessible to doctors. Certainly her John had dissection as a vital part of his training. Here in Detroit, at the fort, there were always bodies available, whether from wounded or sick soldiers, or from the members of the public who had died, and whose families showed no objection. She finished by stating that "it was unfortunate that Herman had to resort to taking that body from her grave, but I'm sure that the lessons he has learned from such work have helped him to save many lives!"

That evening, over their tea after dinner, Marie moved her chair closer to Herman's than usual, leaned over and took his hand. He took the gesture as one of happiness over her pregnancy, and was surprised when she spoke of another subject entirely.

"Rita tells me that you and John have been doing some dissections at the fort."

Herman's face fell into an expression of guilt. "Oh my dear" he gulped, "yes, I have. I'm so sorry. I know how you feel about it. I had hoped that you wouldn't find out."

Now it was her turn to interrupt. "No, no darling, don't feel bad. Rita and I had a good talk about it, and she showed me how important it is to you – to all doctors. I was wrong to be so negative about it back home in Longueuil. I should have been encouraging you, not criticizing. I'm so sorry."

He paused, tongue-tied. Then: "you are so wonderful, Marie. You really are. I must admit, you know, that it does seem like an unpleasant practice, a terrible way to treat someone's body. But believe me, it really is as important as I have said in terms of our learning our profession. Without it we are almost ignorant of what we are doing. For if we don't know how our bodies work, how can we fix them?"

He paused once again, seeking the right words. "Well, my thanks go to Rita for helping us deal with this thing between us, and to you, my darling Marie, for being so understanding."

They smiled at each other, and she squeezed his hand before withdrawing it and returning her gaze to the fire. But her mind was racing now. They felt so close at that moment. Was this a good time to raise her concerns about his attitude as Acting High Sheriff?

The problem simply would not go away. Even in this bad weather Herman had a considerable amount of work to do in that capacity, and his attitude continued to worry her. She did not mind him wearing his formal clothes when delivering summonses or visiting Justices of the Peace in their areas, but his outfits for appearances in the courts had progressed to the point that she felt thoroughly upset. He would wear a cocked hat, a black velvet coat, knee breeches, a yellow brocaded waistcoat and a sword. He felt proud of this outfit, which befitted an important official in Europe. But here in Detroit Marie saw it as pretentious, and it embarrassed her. And she had heard enough comments at church events to know that others in the community felt the same way.

But no, this was not the time. Perhaps he would come to his senses once the thrill of new office was gone.

The winter weather receded as April launched the first signs of spring. Once again the supply ships came to Detroit, filling the shops with welcome produce and supplies. Fishing and hunting were taken up with renewed energy, and the farmers looked to their early plantings. Marie welcomed the warmer weather, even as the new crop of black flies and mosquitos appeared to dampen their spirits. The children loved to go outside for play, and learned that a coating of grease on their faces helped them to survive the attacks of the insects.

Official life in Detroit proceeded at a good clip as the governance of new Wayne County was developed and fine-tuned. John Askin's list of signatories to the statement that they intended to continue as British subjects grew slowly, becoming quite substantial. He had handed three parts of it to the Prothonotary of the County Peter Audain, and rumour had it that he was still working on one final part. He also sent copies of the list to Peter Russell, Administrator of Upper Canada in the absence of the Governor.

These activities did not worry Marie, as she felt confident that Herman could easily handle the question of nationality. What did worry her was the outbreak of scarlet fever in the town. It was a severe illness for children, in some cases causing death. There were rumours of several cases in Detroit and in the surrounding area. Some children had already died from it. Every parent was on watch for signs of it in their children, or the friends of their children.

Scarlet fever came to the Eberts home on May 4, on a bright, sunny spring day. Joe and Guillaume arrived home shortly after 11am in the morning, coming in the front door just as Marie was finishing up her housekeeping and preparing to go to the market with Françoise. Guillaume scurried in the door ahead of Joe and called to his mother "Maman, we have scarlet fever! I mean, one of our friends at school has it! So we had to come home and not come back until next week!"

Marie crossed herself. It had arrived! "Oh dear, boys. Tell me, what has happened? Who has it?"

Joe moved ahead of Guillaume, pushing him aside. "It's Peter Tomkins. His mother came to the school this morning to say that Peter came down with it last night. She told teacher that Peter has all the signs of it, and he might have given it to some of us! So teacher told us to go home and stay home until he lets us know that it's alright to return."

Now Guillaume pressed forward. "What's it like Maman? Does it hurt? What does it look like?"

"I don't know much about it. Your father will be able to tell us when he comes home. But I hear that it gives children a red rash, and they sometimes have red faces and white tongues. I believe that they have a temperature and a sore throat, and sometimes feel sick in other ways. Oh dear, how terrible this is. Boys, you were in contact with poor Peter, so you'd better stay home, and try to stick to your room as much as possible unless you are outside. We'll just have to wait and see if you've caught it. God help us!"

The boys settled in at home, their worries about the disease nicely balanced by their happiness at having some days off school.

When Herman learned of the case upon his return home from the courts that afternoon, he showed more concern than Marie had hoped that he would. "It's not just a simple childhood disease, I'm afraid. It can be very serious. There have been at least two deaths from it in the farms out near the Raisin River. Let's just hope that this case in the school has gone no farther than that one boy."

They discussed what to do as they waited for the disease's incubation to end. Herman told her that by Tuesday at the latest they would be through the last of the incubation period. If they didn't have it by then they would be fine. In the meantime it would be best to keep the girls away from them on the chance that one of them did have it, and so might pass it on to the girls who had so far had no exposure to it at their school or with their friends. They decided to impose upon Rita Plummer to take the girls in for a week. Rita was quick to agree, and Marie packed some belongings for each of them, and diverted them on their way home from school directly to the Plummer home.

Then they waited. As the weekend passed, Marie felt increasingly confident that the disease had passed them by. The boys were fine, and growing restive to return to their studies and their friends. On Monday they had a message from the school that Peter Tomkins had recovered. He would not be back for another week as he was weakened, but the other boys could return to school next day.

But in the early morning of Tuesday, May 9, Herman and Marie were wakened by Joe's loud knock on their bedroom door. "Maman, Papa, Guillaume is sick. He looks funny, and says that he has a terrible sore throat! Please come..."

They rushed upstairs and found the boy lying on his side with his arms covering his face, crying softly. Herman examined him as Marie watched. Even without the formal doctor's opinion, she could see that Guillaume had come down with the fever. The boy knew how serious the disease was – his parents had talked about it openly over the weekend, assuming that it had passed them by. Now, as his father confirmed his diagnosis, Guillaume burst into loud tears of mixed pain and fear.

Marie sent Joe scurrying out of the house, and then went to the kitchen to heat the kettle so that there would be warm drinks for the patient. She could hardly see what she was doing as tears coursed down her cheeks, all but blinding her. Her fear was so strong she thought her heart would burst.

Warm tea with honey in it seemed to help somewhat, easing Guillaume's sore throat. But it was a token weapon against serious odds. As the day progressed Guillaume's body was consumed by a vivid red rash, and his tongue turned a chalky white. He was in pain, and his parents were helpless to do much about it. They sent Joe over to the Blacks' home, and then started in on five days of constant care for their little Squeaky. He was unable to take most of the foods offered to him, existing on soups and sweetened tea. He slept a lot, and had little interest in reading or talking when he was awake. He fell quietly into Marie's frequent, lengthy embraces.

By the following Monday Guillaume seemed to be recovering. His tongue was back to its normal colour, his sore throat had gone, and his rash was fading. He took some food, smiling hopefully at his parents as he did so. But he was badly weakened after that hard week, and had virtually no energy. As evening came on his breathing became louder than usual, and he started to cough occasionally in a low, harsh tone. Herman had been out that day attending some patients in other homes. When he came through the door he stopped to listen to the sounds from the bedrooms upstairs. He heard the cough and slumped into a chair, his head in his hands.

Marie heard him and left Guillaume's side to come down to him. She saw the despair in his eyes and rushed to him. "What is it Herman? Tell me!"

He looked up into her eyes, and she saw the tears starting down his cheeks. He reached for her and pulled her roughly against him. "That cough. Oh my dear God, that is pneumonia. I would know its sound anywhere. Oh Marie, I thought that he was better, but now I truly fear for his life."

Marie straightened up, pulling away from his embrace. "Oh no, Herman. No! It cannot be. I will not let it happen. Surely there's something we can do? Please Herman…what should we do?" She was yelling now, gripping the lapels of his jacket as if she would drag a cure right out of his chest.

Herman did his best to calm her. "We must keep him warm and full of fluids. He'll be sleeping a lot, and that's good. But I'm afraid there is no cure for it. He will just have to survive it through his own strength and perseverance."

Marie nodded dumbly and stood in silence, thinking what she should do next. Then, with a sudden bolt of energy, she went to work. While Herman sat with Guillaume, she made more soup and tea, and put together the makings of a meal for Herman and herself. It was better to act than to sit and worry! Then she left Herman in charge and visited the Plummers and the Blacks to give them the news, and ask them to extend the visits of her children for a few more days…"just until Guillaume is out of the woods". All of her friends expressed alarm, agreed immediately to keep the Eberts children as long as was necessary, and offered to send any food or supplies that might be needed. Warmed by this display of neighbourly affection and concern, she returned to her house and her desperate work to save her son.

For four nights and endless days Marie nursed Guillaume, sleeping next to him at night, feeding and bathing him, and reading to him in his lucid moments. Herman had to be away most of the days, but he came home as soon as he could each evening, and gave Marie a chance to rest.

Guillaume died at 10:30am on Friday, May 19, 1797. His laboured breathing simply stopped suddenly as Marie was reading to him. She looked up and knew instantly that he was dead. They had lost the fight. She sat there for some time, dry eyed and in shock, gazing lovingly at her gentle little Squeaky, now gone from her forever.

The family gathered back at the house and started into a period of mourning. They moved silently around the house, wept at the slightest provocation, and the children hugged Marie whenever she was nearby. She visited the church every day to pray. Her closest friends came by to offer their prayers and condolences, to bring food dishes for their table, and to talk to them with a view to helping them work through their sorrow. William and Effie Baker made a brief visit to Detroit just to be with them.

It was difficult for them to sooth Marie. She had produced seven children, but there were just three left in the home. Ignace had abandoned them, and Phillip, Antoine and Guillaume had died. Marie was now showing her pregnancy, expecting in August. "My Lord" she exclaimed to Herman one night, "it's like replenishing a jug of water that has a hole in it! The more you pour in, the more you lose."

But life did slowly return to a semblance of normal. The children returned to their schools. The weather improved, and Herman was able to get out for long trips into the countryside. He pursued his official and medical duties with determination, and as long as she was in mourning, Marie forgot to worry about her husband's attitude to his work. She wrote long letters to her mother and to Yvette, pouring out her sadness as she tried to keep her tears from smudging the page. She also wrote to Ignace and said that the family needed him desperately.

Of course, while the Eberts family mourned, life was proceeding elsewhere in Detroit, and across the river at Sandwich and Amherstburg. William Baker reported that work on the naval yard at Amherstburg was going well. The project up the Thames was a different matter. They had laid out a plan for the stockade and the town, but made little progress beyond that. They simply did not have the workers to move things forward. Even the previously idle men in the Sandwich area were fully occupied now, helping with the developments in that town with its sudden influx of new citizens. Furthermore, following up on Jay's Treaty, there was now a major program of fort and road building in the Canadas, initiated to secure its safety from the United States. Military roads were being built connecting Amherstburg, London, Niagara, York and Kingston. Fort George was constructed to compensate for the loss of Fort Niagara. Trade and travel were facilitated when the portage on the west side of the Niagara River was constructed.

One of the new landowners in Sandwich was Angus Mackintosh. He had an oft-stated wish to build a substantial trading post and family hall which he would call 'Moy Hall' after his ancestral home back in Scotland. With his main business connections in Canada, he decided that it would be best to move back there, so in May he purchased a large property in Sandwich. It would take some time to build the facilities that he required, so he kept Archange and their seven children in Detroit, set up a camp and went to work on the new property.

Detroit and its surrounding area was proceeding through a late spring and early summer that seemed promising for the farmers. Trade in furs and other goods was doing well. The fort with its heavy load of soldiers was a strong market for all sorts of products, and the soldiers were avid customers at the town's taverns.

Herman's official duties started to dominate him, leaving him little time for medical work. This worried him, but he enjoyed being an important official, and figured that he would not lose his medical skills over the few years that he was likely to hold the official jobs. He could then return to a fuller medical practice. But his work as Acting Sheriff was not without its annoyances. On June 8 he was at court for the case he had brought against Francis Navarre, the man who had refused to raise militia to help him carry out his official duties back in October. Herman had charged the man with refusing to obey his orders. Navarre made an eloquent plea in his defense, stating the facts of the case, including a listing of 'coercive actions' that he claimed Herman had taken in carrying out his duties. These actions were illegal in his view. The court agreed with Navarre's position and released him. When Herman told Marie about the case that evening, still angry at the insinuations and the outcome, Marie simply nodded. She could not concentrate on the story beyond a general sense that, once again, Herman had not acted well in his public duties.

Another issue that Herman had to deal with at that time was that of nationality. In mid-June John Askin delivered his final list of those wishing to retain their status as British subjects. Herman and several other influential citizens found out that the total number of signatories was much greater than had been anticipated, representing a substantial portion of the English-speaking population of Detroit. They saw this as the result of strong sales tactics on the part of Askin, and suspected that by no means all of the signers were really serious about retaining British citizenship in the long term. But in the meantime, the situation posed a threat to the stability of the community, for if so many of the people insisted upon remaining British, then just how loyal was Detroit to the United States of America? Would it be possible to raise a militia should it prove necessary, and how loyal would the militia be if ordered to oppose Canadian forces?

Herman met with eleven other men who wished to be citizens of the new country. They were concerned that the senior official people in Wayne County were not fully seized with the importance of this situation, and decided that they should lodge a petition of their own. On July 12, 1797 they presented a note signed by all twelve of them to Secretary Winthrop Sargent.

Sir: - We, the undersigned, magistrates and sheriff of Wayne County, in the territory of the United States of America, impressed with every degree of attachment to the government of the United States and most sincere wishes for the safety of this country and its inhabitants, have sincerely to regret its

present situation, and for its safety disagreeable apprehensions for the dangers that at present menace its tranquility from an approaching enemy as well as from internal and increasing factions.

Twelve months ago we knew of no more than ten of the inhabitants that were avowed British subjects, they remaining here for one year after the evacuation of the place by the British. During that period they, with some other emissaries, found means of indirect insinuations and circulating papers, to corrupt the minds of the inhabitants and alienated their affections from the government of the States to such a degree that it was with difficulty that the sheriff could procure a jury of real citizens to attend the last sessions, or bailiffs to do their duty. Some score (it is said some hundreds) of the inhabitants have signed the said circulating papers declaring themselves British subjects, which gives us reason to fear that little or no dependence can be put on the militia of the country if called upon. This being truly the state of the country, we feel the greatest anxiety for its safety. We therefore conceive it our duty to transmit to you every part of our apprehension and the causes exciting them, hoping that you will see the propriety of vesting sufficient power in the commander-in-chief here or the commanding officer for the time being, to take such steps as may check the progress of the present prevailing faction and prevent a further complaint of the inhabitants, we, by experience, finding it out of the power of the civil authority at present, to do it.

Herman described the petition to Marie the evening it was presented. Now heavily pregnant, she was still downcast and virtually uninterested in matters beyond the family, but she sensed her husband's enthusiasm and asked him to explain it to her. Why did they think it necessary to tell the government how to do its business?

"I suppose it goes back to the early, immature situation in this country. The government people are still trying to develop the right systems for such a huge area, and so are preoccupied with official matters. I'm on both sides of the fence; I have an official position, but I am also a private citizen with my medical work. I suppose that gives me a realistic perspective."

Marie smiled at him for the first time in a long while.

Encouraged, he continued. "You'll notice that I'm referred to as 'Sheriff', even though I'm really only acting. And George MacDougall was not even included in the discussions! But as to why we felt we should submit this petition, we felt that the senior people like the Governor and the Secretary were not seized with the seriousness of what Askin has done. They could actually interpret it as treason, you know, and that without even knowing about his work with the Canadian militia! So in our view the military should be involved, and stop these actions.

"Oh, and not only that, but have I told you that Askin and some of his colleagues are trying to buy up big tracts of land from the government in several places including around Lake Michigan? If you put all this together, you could say that he is seeking to take big sections of land away from the government, while at the same time causing disaffection amongst the local population and, simultaneously, raising the preparedness of Canadian forces. It's a nice basket of treason, is it not?"

Marie was impressed with Herman's insights. "It is indeed. My goodness, what a thing to be happening so soon after the Americans have taken over! Surely the authorities will take some action now?"

"Oh, I'm sure of it. Askin is at the heart of much of this disaffection, but by no means all of it. I'm told that there have been a substantial number of desertions from the fort, probably by soldiers so bored that they would rather go over to Canada than stay here. Or so drunk, I should say. Plummer tells me that the problem of drunkenness amongst the soldiers has become so serious that they're thinking of denying them access to the taverns! Can you imagine? But then, Baker has told me that there's been a problem of desertions from the British forces over there as well. I suspect this would be soldiers who have established homes or friends or loved ones over here, and wish to return. Who knows? But Baker thinks that the authorities over there are cooperating with ours here to stem this desertion problem."

The next day Herman told Marie that the fort had issued general orders prohibiting anyone from selling liquor to soldiers, or enticing them to desert. "Here's what they say about desertion:"

...Any person detected in attempting to inveigle a soldier from his duty, or in advising him to desert, shall receive 50 lashes and be drummed out of the fortifications.

But General James Wilkinson, Brigadier General and Commander in Chief of the Troops of the United States, went further than that, proclaiming martial law in Detroit. Under this order all citizens would be considered *...followers of the army and treated accordingly...*

Two days after that he had more news. "They've now decided to take some interesting steps concerning deserters. Deserters from the British ranks are ordered to leave town within twenty-four hours. Our forces here may not enlist deserters from any other nation. On the other hand, deserters from our own ranks will be granted a full pardon if they return and admit their sins. I think that much of this relates to the actions of John Askin. It's feared that he's been seeking to create confusion and disruption with his lists, and has used liquor to persuade people to do things they would not do in more sober moments."

As time went on Herman reported several stages of the battle over control of the soldiers, and ways to curb their access to liquor. The British element still in Detroit did not like the idea of martial law, and a number of them, including Angus Mackintosh, sent a lengthy letter to the General asking him to modify his order. Not receiving an acceptable response from General Wilkinson, they then petitioned the War Department, and had some satisfaction in separating the martial governance of the troops from the regular governance of ordinary citizens.

Marie found that she was increasingly able to focus on these important issues affecting their lives, and to put aside for quiet moments her mourning for Squeaky. She had to rest for long periods every day, leaving most of the work around the house to the children. Then on August 8 William Henry Eberts was born at noon, noisy and lively. Herman attended the birth with one of the local midwives. As it was a Tuesday, Thérèse and Joe were at school, but Françoise knew what was about to happen and begged to stay at home. She was shooed out of the birthing room, but ran to her mother's side as soon as permitted, and joined in the joy at the appearance of a new brother, younger than her!

Jennifer Black dropped in soon thereafter to visit Marie, and when she heard the news she rushed out, found Rita Plummer, and together they brought a wonderful cooked dinner to the Eberts home. By that time Herman was able to let them have a brief visit with Marie and the baby, and they joined the children seated around Marie's bed. They all admired William, but at the same time the irony of the situation was not lost on any of them – his arrival so soon after they had lost Guillaume. Françoise's innocent comment "Oh I wish Squeaky was here to see William" unleashed a flood of tears from all sides. They decided to call the baby Henry rather than William, which was too close to 'Guillaume'.

But ironic or not, the baby gave Marie a new reason for hope. Her life that had seemed so desperately sad and hopeless back in May now had a new beginning – literally, a re-birth. She flung herself into this opening of the gloom that had surrounded her with all of the energy she could muster, helped along the way by her friends. The baby was wonderful, the other children loved him and took turns caring for him, and Herman was smiling and even singing quietly to himself when he thought that nobody would notice.

18

FRONTIER LIFE

Two weeks later Herman was commissioned as Sheriff of Wayne County in place of George MacDougall, who had resigned. The authorities felt that it was not right to have such an important position in the hands of someone on an acting basis. MacDougall had told them that he was too preoccupied to do the job himself. Herman could not, however, carry out the job of Coroner as well, so that position was given to John Dodemead, a tavern keeper.

One of the first actions by Herman following this appointment was delivering a summons to the famous John Askin to appear in court to answer charges that he had used undue pressure in securing signatures from people concerning their wishes to retain their British citizenship. This was the start of a series of problems faced by Mr. Askin, but he was a clever and well-connected man. He escaped from all charges laid against him, retained the goodwill of the authorities on both sides of the border, and moved to Canada a few years later.

With her spirits raised by the arrival of baby Henry, Marie emerged from the cloud of mourning and showered attention on her family. She wrote Ignace regularly, receiving no positive relies to her pleas to come to Detroit, but she had grown beyond caring about it as a central theme in her life. Yvette kept her up to date on her parents. Her four children, here with her and relying on her, were the focal point of her being.

Herman had suffered from Guillaume's death, and Marie saw that he too was drawn closer to the four surviving children, and to Marie herself. He was most attentive to her, spending as much time with her and the children as he could. But his time was limited, for his duties were heavy in both official and medical spheres. Unfortunately, as time went by she began to see once again the signs of arrogance in his official persona that harmed his popularity in the community.

The authorities liked him because he carried out his duties efficiently and with great energy – perhaps too much energy at times. The word went around that one scholarly official had accused him of 'contumaciousness'. When questioned, the unnamed official said that it referred to a contempt for and opposition to lawful authority. Stated another way, he was known to press cases that were not ready to be pressed; to take actions in ways that were not always in strict conformity with the official procedures for court officials. It was seen as being similar to upper class people in Europe who scoffed at the petty rules and laws designed to keep the lower classes in order, and did things 'their own way'. One man who had suffered from a summons delivered in a particularly energetic manner by Herman was quoted as saying "...the man's a bully".

The reputation did not affect Marie directly, for the most part. Her friends were all fond of her and her family, and her life proceeded as pleasantly as could be expected in backwoods conditions. But she knew that being the wife of a liked and respected doctor was different than being the wife of a generally disliked official of the law. She noticed that whereas shopkeepers would give the wife of the 'good doctor' an extra egg or measure of salt, they had no such generous tendencies for the wife of the Sheriff.

Friends such as Angus Mackintosh, John Plummer and William Baker were not affected, but Curtis Black, described by Herman as a 'working tradesman', pulled back from the family connections. Marie was not happy with the situation, but was still hesitant to challenge Herman on it. He was a loving husband to her, and father to the children, and she was not prepared to disturb that state of affairs.

The government people were, however, aware of Herman's actions and resulting reputation. With criticism growing, they finally took action in August of 1798.

> *August* 20th *[1798] the Governor was pleased to revoke the Commission of Herman Eberts, Esquire, the Sheriff of the County of Wayne, the said Eberts having misdemeaned himself in the Execution of the said Office by refusing to execute certain writs issued out of the Court of General Quarter Sessions of the Peace for the said County, and Lewis Bond, Esquire, was appointed to succeed him and commissioned accordingly.*
>
> *Territorial Papers of the United States*

"Damn then for the bureaucrats that they are" cried Herman when he arrived home that day. "They warned me about this, but I simply did not believe it. How the devil do they think they can run this place without strong rules and strong implementation of the rules...and no silly frittering away time with unproductive efforts like those silly writs I refused to execute?"

As Herman slowly calmed down over a glass of wine, Marie was secretly thrilled with the decision. It would return Herman to the work that he was best at, and surely his reputation would be repaired over time? He could put away his cocked hat and silk stockings and become a real person again!

Which he did. Herman set about to rebuild his medical practice in Detroit, the surrounding areas, and across the river in Sandwich and Amherstburg. He was still a proud man, but he learned to refer to his 'brief fling as an official' that he was 'very pleased to be finished with'. This satisfied most people. His medical skills were unquestioned, but there still hovered over him the sense that deep down he was more comfortable with the British way of life; that the egalitarian approach to society that was being pursued in the United States was not the best way to approach things. Was he loyal to the United States? He never said that he was not, but there were suspicions.

In May of 1799 Marie announced to the family that she was pregnant again. She was thrilled with her condition. Little Henry was approaching two years old, and was a joy to the whole family. Françoise treated him as her own live doll. She had started school that spring, but would rush home to help care for Henry. Now she could look forward to another baby to cuddle.

That summer Angus Mackintosh completed Moy Hall at Sandwich, and moved his family over to Upper Canada. It was a blow to Marie, as Archange Mackintosh was such a good friend, and she missed her as soon as the family completed their move across the river. The only compensation was her decision to travel occasionally, with children in tow, to Sandwich to visit friends. Herman was there frequently on business, and would accompany her when possible. He did not like the idea of her travelling alone across the river, but he knew that their friends over there would take good care of her. She would walk to the ferry, and they would meet her with a carriage on the other side.

Sandwich was still small, but it had grown impressively with the outflow from Detroit and the tremendous work proceeding at Amherstburg. Her first visit to Moy Hall was great fun. She had come over with Herman, leaving the family running itself back in Detroit, with an occasional look-in by Jennifer Black. The Hall was a large wood-frame building, impressive in appearance and well designed for business. Mackintosh showed it off proudly, describing his work there. He was the main representative in this area of the Northwest Company, trading and selling. He also had more plans for the large property, which was on the river. He would be building a distillery to process grains 'for more efficient shipment', and might even try his hand at ship-building. "These lakes are like oceans, you know. There will be a huge demand for ships of all types as time goes by. Well Sir, the folks at Amherstburg can build the warships. I'll build the rest!"

The Mackintosh house was on a nearby lot. It was a substantial structure as was required to house the nine-member family, with another on the way. Archange said that facilities such as schools and shops were still at an early stage in Sandwich, but changing fast. She said that it was nice to be back in British North America in spite of the primitive conditions, and wondered if the Eberts family would ever think of moving back. Marie and Herman were non-committal. In answer to Angus's question about Joe, Marie said that the boy was tall and strong like his father. Angus said that there would be much work to be done at the Hall, and never enough people to do it. If the boy would ever like to do some hard work when out of school, he would be glad to take him on.

On another trip several months later, Marie took Thérèse and Joe with her for a stay with the Bakers. Thérèse was now seventeen and Joe fourteen, and they loved getting away from Detroit and seeing the Bakers again. Catherine Baker and Thérèse were very friendly with each other, and Marie noticed that Joe now showed some interest in young Ann Baker.

Over tea, William told them about his work. "At Amherstburg the naval yard is finished, and we're setting up to build ships. Work is already proceeding on Fort Amherstburg, which will protect the shipyard. I can tell you, with the Americans in Detroit now, and the French sniffing around to see if they can cause trouble, we're seeing a very active building program here in Canada. We're getting new military roads and forts, and this naval yard is another example of how quickly things are happening.

"But things aren't going so well at the site up the Thames. We have the townsite laid out and some people settled there, but it's taking a lot of time to start up the boat-building. As I told you before, the major problem is lack of skilled people. There is so much going on here that very few wish to go and live in the woods there. We also have the problem of finding the right wood, properly dried. So we keep working away at it, but the senior people don't seem quite as anxious to get it going now that we have the facility here at Amherstburg. I guess you could say 'better a ship from Amherstburg than a gunboat from Chatham'!"

Richard Duncan Eberts was born the morning of November 11, 1799. He received the usual noisy welcome from the family, and Françoise took on her role of managing the baby as much as permitted. With two baby boys to control she was in her element.

The winter of 1799 was relatively mild; either that or they were just getting used to them. Marie wasn't sure. But she was wonderfully organized now, with babies to care for and older children to oversee. She volunteered at the church, and ran the house so well, with all of the children playing their prescribed roles, that Herman could devote all of his time to his medicine and trading, and bring visitors to the house whenever he wished.

As springtime broke over the cold land in the year 1800, Detroit and the surrounding area had a population of around two thousand, with over five hundred families. That May the Congress created the Territory of Indiana, which embraced all of the Northwest Territory west of a line drawn due north from the mouth of the Big Miami River. General William Henry Harrison was appointed Governor of the Indiana Territory, whose capital was at Vincennes, four hundred miles from Detroit. This left Detroit in the Northwest Territory, which was administered by a legislature at Chillicothe, Ohio.

Herman explained these events to Marie, but she was far more interested in local events and issues. One key issue was simply the state of the town and the surrounding areas. There were no proper roads outside of the town, so that more distant communities could be visited only by boat for most of the year. Indeed, most of the land around the town was in Indian hands, lending a sense of potential danger for travelers. The town itself seemed to be in a permanent state of decay, the streets dirty. The town had, moreover, a sense of disorder and even danger due for the most part to the presence of such a large number of soldiers with little to do but idle away their time drinking and fighting. They were under military law, so the civilian population could do little about them beyond filing complaints. Marie made certain that her children steered clear of the main trouble spots, namely near any of the taverns, and were home before dark.

She admitted to herself and to Herman that while life in Detroit had a precarious feel to it, she was not unhappy. She liked the feeling of adventure, the sense that she had to take active measures to protect her family, and was quite capable of doing so. And of course she could hold her head high in society once again now that Herman was back working in his true profession.

Her older children were now at ages where they were becoming attracted to the opposite sex, and that called for careful watching. Thérèse was a beauty, reminiscent of her mother at that age. Her dark eyed, slim good looks caught the eye of every young man in the town, and unfortunately of all of the soldiers as well. The only young man who actually called upon her was Jonathan Black. The trouble was, there just wasn't much to do for such a young couple, and anyway, she didn't really like Jonathan that much. He was too direct and forceful, with strong opinions on things she didn't agree with.

That summer Thérèse's greatest pleasure was a month-long visit to the Bakers at Sandwich. She and Catherine had become best of friends. They gossiped endlessly, attended several parties where there were some presentable boys from good Loyalist families, and even went and helped out at Moy Hall, which was fast becoming a thriving trading post. Angus Mackintosh was grateful for their help. They were good at organizing, counting and displaying goods, and selling clothing – skills not readily available in many of the local people.

Joe also enjoyed a month with the Bakers following his sister's return. Marie did not want them both to be away at the same time, as they were of such valuable assistance to her, but she was delighted that they had this outlet for their energies. Starting this summer, Joe's visits with the Bakers became an annual event, much looked forward to for three reasons. First, it was a refreshing escape from the stifling confines of Detroit to the woods and fields of Sandwich. Second, like his sister he was welcomed at Moy Hall as a 'family helper', as Angus Mackintosh called it.

Third, and of increasing importance as the years went by, was the presence of sweet Ann Baker at the Baker home. The natural attraction between the two was so obvious that Effie Baker had to laugh every time she saw them together. They gossiped and joked, played games and read together. They even went for walks through the woods and along Sandwich's many dirt roads, giving no thought to possible dangers. Effie did not see them ever hugging (or worse!), and was confident that Ann had a strong moral sense, and would not do anything silly. And Joe was probably the same, although less predictable.

Marie corresponded regularly with her parents, and with Yvette and Ignace. They were all well, missing her but clearly quite happy with their own company. In one of his letters Ignace mentioned that he was developing an interest in the army, perhaps in joining one of the militia regiments in Lower Canada.

Thérèse and Joe had their visits to Sandwich in the summer of 1801. Near the end of the summer William Baker said that Fort Amherstburg had been completed and manned, and the naval yard there was now turning out vessels 'full tilt'. Joe had now finished school, and spent his time working at Herman's trading company. With his work there, and then at Moy Hall in the summer, he was developing into an astute businessman.

In August the Eberts had a visit from a merchant from Montreal, who was visiting Detroit and Sandwich on business. Jean-Louis Biron was an elegant man, of medium height and with a look of great physical strength. He was travelling to secure sources of supply for his selling activities in Montreal, and he told his friends that he had come to the trading and sales business the hard way, by hauling heavy crates in warehouses and toiling on the docks. But he had been intelligent in his work, found his way into managing his own enterprise, and was now happily prosperous.

As they sat over a glass of wine before dinner, Marie guessed that he was probably in his late twenties. She liked him, with his warm smile and ready laugh, his articulate speech and good manners. The family drank in his news about Montreal and Lower Canada, the hard news and the gossip. As the evening progressed Marie noticed that his eyes strayed often to Thérèse. Biron parried all of her questions and comments with seriousness blended with good humour, and she responded with smiles and occasional blushes. *This,* Marie said to herself *is modern day courting. He's courting her right in front of our eyes! He is a clever one! Well, she doesn't seem to mind, and I must say…*

Biron returned to Montreal in early September with assurances that he would be back next year. He had visited the Eberts home several times during his stay, and clearly enjoyed his growing friendship with Thérèse. Marie saw in their relationship a direct parallel with her own courtship with Herman.

In mid-September Marie announced that she was pregnant again.

Pregnant again! Marie had known several families back in Quebec that had numbered over ten children. At the time she had thought little about it; it was the way it was, the method that parents used to ensure that they would have sufficient children around to care for them in their old age. Infant deaths, childhood diseases, accidents – there were so many ways that children could be lost to you that it was important to start with a large number.

She was well on the way to proving this theory. At thirty-five years of age she had been pregnant ten times, and had produced nine children, with one on the way. One had left the family and three had died, leaving her with five at home now, soon to be six. Thérèse and Joe had reached early-adult ages, and might well leave the home soon, but hopefully they would be nearby. That would leave four small children for her to care for. Françoise was now ten years old, and continued as a wonderful, happy girl who loved to take care of the younger ones – bless her! They used to call her their 'little doll'. Now they called her 'Dolly'.

Henry was now four, and baby Richard would turn two in November. The new baby should arrive next March, giving her and Françoise three small children to look after. The prospect was quite delightful to Marie, for the little ones made her heart sing, and toiling with Dolly in the kitchen and the baby room was, well, just plain fun. She blocked from her mind the children lost to her. She lived in a tough, frontier town, in another country far from her old home and her parents. She ran the house and family through frigid winters and sweltering summers, travelling through dangerous streets, protecting her young. She was a frontier woman, and proud of it.

And proud of her man, too. Herman had recovered from his bout of officiousness. He was still a sophisticated man, by no means a crude frontier fighter, but his medical work brought him close to people rich and poor, and he had a compassionate streak in him that pleased Marie greatly. His trading store was doing well, especially with medicines, but also with furs and, unfortunately, spirits. Like it or not, however, this trade brought in a good living, and Marie felt confident and happy because of it.

She continued to love Herman deeply and, on occasion, with great passion. She knew that he would never be popular with everyone in Detroit as he was just a bit too sophisticated, and in the eyes of many of the town's inhabitants, some of them people of rank, he was still sympathetic to the

British. This concern was well founded, for both Marie and Herman often spoke fondly of their lives and friends back in Quebec, now Lower Canada. Detroit was livable, but by no means an ideal place for them to be living and raising a family. They knew that they could move to Upper Canada without any problem. They could cross the river at any time – just pack up and leave.

But they were well settled, prosperous and healthy. Sandwich had developed rapidly over the past five years, but it was still more a gathering of lots in the woods than a real town. Detroit was larger and more settled, and they were satisfied to remain there for the present.

Detroit was incorporated as a town by the legislature of the Northwest Territory at Chillicothe, Ohio on January 18, 1802, effective February 1, 1802. Government was administered by a five-person Board of Trustees and there was no office of Mayor. The original incorporation provided for a Board of Trustees to govern the town, the Chairmanship of which was the highest governmental position.

Herman was pleased when, in late February, the new Board of Trustees adopted a fire code that required all residents and business owners to sweep their chimneys often. It provided buckets and ladders to residents, who were required to turn out to fight any fires. "They seem to have their priorities well organized" he said to Marie when the decision was announced. "I've been in so many houses and stores in this place, and many of them are in real danger of having fires. There's a lot of old, dry wood in them, near hot stoves and fireplaces sparking away happily. Let's hope that everyone obeys this rule."

Marie agreed, but had more urgent things to think about, for on March 18, 1802 she gave birth to Josette Felice Eberts. "It's a girl" Herman announced to the waiting children, and Françoise almost hit the roof in her delight. "Oh how wonderful" she cried, running to Thérèse and throwing her arms around her. "Now there are three of us and, and…three boys as well! Oh, what fun we shall have!" She decided that the baby should be called 'Phillis,' and the name stuck.

They waited breathlessly for permission to see the baby. When Herman finally opened the door and called them into the bedroom it was Françoise who led the way, clinging tightly to Thérèse's hand. They gathered around the bed where Marie lay, tired but happy, the baby in her arms. She smiled at the children and said "well my darlings, here is your new sister." They chatted and stared until the midwife shooed them all out of the room, leaving Marie to her work and her sleep.

That summer Jean-Louis Biron was back in Detroit on business, which included some sourcing of furs through Herman's company. He was quick to accept Herman's invitation to dinner, and immediately re-started his courting of Thérèse. As a visitor only, he was not in a position to court the girl in the formal sense, requesting permission of her parents and so on. But on the other hand he picked up the sense of informality that pervaded the new society in the United States, and felt free to speak to her, to go for walks with her, and on one magic occasion to join with her in a day visit to Moy Hall in Sandwich. This was on business, of course, but with definite social overtones as far as he was concerned. And he knew that Thérèse enjoyed herself as much as he did.

On the eve of his departure in August, Biron took Thérèse aside for a brief farewell chat in which he asked if he might correspond with her during the winter. She was pleased to accept, and he left with a kiss on her hand and a promise to be back the following year.

Marie observed all of this happily. She knew how limited were her daughter's prospects here in Detroit, and she saw in Biron great promise for the future. Joe was also pleased with Biron's attentions to his sister. He liked the man for his good humour and energy, and on two occasions they went outside of the town for productive hunting expeditions. He and Ann Baker continued to be fast friends.

The year 1803 passed by with much of the same rhythm for the Eberts family as the previous year. The family grew and remained healthy. Françoise turned twelve in May, and was developing into a slim, energetic and attractive young woman; not a beauty like her mother or Thérèse, but a delight to everyone who knew her. She lorded it over the three youngsters, and had no patience with Henry, turning six, who occasionally was bold enough to object to being bossed around by his sister. But that was a minor problem; in general the children were devoted to Dolly.

Herman's practice prospered, as did his trading activities. Jean-Louis Biron arrived right on cue in late June, and this year he wasted no time in seeking the approval of Herman and Marie for courting Thérèse. They agreed, and Biron was a frequent and welcome visitor to the Eberts house. One evening he said that his business was now such that he was seriously considering moving to Detroit, or perhaps Upper Canada. Marie glanced at Thérèse to see how this news would affect her, and saw that the girl was already aware of the prospect, and could scarcely contain her happiness over it.

Joe had another enjoyable summer visit to Sandwich, where he pursued his friendship with Ann Baker with energy and great good humour, but as yet without any sign of serious intent. When he came home in August he told Marie that the Bakers would be moving soon to Amherstburg. "William is spending so much time there now that it seems silly for them to remain in Sandwich. It's not far away, of course, but it's too far for him to come home every day. So they've arranged for a house near his new naval yard, and will be moving in this fall. It's too bad; I'll miss them when I go over to Sandwich."

In November Marie announced that she was pregnant again. She smiled, but with a tired expression on her face. Thérèse actually frowned at the announcement. Surely Maman was growing a bit old for this sort of thing?

The international scene in 1803 took an important turn when Britain declared war on France on May 16. This raised a variety of concerns in British North America (BNA) – the colonies of Newfoundland, Nova

Scotia, New Brunswick and the Canadas. One was that the French might seek to regain at least parts of BNA, counting on the loyalties of the French-speaking inhabitants there, who were still in the majority. Another, related concern was that Britain would not be able to spare more troops for North American operations due to the priorities in Europe. That would weaken BNA in the eyes of the French and also, of course, the Americans.

Responding to this crisis, the British granted authority for the colonies to raise regiments of cavalry and infantry. They would be called 'Fencibles', a name drawn from 'defensibles', meaning regiments for local defense only. The idea came from earlier situations in Scotland, where there was no local militia until 1797. The Fencibles were more than militia, they were units of paid and trained soldiers used generally for garrison and patrol duties, leaving the regular troops free for offensive duties. However, some Fencible units had volunteered to replace overseas units of regulars during the war with revolutionary France, setting a precedent that would be followed in British North America.

19

HAPPY AND SAD – 1804

1804 was a year of mixed happiness and sadness for the Eberts family. It started well with an early, pleasant spring. On May 6 Marie produced Robert Michel Eberts, another boy to add to the substantial collection already filling the house on St. Ann Street. Even Françoise seemed somewhat overcome by this latest addition to the family. "How many more children will you have, Maman?" she asked in her usual direct manner. "We're running out of space, you know!"

Marie was only too aware of that fact, as well as the more basic fact that her body was telling her in several different ways that it was time to stop childbearing. Fortunately, Herman agreed. He was aware of the strains upon his wife, and also of the fact that the house was now much too small for such a substantial family. Unfortunately there were not any options in Detroit. The town was busy, with every larger house full and no real space to expand.

That being said, tiny Robert fitted in well with the other children. Even two year-old Phillis found a way to care for him, holding his tiny hands and humming softly to him.

Jean-Louis Biron appeared in June as usual, this time with the wonderful news that he was moving to Detroit. His business demanded it, and he was only too pleased to do so. His letters to Thérèse during the winter had spoken of love and devotion, and by early August the two were engaged to be married, the date set for next spring. In September Biron purchased a small house two blocks away from the Eberts home, and went about the complex task of finding sufficient furniture to make it a home.

Joe had his usual summer visit to Sandwich, staying with the Mackintoshes, and his platonic friendship with Ann Baker pursued its quiet way. He was now actively involved with business affairs, and had little time for romantic pursuits. Marie asked him several times about his relationship with Ann, but had no satisfaction. He simply said that she was a great friend, but that he was very busy and determined to make something of himself before becoming involved with her, or with any girl for that matter.

The news from Ignace was troubling. Marie had hardened her heart concerning her first-born, but his letter received in late September set her heart racing once again,

August 14, 1804 *Fredericton, New Brunswick*

Dearest Maman

You will be surprised to see that I am writing to you from Fredericton, in the colony of New Brunswick. I have come here to join the army!

I am now a recruit in the New Brunswick Fencible Infantry. I wanted to join the army in Montreal, but I did not want to be in the militia which is not paid very well, or sometimes not at all, and is not always reliable. This regiment had posters saying that there was a need for recruits. We would not be regular army soldiers, but would be paid and trained to fight. 'Fencible' is short for 'defensible'! Is that not amusing? It means that we are here to defend our own land, but not to go away and attack somewhere else. That is fine with me, as I think that my responsibility is to protect our own place.

They provided transport for all of us who volunteered, and we are now living in tents here in Fredericton. As part of our training we are helping to build some barracks, and I hope we will have them finished before winter. I have a uniform, and we drill and train, and shoot our muskets at targets.

Grampa and Gramma were sorry to see me leave, but I know that they are proud of me. I hope you are too. I am able to write to you now, and to receive your letters, as we are not at war. If that happens, then it will be more difficult.

Please give my love to all the children, and especially little Phillis.

Your loving son,

Ignace

Yvette added some detail in a subsequent letter.

...your parents are saddened by Ignace's departure. He seemed to them to be their constant family, their companion for life. Then one day he was gone! Mind you, your Papa is very proud of him joining up, even if it is in a far-away place. But then at times he seems bewildered with it all, Aunt Judith even more so. The poor souls.

So my dear, I am visiting them at least weekly now, and Josie drops in when she can. The house seems so empty. Is there any chance that you might return for a visit?...

It was a lovely fall in Detroit, with warm breezes, sunny skies and clear, chilly nights. The Eberts family was happy and busy in its house on St. Anne Street. But on December 3 a storm cloud appeared on the family's horizon – a storm that would sweep away the happiness and confidence that they had been enjoying.

Françoise came home from school with a cough. She told her mother that two other children had been absent from school the previous week, and the teacher had told them that the children had bad coughs and would have to stay away until they got better. The next morning the cough had deepened into her chest, and she was hot and uncomfortable in her bed. Herman was away at Amherstburg for two days, so Marie had to do the diagnosis. She decided that Dolly had a bad cold, put her in a room by herself and plied her with warm drinks. The girl slept a lot of the time, and when she was awake she was restless and badly disturbed by the cough that seemed to be sinking deeper and deeper in tone. Rita Plummer dropped in that evening to see how the girl was faring, and when she heard the cough she rushed home and returned with her husband.

Dr. Plummer examined Françoise, and told Marie that it sounded like bronchitis. The child must have complete rest, and be isolated from the other children. The danger was that it might progress into pneumonia.

Herman arrived home the following afternoon and found that Thérèse had the young children in a sort of dormitory in the parents' bedroom downstairs, Joe had a room upstairs, and he and Marie had another upstairs bedroom. Françoise was in the other upstairs room, and Marie was with her virtually all of the time. Herman did his own diagnosis and agreed with Dr. Plummer on all counts.

The next day Dolly's cough had turned harsh and growly, and the worried parents could hear that she was fighting against a wave of fluid in her lungs. Herman told Marie that it looked like this was pneumonia. It had come on so quickly! It was so cruel! Marie changed from providing warm drinks to administering cold cloths, seeking to cool the girl in her fever. Thérèse and Joe ran the house now. Marie was frantic with fear, but only Herman knew it, as she maintained an outward appearance of calm and confidence.

Friday was the same as Thursday, the harsh coughing from upstairs echoing throughout the house. At noon Rita Plummer came and took the little children and Thérèse to her home, insisting that they settle in and stay until Françoise was better. That night the girl was in crisis – hot, in pain, rasping coughs, and convulsing with fever.

Early on Saturday Marie asked Herman to bring the priest, Father Gabriel Richard, to administer the last rites. He did not like it for he was no Catholic, but he could not deny Marie's command. The priest came and did his duty, and Françoise died as the bell in the church struck noon on Saturday, December 8, 1804.

Marie had lived through the deaths of three young sons, and had grieved for them all, but this was too much to take. Losing Françoise, her wonderful friend and daughter and companion, drove her to the dangerous edge of distraction. When Herman confirmed the death, she leapt up screaming, tearing at her hair, leaping around the room like a wild animal. In tears himself, Herman had to capture and hold her to prevent her from injury. She convulsed in his arms for several minutes before calming down to a menacing silence.

"I must pray" was all she said, all she could say. She pulled away from his arms and sank down beside the bed. Tears streamed down her face, and she took great swallows and gasps of air as she started in to pray for the soul of her daughter. When he saw that Marie had calmed down sufficiently, Herman left the room and went about telling the family and friends of the tragedy and making plans for the funeral, all the while dealing inwardly with his own sorrow. Before he left he told Joe, who was weeping noisily at the bottom of the stairs, to not let anyone upstairs until he returned. He decided to leave the children with the Plummers until Marie was able to deal with them.

Marie prayed for Françoise all that night, pausing only to sip water and stretch her knees. Herman kept the door to the room open, and placed candles to illuminate the body. He dozed fitfully in the next room, with the doors open between them so that he could be alert to Marie's situation. He posted Joe downstairs in the big bedroom to keep an eye open for any visitors.

Early next morning Herman awoke with a jerk from a terrible, cloud-filled dream, and realized at once that there was no sound of Marie praying. He went in to her and found her slumped on the floor, under a blanket and in a deep slumber. He was relieved to see her resting at last. It would take time to recover, but at least she would have some strength to sustain her through the ordeal of the days ahead. He picked her up and carried her downstairs to their bedroom. He put Marie into bed, closed the door and left her to sleep. Joe came out of the kitchen where he was preparing breakfast, and finally Herman had a chance to hug his son and share with him the intense sadness that would hobble the family for weeks to come.

As 1804 moved into 1805, the Eberts family slowly recovered from the loss of Françoise. It was a hard time for all of them as Dolly had been so much a part of all of their lives. The main thing that rallied them was the state of their mother. Marie had suffered a blow from which she had trouble recovering. They all had, but as time went by they realized that she needed every possible support that they could provide if she was to regain her spirits. She ate hardly anything, losing so much weight that Herman worried about her strength.

She watched Herman, Thérèse and Joe looking after the four little ones, but only occasionally involved herself in the work. For most of the time it was as if she wasn't there, that her mind was far away, outside of her body and beyond the regular cares of the day. It was in mid-January that Father Richard finally broke through to her and started the healing process.

Thérèse was talking with Marie one morning as she fed her mother some tea and bread. She had decided to be firm in an effort to break Marie out of her reverie. But when she suggested that it was time to move on, Marie burst into tears, and through her sobs revealed to Thérèse the core of her problem. "Oh Thérèse my darling, you do not know, you cannot know what I have done. I have sinned! I have sinned in the eyes of God, and he is punishing me! Oh..."

Thérèse leaned forward and took her mother by the wrists, seeking to shake her out of her fit. "How have you sinned Maman? How? What have you done? Tell me, for God's sake. Tell me!"

Marie fell quiet, and then spoke in soft, defiant tones. "I don't know, but what I do know is that I am being terribly punished. Look Thérèse, look! I have lost four children. One was a baby, two little boys, and now Françoise. The Lord has taken them from me, and why? Why would He do so? How have my sins led to this? What have I done? Is He calling me home to join my little ones?"

She renewed her sobbing while Thérèse sat back and watched her. It was a revelation to her. She knew that her mother blamed herself for the deaths, but she had not realized how deeply the sense of sin, as preached by the church, had affected her. And that last question that Marie had posed, was it a warning? Would her mother harm herself in her grief?

When Herman came home Thérèse told him about the conversation. Herman was terrified, for he simply did not know what to do. Try as he might, he could not seem to help Marie. Medicine was not the answer, nor were warm family scenes, and a good, firm talking-to had failed several times. Herman had never gone to St. Anne's Church, and was suspicious and even contemptuous of the control that the Catholic Church seemed to have over its members. But now he realized that he had run out of options. He sent Thérèse hurrying to the church to seek a private consultation for Marie with Father Richard.

Within the half hour Thérèse returned with the priest. Herman was impressed with the man's sense of devotion and of service, and welcomed him warmly. He asked Thérèse to go into the bedroom and prepare Marie to meet the priest, and then sat with Father Richard to wait. Thérèse soon emerged to say that Marie was up and prepared, seated in the bedroom as the only private place in the house. The priest rose and entered the room, and as he closed the door behind him Herman had a glimpse of Marie moving onto her knees, her hands folded in prayer.

Herman gathered the family in the kitchen so that they could be together in this time of crisis, and also to have them as far away as possible from the consultation room. Even so, as they sat silently on chairs from the dining area, young ones on the laps of older ones, they could hear occasional sounds of sobbing and the gentle murmurings of the priest. Thérèse wept, and even Joe gave up on being brave. All of them except the youngest knew that the happiness and even the future of the family were at stake in that consultation.

Finally they heard the door open. Herman left the kitchen, signaling the children to stay where they were. He met Father Richard at the front door, and for a moment they just stood there, staring at each other. Then the priest spoke.

"Dr. Eberts, your wife has not sinned. Madame Eberts is a fine woman, a pious woman, of an open and friendly spirit and dedicated to the happiness of others. I have come to know this through observing her work at the church, and receiving the comments of her many friends.

"I have assured her of this, and I believe that she has accepted my words. Yet how do we explain the cruel fate that has befallen this family, and that she has taken upon herself as a sign of God's disfavour in her? We cannot, Sir, for we cannot know what God has planned for us. He is a merciful God, and will reveal his plan for you and Madame Eberts in his own time. For now it is important that you continue to serve people and lead good lives. You will, in the end, have your reward.

"Dr. Eberts, I believe that I have convinced your wife of this truth: that she must forget her concerns of sinning and inviting God's wrath, and return to her life and continue to serve God as she has in the past. It helps nobody to continue in such a sad manner, affecting her own life, but also the spirits and the lives of her family and others who know her and love her. I know that you will help her to understand. I will call again soon to visit you, and I will help you in any way I can. Good evening Sir."

He left the house, and at the sound of the door the family came out of the kitchen and crowded as silently as they could around their father. He told them what the priest had said, and they listened carefully and with relief. He sent them to their rooms or to the kitchen to prepare dinner, and then he went into the bedroom and closed the door.

Marie was sitting in her chair, her hands in her lap. As he entered the room she looked up at him, and watched him as he came over to her, sat on the edge of the bed and gazed into her eyes. The room was silent except for the slight scuffling noise of the family moving about the house.

Slowly, quietly, a smile curled the edges of Marie's lips. Herman was mesmerized, not knowing what to do. How to respond. But she soon broke the silence.

"My darling, I am hungry."

20

FIRE! – 1805

With her spirits on the mend and the constant, loving help of her family, Marie returned slowly to health and to her active role in the family and in the community. Her friends played their roles with visits and invitations to tea. She took over the family affairs, regretting bitterly the absence of dear little Dolly, who had always been so helpful. But she learned, once again, to lock her regrets away in her heart, and to look on the bright side of things.

She did not care much about political issues, but had to admit that the news that President Thomas Jefferson had approved the establishing of the Michigan area as a separate territory, with Detroit as its capital, was exciting. William Hull was appointed as Governor, and would soon move to Detroit. One of Hull's major tasks would be to purchase land from the Indians to make way for more American settlers. The government of the new territory consisted of the Governor and four territorial judges. This would all become effective as of June 30, 1805. So Detroit was becoming more important, and there were rumours that Congress would be passing an act authorizing the territorial government to lay out a new and much larger town that included all of the old town of Detroit, based on the layout of Washington.

The wedding of Thérèse and Jean-Louis Biron was the perfect antidote to the sadness of the previous winter. As the early spring brought out the blossoms (and also the mosquitos), Marie and Thérèse planned a small wedding, one as elegant as could be arranged in tiny Detroit. The wedding ceremony was at the church, administered by Father Richard and attended by over fifty family and friends. Then it was off to Dodemead's tavern for the wedding supper. It was a wonderful occasion. Thérèse was lovely and Jean-Louis was handsome, and amusing in his happiness. Marie enjoyed herself throughout, sipping wine with evident enjoyment, and clinging proudly to her husband's arm as they greeted guests.

The happy couple then ferried across the river to Sandwich, accompanied by the Mackintoshes who took them to the newest inn for their honeymoon stay. Two days later the Birons returned to Detroit and moved into the house previously purchased by Jean-Louis. This gave Marie yet another place to visit in the town, which in the confines of Detroit was a truly positive benefit.

This enjoyable state of affairs did not, however, last long. On Tuesday, June 11 a careless bakery worker was harnessing horses in the company's barn, preparing for the usual 9am delivery run, when hot ashes from his pipe fell into a pile of dry hay. Three hours later the entire town of Detroit had disappeared in a mass of flames and smoke.

By a stroke of good luck, Herman was still at home that morning, going over some order lists with Joe before they headed out, Herman on his rounds and Joe to the store. Marie had the four little ones in the dining area, drinking juice and playing with a toy horse that Herman had brought home the previous day, a gift from a grateful patient who was a carpenter. They all turned when the front door flew open and Jean-Louis and Thérèse rushed in, followed by a stream of smoke. "Papa, Maman" cried Thérèse, "there's a fire! Just along St. Anne Street and it's coming in this direction. Quick, we must all get away!"

The young couple had some of their personal goods – papers, some utensils, some clothes – in their arms. Herman put his papers into his instrument bag while Joe rushed to help his mother and the Birons gather up some clothes and other family treasures. As they passed on the stairs, Herman asked Jean-Louis "where should we go? Do you have any sense of how the fire is moving? My God, this place is a tinder box!"

Jean-Louis called over his shoulder "it seems to be moving quickly, coming this way and spreading out. Most people are heading for the gates up and down the river, and it'll be a stampede soon! I think our best bet is to head straight down to the dock. Our company has a boat there, loading furs. If we move quickly we should be able to get to it before the crowds overrun it and any other boats there."

They left the house and plunged into a cloud of choking smoke. Herman had Phillis and Robert in his arms, and Marie had Henry and Richard clinging to her hands. They each carried small sacks of goods handed to them by their frantic mother. Joe and Thérèse followed with their arms full of bags. Marie glanced back once at the house that had sheltered them for nine years; it would soon be a pile of ashes! But there was no time for mourning. Their eyes were smarting from the smoke, and they had to brush off the hot cinders that floated down onto their clothes.

Jean-Louis took the lead and walked quickly down the streets, clogged with other citizens in similar flight, to the dock. As he had said, most of the people were heading for the gates of the town, realizing that there was little chance of escaping through the dock. His company boat, a sloop named the *Camilla,* was tied up at the far end of the dock, surrounded by bales of furs and other goods waiting to be loaded. The crew was working feverishly to load the goods, and the few people who had so far come down to the dock were still seeking out other craft. Biron led the family along to the *Camilla,* handed them on board and took them into the Captain's cabin. Marie sat down on a bench in the corner of the cramped cabin, Robert on her knee and Phillis standing beside her, clutching her skirts. The two older boys stood beside Thérèse, chirping with excitement as the smoke seeped in from outside.

Biron and the Captain agreed to try and complete the loading if they could, but to fend off as soon as safety demanded. The Captain also agreed to take on as many other people escaping the fire as the boat would hold, on the understanding that they would all be let off across the river at Sandwich. They waited for another twenty minutes while the smoke thickened, and hot ash started to rain down on the decks. Joe and Jean-Louis took buckets to douse any fire spots on the decks. Finally the goods were all on board, and the Captain waved to a number of families who had rushed onto the dock and come along to see if they could board. Ten minutes later the sloop *Camilla*, loaded to the gunwales, fended off from the dock of what had been the town of Detroit, hoisted sails and tacked across the river to Sandwich.

The dock at Sandwich was in chaos. People coming from the town and local areas to see the fire across the river mingled with the families landing from boats ferrying people escaping from the inferno. Some had managed to bring substantial bags of personal effects, and these together with the numerous children presented a complicated mass of obstacles under the feet of the struggling adults. The captain of the *Camilla* moored the craft at the northern tip of the dock, and immediately called for his passengers to alight. He was desperately keen to get away from this scene of chaos, to sail his valuable cargo out onto the lake and on its way to Montreal.

Herman and Joe helped Marie and Thérèse move the children from the suffocating cabin to the deck, and thence to the dock. Jean-Louis handed them their parcels, and then left them for a few moments while he exchanged final words with the captain. Then he leapt ashore as the sloop moved away from the dock and headed safely downstream.

With Herman holding the two babies and Marie clinging to the two youngsters, and Jean-Louis still dealing with the company sloop, Joe took the lead in moving them away from the waterfront. The dock was at the foot of Mill Street, and he led them up it to the edge of the tiny town. Jean-Louis soon followed. When they were clear of the crowds they stopped to get their bearings and rest. They sat by the side of the road, soot-covered and distraught. In a very brief period of time they had lost their home and even their entire home town, all of their furniture and food, and most of their clothes and personal things. What to do now?

That question was answered by the miraculous appearance of Angus Mackintosh, driving his company wagon down the road toward the dock to see what he could do to help. His oldest son Angus Jr. was at the reins. He pulled to a stop beside the family and Angus jumped down, bellowing his greetings. They gathered around him as he asked questions about the fire.

"It looks like a disaster to me, at least from over here. What the devil has happened?"

Herman replied. "We don't know how it started, but it was spreading quickly when we left our house. You know how dry all those houses were over there. They were so much tinder, and I fear that soon they will all be ashes. I don't see how any building can avoid those flames. There are an awful lot of people without shelter now, and probably stone broke as well, for many have lost everything. We've managed to keep enough money with us to tide us over, so we'll be fine. But it really is a terrible tragedy."

"Do you think many people have been killed?"

Herman could only guess. "There was ample time for most people to escape, but I suppose there will have been a few deaths. The big problem now will be sheltering all of the people who have lost their homes, and finding enough food to keep them alive. Hopefully the fort has been spared, as it's far enough away from the town. There aren't a lot of troops there at the moment, so that will provide some space for people. Otherwise they'll be coming over here, or just heading out into the countryside."

Mackintosh was astounded, but as the whole group turned to watch the smoke rising on the far shore, he came to his senses. Turning back to Herman, he asked where they intended to stay until they could arrange for a new home. "And don't tell me the local inns. We have very few, and they're already full and have lines of people outside hoping for rooms. I think, in fact, that all of the houses over here will have guests for a while. In fact, I would like you to come to Moy Hall and stay with us until you find a place elsewhere. Our house is full of course – you know that wife of mine keeps producing more children! But our trading post has lots of room. We'll put some pallets down, and there are washing facilities at the back, and a privy, and you can join us for meals at the house. What say you?"

Marie almost fainted with relief. She had been despairing over their prospects of having a roof over their heads. Now this wonderful man was saving them! She did not wait for Herman.

"Oh my dear, dear Angus. You and Archange are surely blessed! In the midst of this terrible tragedy we find your friendship and generosity overpowering. Yes, we will certainly accept your kind offer. Thank you. Yes."

Jean-Louis glanced quickly at Herman, surprised that Marie would take such an initiative, but Herman seemed to be perfectly happy with it, nodding his head in support. The doctor handed Phillis to Joe, and then stepped forward and shook Mackintosh firmly by the hand. Marie was not surprised to see tears in her husband's eyes as he mumbled "thank you, my dear friend", and then they moved to the wagon to load up for the short trip to Moy Hall.

21

A SANDWICH WELCOME

The Hall was not an inn, but it had a roof and a floor, and enough space in its several rooms to place pallets for the family to sleep. Marie managed the distribution of children, with Jean-Louis, Thérèse and Joe amongst them to maintain peace and order. They borrowed clothes, bedding and other necessaries from the Mackintosh family, and the older ones helped with the cooking at the house. Marie and Herman were treated royally, for Archange refused to have them sleeping on the floor in the Hall, and pushed three of her sons out of their room in the house to make way for them.

The place echoed with activity and gratitude as the two large families settled down for...how long? Nobody knew, so nobody mentioned it, and in spite of the disaster that had overtaken them they all had a great time, the families mingling delightfully. The meals were more like great feasts than simple family affairs. The kitchen at the house was a steaming, crowded, frenetic place as the mothers and older children laboured to feed the multitude.

The next day, as Marie, Archange and Thérèse managed the large brood of children at Moy Hall, Mackintosh took Herman, Jean-Louis and Joe out in the wagon to look around the area of Sandwich. The town itself was tiny, with most of the homes spread out along roads winding into the country-side. Some were on smaller lots; some were on lots of many acres. There were many signs of overcrowding in the homes, with some temporary tents in lots and unhappy children staring out at the roads. Mackintosh showed them three houses that were for sale, one of them on a large property downriver from the town centre. "If you have any intention of moving over here, now's the time to be buying" said Mackintosh, laughing at his bold-faced truism.

But that was the theme of the conversations back at Moy Hall that evening. Angus Mackintosh, in his typical forceful way, raised the obvious question as the adults enjoyed their turn at the dining table.

"Well now Doctor, and Marie, and you too Jean-Louis and Thérèse, what might be your thinking about living arrangements for the next year or two? Don't get me wrong, you're more than welcome to enjoy the comforts of the trading hall, but it may be more comfortable for you to find better accommodation before the winter sets in. Not to mention our need for some space to do some trading, of course!"

He laughed politely as he said this, and the family laughed with him. They knew that what he said was true, and they were gratified that the subject was out on the table so quickly and easily. The family had not discussed it so far, although the issue had been on their minds from the outset. So they naturally turned to Herman to start the reply.

"Angus my dear fellow, you and Archange have been our saviors, and we are most thankful to you, as we have said already several times, I am sure! And yes of course, we must start thinking about that very question. Mind you, it's not a simple question, for we really must start by asking ourselves whether we want to return to Detroit when we can, or elsewhere in the United Sates for that matter, or is it perhaps time to come back to British North America? I have some thoughts on the matter, but I would like to hear others first. Jean-Louis, how about you?"

"Ah Doctor" said Jean-Louis, "it's a good question. My Thérèse and I have enjoyed Detroit, and I think we might like to return to it when it's possible. Yes my darling?"

Thérèse nodded, but tentatively. "I suppose so, although I must say it does feel good to be here on our home soil. Well, not exactly our home soil, but at least in the Canadas. I'm sure it will take a long time for Detroit to be rebuilt. And what will happen to our property? Well, anyway, we have to wait and see."

"Quite right" said Jean-Louis. "It's too soon to be making such big decisions. I suppose that, in a way, it doesn't make too much difference from a business point of view. We're involved on both sides of the river, so we could live on either side. Mind you, if there was ever another war it would be inconvenient to be over there." He came to a stop, and Marie burst into the conversation.

"I have a view, I can tell you. We have lived safely and quite well in Detroit, but it has never seemed to be home. I still think of Quebec as home, but of course that's out of the question. And as Thérèse says, at least we are back in the Canadas. We can probably never go back to Lower Canada, but Upper Canada is just fine. Detroit will be rebuilt, and will probably be much better than it was before. But the thing that makes me feel that we should remain here is the fact that the United States is growing stronger by the day. There seem to be new territories and even states proclaimed every week. The courts and the government and the army – all are growing and becoming better organized.

"The Americans are proud of their new country, and suspicious of those who feel otherwise. I believe that we can return to Detroit if we wish, and be accepted again into the community, but there will be continuing suspicions that we are actually Loyalists, staying in the United States simply because it's good for us. Eventually that will not be acceptable. They'll see where we rushed to in the time of trouble – right back here to Upper Canada! So my answer to the question is that it's best for us to remain in Upper Canada. It's too much to say that God has given us a sign but, well, perhaps he has?"

This last comment brought on an extended silence around the table. Then, as Herman cleared his throat, Thérèse suddenly spoke up for a second time. "Oh Maman, you've said it so well. For myself, I've been thinking that we've had such a warm welcome here; would we be welcomed back with the same spirit? What would people in Detroit say when we suddenly returned from Sandwich, safe and sound while they had to clean up the mess over there? I doubt that they would be very pleased. And anyway, I do like the feeling of being here in Upper Canada. I agree Maman, it's not Quebec, but it is our people, our laws, our government. So, that's how I feel."

It was finally Herman's turn. "I have been thinking about this question constantly since we arrived over here. I have leaned towards returning to

Detroit when we can. It has been good to us, and we have so many friends over there, and excellent business prospects. But now I find that I must agree with my women. As they have said, it feels like home here. People are loyal and polite, we have the Redcoats to comfort us, and we are welcomed for who we are, not because I manage to do some good doctoring and we are acceptable company. So yes my love, my two loves, let us stay here and make a go of it as Loyalists."

Angus jumped to his feet. "Bravo my dear friends! Bravo! Come, let us drink a toast in this excellent rum to the return of the Eberts family to civilization!" And with that they drank and then sang and danced around the table, hugging and proclaiming their happiness.

The next morning it was down to business in earnest. As the extended family proceeded through its noisy morning, Herman, Angus and Jean-Louis met in the Hall's office to discuss housing. As usual Angus Mackintosh had a solution in mind.

"You remember the three houses that I pointed out as being for sale? Well, I do believe that the large one, which has around twenty-five acres of land, would be perfect for you. It's a good house – I have been there many times – and the property is good. It has one large out-building and a barn, and it's all in pretty good condition. The owners, a family named Brazeau, had to leave last fall, and it's been up for sale ever since. The papers are held by my bankers in Mill Street."

Herman was interested, but cautious. "That would be excellent, Angus, but you know I've taken quite a hit with the fire, and it will take me awhile to build up my funds again. Surely that place is expensive?"

"Not as much as you would think, my friend, for it's been empty all winter, and the owner, who is now in Montreal, is evidently keen to sell it. It would be good to buy it immediately if you are interested, before somebody has the bold idea of raising the price. As to the funds, I can assure you that my banker will have no trouble standing behind you, particularly with my encouragement. His name is Thomas Magee. He's Irish, as you can see, but he's a good fellow nevertheless. And I also think that if you, Jean-Louis, were to join in at least at the outset, your business concerns would add to our ability to finance the arrangement."

Jean-Louis replied with a broad smile. "I would be more than pleased to assist with this transaction. I assume, of course, that the house will have a room for Thérèse and me to use, at least for a while?"

Angus grinned. "Of course, my friend. There are plenty of rooms for all. Well done! So, what say you, Herman?"

Herman thought for several minutes, striding up and down the small office. Finally he turned to Angus. "Let's do it Angus. Of course, I must speak with Marie about it first."

Marie was thrilled with the idea. The location was not ideal, being down along the road to Amherstburg, a brisk walk or carriage ride away from the town centre. But to have it available now, with all of that space for the children and to grow things, and for Herman to do his business there, seemed like the godsend to which she had referred the previous evening. With her assurances ringing in his ears, Herman joined Angus and Jean-Louis and they walked to the bankers' office. By the end of the day the Eberts family was in possession of a big, well-kept house on a large, partially wooded property just south of Sandwich.

At this stage in the family's life things became truly chaotic. Herman had to press forward with his medical practice on both sides of the river. He would spend long days at Amherstburg, in and around Sandwich, and across the river in the rural areas. He was requested on occasion at the fort. John Plummer kept him apprised of the situation there, and assisted with the cases that required his attention. The Plummers had cramped quarters in the fort, with promises that the army would assist them to build a new home when Detroit was restored. There was no word of other friends including the Blacks, whom they assumed had found refuge with friends in the countryside.

Herman's trading business was totally lost in terms of inventory, as all had been destroyed in the fire. Fortunately that whole inventory of goods had been paid for, so he had no debts outstanding, but he had to work with Joe to rebuild his orders for new supplies of medicines, and to prepare the out-building on the property as his trading house.

Jean-Louis continued to pursue his business interests. He had lost little in the fire except his own small house, thanks mainly to the fortuitous timing of the departure of the sloop *Camilla* with the latest inventory of furs. But he had supplies coming in soon and shipments to organize. He would need storage space for his goods, so he pitched in eagerly with Joe to prepare the out-building to receive supplies.

This left Marie in full charge of the move to the new Eberts home. She had Thérèse to assist her, while Archange Mackintosh handled the children. She also had occasional access to the workers at Moy Hall and, through the good services of William Baker, carpenters from the naval yard at Amherstburg. This latter offer was of particular importance, as the Eberts were starting their new life in Sandwich without a stick of furniture. The naval craftsmen could turn out furniture quickly and proficiently, using well-dried wood from the navy yard, all under Baker's orders.

Marie and Thérèse took the cart from Moy Hall and one worker with them, a large, jolly man named Gabriel, and went to the house. The sight that greeted them as they stopped in front and walked into the overgrown front yard was a daunting one. The house was large and well-built, two stories high and made of dovetailed black walnut logs, and all of the windows were intact. But everything was dirty, from the front porch to the windows, and the rooms inside were the same. There was no sign of vermin in the house, but it had a dank, mouldy air to it that would clearly welcome some cleaning and airing.

The out-building was one hundred yards away down the road, accessible via the road or by a rough dirt path on the property itself. Marie did not dare to venture there as she was all but overwhelmed with the job ahead of her at the main house. In any event she knew that Joe and Jean-Louis were there; their cart was outside, and she could hear hammering. Turning to go into the house, she heard the sound of horsemen riding up the road from Amherstburg. Her heart stopped for a moment as she saw that it was a party of Indians. As the riders approached she nervously asked Gabriel what to do. He was perfectly calm. He waved to the passing riders, telling her that this was just a party of Shawnee coming from Amherstburg to see what was going on in Sandwich. The leader waved back at him, so Marie realized that they were friendly, and she said so to Gabriel.

"Oh yes Ma'am, they're fine. They don't think much of the Americans, so there are a lot of them over here, particularly down around Amherstburg. We've tried to keep on their good side, and it seems to have worked. We trade with them, of course. You'd better get used to them, as you'll be seeing lots of them from now on."

Marie then went with Gabriel into the house, and called Thérèse downstairs for a brief meeting. She instructed Gabriel to work around the outside of the house, cleaning up the garden area, mending any fences that needed it, cleaning the verandah and washing the windows on the outside. For Thérèse it was cleaning of the hardest type – scrubbing floors and walls, washing and airing closets, washing windows and swiping cobwebs out of corners. Many places needed painting or papering, but that would have to wait until they had moved in and had the time. Fortunately the water well beside the house had been protected, and the pump worked after some hard priming. The privy at the back needed cleaning, but was still usable.

She would be helping Thérèse later, but for the moment she worked with quill and ink to make a room plan for the family, which would include Thérèse and Jean-Louis for a while at least. Then she made a list of furniture they would require divided into two parts: needed immediately and longer-term needs. The only furniture that had been left in the house was a massive wood stove in the kitchen and a double bedframe in the master bedroom.

The list completed, she pitched in with Thérèse, sleeves rolled up and hair captured under a cotton hat borrowed from Archange. They went back to Moy Hall for a break at lunch, and Marie went over her plans with Archange while the children ate their meal. The plan and furniture lists agreed upon, Marie and her two helpers returned to the house to do more work.

That evening Marie went over the plans with Herman and Jean-Louis, who made a few suggestions. The next day Marie went with Thérèse in a Moy Hall carriage driven by Gabriel on the long road to Amherstburg. They went over their plans with William Baker, and left him with the agreement that he would have the 'immediate' furniture made and sent along as quickly as possible. This would bring welcome extra pay for some of his workers, who were quite prepared to continue working in the navy workshops after official closing time.

The immediate furniture arrived in three weeks' time, giving the family the chance to leave the overcrowded residence at Moy Hall. Marie had spent those weeks buying clothes, household goods and utensils, linens and foodstuffs. Some she could buy at the shops in Sandwich, although many of the shops were sadly out of stock due to the heavy demands on them from the new arrivals. Some she had to buy from friends around the town who were willing to help. Several supply ships arrived over this period, so that relieved some of the scarcities. She was welcomed at all of the shops and permitted to make her purchases on credit, for everyone knew of the fine reputation of Dr. Eberts, not to mention the added security of his businesslike son-in-law and the precious goodwill of Angus Mackintosh.

The family moved in with great excitement on the part of the children, and relief for the adults. Marie and Herman had a bedroom on the main floor, set in similar location to theirs in the smaller Detroit house, but much more spacious. The other rooms on that floor were larger as well, and more comfortable. Upstairs, Thérèse and Jean-Louis had a large room at one end of the hall that ran across the house. It had obviously been built as a separate apartment of sorts, perhaps for aged parents, for it had some closets built in along one wall, and large windows looking out over the woods. Joe had his own room at the far end of the hall, and in between there were four smaller bedrooms for the young ones: Henry (eight), Richard (six), Phillis (three) and baby Robert.

The immediate furniture had included bedframes for all, some basic tables and chairs, one closet for each room, and the dining table and chairs. There were still a lot of gaps in the furniture, and therefore a lot of goods and foodstuffs still sitting on the floor along the walls of the various rooms. There was still much to do, and Marie continued to manage the process that would, over the coming months, involve such activities as receiving and placing the 'long-term' furniture that gave the house the ability to actually offer comfort to its inhabitants; painting and repapering the rooms that needed it; sewing mattress covers to add softness to the beds; and turning the kitchen into a useful, efficient place. She also directed all work being done to fix up the exterior of the house and the surrounding garden area.

She had Thérèse and Joe to help her with these many tasks. Herman was away too much to be of any real use. Jean-Louis was totally preoccupied with his own business affairs, and fixing up the out-building to handle the family businesses. They were all able to borrow Gabriel when they needed him for heavy work, but used him sparingly as he was a valuable worker at Moy Hall.

22

GOOD TIMES, WORRYING TIMES

Marie was happy – so happy that she felt guilty. The Eberts family had come through a serious calamity unscathed, and when she looked around her at the lot of so many other people, she knew how fortunate they were. Herman told her that the situation on the other side of the river was desperate, for many of the people who had fled the fire through the gates of Detroit into the nearby countryside had not been able to find a place to settle comfortably. They had lost everything in the fire, and most of them had no money to buy their way into better conditions. They were forced to beg for their shelter and food, seeking any way they could to start rebuilding their lives. It was still the warm, pleasant summer. Heaven help them when winter arrived!

Marie worried about them, and insisted that Herman seek out the priests from the destroyed St. Anne's Church and make a substantial contribution to their welfare and, through them, the welfare of some of the impoverished parishioners. But she still was pleased in her new home. The furniture had fitted in nicely, giving all of the family the space that they needed. Even Thérèse and Jean-Louis, confined to one room on the second floor, were not complaining.

The area around the house had cropped grass and some flower beds, and a large vegetable patch at the back. Thérèse took charge of the patch, and it was soon neatly weeded and planted. Past the rough wood fences that surrounded this inner property there was a substantial field suitable for grazing horses or cattle, and then woods. After the cloying, almost claustrophobic streets of Detroit this seemed to Marie like a dream come true. Her family had light and air, space to run and play, quiet at night and, soon, fresh vegetables at their doorstep.

In front of the house was the road between Sandwich and Amherstburg. It was never crowded or noisy, but did have occasional passers-by – business people in their carts, soldiers, groups of Indians on horseback, occasional itinerants seeking a handout or a chance to work for pay. It was just enough to give the place a feel of being connected to civilization, but yet free of the inconveniences of crowded towns.

As the house rounded into shape, Marie had in her mind a short list of important items that needed attention. One was the young children. They had enjoyed the freedom that they found at first in the new house, playing in the rooms and outside, helping in their own childish ways. But now it was time to take a more concerted look at their care and keeping. The older boys were ready to start some schooling, but unfortunately there was no prospect of formal schooling as yet in Sandwich. Aside from that, she felt the need for some assistance in tending them day-to-day. She and Thérèse enjoyed taking care of them, but they had many other things to do at the house, and also assisting in the business in the out-building, and developing social networks in Sandwich and Amherstburg. Their husbands were well known and respected men, so people wanted to meet them – to visit and be visited, to entertain and be entertained.

It was not difficult to find a girl in the community interested in helping out with the children, as so many families had been displaced and were in trouble financially. She simply said a word at Moy Hall about looking for someone, and quickly had several candidates knocking on the door. She did not see any of them as suitable to live in with the family, but she found one girl, a 16 year-old named Claire Parent, who seemed intelligent enough and strong, and she engaged her to come during the days, and in the evenings when required.

Schooling was a more difficult challenge until she met an experienced teacher who had just moved to Sandwich from Quebec. The wife of a government engineer, she was pleased to have some teaching to take up her time.

The other main issue that Marie had to deal with was transportation. The house was just far enough out of the town centre that it was inconvenient to walk there for visiting or shopping, trudging along in her long skirts, shopping bag under her arm. Herman and Jean-Louis had purchased two horses from a local farmer for their business purposes, and they had a rough cart for their businesses, so they were adequately served. Joe fixed up the barn for them, and used one of the horses when available. But for Marie and Thérèse, something had to be done. She set Joe to work on the problem.

Through the good services (as usual) of Angus Mackintosh, Joe located a smallish, nicely built cart that could be painted and fixed up to serve the needs of the women, and also be useful to the businesses at the out-building as back-up transport when required. They purchased the cart from the owner, who wanted a larger model, and also bought one more horse from the farmer. The transportation issue was resolved. It was not elegant, but practical and appropriate for this rough part of the country.

Thus by the end of September of 1805, as the cool autumn winds started to blow, Marie could look with satisfaction at the new life they had been able to rescue out of the flames of Detroit. She had a thoroughly delightful house, an able assistant and a teacher for the children, businesses operating on the property, old friends nearby in Sandwich and in more distant Amherstburg, and some new neighbours and friends in the town. And to top it all off, she had acquired the new skills of horseback riding and wagon driving.

She was also grateful for the personal benefits that had come from their move from Detroit. She loved having Thérèse back under the family roof. Jean-Louis was also a positive addition to the household. Joe was busy around the yard, cleaning and pruning and planting, employed part time at Moy Hall, and providing Marie with a strong arm when she needed help. He would occasionally go down to Amherstburg where he maintained his friendship with Ann Baker.

Most important of all was the change in Herman – in his status, and in his demeanor. In a poetic sense, the flames of Detroit had swept away the clouds that had hovered over his life there. No longer was he under suspicion as a possible Loyalist still living in the new United States. The sense that he had been a rather objectionable official, and therefore suspect as a person, had disappeared. Now he was back in British North America, admired for his loyalty to the Crown. The military establishment at Amherstburg welcomed him as a fine medical practitioner and a gentleman, as did the people of Sandwich. His growing store of medicines and medications was invaluable. He and his charming wife were welcome guests in many of the homes at Sandwich and the surrounding area.

So he was happy, and showed it in his affection for his active household and his love for Marie. The large bedstead in their bedroom, with its soft, hay-filled mattress, had its goodly share of activity, but with one change from former times. Marie had told Herman that at forty years of age she did not wish to have any more children. He had agreed, and from then on their lovemaking was well enough spaced that their agreement was successfully implemented.

This happy state of affairs flourished in an environment that was ostensibly peaceful, but wherein there were hints of troubles to come. Since Britain had declared war on France at the start of Napoleon's conquests back in 1803, the authorities in British North America had been concerned about the effects these events in Europe might have on relations with the United States. There were grievances on both sides.

The Americans were annoyed over the British policy of refusing to let ships of neutral countries (such as the USA) enter ports of French-dominated Europe, searching them on the high seas for contraband and deserters, and impressments of American seamen. They also disliked Britain's practice of inciting American Indians to attack U.S. settlements on the western frontier.

Britain feared the American desire to gain territory by invading and annexing the BNA colonies. British spies reported that there was a feeling in the United States that control of the entire North American continent was their 'manifest destiny'. They actually felt that if they were to invade, Canadian colonists would rise up and support them as liberators.

The authorities in the British colonies knew that they needed more troops to defend BNA properly, but that British armies were fully engaged in Europe. With little help forthcoming from that side, they pushed to increase the local forces in BNA itself – outfits like Ignace's Fencibles in New Brunswick, and militias in other parts of the colonies.

The Americans were constantly seeking to lure men to desert to the USA, a serious problem for the British. The problem was reported by Colonel Isaac Brock early in 1806 when he was temporarily in command of the entire British army in BNA. Brock felt that Quebec City should be the concentrated centre of defense of BNA. In December the 10th Royal Veteran Battalion was formed for service in BNA. It had ten companies totaling six hundred and fifty rank and file coming from re-enlistments and volunteers from other battalions.

Thus while there was still a free flow of people and goods across the Detroit River, there was a slowly-growing sense on both sides that, perhaps soon, things might not be so friendly. William Baker told the family in the spring of 1807 that they were building vessels at a furious pace at the Amherstburg naval yard. "Our commanders feel that if (perhaps I must say 'when') war breaks out with the United States, control of the lakes will be the key factor. If we control the water, we can control the land. So we are ordered to build as many warships as we can. Our friend Mackintosh is turning out some good vessels at his yard at Walkerville, and they might be useful as supply ships and transport. But there's nothing like decks full of cannon to keep things on an even keel...so to speak."

"Of course" said Jean-Louis, "that is clear. Without roads, it's ships that will win the day. But William, a question. I hear that Fort Amherstburg is being called Fort Malden now. Is that so?"

"It is" replied Baker, putting down his cup so that he could wave his hands as he spoke. "The fort is in Malden Township, so the name has evolved quite naturally. It's quite useful, in fact, as it separates the fort from the town of Amherstburg in conversation and written materials. And speaking of written materials, what's the latest news from Detroit? I hear that Governor Hull is working on a grand plan for the rebuilding of the town. Perhaps it will eventually look like Washington itself! I hesitate to go over there now. Herman, what have you heard about this?"

Herman said that the townsite that was Detroit was still a wasteland. Army work parties had joined groups of citizens to clear the wreckage from the fire, and there were surveyors starting to lay out streets along a new design, but he did not have details. "It's a hard business, I can tell you.

There are so many people still in serious trouble, without proper shelter or even means to feed themselves. I have lots to do in and around the townsite, but there are few fees to be earned from those wretched people. The fort is the only reliable source of income for me on that side of the river. Oh and incidentally, John Plummer sends his regards to you, William. He's soldiering on, living with Rita in a stuffy little room in the fort."

"Poor Rita" said Marie. "She had such a nice house, and now to be penned in at the fort – what a difficult time for her! Herman has told me that she's doing some nursing now, helping with some of John's cases at the fort and in the homes nearby. I wonder if she will ever have a real home again, at least for a long time to come."

Herman said that the Governor was considering a plan whereby owners of properties in Detroit before the fire would, when the new plan had been laid out, be offered lots to build on. Fortunately the town property records had been saved from the fire, so this approach would be possible. "So if John and Rita can stay there for a while, they will have a lot and can rebuild. I certainly hope that they do, as John is a wonderful source of information on what the Americans are thinking."

1807 was an interesting year for the Eberts in terms of family activities. The occasional letters from Ignace told of heavy training and progress for him to the rank of Corporal. Marie no longer bothered to share his letters with Herman, but Thérèse and Joe were pleased to hear of him. But she had bad news from Boucherville: her mother Judith Huc died in February. Yvette broke the news to her.

Montreal *February 23, 1807*

Dearest Marie

It is so sad to have to tell you that your dear Maman died on Monday. She had taken to her bed the previous week, but I don't think she was ill. Her life had just run its course. She was tired and needed to rest. Your father was with her at the end.

I saw her when my Maman and I visited just two days before she died. She was very subdued, but not unhappy. She spoke fondly of you and your family, saying that your successes in Detroit were a great comfort to her. Josie held her hand and was very brave. Braver than I was, I'm afraid. I do miss her. She was such a dear woman!

So Uncle Gregoire is on his own now. He is still involved in the business, so there is some income coming in for him. He wants to stay on in the house, and has taken on a woman to do some cooking and cleaning for him. He says that he will write to you soon, but I doubt it.

I hope that all is well with you…

Marie and her family mourned for Judith, and she sought out the priest over on the Detroit side to say prayers for her soul. She longed to travel back to Boucherville to comfort her father, but knew that it was just not feasible.

Starting that spring Thérèse and Jean-Louis showed signs of restlessness being confined to one room in the Eberts house. Large and comfortable as it was, it was no real substitute for the home that they had owned in Detroit. Sandwich's growing population needed everything, so Jean-Louis' trading business was flourishing, and he could afford to take action. In the early summer he agreed with Herman that they would carve a lot out of the large Eberts property, and build their own house there. As they felt that they might well want to return to Detroit in the future they built a small, one-storey cottage, completed before the first snows fell in November.

Joe, now an experienced twenty-two year-old, also wanted to leave the family home. On his occasional trips to Amherstburg he found increasing enjoyment in visits with the Baker family. His friendship with Ann flourished, but had not yet flowered into romance. He was a cautious man, and wanted to have his own home and income before he took on the responsibilities of marriage. He had worked for Angus off and on for several years now. In June he asked Angus two things: might he have permanent employment with the Northwest Company, and might he buy (over time) the small cottage situated on lot ninety-three at Moy Hall. Mackintosh agreed on both counts, and immediately appointed Joe in charge of the company's Wabash and Indiana district. After some tidying up and painting, Joe moved into his cottage in late August. He started in on his work for the company, which was more demanding than he had imagined, and took him away on long trips through his district. He had very little time for visits to Amherstburg.

Aside from these moves, and the happy state of her new home, Marie always had at the back of her mind the changing political situation. She knew that there continued to be bad feelings between Britain and the United States. With his good connections at the forts on both sides of the river, Herman was able to keep up-to-date with the various movements and concerns and decisions that defined the situation. But it was complicated, and she generally preferred to fall back on the notion that the people living on the two sides of the river were good friends and even, in some cases, relatives. Surely they would be spared the unpleasantries of international turmoil.

This thought was laid to rest one chilly evening that fall when William and Effie Baker came to the Eberts house for dinner. Thérèse and Jean-Louis joined the table, and the conversation soon turned to the strategic issues that overlaid the seemingly peaceful scene. The spark was William's remark that he had not been able to visit recently, as work on new warships had reached a fever pitch at Amherstburg.

"We've laid out the townsite up the Thames that will be called Chatham, but the boatbuilding is going slowly there. Our resources are by no means unlimited, so our main focus has to be Amherstburg. We know that the Americans are busy building their own ships, and we must keep ahead of them!"

He paused to sip his wine, and Jean-Louis interjected. "Yes of course, William. We both, the Americans and ourselves know how important the lakes are. But can you give us some information on the general state of things? Why does the tension between our two countries seem to be rising so steadily?"

William put down his glass and sat back. "You are of course aware of the general state of affairs in Europe. Napoleon is rampant, and we must do everything we can to defeat him. One of those things is blockading his ports, and that angers our American friends who like to trade with the French. We are also blocking shipping into and out of American ports on the pretense that we are protecting the United States from the French. And related to that, our ships seem to enjoy boarding American ships to look for trade goods that we call 'illicit' or 'illegal', and for deserters who have gone over to the Americans. This used to be quite easy to do, but the Americans are now producing some very fine warships, many of them large and powerful frigates, so the balance of power on the seas is starting to shift. Have you heard about the incident between the *Leopard* and the *Chesapeake* in June?"

"We've heard that there was an incident" said Marie, "but tell us."

"It was part of the British attempting to stop its seamen from deserting to the American side. Keep in mind that the two countries are not yet at war, at least technically. But off the coast at Norfolk, Virginia the British Frigate *HMS Leopard* took a warlike step. It requested permission of the American frigate *USS Chesapeake* to board in search of British deserters. The *Chesapeake* commander, Commodore James Barron refused, and the *Leopard* opened fire with broadsides! The *Chesapeake* had its decks covered with freight in preparation for a long voyage, and couldn't return fire, so had to surrender. The British boarded and took away several deserters. They were later tried, and at least some were hanged.

"Needless to say this has infuriated the Americans. It was an act of war without war having been declared! Many are demanding that they declare war, but President Jefferson is taking a calmer approach. For one thing, this has accelerated the shipbuilding program in the country. They're turning out many more ships like the *Chesapeake*. I believe that in time they will actually challenge the British fleet, at least in American waters."

Marie felt, as she had so often in the past, the spectre of war hovering over them like a dirty cloud. She could scarcely contain herself. "So now we have war without war! Is that it William? Do you think this sort of 'incident', as it seems to be called, will happen again and again? Are we doomed to have another war, or will it just be unexpected and unpleasant incidents? Will our friends over on the Detroit side send gunships over to set fire to our houses?"

Herman broke in, as much to settle Marie down as to purse the conversation. "I think it's a good question, my dear. If there is not a major fire, then perhaps we will have a series of damaging little campfires! Well, let me add something to what William has said. John Plummer has told me that the Americans at the fort were scandalized when they heard the news. They are perplexed that, with such a huge land mass to tame and settle, and to fight over with other claimants, many major issues will be settled offshore in ships, not on the land! We do of course have our grisly little skirmishes in the woods, but the British navy is still our glory and our protector! But William, I have another question for you...after you have had a good quaff of your wine, of course."

He refilled all of the glasses while the table resettled itself with small comments and asides. Then Herman returned to his question. "Now then, William, we've heard that the Indians have made certain overtures to our side down at Amherstburg. We've been fortunate to have them on our side until now. What seems to be happening?"

William shifted in his chair, less comfortable with this question than dealing with naval matters. "As I understand it, the Indians in this northwestern part of the United States continue to be unhappy with their situation. They're being hemmed in by the American settlers, and have been forced to sell much of their land in order to survive. Some of them have even taken on a sort of religion that preaches that the great spirits will help them free up their lands, but of course, that's just superstition.

"The name that keeps coming up as a leader is the Shawnee 'Tecumseh'. He was at Fallen Timbers, and has appeared all over the place, seeking to have all the tribes join in an alliance powerful enough to reclaim their place in the land. But at the same time he seeks peaceful means of achieving his ends. This appears to mean that they are not yet ready for war.

"Our authorities consider the Indians still to be allies. For one thing, the disputed lands are below the lakes, and for another, having the Indians friendly allies on our side keeps the Americans on edge. As it should, for they are good fighting allies, and terrible foes to deal with in the forests. As I understand it, we're taking steps to strengthen our alliance with them. The Indian Department is recruiting the friendship of the various tribes. The feeling is that if we don't ensure that they remain with us, we might find ourselves fighting them in the future."

"You mention 'the feeling' William" said Herman. "At the more general level, what is the feeling at Fort Malden about our chances should war break out with the Americans?"

Baker was even more hesitant to answer, but could not escape. "I would have to say that the conventional wisdom at the fort is that Canada would fall quickly in the event of an invasion. We're doing the best we can to strengthen our forces and our fleet to give us a fighting chance, but our senior people are not optimistic."

This last comment left the table in silence except for the sounds of wine being sipped. Thérèse left the table for the kitchen, where dinner was bubbling on the stove. Marie followed, and they heard the conversation turn away to a subject only slightly less grim, namely the state of the former citizens of Detroit, still settled uneasily in the areas surrounding the townsite.

23

DARK CLOUDS – 1808

Through the winter and into the warm summer of 1808 the young children flourished. Henry was a strong young man, now eleven years old. He was steady at his lessons and his reading, and was a great help around the house. Richard was quite different. At nine years of age he was still short and slim, but strong and wiry. He had a quick, almost mercurial intelligence, moving through his lessons in a way that the teacher described as "almost as if he has already learned them, and is just refreshing". Like all the children he was perfectly fluent in English and French, but he was also learning several of the Indian languages. He seemed to absorb them through his skin when he heard them, never hesitating to approach Indians riding by or in the town for a bit of conversation. He was a good athlete, fast on his feet and already an excellent rider.

And then there were the young ones – sweet little Phillis and four year-old Robert. They played together, roaring around the house and the yard outside, and even talked Henry into helping them to build a secret house in the woods, a lean-to made of branches with an evergreen bough roof.

Herman and Jean-Louis pursued their professional and business interests with great success. Thérèse loved her small house, and decorated it with good taste. Marie liked to visit her for tea and chats, and Thérèse would return the visits for the same, plus joyful romps with her young siblings.

Joe's work under Angus Mackintosh prospered, and happily it took him on occasion to Amherstburg. He said nothing to Marie, but Effie Baker reported to her that Joe's friendship with Ann had finally evolved into something closer and more intimate. He had started to court her, in fact. Joseph was hardly a romantic, but Effie could tell from the tone of their talking, their laughing together and the lengths of their walks along the wooded roads of Amherstburg, that something was up.

"And about time too, wouldn't you agree Marie?" said Effie over tea and scones. She laughed as she said it, and Marie joined in happily.

"I should say so. My goodness, Joe is certainly slower than his father in the matter of love. Herman, you know, was courting me just a few months after we first met. Joe seems to take forever to make up his mind. Or perhaps he made up his mind some time ago, but is just slow in acting. I don't think he's shy. Do you?"

Across the river, Detroit was slowly recovering from the 1805 fire. The new town plan was not the grand design that had been proposed to copy Washington. It was similar in size to the town before the fire, but at least it was done, and rebuilding could begin. During the summer of 1808 the Governor and judges in Detroit distributed lots among the citizens who had lived in the town before the fire. The Eberts and Biron families both took title to their lots, even though neither had plans to build any time soon.

But the political tensions between the two sides continued to fester and grow. From his visits to Amherstburg Herman learned that Tecumseh had come to Fort Malden in June to meet with British officials. He had told them that he was working on developing a grand alliance of tribes to defend their lands. His forcefulness was bolstered by faith in the 'millinarian' religion preached by his brother, the prophet Tenskwatawa. The Great Spirit would intervene to save the native people from their white oppressors. Tecumseh had said that the Indians did not wish to be involved in a war between the two nations, but if called upon they would stand by their friend, the King.

Herman also learned that General Isaac Brock, acting commander of British military forces in British North America, was pushing the administration in Lower Canada to call out sufficient militia to repair the crumbling defenses of Quebec, and to train for an emergency. The response was slow, as it often was in dealing with militia. It did, however, show that the senior military was concerned about the situation. Counting on the militia had its risks, for they were not generally well-trained as combatants, and tended to slip away home when the crops needed tending. There was also some concern about the Loyalists who had come to BNA from the United States. By coming to the colonies they had shown their loyalty to Britain, but many of them had tasted the spirit of freedom and equality that was prevalent in the new country. Would they continue to be loyal under the more rigid discipline of the British administration?

The war in Europe was dragging on, so they could not expect many reinforcements from Britain. It was some consolation, however, that spies in Washington were reporting that the American army was at low ebb. The people were tired of war, being more interested in building their vast new nation.

Herman found in his discussions with John Plummer that the concerns on the American side mirrored those in BNA. The American army was not strong, and much of the country's security depended on militias raised in the states. Some of them were good fighters, but they were subject to the same problems as in BNA – drawn to their domestic problems such as harvesting crops at times that were often inconvenient from a military perspective.

The Americans were particularly concerned about the continuing relationship between the British and the Indians. They knew that the Indians wished to hold onto their lands, but also that they, the Americans, must continue to purchase land to make way for their settlers. Tecumseh and other Indian leaders stood in the way of their progress, and having the British supporting those efforts was intolerable. The Americans were still formally at peace with the Indians, but how well that peace would hold was anybody's guess.

1809 came in gently and passed relatively quietly. The rebuilding of Detroit proceeded, and Sandwich prospered. On the political front, the Americans celebrated the inauguration in March of James Madison as their new President. They continued to be angered by British actions on the high seas and with the Indians, but also to be frustrated by their inability to fund a substantial army.

There was little change in the family situation, except for the happy occasion of Joe's engagement to Ann Baker, and the sad news of the death of Marie's father Gregoire Huc. Not long before she received the news from Yvette back in Montreal, Marie had actually received a note from Gregoire. It had been more of a scrawl than a letter, and Marie had longed to return to Boucherville to nurse him. Now Yvette said in her letter that Marie should consider coming back at some point to help sort out the family affairs. By the time there had been several exchanges of correspondence on the subject it was early 1810, and Marie knew that she had to take action.

She prayed that the current peaceful conditions would continue. They did in that no war was declared, but it was clear on all fronts that war could not be far off. Lieutenant General Isaac Brock, the big man with the reputation for strong leadership, was placed in charge of all forces in Upper Canada. His priorities were strengthening defenses and training troops and militia. The American preoccupation with British support for the Indians gained strength. General William Henry Harrison, Governor of the Indiana Territory, authorized further purchases of Indian lands. Tecumseh met with him to warn him that this was not acceptable to the Indian confederacy, but no agreements were reached.

Tecumseh then came to Fort Malden in November and said that he was now ready to go to war with the Americans. This was not what the British wanted at that time, for if the Indians acted precipitately it might force the Americans to launch an attack on BNA, and the British were not ready for it. They urged patience.

24

HOME LEAVE – 1810

Marie's home front continued throughout 1810 in a positive manner, but she missed half of it. On July 24 Joe married Ann Baker at the family home in Sandwich. The two mothers chuckled as they agreed once again that it was about time!

In mid-August Marie took ship for Boucherville. She had sent a letter to Yvette telling her when she expected to arrive at her old home, and she hoped that her cousin would be there and prepared to help out. She looked forward to seeing Aunt Josie.

The trip took three weeks, drawn out by annoying delays at Niagara. In early September she stepped onto the dock near Boucherville where, to her delight, Yvette was awaiting her. After embraces and kisses, and exchanges about each other's families, Marie asked "how on earth did you know to meet me here today?"

"Ah my darling Marie, it was simple. From your letter I was able to tell Maman when you would likely be arriving, and she found out, somehow, about the lake arrivals over the two-week period that ends four days from now. Josie has so many contacts, you know, and I never question her about them. I just put in the questions, and out pop the answers after a brief period of 'sounding out with friends'. So, yours is the third ship I have met over the past five days. Not too bad, I would say!"

Yvette took Marie to the old family home in her carriage. As they approached the house, Marie asked her to stop for a moment so that she could gaze at the place that had been her home during her childhood. Fond memories flooded her mind. She could almost hear Gregoire's rough voice calling her out to help him with the roses; her mother's more gentle voice coaxing her through the intricacies of baking bread. The yard was well kept – obviously Yvette had employed a gardener to keep it presentable. What a joy it was to have a cousin like Yvette! She was so thoughtful; so helpful during the long absence at Detroit; so loving and friendly, softening the hard edges of Marie's visit.

Little had changed in the house. The relatives had put sheets over most of the furniture so it was protected from the dust that hung in the air and coated the floor. The two women wandered around the house, reminiscing over family scenes: celebrations, victories and problems, fun and contentment. The spirits of Gregoire and Judith lingered in the air, resting in the rooms, bringing occasional tears of laughter or of sadness.

Yvette had come in a few days previously and cleaned and aired the kitchen and one bedroom. She had also put some food supplies in the larder. "Francois and I would love you to stay with us, Marie, but I know that you would prefer to settle in here. So at least it's livable, and of course will be more so with a bit more work."

"Oh Yvette, you are such a treasure. Thank you. Yes, I would prefer to be here as I plan to go to work at once, so that I can return to Sandwich as quickly as possible. Now then, may I offer you a cup of tea?"

Over tea, Yvette said that she was free to help out in any way Marie should wish. Francois could help with the legal issues. Marie should not hesitate to ask. They loved having her home, and wanted to see as much of her as possible during her stay. Marie thanked her, and asked after Aunt Josie.

"She's fine but, well, not the Josie you will remember. I'm afraid that ever since Papa died three years ago she's lost most of her energy, so she seldom leaves the house. She still eats well, but seldom leaves her chair except to retire to bed. She can't wait to see you. Perhaps you can come with me later today for a visit? And she will want you to stay for dinner, of course."

Marie set to work, learning first-hand the complexities of settling a family's affairs. Gregoire had sold half of his company to his main helper, who wished to carry on the business. He tried to force Marie out, and there were some legal disputes that she had to deal with. Yvette's husband was great support in the dealings, helping her to instruct her lawyer, and advising her based on his sound business sense.

Then there was the house and all of the personal effects of her parents. Gregoire had not sold off any of Judith's clothes or other things such as books and china, so with help from Yvette, Marie was introduced once again to selling goods in markets. And then she had to sell the house. Fortunately it was in good shape and the market was strong, and it sold quite quickly. But everything seemed to take time with the work, the sales and the frequent and enjoyable visits with old friends. Soon, Marie found herself stoking fires against the chill of the winter of 1810/11.

Her visits with Aunt Josie were troubling, yet rewarding. Josie was not, as Yvette had forewarned, as Marie remembered her. She sat quietly and listened more than speaking, which was unheard of. But when she did speak she showed that the old sparkle was still there – the intelligence, the insights, the understanding. Marie tried to visit her at least once a week, and they had a fine time during Marie's stay over Christmas.

One event during the visit to Boucherville came as a stunning, emotional surprise. Aside from the necessary work of settling the family affairs, it made the trip supremely worthwhile.

On a bright, chilly Tuesday in October, Marie was in her parents' old bedroom sorting through Judith's clothes when she thought she heard a horseman approaching the house. Sure enough, there was a knock on the front door. She opened it and faced a tall soldier, a Redcoat. He looked thin and tough, a man who had seen heavy training, and perhaps war. He was smiling at her, and he was beautifully familiar.

Marie gasped, screamed, and fell into the arms of her first-born son Ignace.

"Why do we weep so much when we are so happy?" Ignace was sitting next to his mother, who was busily mopping her tear-stained face. He had already dried his face, and sat clutching his mother's other hand. "Oh Maman, it's so wonderful to see you again after all these years!"

Marie glowed. "Ignace my darling son, you're here! How? How did you know that I would be here? Does the army know that you are here with me? Oh, you're not deserting, are you?"

"Maman, of course not! No, I am not a deserter. After all, I am a Sergeant! How could I? No, as you probably know I've kept in touch with Yvette. When you told her about your visit she let me know, and I was able to negotiate this visit to Montreal. I've come bringing some messages from my commander to the bigwigs in Montreal. I'm not a regular messenger, of course, but my Lieutenant let me come when I told him about you and our family. I have just this one day here, from now until tomorrow noon, but it's wonderful, isn't it?"

And so it was. From that moment until noon the following day they talked non-stop, eating as necessary, snoozing in front of the fire when unavoidable. Yvette joined them for tea late in the afternoon, sharing Marie's joy for a noisy hour. She commented on Ignace's red coated uniform, and he told them that his Fencible unit had recently been upgraded by the army to a regiment of the line, renamed the 104th Regiment of Foot. So he was officially a Redcoat.

This prompted the obvious question from Yvette: "why have they done that?"

"Because our leaders believe that we will soon be at war with the United States, with all of the complexities with France, and our navy annoying them so much. We believe that the Americans will soon have had enough of it, and will decide to take British North America and say good-bye to the British."

"Oh dear" said Marie, unable to contain herself. "Another war! Oh, of course I know about it, Ignace. It seems to be all we talk about back at Sandwich. When will the Americans attack? How can we stop them?" Her tears started to fall, tears of anger.

Yvette came to her rescue. "Come now, Marie. You know how it is. There's so much at stake here in North America. We are, after all, fighting over who will own this great continent! So Ignace is part of a great cause, and you must be proud of him."

"Oh, I am" said Marie, chastened by her cousin's comment, and by the unhappy thought that her son had in fact been training for war for several years, and seemed quite happy with it. "All I can say is I hate war and what it does to us. I'm proud of you, Ignace, for the service you are giving our country, but at the same time I fear for you, for your safety, for your life. And for the lives of your father, and all of my children! War seems to dominate our lives no matter where we live!"

There was no answer to this, and they sat in silence for a while before Yvette rose and took her leave, and Ignace picked up the conversation again in safer territory.

Marie saw Ignace off next morning, dry-eyed and happy. She would cherish his brief visit in her heart forever. Then it was back to work, slowed for a while by winter weather. By the time it was all completed to her satisfaction it was late March of 1811. She said her goodbyes, and took ship back to Sandwich in mid-April.

On her arrival at Sandwich she was greeted by a family gathering that warmed her heart. They all turned out at the dock to greet her ship. There were great hugs and kisses all around, including from Joe's new wife Ann, who was heavily pregnant. They went home for a wonderful great dinner, with little Phillis and Richard proudly helping in the kitchen.

The family was excited to hear about Ignace, and their own news was all good.

Ann Eberts produced her first child, William Duncan Eberts, at Moy Hall on July 17, 1811. After the joyful event had been celebrated, Marie came home and looked at herself in her mirror. Looking back at her was a forty-six year-old grandmother!

On the political side of life, 1811 was seeing a slow but sure escalation in tensions.

In June General Brock was promoted to Major General, and in October he was sent to Upper Canada as Senior Officer Commander of the Troops and Senior Member of the Upper Canada Executive Council, putting him in charge of both the military and civil authorities. As Upper Canada's administrator, Brock made a series of changes designed to help Canada in the event of a war. He amended the Militia Act, allowing the use of all available volunteers, and ordered enhanced training of these raw recruits. He continued strengthening and reinforcing defenses, and began seeking out Indian leaders such as Tecumseh to see if they would ally with him against the Americans in the event of war.

Tecumseh's confederacy was attacked by the Americans late in the year, and the outcome of the fight ensured that the Indians would support the British when war broke out. As tensions and violence between the Indians and the Americans increased, Indiana Governor Harrison marched with an army of about 1,000 men to disperse the confederacy's headquarters at Prophetstown, near the confluence of the and Tippecanoe and Wabash Rivers.

The Battle of Tippecanoe was fought on November 7, 1811. Tecumseh, not yet ready to oppose the United States by force, was away recruiting allies when Harrison's army arrived. Tecumseh's brother Tenskwatawa, a spiritual leader but not a military man, was in charge. Harrison camped near Prophetstown on November 6 and arranged to meet with Tenskwatawa the following day. Early the next morning, warriors from Prophetstown attacked Harrison's army. Although the outnumbered attackers took Harrison's army by surprise, Harrison and his men stood their ground for more than two hours. The natives were ultimately repulsed when their ammunition ran low. After the battle they abandoned Prophetstown. Harrison's men burned the town and returned home.

When Tecumseh returned to Prophetstown and found the scene of carnage, he began preparations for the war that surely would come. News of the battle quickly reached Detroit, and caused near-panic. They felt isolated and, now that there were actually hostilities with the Indians, vulnerable to attack.

25

WAR – 1812

"It would be an amusing spectacle if it weren't so dangerous" said Herman, sipping his tea in front of the fire where he and Marie were enjoying a quiet afternoon in early February of 1812. "I tell you, my dear, it's like two fighters, both seriously underweight and in no condition to fight, strutting around each other, insulting each other and daring the other to come and be thrashed."

Marie was amazed. "But Herman, what a strange way to describe our two great countries! I do realize that our forces are not large or robust, but what exactly do you mean?"

"Well now, let's take our side first. You know, there are still many British, even some in high places, who believe that the United States will not last long as an independent country. They see the American insistence on independent thought and deed, on fully democratic government and free speech, as weaknesses that will soon catch up to them, and they will long for the more ordered system that we have under British rule. So we keep the pressure on them. Our navy keeps harassing their shipping, quite unfairly and even illegally. And of course we continue to bait the Indians to upset the American drive for control of these vast spaces. Yet British troop strength over here is very weak, and our leaders are forced to cobble together militias of ordinary citizens just to protect our land, much less attack. If it weren't for the Indians supporting us, I doubt that we could hold out for a day against any sort of American invasion."

"Oh dear" said Marie. "What a dreadful thought!"

"Yes it is" replied Herman, "but then look at the Americans. Their hawkish citizens are urging that they invade us, but you know, I'm told that their army numbers no more than four thousand troops! That's fewer that our Redcoats! Their congress has approved increasing the army tenfold, but they'll have a devil of a time raising that number. They have to get everyone to agree to it, and in the states there are many who don't agree. They're too busy building their own communities, and anyway, they have their local militia." He laughed, and leaned forward towards the fire. "Can't you see it darling? Our militia made of farmers and fishermen battling their militia made of the same material? They'll fight for a few hours, and then break off by mutual consent and head home to milk the cows!"

Marie laughed at that. She had seen some of the local militia, the Essex Militia, drilling in a field near Sandwich, and it was not a sight to fill the soul with confidence.

"But surely the leadership on both sides will set things right? I understand that General Brock is a very strong man, and he won't let us down."

Herman nodded. "I do agree with you on that score. Yes, he is a strong fellow. I attended a meeting at Fort Malden last month where he presided, and I must say it was impressive. He's a big man, and he speaks forcefully. And he certainly is loyal. The rumour is that last year he asked for permission to return to England, but when that permission came through recently he turned it down. I take it he sees it as his duty to defend Canada. I also understand that his idea of defending Canada includes attacking into the United States when necessary, and that Governor-General Prevost doesn't agree. He feels that our emphasis should be on defense, not attack, and should be focused in Lower Canada. In other words, we will probably have to give up Upper Canada, but let's at least hang onto Lower Canada. You can imagine how Brock feels about that!"

Marie had to agree, and asked about the Americans.

"I mentioned the agreement to increase the size of the regular army. Well, I've just learned that the army in this Northwest Region has been placed under the command of Governor Hull. Plummer told me, in strictest confidence of course, that the rumour is that Hull believes that we on this side of the river would welcome the Americans should they venture over here. After all, many of us have spent much of our lives on the American side. I have to believe that he is mistaken, but there you have it."

Marie sat back and smiled. "Well I now see what you meant about the two underweight fighters. Goodness what a strange situation! But Herman, to be practical, whatever happens will affect us here. What do you think we should be doing?"

This question set Herman back in his chair. After a pause he looked at Marie with a worried look on his face. "Yes my love, I have thought hard about that very question. First of all, I don't believe that we'll give up without a fight, no matter what the Governor says. We do, after all, have some troops here at Fort Malden, and over at Fort George, and elsewhere, and some more will surely come in time. We do also have some militia already raised and training, and the authorities are making strenuous efforts to increase their numbers. And then of course we have the Indians. That's on land. We must also remember that our navy controls the lakes, so our forces can be much more mobile that theirs. This balance of power on the lakes is a serious matter, as you can imagine.

"I think that Brock is a strong leader, and probably a good military strategist as well. On the other hand I've heard contradictory stories about General Hull. He is rumoured to be indecisive. So all in all, I'm inclined to be optimistic about our chances to do well in a scuffle with the Americans. Of course they have the potential to throw great numbers of troops at us, but they have to raise them and train them first, and that will be difficult.

"So then, you've asked me what we should be doing. That brings the issue down from the high level issues to what we should do to protect our own property, and serve our country as well." He paused, gazing into the fire. "I believe that we should keep our home well stocked with food, some of it well hidden, and we should have horses sufficient to give us mobility should we need it. Indeed, I've already asked Henry to see if he can find two more horses that we might purchase. As to serving the country, I believe that we men of the family should, in fact must volunteer our services."

Marie sat up straight, her face a mask of concern – the familiar face of a mother whose family is threatened. "Herman, what are you saying? You're all so busy and needed here. Surely you don't mean..."

As her words trailed off, Herman leaned toward her, placing his hand gently on her arm. "Yes dear, I do. We can't sit here, going about our business, while our friends and neighbours are doing the fighting on our behalf. This place has been good to us. It's our duty to help defend it. So yes, I do believe that we must do what we can. I intend to have Joe join the militia that is being formed here – the Essex Militia. And I'll suggest to Jean-Louis that he do the same. As for me, I'll be going to Amherstburg in a few days, and I intend to inquire at the fort as to whether they might have need of my services. I'm rather old to be joining the army, but I know that they will need me."

Marie stared at him. "And Henry? He will be fifteen in August. Surely that is too young!"

Herman was uncertain, but decided to speak firmly. "Oh yes, he certainly is. As is Richard. Yes, we'll still have our four youngest with us, no matter what happens."

Marie pulled her arm out of his grasp, but then leaned forward with a brave smile on her face. "Of course, my love. Of course. We will do it, and we will see it through. And who knows, there might not even be any fighting!"

Jean-Louis joined the Essex Militia not long after that conversation. He went to the recruitment office in Sandwich, and within two days he was out in the local field, starting his training. Joe was away at the time, travelling down in the Indiana Territory. When he returned he told his family that the conditions for his doing business down there were deteriorating quickly as anger against the British grew, so it was timely for him to follow Jean-Louis into the militia. Angus Mackintosh had no objections. He knew what war meant, and that every man counted. But he insisted that when Joe was not training he would be needed at Moy Hall. They had to prepare for war as well.

Young Henry pestered his father to let him at least try to sign up, but Herman would have none of it. He told the boy that he was needed at home to support his mother, as was his brother Richard. Henry was mollified, but only just, and whenever he could he stole away to watch the militia training.

Herman spoke about his own situation with William Baker at Fort Malden, and William brought him to the Commandant, Lt. Colonel Thomas Bligh St. George. Herman knew the Commandant, but was surprised to find General Brock also there. Brock said that he was pleased to meet the doctor. He had heard much about him, and knew that surgical skills of his high level would be most welcome should war break out.

Thinking about it for a moment, Brock then invited Herman to join his personal staff as surgeon and medical advisor. He would be commissioned in the army as Major, and hopefully would be prepared to move around with the General to ensure that medical service was always near at hand for the senior officers. He expressed it all as 'hopes' and 'invitations', but Herman, an old military man himself, recognized an order when he heard one. It would be unwise to refuse, and in any event he found the prospect of such an appointment exciting. By the time he left Amherstburg he had already been measured for a new uniform.

The patience of the Americans was finally exhausted when the British navy simply ignored President Madison's proclamation warning British vessels away from American waters. On June 1, 1812 the President sent a message to Congress recommending a declaration of war. The act declaring war with Great Britain was approved by President Madison on June 18, 1812.

General Brock learned of it at York on June 25.

On June 29 a dispatch rider from Fort Malden stopped in at the Eberts home on his way to Sandwich, seeking Herman. Marie sent him over to the out-building where Herman was working. She stood on the verandah and watched as the rider spoke briefly to Herman, and then rode away. Herman immediately strode over to her, and she knew even before he spoke that it was bad news.

"War has been declared, my dear. They've just heard about it at the fort, and are organizing for defense. I am ordered to ride there immediately, and they're calling out the militia. I believe the Essex will be gathered at Sandwich, but I'm not sure."

Marie hugged herself hard, forcing herself to be strong. "So here we are. It is a fact, after all these months of waiting." She paused and her face brightened. "My goodness, I'm almost glad to have it finally happen. The tension, the unknown, was hard to bear." She moved to Herman and they embraced. "So my dear, you're off to the fort. My husband is off to war! Come, I'll help you prepare your things."

Before Herman rode off in his splendid new uniform, they talked about preparations at the house. They knew that, should the Americans invade (as they surely would), they would come looking for food and other supplies. Many of them were bound to be militia, so they would probably be ill-equipped, looking for any weapons or other gear that they could take. They agreed that Marie should organize the older boys to take much of their food and implements and supplies of potential use to the Americans and conceal them in the woods. "You must leave some here so they don't become suspicious and go searching through the woods" said Herman. "They'll be in a hurry, so leave just enough so that they can be satisfied to take it and move on."

As Herman rode away, Marie called the family together and explained what was happening. She saw that Henry and Richard were excited with the turn of events. "You see boys, you're part of our war effort, even if you're still too young to join the militia!"

They went to work, placing most of the non-perishable food, apples and root vegetables, medicines, half of their utensils, and three of the five muskets with powder and shot into bags. The boys took the bags out past the field and into the woods beyond. It took several trips, and then they looked thoroughly pleased with themselves. They told Marie that everything was well hidden, but could be reached easily if needed. They wished that they could hide the animals too – the horses, chickens, pigs and three cows – but knew that would be impractical.

Several days later Herman returned from Amherstburg, and the family crowded around him to hear the news.

"The troops at Fort Malden are scurrying to strengthen the fortifications, and preparing for attack. It does look like there will be an attack of some sort."

He said that two days previously on Lake Erie a British ship had captured an American schooner full of baggage, official papers and sick American militia men. The Americans were surprised by the attack, as they were not aware that war had been declared! They had been returning to Detroit from where General Hull was isolated in the woods, marching to Detroit with three regiments of Ohio militia and one of regular troops. That gave them around three hundred regular troops and twelve hundred militia. Evidently it was a hard march through the woods, and they were probably terrified of the Indians. So General Hull would soon be at Detroit, thoroughly annoyed at losing his letters and baggage, but with lots of troops.

"He will learn soon, if he hasn't already, that we're at war, and he'll be bound to pay us a visit."

Marie told him about the preparations they had made, and he was greatly impressed. "Well done my love. And boys, well done to you! As you can see, in this war we all have important roles to play! And tell me Marie, what's the word on the militia. Our men aren't here right now. Are they off drilling?"

Marie said that Jean-Louis and Joe had been away training every day. Herman said that he had heard that if the Americans should come across the river at Sandwich, the Essex militia, and probably the Kent Militia as well, would try to stop them."

"What?" cried Marie. "Stop all those Americans? But how would that be possible?"

Herman stepped in. "This has been discussed at length at the fort. They would, of course, like to see our brave boys repel the Americans, but they're realistic. The dominant thinking is that our militia would not have a chance against a force of fifteen hundred Americans landing at Sandwich. They can try, but will probably be forced to retreat. If they do, they'll be marched to Amherstburg to assist with the defense there."

"How could they hold them away from Amherstburg?" asked Henry, perched precariously on the edge of his chair.

"The Americans are likely to do some pillaging first, as they will be short of food and other supplies. Then they'll probably turn on Amherstburg, hoping to gain full control of this end of the lake. So as I understand it, we plan to form a defensive line on the south shore of the Canard River, about five miles this side of Amherstburg. With our regular troops from the fort, plus the militia and a good force of Indians, we should be able to hold them there. Then when the time is right, we can drive them back over to Detroit."

On July 12 Marie was on the front verandah shaking out rugs when a large body of men appeared, hurrying down the road towards Amherstburg. They were a ragtag looking bunch, carrying their bags and packs of possessions, and only some of them with weapons. They were driving a small herd of cattle before them, and had several wagons laden with supplies. Marie hurried to the edge of the road to watch for her men. The first past was Joe. He stopped just long enough to gasp out that the Americans had landed at Hog Island upriver from Sandwich, and were approaching fast. So the Essex had been ordered to head straight for Fort Malden.

Then he was back on the road, soon to be followed by Jean-Louis. Marie saw Jean-Louis pause briefly by the side of the road at his own house for a quick word and kiss for Thérèse before returning to the column. As soon as the last men were by, Thérèse ran along the road to huddle with her mother.

"Our men have all gone down to Amherstburg now" said Thérèse. "So it looks like what Papa said is going to happen. We won't fight the Americans at Sandwich, but we'll stop them before they can get to Amherstburg. I suppose we should just go about our daily chores, and be polite when the Americans come to call."

"Yes of course, dear" said Marie. "My, isn't it a strange feeling to know that perhaps some of our old friends and neighbours may be coming to steal our things, and to shoot at our men?"

Thérèse returned to her home, and Marie told Henry and Richard to sit down in the parlour with their books and do some studying. The boys were outraged. How could they sit there calmly in time of war?

"I understand how you feel, boys, but remember that while you may be too young to join our forces, you both look mature and strong. If the Americans find you outside working or even playing, they might take you for potential soldiers and arrest you. So I want you to look small and young, and be studying like good children."

The boys laughed at their clever mother and obeyed without further comment, but as it turned out the precautions were unnecessary. Squads of American soldiers appeared, setting up defenses and pickets, but none of them came in to bother the family. The next day Marie learned why when she went into town in the company wagon, and heard from friends that the Americans had orders to take supplies only from official stores and large commercial establishments. General Hull, it seemed, wished to maintain friendly relations with the people, proving the earlier rumours that he believed that his forces would be welcomed in Upper Canada. The General's intentions were clearly laid out in a pamphlet that was being distributed that day by American soldiers.

By WILLIAM HULL, Brigadier-General and Commander of the North Western Army of the United States.

A PROCLAMATION

INHABITANTS OF CANADA: after thirty years of Peace and prosperity, the UNITED STATES have been driven to Arms. The injuries & aggressions, the insults & indignities of Great Britain have once more left them no alternative but manly resistance or unconditional submission. The Army under my command has invaded your country & the Standard of the Union now waves over the Territory of Canada. To the peaceable unoffending inhabitants, it brings neither damage nor difficulty. I come to find enemies, not to make them. I come to protect, not to injure you.

Separated by an immense Ocean & an extensive Wilderness from Great Britain, you have no participation in her Counsels, no interest in her conduct. You have felt her Tyranny, you have seen her injustice, but I do not ask you to avenge the one or to redress the other. The UNITED STATES are sufficiently powerful to afford you every security, consistent with their rights & your expectations. I tender to you the invaluable blessings of Civil, Political and Religious Liberty & their necessary result, individual and general prosperity: that Liberty which gave decision to our counsels and energy to our conduct in our struggle for INDEPENDENCE, and which conducted us safely and triumphantly thro' the stormy period of the Revolution. That Liberty which has raised us to an elevated rank among the Nations of the world, and which has afforded us a greater measure of peace and security, of wealth and improvement, than ever fell to the lot of any people.

In the name of my country and by the authority of my Government I promise you protection of your persons, property and rights. Remain at your homes. Pursue your peaceful and customary avocations. Raise not your hands against your brethren, many of your fathers fought for the freedom & independence we now enjoy. Being children therefore of the same family with us, and heirs to the same Heritage, the arrival of an army of Friends must be hailed by you with a cordial welcome. You will be emancipated from Tyranny and oppression and restored to the dignified station of freemen. Had I any doubt of eventual success I might ask your assistance, but I do not. I come prepared for every contingency. I have a force which will look down all opposition and that force is but the vanguard of a much greater. If, contrary to your own interest & the just expectation of my country, you should take part in the approaching contest, you will be considered and treated as enemies, and the horrors and calamities of war will stalk before you.

If the barbarous & savage policy of Great Britain be pursued, and the savages are let loose to murder our Citizens, & butcher our women and children, this war will be a war of extermination.

The first stroke of the Tomahawk, the first attempt with the scalping knife, will be the signal for one indiscriminate scene of destruction. No white man found fighting by the side of an Indian will be taken prisoner. Instant destruction will be his lot. In the dictates of reason, duty, justice and humanity cannot prevent the employment of a force which respects no rights, & know no wrong, it will be prevented by a severe and relentless system of retaliation.

I doubt not your courage and firmness; I will not doubt your attachment to Liberty. If you tender your services voluntarily, they will be accepted readily.

The UNITED STATES offer you Peace, Liberty and Security. Your choice lies between these & War, slavery and destruction. Choose then, but choose wisely; and may He who knows the justice of our cause, and who holds in His hand the fate of Nations, guide you to a result most compatible with your rights and interest, your Peace and prosperity.

By the General

A.T. Hull *W. Hull*
Capt: 13th U.S. Regt of Infantry and Aid de camp

"It's an interesting note" said Henry, sitting with Marie supervising the early supper for the little ones. "The Americans talk about their 'freedom' as if we're in chains here! It seems to me that our laws are fair, and we're free to live the life that we wish. We have politics, as do they, but from what I've heard theirs is so complicated it takes a long time to come to any sort of decision on anything."

Marie nodded. "I think I agree with you, although these government things make my head spin. Over in Detroit we never seemed to know who was doing what, and where! Were we a territory or a state? Or a region? Were we a town or...what? But I suppose we must respect the Americans for what they've done in spite of their confused politics. After all, they did break away from Britain!"

It was Henry's turn to nod. "Yes, true. But look here, Maman, something else that's most interesting in the note. It shows how much they fear the Indians. They make no mention of our Redcoats or militia, but they make a great thing about the Indians, and how awful it will be if we fight on their side."

"You can't blame them. The Indians are truly terrifying in their war outfits. And you know, they really have done some terrible things."

Two days later, to their surprise, their conversation was joined by Jean-Louis and Joe. They arrived on foot near the end of the day, having walked all day in ordinary clothes, looking like shabby farmers. They told their surprised women that Hull's proclamation had made it clear that the Americans had no argument with ordinary Canadians, just with the military and the Indians. This had led over half of the militia at Amherstburg to return to their homes to catch up on their chores. It seemed to be quite all right, as General Hull was taking his time marching on Amherstburg and Fort Malden. The soldiers of the 41st Foot Regiment who manned the fort were working hard to improve its defenses, but they could not hold the hundreds of militia members who had urgent work to do at home. They had taken the opportunity to come home for a visit, planning to return in a couple of days. Herman could not join them as he was now a serving member of the army.

They had a happy reunion, and then Joe left them to continue on to Moy Hall to see Ann and the baby.

As the days went by there were numerous groups of American soldiers moving up and down the road. The families were certain that this would all lead to a major attack on Amherstburg, and then the war would be over for them. But that did not happen. Rumours were flying in Sandwich that General Hull, a cautious man, preferred to wait and see, to be certain of his position rather than taking risks. This lack of boldness on his part, which must have driven some of his veteran officers mad with frustration, was giving the British time to strengthen their fort and take other actions to improve their position.

Near the end of July a passing militiaman named Armstrong stopped for a drink of water, and told the Eberts people an amazing story that had just come to light at Fort Malden. It seemed that General Brock, ignoring his orders not to take any offensive action, had sent orders by canoe to Captain Charles Roberts at the British outpost on St. Joseph Island at the northern end of Lake Huron, allowing the commander to stand on the defensive or attack the nearby American outpost at Fort Michilimackinac at his discretion. Roberts had immediately attacked with a small force of regulars of the 10th Royal Veterans, some fur traders and Indian warriors. The American garrison was taken by surprise, not being aware that war had been declared, and surrendered without a shot being fired. Roberts decided to hold the fort as it was in a better position than Fort St. Joseph, and he sent the Americans back to Detroit.

Armstrong said that the news of this easy victory had been well received by the Indians at Amherstburg, confirming their feelings that the British were good and reliable allies. In fact, they heard later that this action helped to move the defensive policy of Governor-General Prevost to a more aggressive stance when he saw the positive effect that it had on the Indians. It showed that Brock was a strong and decisive leader, ready to interpret his orders as required to fit the needs in Upper Canada. Armstrong also told them that Brock had appointed a new Commandant at Fort Malden, Colonel Henry Proctor, who was expected to be equally audacious.

Not so General Hull. After many feints and countermoves, and delays blamed on shortage of artillery and every other excuse, on the night of August 7 and the morning of August 8 Hull withdrew his troops back to Detroit. He left a token force in Sandwich with hopeless orders to hang on there. The word was that his officers were desperately unhappy with this turn of events, this ignominious retreat without any real battle being joined. And there was worse to come!

The Eberts family continued to monitor movements along the road, and to question every British or Canadian person passing by. They were able to piece together an exciting, if occasionally garbled picture of the next moves in the war. One neighbour, a farmer who had gone over to the Americans after their arrival and then returned to his own side when he saw the weakness in the American leadership, told them that one of the reasons that Hull had ordered the retreat to the other side was that he was afraid of being cut off from supplies and munitions. It was, admittedly, a hard trip from American supply centres to Detroit, through woods likely to be teeming with Indians and British soldiers.

But even being safely back on the other side did not yet guarantee Hull his supplies, for the British could cross the river below Detroit and cut them off, and British ships could shell supply trains from the safety of the river. This, in fact, happened in the second week of August. The attack by the British and their Indian allies was not particularly successful, but it forced Hull to send a large body of troops away from Detroit to protect the supply lines. He also recalled to Detroit the troops who had been left behind at Sandwich.

Then, almost by written script, General Brock arrived by boat at Amherstburg on August 13 with fifty regular troops, two hundred militia and an artillery piece. He had an historic first meeting with Tecumseh and, as later reported by Herman, his eyes flashed as he saw his opportunity to strike a major blow against the Americans by taking Detroit.

The Eberts men had long since returned to Amherstburg, so the women knew that if there was to be action, their men would be involved. For the first time they were likely to be firing on Americans, and being fired upon in return. The idea frightened them, but also thrilled them. Thérèse said that "with General Brock leading them, they will be just fine. Jean-Louis says that he is an amazing man, so aggressive and full of ideas. I would hate to have our men fighting against him!"

The attack on Detroit under General Isaac Brock was a classic exercise in military mischief. Brock had three hundred Redcoats, four hundred militia and six hundred Indians as his force, hardly a match for Hull with his five hundred and eighty regular troops and sixteen hundred militia from Ohio and Michigan. But Brock had some important elements in his favour, aside from his own superiority as a military leader. His spies had told him that around four hundred American militia had been sent away to the Raisin River area to meet and protect a supply column heading for Detroit. Second, he knew that the Americans were terrified of the Indians – what they would do if unleashed upon the American troops and civilians. And third, he had red uniform coats for the Canadian militia, so that from a distance his force would appear to have seven hundred Redcoats rather than just three hundred and a group of militia.

He played the Indian card boldly in the letter he sent by messenger to Hull on August 15, demanding surrender. He stated that "*...It is far from my inclination to join in a war of extermination, but you must be aware that the numerous body of Indians who have attached themselves to my troops will be beyond my control the moment the contest commences...*" Hull did not give up immediately, but this warning clearly affected his thinking.

When Hull sent a return note refusing to surrender, Brock ordered his small artillery unit at Sandwich to open fire on Detroit. The Americans returned the fire, but there was minimum effect on either side.

Brock then ordered the attack, with Colonel Proctor as his field commander. That night the six hundred Indians crossed the river at its narrowest point at a place called Spring Wells, south of the town of Detroit. Their landing was unopposed, as Hull had ranged his militia close to the walls of the town, most facing inland, and his regulars within the town or at the shore batteries. The next morning the seven hundred red coated troops crossed over, protected by more artillery fire from Sandwich into Detroit, and the guns of two British ships sitting in the river off Detroit. The British force advanced to within a mile of the town, well spread out so that they would look like a larger force than they really were. Brock made certain that the Indian forces showed themselves to the fort, terrifying in their numbers and their savagery.

The Michigan militia deserted their posts, and then a shell from the artillery at Sandwich landed in the officers' mess, killing four. Faced with what he thought was a formidable force, and with the Indians lurking in the woods preparing to attack, Hull decided to surrender all of his forces, including those still returning from the Raisin River. In fact, he surrendered the entire Northwest Region of the United States, which was under his command.

"Brock's orders then came thick and fast" said Herman, back home for a brief visit before returning to the General's staff. Marie held his hand as he told the family about the taking of Detroit, and Thérèse did the same with Jean-Louis, who had accompanied the doctor.

"He put Hull and his troops on board two of our ships and sent them away to Quebec, where they'll cool their heels until the war is over. He also released the American militia, on their parole, to return to their homes. He sent some of our men with them to ensure that the Indians would not attack them on their way."

"What does 'parole' mean, Papa?" asked Henry.

"It means that they give their word not to attack us again. They're given a choice: either be imprisoned or even shot here, or go home free men, but with a promise not to bear arms against us again."

"Is that forever?"

Herman laughed. "Probably not, Henry, but it should work for a while at least."

He went on to say that they had captured a valuable store of arms and ammunition at Detroit: "thirty-three artillery pieces, twenty-five hundred muskets and a large supply of military stores, to be precise" said Jean-Louis. "Oh, and we also captured one of their ships that was docked there. I believe it was the brig *Adams*."

Turning to Thérèse, he added that he had gone to see the plot of land in Detroit that had been allotted to them. "While I was there an American fellow, a miller named Joseph Campeau, was wandering around nearby. When he saw me standing on the property he came up to me and said that if I was interested, he would like to buy it. That had me really thinking about it for the first time. Do we really want to return there to live? We would have to build our house, and presumably would eventually be living back in the United States. You never know, of course. At any rate, he offered to pay us $50 if we were interested. I said I would come back to him with an answer after I had spoken to you."

This set the family talking about what would happen next, and where they would like to go once things settled down. The consensus emerged that while the British had the upper hand in the territories across the river at the present time, the Americans were not likely to put up with that forever. They were too big and too proud to give back territory that they had already settled and governed. That being the case, the Eberts family would be better to stay in British North America.

Herman and Jean-Louis returned to Detroit the next day to take up their duties, and Jean-Louis sold the property to Campeau.

26

WHAT NEWS?

Living outside Sandwich, Marie knew that she would be totally isolated from news of the war unless she took steps to deal with the problem. There were the usual delays of any news reaching anywhere quickly, so that an action at, say, Niagara, might not be known of even at Amherstburg for another week or so. And then it would have to filter through the military system, which always tended to be cautious and close-mouthed about letting out information. Delays in news were a common feature of life in 1812, and the delays were accentuated by the war.

Yet now she felt that she simply had to know what was going on, for her men were involved. Immediately after the taking of Detroit, Herman had left with General Brock for the Niagara area. Brock had appointed Colonel Proctor as Governor of Michigan, and he soon led a force down into the territory to confirm British control there. To Marie's relief, Joe and Jean-Louis were left behind with the militia force occupying Detroit and defending Sandwich and Amherstburg.

So Marie had these two warriors to count on for the latest news from the military. She also had William Baker at Amherstburg, who had the ear of the remaining forces there. Indeed, it was William who reminded her just how complex the war was. "It's a long way from here to Halifax, as you know Marie. And the war is being fought, or will be fought, at places all along the border. Now mind you, there are no huge armies involved as there are in European wars, but there are enough forces to make this a nasty affair. Fortunately the Americans are having trouble raising troops, but that will be resolved. So in the meantime it's important that we do well and take the initiative.

Marie nodded. "I see. But tell me William, do we still control the lakes?"

Baker frowned. "That's not clear. We know that they've been building ships at Sackets Harbour, so our numerical advantage may be diminished. And we've just heard that a new man, Commodore Isaac Chauncey of the US Navy, has assumed command of their naval forces on the lakes. He's a good man; I knew him years ago when I was in New York. So they're taking the issue seriously."

Stories came in every week of things happening, some small, some major, some amusing, some tragic. There was news that the Governor of Indiana, General William Harrison, was in the field against Colonel Procter, and was having some success.

Then in the third week of October came news that stunned the community. British and Canadian forces under General Brock had taken on American forces in a major battle at a place in the Niagara region called Queenston Heights. "Our side prevailed" said Joe, with tears streaming down his face, "but General Brock was killed. Oh my god, what a loss! Oh Maman, he was such a genius! We all loved him, you know. We would have followed him anywhere!"

The mood around the family table was heavy. Ann held onto Joe's arm. Jean-Louis and Thérèse sat staring across the table, hands clasped together. The young children, Phillis and Robert, sat quietly, watching their mother. It was Henry, strong, happy Henry who broke the silence. He jumped to his feet, pounding the table, his eyes splashed with tears. "Damn those bloody Americans! Damn them to hell! I hate them – all of them. And I'll get them!" He turned on Marie, who stared at him in open-mouthed disbelief. "I'm going to join the forces Maman. You can't stop me. I'll do it, and we'll beat those..." He stopped before he swore again, and strode out of the room. Richard followed close behind.

Marie was stunned. In those few seconds of fury from an unexpected source she had learned several important things. One was how truly dangerous the war was to all of them, and how their trust and hopes had been focussed on one man, General Brock. With all the big things out there

– the large areas under dispute, the potentially huge size of the opposing forces, the seeming impossibility of it all – they had come to see a ray of hope in the form of one British General who had chosen to stay and fight for Canada rather than return to England. With him gone there was a gap, a dangerous gap that could prove decisive.

Another revelation was the force of feelings in her son Henry. He had been saying all along that he wanted to join the militia, and she had fended him off relatively easily by reminding him that he was not yet sixteen, so was not eligible to serve. He had seemed to accept it, but now she realized that he had just been putting on a face to make her happy. He was in fact a young man in turmoil; how could she have been so stupid? He was a tall, strong fifteen year-old lad, bigger than half of the men in the militia. His father was away at war. His brother Joe was in the forces, and so was Jean-Louis. What was he, a big baby sucking his thumb in comfort while they did all the hard stuff? She realized only now why he had for the past several months been hesitant to go into town. People had probably seen him and wondered why he wasn't serving, and if they asked him he had to make the embarrassing excuse that he was too young.

The third revelation, akin to the second, was that Richard obviously felt the same way. He was a year younger than Henry, but under the same pressures of having loved ones doing the fighting while he could only watch. And Richard was a very capable young man. He could ride and shoot with the best of them, was amazingly fleet of foot, and had his wonderful language skills. Surely he could be of use?

All eyes were on Marie to see how she would react. She finally managed a weak smile. "Well, I suppose we're all under pressure these days. But I must say, the strength of Henry's feelings has come as a surprise to me. What do you feel?"

With that question, she had another revelation: for the first time she was made truly aware of the divide between generations. All of the other people around the table were a generation apart from her. They were the next wave, the next level, and they had their own ideas and sensitivities that were, in some ways, different from hers. Thérèse broke the news to her.

"Oh Maman, I don't think we're as surprised as you are. Certainly Jean-Louis and I have had Henry at our home several times when he has exploded like that. But we've always tried to calm him down, and he has so much respect for you that he's done so. But, well, Joe...?"

"It's true" said Joe, embarrassed to have to say so to his mother. "It's a difficult situation, you know. I mean, here you have Thérèse and me, much older than Henry, but still his brother and sister. So we have a different relationship with him than do you."

Jean-Louis and Ann were nodding as he spoke, so Marie knew that he was right. Strange – she was the head of the family (in Herman's absence), but her children were the ones who really knew what was going on. Her next step was obvious; she asked them what they would suggest.

They said, and she agreed, that it was time to stop opposing Henry in his wish to join up. He would not yet be eligible due to his age, but he could start moving in that direction. And the same could be said for Richard. Joe agreed to speak to the Captain of his unit to see if he could bring Henry and Richard to their training sessions so that they could at least start learning the trades of war.

As Henry and Richard proceeded with their training with the militia, news continued to filter in of actions along the border. Colonel Proctor campaigned into the Michigan territory, seeking to strengthen British control of Detroit and the surrounding areas. His opposition was led by Brigadier General William Henry Harrison, who was forced to wait for supplies before moving to retake Detroit.

The American naval forces were now considered to be a match for the British on the lakes, changing the strategic balance. There were actions along the frontier, notably at Niagara and near Montreal. In the latter case, the attacking Americans were frustrated when their militias from Vermont and New York refused to cross the border into Lower Canada. They insisted that militias were engaged for defensive purposes, not attacks on foreign nations.

As 1812 came to a close the authorities in British North America could claim with some satisfaction that not one American soldier remained on their side of the border, aside from the prisoners who were incarcerated in Lower Canada. There was a general sense of confidence in the Canadas, although the authorities knew that the American government would not put up with such a poor showing for long. The growing strength of the American navy, on the ocean where it could threaten the Atlantic colonies of British North America, and on the lakes where it was gradually changing the balance of power on and around the lakes, was a concern. This was especially so as the Provincial Marine, the British navy in the Canadas, was woefully short of trained seamen, supplies and weapons.

Winter weather slowed operations in early 1813, although not completely.

Colonel Proctor's work in Michigan had resulted in the British forces occupying a small place called Frenchtown, twenty-six miles south of Detroit. It was then lightly defended by a few Canadian militia and Indians, and on January 18 it was re-taken by an American force under Brigadier-General James Winchester, who came under the over-all command of General Harrison. Colonel Proctor promptly counter-attacked with a force that included two hundred and seventy regulars, sixty-one Fencibles, two hundred and ten militia and six hundred Indians. The Americans took heavy losses, and had five hundred of their troops taken prisoner, giving up when Proctor warned Winchester that his Indians might get out of hand if the Americans did not surrender immediately.

Harrison withdrew his forces. Proctor paroled the Kentucky militia back to their homes, and then withdrew his own force to Fort Malden, where he was soon promoted to Brigadier-General. Marie had three of her family involved in this action. Herman was with Proctor's commanding unit, and Joe and Jean-Louis were both there in their militia unit. They all came through the action safely, and were welcomed home by a relieved Marie and family.

In February there were attacks in both directions over the ice of Lake Ontario, resulting in some useful but by no means decisive destruction of American naval ships and related supplies. These were interesting stories for Marie and her family as they filtered through Fort Malden and the friendly hands of William Baker. Then in late March came astonishing news that affected them directly. In order to strengthen British forces in the Canada's, the authorities in Quebec had ordered an artillery detachment and six companies of the 104th Regiment of Foot, five hundred and fifty men in all, to proceed from New Brunswick to the Canadas. With the St. Lawrence River frozen over, they had to march three hundred and fifty miles through the snow to Quebec City. When William Baker described this epic march to the Eberts family, listening to him in breathless silence, he said that the force had subsequently been sent on to Kingston, another three hundred and sixty miles! They were enroute now, expected to arrive in Kingston in mid-April.

This was Ignace's unit! Ignace was coming!

Herman was silent as this story was unfolding. Marie, sitting next to him, felt upset and yet thrilled at the same time. She knew that the unit would be suffering unbelievable hardships on the march, but at the same time there might now be a chance of seeing her firstborn son again! Mind you, Kingston was still a long way from Sandwich, but you never knew what might happen! Knowing Herman's views on that subject she kept her silence and a straight face, but others around the table were not so diplomatic.

As springtime came on with warmer temperatures, melting snow and mud, military action intensified along the border. The news of engagements, usually late and often inaccurate, kept the family in suspense, particularly as Sandwich was so close to the border with the United States.

In April and May General Proctor besieged General Harrison's forces at Fort Meigs, in Ohio but close to Detroit, up the Maumee River. This action was not successful, but then on May 5 Proctor and his Indian allies inflicted a devastating defeat on the Americans at the Battle of Miami Rapids, down the Maumee River from Fort Meigs. But Fort Meigs remained in American hands, and in June Proctor returned to Amherstburg and released the militia to their farms and homes, which sorely needed them.

As these actions were taking place, the Americans were establishing an even stronger naval presence on Lake Erie. This strengthened their strategic position on the lake, as they could more easily serve and protect supply depots at places like Sandusky, Presque Isle and Fort Meigs.

General Procter attacked these areas in July, seeking to disrupt the supply lines of General Harrison who, it was assumed, was preparing to retake Detroit, and probably even attack into Upper Canada. Unfortunately the British attacks failed, and the British forces at Fort Malden were now desperately short of the supplies that were waiting for them at Long Point at the far end of Lake Erie.

On August 8, 1813, his sixteenth birthday, Henry Eberts joined the Essex militia as a private. He had been training for a year, so was able to move into the unit easily, confident in his duties and determined to do well. Richard, who would turn fourteen in November, was still officially too young to join up, but he had been noticed by the militia officers when he participated in training exercises. Communications in the military were based on human speed, whether on the water in fast ships or on land with fast runners or skilled riders. Richard was already one of the fastest runners in the group of trainees, and was the best rider of the group. His language skills were also formidable and potentially valuable for dealings with the many Indian tribes allied to the British. Thus the authorities engaged him in the militia as a confidential courier, to be available when called upon.

Joe and Jean-Louis had come home with General Proctor's release of the militia in June. Joe had then been posted to Detroit as part of the occupying militia force. Henry was posted there immediately upon signing up, so had the satisfaction of joining his brother in his first active duty. Richard and Jean-Louis were based at Fort Malden.

With all of these family members involved, Marie now had the feeling that her family was almost running the war for Britain – for Canada. This left her with a sadly depleted family table whenever she was able to bring it together. There was Phillis, now a blossoming eleven year-old, and nine year-old Robert. Thérèse was there, as was Ann with two year-old William on her knee, and newborn Walter in his bassinette.

Thus the summer passed in a state of hot weather and nervous tension. The men would appear occasionally, as permitted by their commanders. Herman was almost never there. Even William Baker, their priceless source of information, seldom appeared. He was making a name for himself as a fearless, tough fighter as well as a ship builder. He would go out on the lake in a gunboat with volunteer shipyard workers armed with rifles and axes to take on marauding American boats.

But it was Baker who told Marie during a visit in early September that the situation at Fort Malden was desperate. They were low on all supplies, and unless they could soon be re-supplied from the stocks at Long Point, they would probably not be able to hold Detroit, nor Amherstburg for that matter. This seemed inconceivable to Marie, and to many at Sandwich, who had come to rely totally on the abilities of the British forces at Fort Malden, their militias and their Indian allies. But it proved to be an accurate prediction. General Harrison had a substantial body of troops and strong supply bases close to Detroit and Amherstburg. Unless the British could re-supply quickly it would be no contest, and even if they could it would be a hard fight.

On September 9 British Captain Robert Barclay departed Amherstburg with a fleet of three warships and three armed schooners. His destination was Long Point for supplies, but he was met and defeated by an American fleet under Commodore Oliver Perry. When news of this defeat reached Amherstburg, preparations were made to leave Detroit and Fort Malden. The troops were pulled back from Detroit, the militia was dispersed, and on September 22 General Proctor led his nine hundred Redcoats away towards the mouth of the Thames River. His objective was to travel up the river and then overland to the British post at Burlington Bay, at the west end of Lake Ontario. Tecumseh saw this as an ignominious retreat.

Some of General Harrison's troops marched into Detroit; others landed from Perry's ships at Amherstburg. They immediately burned Fort Malden and the navy yard there, and then started their pursuit of General Proctor, foraging for supplies along the way.

27

LOST

The war finally touched Marie directly on September 26, 1813.

Over the past few days there had been an endless stream of British forces – Redcoats, militia and Indians – moving past the house, heading for Sandwich and beyond. The Redcoats were deadly serious, rushing their retreat from what would be a rampant American army. The militia were composed and serious, heading for their homes in an attempt to hide from the conquering Americans, preparing, hopefully, to fight another day. The Indians were in surly mood, contemptuous of the order to retreat.

Marie knew that this would happen. News of the American attack and Proctor's retreat had spread quickly. Herman had stopped in briefly as Proctor's group rode by, but had no time for anything but a quick word with Marie and kisses for family members present.

The citizens of the area around Amherstburg and Sandwich kept their heads down, hoping that the Americans would move through them without causing too much damage to the local population. Militia members hid any uniforms and weapons they had, and went back to work in the fields and the woods, keeping out of sight as much as possible.

On the previous day some American scouts had come along the road, heading for Sandwich. They had left the Eberts houses alone, but were a portent of things to come. General Harrison's army was sure to follow soon. On this morning Henry, Richard and Jean-Louis were out collecting wood in the forest beyond the field at the back of the house. It was chilly and raining lightly, and Marie was sweeping the verandah at the front of the house, helped by Phillis and Robert, when an American foraging team came along the road. The familiar sounds of men on horseback – talking, the whinnying of the horses, the creaking of saddles and jingling of bridles – echoed over the fields and surrounding woods, heralding in advance the troubles to come.

Marie saw them stop at Thérèse's house, leave a wagon there with two soldiers, and send Thérèse out into the field behind the house. The main body of wagons and soldiers then moved along to Marie's house, and she went down to the road to greet them. The nine tough-looking soldiers looked tired and edgy. They were accompanied by four large horse-drawn wagons, gaping empty behind their drivers. She knew that they were professional soldiers because, unlike the ragtag Kentucky militia she had seen once from a distance, they had smart uniforms, not yet overly dirty. So far, so good.

She was also relieved to see that she knew the Sergeant in charge. It was Jonathan Black, whom she had known back in Detroit. Young Jonathan had been a boy of twelve when the Eberts family moved away from Detroit to their home in Sandwich. Now here he was, a grown man and Sergeant in the United States Army.

"Why, Jonathan Black" she cried, putting on her best smile, "how good it is to see you again. I do hope that your parents are well?" Her knees trembled under her skirt and she prayed inwardly, but she bluffed a welcoming demeanor and sense of confidence.

Black stared at her for a moment, and then glanced around the property while his men waited impatiently. For an instant she sensed that he could not decide how to deal with the unexpected familiarity. But not for long. "They are well Mrs. Eberts, thank you. But Ma'am, under the authority of General Harrison I must ask you and your children to leave your house immediately – this house, the barn and the out-building I see yonder. We are under orders to take food supplies and other useful materials in support of our campaign. Please Ma'am, do not linger. My men are not pleasant when forced to deal with opposition."

There was no warm smile or hint of friendship. This was war, and he was a warrior with a job to do. Already his men were spreading out towards the buildings, and the carters were moving into positions to receive goods. They knew that they had come upon a juicy target, and they moved quickly and confidently.

No soldier, not even Sergeant Black, looked at her as she turned and rushed back into the house with the children, struggled to put on their outdoor coats, and then went out the back door. She managed to grab a blanket as they passed the barn, and then Thérèse joined them as they tramped as quickly as they could across the field towards the woods. The rain was growing heavier and the temperature dropping, and Marie was puffing and swearing in equal measure while Phillis wept and Robert cursed with a fluency until then unknown to his mother. He wanted to go back and find his father's musket and teach those damn Americans a lesson, oh yes! Marie kept her silence, and pushed him along through the stubble of the recent harvest.

They paused after entering the woods, dripping wet and yet hot and perspiring, and it was then that Marie thought of the lean-to that her children had built for play. They led her to it, and they were able to shelter from the rain to some extent, although the roof leaked in places and some rain drifted in from the side. They were now cold and wet. Marie hugged Phillis to her, but Robert insisted that he must keep watch, and sat at the edge of the shelter, looking back towards the field. They were soon joined by Henry, Richard and Jean-Louis who had watched the unfolding drama from the woods at the far end of the field, unable to do anything to help for fear of being spotted by the soldiers.

Marie was struck by the situation – the use of the play house for real work. That and the fact that while her husband and sons were fighting in the war, the war had now walked unchallenged into their own home, thrown their family out into the cold, and probably taken all of their worldly possessions and food. She laughed out loud, startling her children. Henry asked her what was so amusing, and she replied "nothing, of course. I was just struck by the irony of our hiding in this play house. But oh, dear Henry, we are going to lose everything! Again!"

Henry frowned. "Yes, I suppose we will. But at least we're safe here. Let's just hope that they treat Joe and Ann as well as they've treated us. Heaven knows what they'll do to Moy Hall."

Marie nodded and grew somber. She was wet through and chilly, shivering under the rough blanket. She felt tired and old beyond her forty-seven years. Why must her life suffer one crisis after another? Is there no peace to be had, even in this miserable wilderness? And in addition, knowing her luck, she would probably catch her death of cold before this was over!

Richard left them and went to spy on the Americans from the edge of the woods. The soldiers finally left just after noon, heading towards Sandwich with three of the wagons laden with goods.

When Richard gave them the 'all-clear' signal the chilled and damp family moved out of the woods and headed across the field to the houses. Thérèse and Jean-Louis split away to their own place, and Richard said that he would check the barn and then the out-building.

Henry led Marie and the two young ones into the house. It was untidy, but not the scene of devastation that they had expected. "It's really not too bad, Maman" said Henry after a quick look around the main floor. "The kitchen has no food left in it – not a bite! And they've taken most of our utensils and buckets and so on. But the furniture isn't damaged. I guess they hope to live with us in peace sometime in the future, so they're not destroying things, just taking what they need. Oh, I'd better check the wood pile around the side."

He went out the back door as Marie went into her bedroom with the children. They found that their blankets, pillows, warm clothing, Herman's shoes and boots, and his muskets and ammunition had all disappeared. Henry joined them as they searched, reporting that all of the firewood was gone. Then they headed up the stairs to find that the upstairs rooms, like the bedroom downstairs, had been stripped of all warm bedding, warm clothing and men's footwear.

They came downstairs and out onto the front verandah. The rain had stopped, but now a cold wind was blowing straight at the front of the house. Jean-Louis came along the road to report the same conditions in his house as had been found in the Eberts house. Marie was now shivering with cold, so she went back into the house with the two youngsters while Henry and Jean-Louis headed up the road to the out-building.

Fortunately, and not surprisingly, the soldiers had not touched Marie's clothing, so she was able to put on some dry, warm clothes. She helped Phillis and Robert to do the same, as their supplies of clothes had also been spared. Just as they finished, the three men came in the front door, followed closely by Thérèse who also had been able to dress warmly. It was obvious that the soldiers who had come by were farm boys, as they had left behind some useful things – all of the cows, three of the pigs, half of the chickens and all of their feed. They had clearly wished to leave the family enough food sources to last the winter.

Henry reported that the barn had lost all but one of the horses, most of the firewood stored there, much of the hay, and most of the saddles and other harnesses for the horses. They had also taken some of the tools that had been kept there. In the out-building all medicines, weapons, powder, shot and other weapons including hunting knives, liquor (not wine), blankets, men's warm clothing and footwear, tools and implements had been taken. What had been left were some valuable trade goods, including several bales of top quality fox pelts. They all laughed, thinking of the soldiers who, men of the land, would have recognized the value of these goods, but been frustrated having to leave them behind because they would be of no direct assistance to an army on the march. As with the other buildings, most of the firewood was gone.

Marie brought the family back to reality, reminding them that the situation they were in was definitely not amusing. They needed food, firewood and some warm clothes and bedding, and the sooner the better. After a quick exchange of ideas, Henry and Richard went out into the woods to the cache they had previously set up in anticipation of such an emergency. They would have enough food to keep body and soul together, although only a few old utensils to cook in. They would also have the muskets to hunt for game. Jean-Louis and Robert took on the task of bringing in more firewood. The house was quickly cooling down as the morning fires and stove cooled and died. The new wood was tough burning, cold and wet, but they managed.

Thérèse went back to her house to start sorting things out, and Marie had Phillis help her seek out clothing and bedding that would enable them to survive the cold, and had been overlooked by the soldiers. It was not yet freezing weather, but it was damp and chilly, a condition often referred to as 'unhealthy weather'. The family worked hard to repair their situation, and were able to go to bed that first night with an unusual but satisfying mixture of food in their stomachs and eclectic piles of light bedding, clothes and rugs keeping them almost warm.

The next day broke cold, but with no rain. The family was up early, coaxing fires in the stove and the fireplace, and preparing a rude breakfast. It was clear that the American army would be passing by soon so the men, including Richard, crossed the field immediately after eating to stay out of sight, but also to secure more firewood and food supplies from the cache, and to hunt for game.

Marie kept the two youngsters busy cleaning up the house, scouring the three buildings for material for warmer clothes and watching the road. They were excited about the situation and went about their work happily, but Marie was a different story. She had never really warmed up from the chilling of the previous day, and now she was shivering, with aches and pains and a headache fed by a rising temperature. By noon she could hold off no longer and took to her bed under a pile of clothes. Phillis ran to fetch Thérèse from her house, and soon Marie was lying in a reverie, sweating under a carpet and being nursed by her two daughters.

Early that afternoon General Harrison's army began its march past the house towards Sandwich. The family kept inside, out of sight, and watched through the windows. It was an impressive sight – a steady stream of men, tough looking and energetic in spite of their long march. Most were uniformed soldiers, but there were also some small units of militia, probably the Kentucky volunteers who seemed to be favored by General Harrison. The stream ended just before nightfall, and the men came back to the house laden with wood, food supplies and three rabbits that they had managed to shoot. Marie was back in bed shivering, her teeth chattering. She could not get warm in spite of the hot water that Thérèse was feeding her.

The family fed her some broth, placed cool cloths on her brow and kept her warmly covered. There was nothing more they could do without a doctor to help them, and their own doctor was many miles away. They remembered the terrible time that little Guillaume had suffered with his pneumonia, and prayed that it was not the case here. At least Marie did not have a sore throat.

But she did the following morning, and her temperature was so high that she was delirious, calling for Herman and Joe and other people, terrified in her heated dreams. The men went out again in search of wood and food, while Thérèse and Phillis watched over her. The rain was back with its dripping cold air, and the house was chilly in spite of the smoky fires in the stove and the fireplace.

Marie's symptoms worsened over the next few days, coming into the heavy, laboured breathing that the family knew was a symptom of pneumonia. There were still American soldiers in the area, occasionally passing the road on sentry duty, but the family knew that they had to send for a doctor. It was a logical assignment for Richard in a war zone. He left the house one morning, slipping along the edge of the road in the mist and rain, invisible amongst the undergrowth and overhanging boughs. While he was gone a large unit of Kentucky mounted riflemen rode by, evidently determined to catch up with the troops who had marched by previously. Two hours later Richard was back, riding proudly in the carriage of one of Sandwich's doctors. As he accompanied the doctor into the house he said that they had sat at the side of the road as the American cavalry passed by. "I tried to look as young as possible, and they hardly even noticed me!"

Dr. Houndsly explained that the Americans permitted him to go about on his rounds, having given his parole that he would report treating any Redcoats. He was an elderly man, well respected in the community, and Thérèse welcomed him gratefully. But her sense of relief ended abruptly when he confirmed that Marie had pneumonia and was very ill indeed. "She is, in fact, in some danger for her life, Madame Biron" he told Thérèse. "Death is a possibility, but I can assure you that it is by no means inevitable. You must keep her quiet, warm and well filled with fluids. Cool her brow if she seems over-heated, but do not let her be exposed to any cold air or drafts. And of course, pray for her."

Not long after the doctor departed another carriage pulled up bringing Joe and Ann from Moy Hall. They rushed to Marie's side, but could do little to help out. Thérèse called the men in from the woods and they had a family discussion over cups of hot water. Joe said that Moy Hall and their home had been dealt with in the same manner as had the Eberts home. The soldiers had focused in particular on food, blankets, weapons and liquor. Angus Mackintosh had stood back and watched them load their wagons, not helping them in any way, but not causing any offense. Like the Eberts, he knew full well that the Americans would probably be around for some time to come, so it was best to be civil with them. After all, they would be customers in the future.

Marie's condition stabilized in the first week of October. Her temperature went down to a reasonable level, her sore throat subsided, and her breathing became less laboured. She wanted to get up and work, but was kept to her bed by Thérèse and Henry, who quoted 'doctor's orders' whenever she put up an argument. On the one occasion when she managed to escape them for a short while and went into the kitchen to see what she could do, she quickly found herself exhausted and retreated gratefully to her bed.

With the Americans now in control of Amherstburg and the lake, there was no longer any flow of information about the war anywhere except here in the western area, and even here the news came in bits and pieces. Sick as she was, Marie tried to keep up with the news. She fretted waiting for any word from or about Ignace, who she presumed was fighting in the Niagara region. Perhaps he might write to her? But how? The Americans would not permit British mail to pass from Niagara to Sandwich. She also waited on tenterhooks for any news of Proctor's forces and Herman. She prayed that they would be successful in their fight against General Harrison and would retake Amherstburg, bringing Herman home to her.

28

DENOUMENT

As Marie's health slowly improved, the news grew steadily worse. First there was a rumour that General Proctor's army had retreated safely up the Thames River, and along with Tecumseh's forces should be able to deal with General Harrison's pursuing army. Then they would return and clear the Americans out of Sandwich and Amherstburg, the militia would be re-formed, and they could once again take the war to the Americans.

But in the second week of October these hopes were dashed when news was received of a terrible battle at Moraviantown, up the Thames River beyond the Chatham townsite. Proctor's forces were not able to withstand the bold attack of the Americans, and over six hundred of them were killed or captured against very minor losses on the American side. The great chief Tecumseh was killed. What was left of the British army, around two hundred and fifty men, escaped and retreated to the head of Lake Ontario, to the British post at Burlington Bay.

Within a day of receiving this news, the saddened Eberts household watched as Harrison's victorious troops marched past the house on their way to Amherstburg. Amongst them, herded like cattle, were their British prisoners. Robert watched the procession go by, and reported that Herman was not amongst the prisoners. "I called out to one man asking about Papa, and he just shrugged and said that as far as he knew the General's staff had escaped and gone to Burlington Bay. So it sounds like he's still alive, Maman."

Marie could only mumble "I suppose so. Thank you dear", and then turn away.

Two days later they received word that General Harrison had signed an armistice agreement with the Indians, and had issued a proclamation concerning his governance in Upper Canada. Civil officials in this area would be permitted to continue in office provided that they took an oath to remain faithful to the United States during this period of occupation, and it pledged security of person and property.

Harrison then sailed off in Admiral Perry's fleet, leaving four hundred regulars and thirteen hundred Ohio militia to garrison Detroit, Sandwich and Amherstburg.

Taking the Americans at their word, the citizens of Sandwich and Amherstburg started to return to a more normal life than had been possible while active war was being waged in their midst. Moy Hall re-opened for business, although it was still difficult to bring in supplies across the lake. But Angus Mackintosh had his distillery up and running, and a good supply of furs coming in from the west, and with occasional ships arriving from the United States with various goods and supplies he was back in business – a good thing for Joe and Ann. Jean-Louis was also able to start up operations again.

The men in the family had no war duties to attend to, so put in useful hours gathering wood supplies and hunting for food. With some late fall vegetables to harvest, the family was able to face the winter with a reasonable degree of confidence.

The problem for them all, the issue that hung over the Eberts home like a dark cloud, was the status of the parents. Herman, if alive, was stranded at Burlington Bay, and there seemed little prospect of his being able to return soon. And of course, Marie was ill – perhaps not ill all of the time, but certainly not well. She had come back from that initial attack of pneumonia quite well, although she did lack energy, requiring frequent rests and a flow of warm fluids. As the weather grew colder, she found that her ability to withstand the cold was not what it should be. She shivered in the slightest draft, and was forever putting on an additional layer of clothing "just to be comfortable". The family worried about her, but not to excess.

She was, after all, with them and on the mend. Their heaviest thoughts and hopes rested on Herman. Was he alive? When would they see him again?

But this balance of worry was misplaced. Herman was fine, just stranded and unable to return or even communicate. But Marie was not well at all, in spite of the apparent evidence that she was on the mend. And it was Richard who recognized this and took action.

One cold, clear morning Henry and the two young children arose to find that Richard was missing. There was a note on the kitchen table – a scribbled note that said simply "I have gone to fetch Papa". Henry told them to wait there in the kitchen, and then rushed out through the light snow to the barn, returning at once to report that the horse was gone. He had stopped in to alert Jean-Louis and Thérèse to the situation, and they followed him back to the house. The family gathered around the kitchen table, out of earshot of Marie in her bed, and discussed what to do.

"Richard has been so unhappy these past few days" said Henry. "I know he's been frustrated about not being able to get back into the war, and also so worried about Maman. So it looks like he's decided to do something about it."

Thérèse was close to tears. "But why would he do such a wild thing? How can he hope to bring Papa back here? We still have Americans patrolling all the time. Surely they'll catch them! Oh dear!"

"It certainly is risky" said Henry, "but knowing Richard, he'll find some way through."

"That's what I've been thinking" said Jean-Louis. "That boy...that man... can go anywhere without anyone noticing. He's so quick and silent when he moves around! Now of course, Herman will not be quite as skillful as that, but I think that with Richard leading the way there may be some hope."

They agreed that Richard would probably go up the Thames River and then overland to the British post at Burlington Bay. They assumed that Proctor's forces, the remnants of that terrible defeat at Moraviantown, would be resting there, awaiting orders to move elsewhere but trapped by the American naval presence on the lakes. In such a predicament it was possible that General Proctor would release Herman to visit his wife. If Herman could find some civilian clothes and borrow a horse, he could then come back down the river with Richard, and thence to Sandwich. It would be hard riding over snowy forest trails, but there was some hope.

They agreed not to mention Richard's mission to Marie. When she asked after him they would explain that he was away helping on a farm near Amherstburg.

By the third week of November Marie was in bed most of the days, with troubled nights giving her little real rest. Family members took turns sitting with her, chatting about their work in the fields and the rumours about the war that were constantly flowing through the community. In spite of the worsening weather there was still some activity on and around the lakes, but there was no hard information that they could rely on. What they did know was that the Americans were in control at the west end of Upper Canada. They could only hope that things were going better in the east.

As time went by Marie's breathing became increasingly laboured. You could hear her fighting for breathe all the way out to the kitchen. Dr. Houndsly confirmed the obvious, that the pneumonia was returning in force. He stressed that there was little they could do now except pray that she could come through the crisis. All of their efforts to care for her had been of only temporary help. She was frequently delirious, ranting about Herman being away on a trip when he should have been planting the potatoes.

With the grudging light of dawn breaking through her bedroom window on November 25, showing a light fall of snow blowing in from the east, Marie stirred in her bed, conscious of a person sitting in the chair next to her bed, which was as usual. But there seemed to be a charge of – something – in the room. She came fully awake with a start, and turned her head to stare directly into the eyes of her beloved husband. It was like one of her many dreams wherein she was unable to speak. Her throat was dry, and she could not find words. She wondered if she was still dreaming.

Herman leaned over and pressed a cup of water to her lips. She grasped his hand, never letting him out of her direct gaze as she gulped the water.

When she was done she was finally able to say "My darling Herman, you have come home".

Major Herman Melchior Eberts, doctor, soldier, trader, Coroner, Sheriff, man of the world, cried like a baby as he swept Marie into his arms.

The family was soon gathered outside the bedroom door, opened just enough to let them know what was happening. Henry had heard the riders when they crept in at midnight, greeted them and helped them to wash and eat and rest. He had then fetched Thérèse and Jean-Louis, who had joined them in the family house while they awaited the morning. Now they all stood there, silent and smiling. Thérèse was hugging Richard so hard that he finally had to beg for mercy.

Herman nursed Marie in the following days, knowing all along that it was a lost cause. He spent every waking moment at her bedside, and when she was able, they talked about the family. Marie refused to mention the war, even though it now dominated the lives of almost everyone she loved. Indeed, every man in her family except young Robert was a fighter in the latest war to affect her life. She could not escape it.

She asked if there had been any word from Ignace, who was probably in the Niagara region. He said no, there had been no word. Joe and Ann were doing fine at Moy Hall, with their two babies, and Joe was working hard for Angus to restore the business. Like Jean-Louis, Henry and Richard, Joe had hidden his militia uniform and equipment, and they were all going about their daily work under the occasional watchful eyes of the American occupiers. The young ones, Phillis and Robert, were thrilled to have their father home, and engaged him in conversation and play whenever they were allowed.

But this happy time did not last long. Marie's condition continued to worsen. In the early afternoon of December 6, 1813, she lost consciousness. The family gathered around to pray for a miracle, but she died just after 3pm. She was forty-eight years old.

29

FAMILY LEGACY

Marie left her family totally engaged in the war with the United States. The men were all able to rejoin the war effort in early 1814. All but one survived the war and went on to their different lives, and the Eberts family was influential in the early days of Chatham, Ontario.

After the war Herman returned to Sandwich and pursued his medical career, focusing especially on the poor and destitute. He died at Sandwich on September 24, 1819.

Ignace was engaged with his regiment until the end of the war, mainly in the Niagara region. After the war he married Elizabeth Anne Thompson. They had one daughter. He died in 1821. He was never reconciled with his father.

Thérèse and Jean-Louis moved after the war to a farm on the St. Clair River. They had one daughter. Thérèse died on March 2, 1822

Joseph (Joe) and Ann moved after the war to a lot above Chatham townsite, given to them by Ann's father William Baker. They had seven children, several of whom played important roles in the early development of Chatham. Joe died on December 21, 1828.

William (Henry) received a Lieutenant's commission in the artillery in 1814. He was killed in an American attack at the historic battle of Lundy's Lane.

Richard completed his service as a confidential courier for the British forces. After the war he married Ann Shepley and they had two sons. He died at Chatham on April 10, 1863.

Josette (Phillis) never married, and lived most of her life in the home of her brother Joe. She died at Chatham on April 18, 1876.

Robert was a trader and adventurer. He married Matilda Meldrum of Detroit in 1835. They produced fourteen children, five of whom reached maturity. He died at Detroit on March 4, 1862.

Appendix 1–

MAP – THE NORTHERN THEATRE OF WAR, 1812 – 14

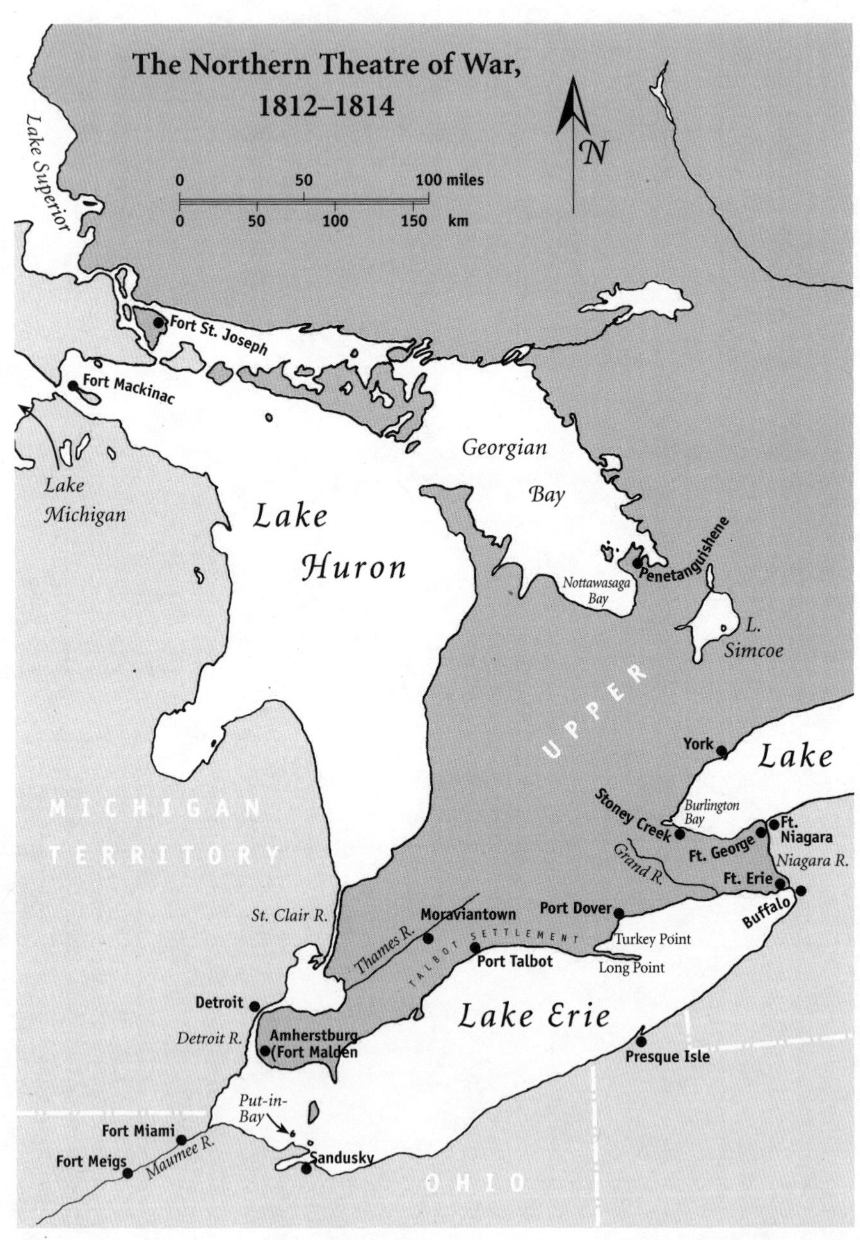
The Northern Theatre of War, 1812–1814
N
0
50
100 miles
0
50
100
150
km
Lake Superior
Fort St. Joseph
Fort Mackinac
Lake Michigan
Georgian Bay
Lake Huron
Nottawasaga Bay
Penetanguishene
L. Simcoe
UPPER
York
Lake
MICHIGAN TERRITORY
Stoney Creek
Burlington Bay
Ft. George
Ft. Niagara
Niagara R.
Grand R.
Ft. Erie
Buffalo
St. Clair R.
Moraviantown
Port Dover
Thames R.
TALBOT SETTLEMENT
Turkey Point
Port Talbot
Long Point
Detroit
Lake Erie
Detroit R.
Amherstburg (Fort Malden
Presque Isle
Put-in-Bay
Fort Miami
Fort Meigs
Maumee R.
Sandusky
OHIO

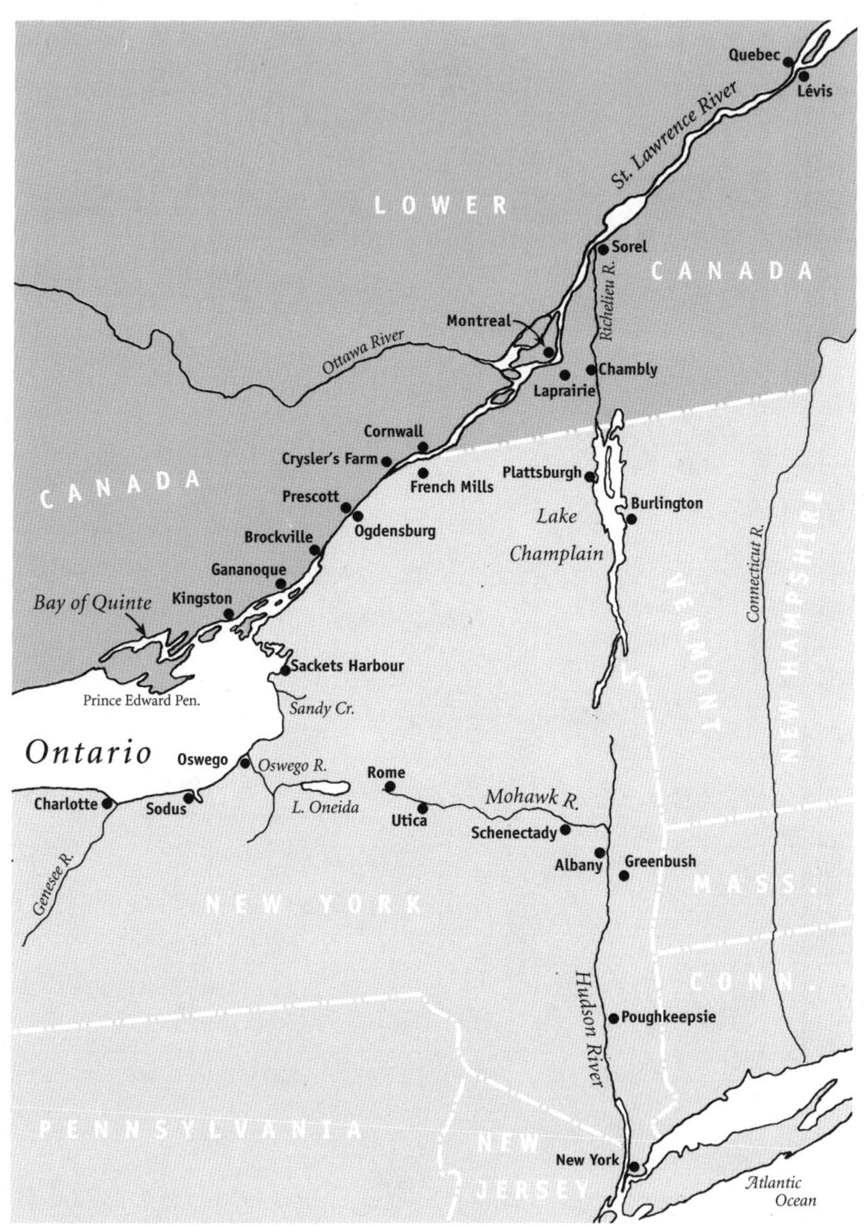
Quebec
Lévis
St. Lawrence River
LOWER
CANADA
Sorel
Richelieu R.
Montreal
Ottawa River
Chambly
Laprairie
Cornwall
Crysler's Farm
French Mills
Plattsburgh
CANADA
Prescott
Ogdensburg
Burlington
Lake
Champlain
Brockville
Gananoque
Bay of Quinte
Kingston
Connecticut R.
VERMONT
NEW HAMPSHIRE
Sackets Harbour
Prince Edward Pen.
Sandy Cr.
Ontario
Oswego
Oswego R.
Rome
Mohawk R.
Charlotte
Sodus
L. Oneida
Utica
Schenectady
Albany
Greenbush
Genesee R.
NEW YORK
MASS.
CONN.
Hudson River
Poughkeepsie
PENNSYLVANIA
NEW JERSEY
New York
Atlantic
Ocean

Appendix 2 – NAMES

The following characters in the book were real people.

All members of the family of Herman and Marie Eberts.

In Boucherville, Longueuil and Montreal:

Gregoire Huc, Judith Cecile Huc, Dr. Christopher Carter, Rev. David Chabrand Delisle, Governor-General Lord Dorchester, Lieutenant-Governor Simcoe

In Sorel:

Col. Ebenezer Jessup, Elizabeth Jessup.

In Detroit:

Major John Smith, Lt. Colonel Richard England, William Baker, Effie Baker, Ann Baker, Catherine Baker, Fr. Dufleaux, General Anthony Wayne, Presidents George Washington, Thomas Jefferson and James Madison, Hon. John Jay, Hon. Lord Grenville, Lt. Col. John Francis Hamtramck, Judge William Dummer Powell, Gregor McGregor, Angus Mackintosh, Marie Archange

Mackintosh, Walter Roe, Charles Smith, George McDougall, Louis Beaufait, James May, Peter Audain, Margaret Campbell, Mr. Brownlee and Joanna, John Askin, Peter Russell, General James Wilkinson, John Dodemead, Fr. Gabriel Richard, Gen. William Hull, General Isaac Brock, General Richard Proctor, Francis Navarre, Captain Moses Porter, Winthrop Sargent, General Arthur St. Clair, Lt.-Col. Thomas Bligh St. George, Capt. Charles Roberts, Capt. Richard Barclay, Commodore Oliver Perry, Brig-Gen. James Winchester, Brig-Gen. William Henry Harrison, Tecumseh, Tenskwatawa.

Appendix 3 –

ABOUT THE AUTHOR

Ian Robertson was born in 1940 in Montreal, and grew up in Vancouver. He studied at McGill University and Harvard Business School.

Ian and Bonnie were married in 1962, and have three children. Their extensive travels followed his career in the federal government, where he was a manager in Canada's international development assistance program, and then his career in Vancouver in international marketing and finance.

They lived in Toronto, Ottawa, West Vancouver, Boston, Philippines, India and Singapore before settling on Vancouver Island in 2003, when Ian retired from active consulting. Finally there was time to write, and Ian set to work on his first book, *While Bullets Fly*. The concept for that book came out of his work on family history, and that history was also the inspiration behind his second book *The Honourable Aleck* and then *Marie Françoise Huc*.

Printed in Canada